Juicy Lucy

Mitch Mitchell, Radio Brum presenter and partner in the Mitchell and Orient detective agency, investigates a bizarre psychotherapy group in the hectic search for a murderer.

Lucy Lessor had stopped crying, so she discharged herself from the psychiatric clinic. Four weeks later her corpse was found belly down in what had once been a padded cell. Burnt-out Roman candles lined two walls, smoke stains funnelling to the ceiling.

Dr Rainbow's psychotherapy group held a funeral for Juicy Lucy, though it appeared she had no intention of staying in her coffin on that hellfire day at the crematorium. 'The devil's got her,' remarked one of the group. And then Mitch found the devil had roped her in, too.

Also by Valerie Kershaw

The snow man (1979)
Rosa (1980)
The bank manager's wife (1981)
Published by Duckworth

Rockabye (1990)
Published by Bantam

'Mitch Mitchell novels':

Murder is too expensive (1993)
Funny money (1994)
Late knights (1995)
Published by Constable

JUICY LUCY
Valerie Kershaw

Constable · London

First published in Great Britain 1996
by Constable & Company Ltd
3 The Lanchesters, 162 Fulham Palace Road
London W6 9ER
Copyright © 1996 by Valerie Kershaw
The right of Valerie Kershaw to be
identified as the author of this work
has been asserted by her in accordance
with the Copyright, Designs and Patents Act 1988
ISBN 0 09 476050 0
Set in Palatino 10pt by
Pure Tech India Ltd, Pondicherry
Printed and bound in Great Britain
by Hartnolls Ltd, Bodmin

A CIP catalogue record for this book
is available from the British Library

RE: PRISONER 563958 (BH)
OPINION TWO

1. By instructions dated July 15 1987 and further to my Opinion dated April 28 1987, I am requested again to advise The Prisoner about a proposed application for leave to move for Judicial Review of the decision to recategorise him to Category C and the decision to transfer him from Her Majesty's Prison Bredon Hill to Her Majesty's Prison Gloucester. This Opinion should be read in conjunction with that dated April 28 which explains the factual background to this case.

Summary

2. I do not believe The Prisoner has any reasonable prospects of success in seeking leave to move for Judicial Review of the decisions to transfer and recategorise him which were taken in April this year.

Initial Transfer and Recategorisation

3. In his letter to instructing solicitors dated April 21 1987, the Governor at HMP Bredon Hill states that:

'The Category D status of The Prisoner at Bredon Hill was changed as a direct result of a report prepared by Charles B. Flower MB BS DPM FRCPsych ... It was reported that The Prisoner complained of "panic attacks" ... "feels he's got to run for it".'

4. I have considered the report of Dr Flower together with The Prisoner's comments thereon.

Dr Flower says that The Prisoner maintains:

'... he doesn't want to go on living ... he has no future and he'd be better dead. He ruminates on suicide.

'When asked how he would kill himself he says he would tape sticks of dynamite to his forehead and light the fuses. He would prefer to use "hundreds of Roman Candle fireworks" but realises these would be ineffective for his purpose of blowing himself "into kingdom come". He says he realises he would blow the building he was in sky high too but he was not in favour of trying to blow himself up in the open because he was not sure how rain or wind would affect his plan and also there was a real danger of his being spotted. What he needed was a room he could lock himself in though this might be difficult to find in a derelict building. He said it would be rotten to blow up a perfectly good building though when he imagined doing it he was always in an empty church standing on the altar but he thinks it would be very wicked of him to take a church with him. He imagined doing it all the time but especially in the mornings when he woke up.

'He maintains he might be decaying "as you do when you are dead". He says he is afraid he is putrifying. If he blew himself up he would have no flesh left and he could be clean again.

'The Prisoner cannot stay at Bredon Hill as I believe he is a suicide risk. I consider he should go to prison at Gloucester.'

I do not consider that the decision to recategorise on the ground of possible self-harm has any realistic prospect of being held to have been unreasonable.

Present Position

5. In regard to further points made by The Prisoner I do consider that they can be validly used to question The Prisoner's continued detention at HMP Gloucester on Category C. The Prisoner states that there are two psychiatrists at HMP Gloucester who will confirm that he was not, at the time of his transfer, clinically depressed. Also, The Prisoner points to numerous inaccuracies in Dr Flower's report and refers to his prison record as showing that he is a person who can be trusted not to abscond.

Conclusion

Given my advice that there are no reasonable grounds for seeking leave to move for Judicial Review in respect of the initial transfer and recategorisation decisions, the 'Description of Legal Aid' on the Legal Aid Certificate should now be amended as follows:

'To apply for leave and, if it is granted, to apply in the Divisional Court for a Judicial Review of a decision made by HM Prison Service to keep the assisted person detained at HMP Gloucester and or to keep him detained in security Category C.'

Should they have further matters to raise, they should not hesitate to contact me.

James Applegate
Percy Chambers
8 Princess Place
Tewkesbury TB9 7QQ

1

Mitch had seen corpses before. If you live long enough it is likely you will see the dead and some of those you love will be among them.

None of them had returned. The memories she had of them were of living people and most of the memories were good ones.

It was the woman who was a complete stranger to her who came back.

She arrived in the morning.

Her murderer came later that day.

She need never have seen the corpse of this woman if Freya Adcock, the station manager at Radio Brum, hadn't decided to do a story on care in the community. A story which Mitch, at the time, gloomily reckoned would be the bore of the year. She had told Digger Rooney: 'It's not my kind of thing. You know? Closing down loony bins and care in the community.'

'I'll get you a gin and tonic. That'll cheer you up. Where do you keep it?'

'Oh. I see. You want a drink.'

'Blossom, one needs something for the shock. Are you absolutely sure Dracula doesn't sleep here? What on earth possessed you to rent this hole?' Digger was looking at the wallpaper. Over the years the pattern had degenerated into weevils in flour. On the window wall a large yellowish stain spread down from the coving round the ceiling.

'I was desperate,' said Mitch.

'The understatement of the twentieth century.' Digger was looking round again.

'You'd be desperate if Freya Adcock was putting you up.'

He poked the spotted purple marble fireplace. 'I had an erotic dream about our revered station manager the other night. I think it must have been because you told me you had to remove her knickers from the rail every morning before you took your shower. Interlock. My God, how cotton interlock knickers can make a grown man groan aloud. Memories!'

'No ice, I'm afraid. The fridge is on the blink.' Mitch was pouring their drinks at a rickety cane side table. 'Stick to being gay. Stokers are so much prettier.'

'I expect I shall. So much more comfortable when one decides to be one thing or the other. Too much confusion and I start to get postural tension. Quite badly, actually.'

'What's that?'

'The feeling you get when the ground goes from under your feet. Terror. You know? Even you must have felt it from time to time. The trouble with you, Mitch Mitchell, is that you're so disgustingly normal you've no idea what we sensitive souls suffer. Bit thin. This gin.'

'You're driving.'

'Anyway, I'd rather do a package on care in the community than host Radio Brum's bonfire night. All the listeners' little horrors trying to blow me to smithereens.'

'I thought a couple of guys from security let off all the fireworks.'

'The kiddiewinkies sneak in their own. Short of strip searching them you're left protecting your goolies as best you may. So this is going to be the new chez Mitch?' He'd wandered over to a door pinned with architect's plans. Below was a series of snapshots of a chapel which had already undergone one metamorphosis and still bore the sign 'In Print' above a door.

'I haven't got planning permission yet. It goes before the committee in a few weeks' time. My fingers and toes are crossed. The place couldn't be handier. Right on the canal bank and a few doors down from the Mitchell and Orient Bureau.'

'I must say that when I first heard you were setting up this detective agency with your little Chinese chappie I thought you were a case for care in the community. I mean, talk about flak-ee! But fair dos and all that. You do seem to be building up a bit of street cred.'

'Thank you for nothing!'

'Believe me, I'm not the only one who's amazed. And envious. All that extra lolly.'

'It's not all that well paid and the work is very lumpy. We're either flat out or sitting on our hands. There is no way I could give up my work at Radio Brum.'

'Would you anyway? Come on, Mitch. If anyone was born to be a broadcaster, it's you.'

'When you've been fired as often as I have you'll get a second string to your bow.'

'You've got to remember you're a lot older than me. I haven't had time to collect that many orders of the boot.' He paused to wonder. 'What will I be doing when I reach my half-century?'

'I'm not that old!'

'Sweet one, you're so far past your sell-by date you'll be coming back into fashion any day now. Not the real thing, of course. Neo. Pastiche. Revisited.' He had a lump of curtain material in his hand. 'What the hell is this? It feels like wire wool.'

'It's fibreglass. Don't dare tell me you're too young to remember fibreglass curtaining. If you don't stop being so nasty to me you won't get another drink.'

'You know I think you're wonderful.'

She eyed him suspiciously. 'For my age? Go on. Say it. You little shit.'

'Absolutely not. And make the next gin stronger please.'

She took his glass. 'Why do I put up with you?'

'Because I'm your bestest chum. Not too many of those in anybody's life. One for all and all for one. And that. Cheers!'

'Fibreglass curtains are sixties antiques. Most are printed with a bamboo pattern. The rest have oblongs and half-moons all over them. Usually in brown and orange.' She found herself fingering the material. 'I wonder when they were last washed?'

'Don't.'

They gazed out of the window, Digger tapping the rim of his glass against his plump rosebud-shaped lips. Birmingham had woken to drifts of drizzle which, late in the afternoon, were still swirling into the city, borne over the Welsh mountains by steady westerlies. One of the reasons Mitch had rented the flat was because she liked the view from this deep bay window. Beyond the weed-infiltrated stone terrace was a sweep of lawn, ragged at the edges but mown, and an overgrown shrubbery. Copper beech marked the garden's boundary. Though it was now October, their leaves still blotted out the milk depot beyond.

'The place does have some advantages, you know,' she said. 'Nice back garden. On the ground floor. Five minutes from Radio Brum and fifteen from the bureau's offices in the Gas Street Basin. This may be a hole but, believe me, I saw tons worse. Acres of nylon carpets, nets, fifties splay-legged furniture, wastebins covered in Dralon with fringes round the top, ovens entombed in grease . . .'

'Oh, don't mind me, blossom. The truth is I envy you. You're on the move. Going places. Quite literally. I feel positively trapped. When am I going to move? When is the next stage in my career going to happen? God knows I've tried to hurry things along. Nobody wants to know. And when I'm not worrying about failing to clamber up the next step of the ladder I'm sweating because I might be knocked off the bloody thing altogether. I don't know if Radio Brum will renew my contract next time round, do I?'

'Don't think I'm not sweating. I didn't want to sell my house in Bristol Road. Hell, that's the place me and Max bought. That's where I brought my daughter up.' She sighed. 'What a rat.'

'Who?'

'Max. Going and dying on me. We had a good thing, you know?'

They continued to look out of the rain-misted windows.

'When's your daughter coming back from America?'

'Next summer. But Cassie won't live with me, will she? I can't see her coming back to Birmingham. And I don't blame her. She's twenty-two. She's her own life to lead.'

'I don't see why you had to sell your house in Bristol Road. I know it was a bit big, but it was a nice house, that. Why fart around with architects and planning committees and renting Gothic horror holes?'

'The money. Why else? I needed some of the capital locked up in that house. You don't set up detective agencies on thin air.'

'I thought Tommy Hung was bank-rolling the venture.'

'He's certainly sunk quite a chunk of his capital into the business. The lease on the premises. Fixtures, fittings and God knows what else. But we need working capital too and I don't fancy a big loan at exorbitant interest rates. I mean, it's all costing something like you'd never believe.'

'I never looked at it in that way.' Digger was silent while he thought about what she'd told him. 'Sounds quite scary.'

'It's the scariest thing I've ever done. When the work comes in you're on top of the world. When it dries up, like now, your heart rate doubles. Still . . .'

'Still what?'

'It's not boring. Whatever else, I'm not going to be bored to death.'

'Well, I don't like being bored but I don't like being uncomfortable, either. And to be honest, Mitch, I've spent most of the nineties feeling uncomfortable. You know. As though the seat of my pants were wet.'

'Somehow, Digger, and I don't quite know how, you've managed to thoroughly depress me.'

'Another gin maybe?'

'At four o'clock in the afternoon? Coffee, my boy.' Mitch disappeared into the cubby hole which her landlord maintained was a small but fully equipped kitchen. 'God,' she yelled as she put the kettle on. 'You can be a wet blanket!'

'You started it.' Digger had followed her and hovered just out of the doorway.

'I didn't.'
'You did.'
'Rubbish!'

'Moaning your head off about this package you had to do. Loony bins closing down and care in the community.'

'One in ten schizophrenics commits suicide. Did you know that?'

'No.'
'Did you want to know that?'
'No.'
'Will Radio Brum's listeners want to know that?'
'No.'
'What will happen to the ratings for my programme?'
Digger turned his chubby thumb down.

'Freya's asked me to do a Mitch Mitchell Investigates on this because the station's light on serious issues stuff and she's a review coming up. She's aware that I know the whole thing's a lead balloon but when it proves to be so it will, of course, all be my fault. I'm not a good enough broadcaster to present difficult material in a way which will keep your average Brummie housewife tuned in. We all know that's a load of old cobblers. Faced with care in the community, God would tune out. But she knows I've got to make all the right enthusiastic noises because the contract I'm on runs out at the end of the month. And as I'm only a part-time employee there won't be any great nasty gap in her schedules if she doesn't renew it. Hell, so near the end of my contract I'd pretend to be enthusiastic about doing a programme on the mating habits of the earthworm.'

'People would listen to that. I would. How do they do it, do you suppose? Do they get it up?'

'I don't know what they do!'

'Rather makes the mind boggle. If you think of what they could do. Considering their shape.'

'Digger . . .'

'All right. All right.' He surrendered, palms out. 'Black. One sugar slightly heaped. Anyway, crazies are not without interest. I wonder how they close down a loony bin? Boot the last patient out on to the gravel and bolt the doors?'

'For a start they're not patients. They're service users. That's what I was told when I made an appointment with John Sargeant. He's the site services manager for Cold Ash. That's the one they're closing down this week. They had some sort of ceremony on Monday but I've fixed for him to take me round the hospital tomorrow. A bit of running commentary . . . not to mention one or two spooky noises. I hope. Colin Parsons will join us at some stage. He's the chief executive of the North-East Birmingham Learning Disability and Mental Health Services NHS Trust.' She was pulling a face as long as the boot of Italy. 'With handles like that who can blame my listeners from tuning out in droves? It's the only sensible thing to do.'

'Blossom, what's through these double doors?'

'See. I've bored you into a state of fidgetiness already. My bedroom's through there. It's what used to be the front room of the house. Gets the morning sun according to the landlord. Can't confirm that. Hasn't been any to date. Here's your coffee.'

'No fibreglass curtains.' He'd opened the doors and poked his head through. He sounded disappointed.

'I moved the bed in front of the fireplace. It's black marble. Didn't want to wake up and think I was staring at my own tombstone.' As he took his mug of coffee from her, she asked gloomily: 'I don't suppose you know anyone who's been mad recently?'

'Well, not offhand.'

'What I need to do is forget site managers and chief execs. What I need is a story. Someone who was in Cold Ash and is now in the tender arms of care in the community. A nice harrowing gruesome tale which has listeners grabbing at their throats in horror. Didn't Derek Ince go off his trolley?'

'I simply can't see madness stopping him being the world's worst bore.'

'Anyway, I remember now. He didn't go into Cold Ash. It was the one on the south side of Birmingham. We've got to know lots of people who have gone bonkers recently. People are always doing it.'

'I suppose they are.' Digger flopped down in one of her armchairs.

'I've been asking around but I've come up empty-handed up to now. You couldn't put out one or two feelers for me?'

'You do your own research. I've my own programmes to get on air.'

'How does it go, honeypot? How did you phrase it? All for one and one . . .'

'I will not tell you what Mitch rhymes with. But you could try the second letter of the alphabet.'

In thirty years of broadcasting she'd learned when it was politic not to hear people. Wriggling her shoes off with delicate thrusting movements of her big toe, she sank into the armchair opposite Digger. As she drank her coffee she found herself studying the marble fireplace. It had the colour and striations of Continental sausages, the smoked variety, she decided. The shape and massiveness of it reminded her of the entrance to a city building. Or was it that storey above the doorways of the town hall? No. Six columns rose above that monumental mouth. Not to mention a few tons of carving and a frieze of painted figures.

Digger had been thinking of other things. 'It's an awful lot of trouble to go to.'

'What?'

'Converting this chapel into a house. I mean, there's only one of you, isn't there? You need someone to share with.'

'Don't I just.' Mitch sighed.

Digger was shifting his bulk about, trying to make himself more comfortable. The way he overflowed the chair reminded Mitch of the time one of her soufflés had performed too enthusiastically. 'Of course, I'd expect to pay you a decent rent.'

In her alarm Mitch almost dropped her coffee cup. 'I'd never take lodgers.'

'Of course, I'm Church of England myself. Always thought chapels infra dig. Other ranks and all that.' He was pretending not to have heard her. 'Still, I'm sure one could cope, blossom.'

2

Sammy Pink was seven minutes late because workmen had part of Bristol Road up. He didn't even stop to look at the two carvings of women at the entrance to the Glick Hope Clinic. In his opinion these two ladies had bostin' good knockers, much better knockers than any of the women in his psychotherapy group, and it was a crying shame that such tasty wares were nothing but stone.

There were two sets of doors and he flew up the steps and through the second set into a two-storey hall which looked like the outer sanctum of a majestic Turkish baths, fancy tiles all over the place and slender wrought-iron columns rising to a glass-domed roof. If only a naked wet girl would pop up through the jungle of palm trees instead of that toffee-nosed bitch of a receptionist who was built like a Staffordshire bull terrier. Yap yap, yap yap. He signed himself in and flew across the tiles to a door in the far wall and then jumped up two flights of stairs. He met the rest of the group toiling on to the landing.

He was spotted first by that porcelain blonde Mirry Vesey, who immediately turned away. She always took care to see as little of him as she could. As if he were the corpse of an animal which had fallen under the wheels of an articulated lorry. Labouring behind her was the dumpy Edwina Grimshaw, but he always felt quite safe with her. As far as he knew, she never saw anyone, let alone talked to them. Her whole life seemed to revolve round the knitting of a peach nylon bed jacket. Sammy thought it was as if she were spinning her own mother's womb about her.

He found he was being looked at by Maurice Pincing who, as always, was leading the members of the group to their attic room. Sammy always felt confused by Maurice. The man seemed in three separate pieces. First there was his face which, in early middle age, was taking on the appearance of a seat of well-worn trousers. The spreading flesh no longer quite fitted. His hair, twenty years younger, was thick and sappy and black. Cut in city whizz kid style, it was parted down the middle and blocked to the top of his ears, the rest closely shaved into the bone of his skull; pieces kept swinging across the top of his eyelids, giving him an intermittent shuttered look. His well-muscled body was as bristlingly young as his hair and looked as if it were about to burst out of the curiously dated dove grey suit he always wore to group meetings. It reminded Sammy of the bell-bottomed seventies though, as he conscientiously noted, the trousers only had a bit of flare at the ankle. In his opinion nothing about Maurice Pincing quite fitted together which, he supposed, was why Maurice had ended up in Dr Rainbow's group. Sammy's bemusement might have been mistaken for idiocy by Maurice. Sammy had never been so totally dismissed by anyone.

Maurice had let Mirry Vesey catch him up. He said to her: 'You have to be fit to come here. Has anyone ever counted all the stairs? Let's hope that all that blood racing about will do something for the old brain boxes, eh?'

Sammy had come up the last of the stairs far too quickly for now he was abreast of Joan Ridley and she was whispering in his ear: 'I wonder when last there was snow at the beginning of October? Such a blessing it has gone.' The way she sidled close, the way she hissed intimately in his ear, terrified him. He always thought she was going to whisper the most indecent things and his dick would stand up in his pants for the whole world to see. But she went on to say: 'My husband doesn't care for snow. Duncan says that all that salt they put down turns a car into a colander. How are you then, dear?'

'I'm fine . . . ' Sammy was escaping crabways towards the wall of the landing.

'We all say that,' said Joan Ridley. 'But we wouldn't be here if we weren't ill, would we? It's being highly strung, that's our problem. If you're too highly strung you're in the soup.'

He suddenly realised he was going to get trapped by the wall and veered off towards the banister railings. He saw Ted Coveyduck's bald spot rising steadily up through the stairwell and then his shoulders. He was followed by Cherry, Dr Rainbow's assistant.

The last to appear was Dr Rainbow. The way that man moved had always fascinated Sammy. The psychiatrist's bones always thought carefully before putting one foot in front of the other. It was alarming to watch such wariness. What did he fear? Plunging down a manhole, skidding on a banana skin? Sammy had never seen a man who thought so deeply about where he was going that his bones thought, too. He had, until then, dismissed this in two of his Aunt Ada's favourite phrases – 'over-egging the pudding' and 'oh, it's ridiculous'. Now, shocked, he saw the doctor hadn't been cautious enough. Two livid scratches, one long, one short, crusted with black blood, ran down his left jowl. A yellowing bruise discoloured his right cheekbone.

He looks as though someone's given him a bloody good hiding, Sammy thought. He almost laughed, though he was frightened rather than amused.

He quickly turned his head and studied the attic room they were entering. Cold northern skies had drained away all the colour and in his mind Sammy always saw this large room as ghostly. There were ten pine-framed hospital chairs drawn in a circle with a coffee table in the middle. The chairs had orange seats and backs. There was an almost dream-like gaiety about them, like deck chairs abandoned by a beach party when teeth began to chatter.

Though the circle of chairs was certainly a circle, Sammy saw it as pear-shaped with Dr Rainbow at the stem end. On his right was his co-therapist Cherry who today wore pants with bib and braces and who had lots of soft red curls which Sammy would have liked to touch because they were so childish. To Dr Rainbow's left was Joan Ridley. When the group had first assembled that chair had been fought over by Maurice Pincing and Mirry Vesey, too. While they had politely jostled Joan had sidled up from the rear and grabbed it. Edwina Grimshaw had established herself next to Cherry and because of the bulkiness of her shopping bags and the needs of her knitting she took up more space and was further away from the others. Sammy's chair had been chosen for him. It was the one the rest of them hadn't wanted. Mirry was to his left, Maurice to his right.

Though the group had only been formed three months ago, one member had already left. Lucy Lessor had been an in-patient at the clinic and had decided to join their out-patient group on being discharged. 'Just to be on the safe side. You can't be too careful, can you?' However, after some eight weeks, she'd decided she was all right. 'I don't cry any more,' she had told them. 'There was a time when I could get through two packets of man-sized Kleenex a day. No trouble at all.' In Sammy's opinion anyone who could wear skirts practically up to her knickers and get away with it had had nothing to cry about in the first place.

After the first two weeks the only thing the group saw of another patient, Ron Saffia, was his empty chair. Each week Dr Rainbow brought news of him. 'Ron has rung my secretary. He's told her he has the flu.' 'Ron was holding a seminar on Franz Kafka's loneliness when a fly got in his eye. He can't see well enough to drive, so he can't come.' 'Ron sends his apologies but he's at Weston-super-Mare today.' 'Ron is taking a wardrobe from his mother's house to his aunt's bungalow in Walsall.'

Each Thursday afternoon's group session began when Edwina Grimshaw got out her strange knitting needle. It had a steel point at both ends but the middle was of thin plastic tubing and the stitches formed a complete ring. There was now quite a lot of peach nylon knitting. Before beginning work she took off her donkey jacket but not her woollen bob hat; at moments of concentration she turned the toes of her cowboy boots inwards. Most of her face was covered by a shock of black hair which fell over her winged glasses, but on one occasion Sammy had caught a glimpse of her eyes. He'd not believed what they'd told him. Light, after all, can be a tricky thing.

He thought of the click of Edwina's strange knitting needle as music to Dr Rainbow's lullaby. The psychiatrist always opened the session with a tale from his week. Today, quite ignoring the dramatic tale scored into his face, he told them about his wife taking off the chintz chair covers and washing them. In his pedantic way he would stop now and then and go back and carefully pick up some small detail he had missed, tease it out and fit it into the proper scheme of things. Then he'd jump forward to where he'd left off. At such times Sammy tended to see him with a bracket in each hand, rounding up some fact which was trying to give him the slip. It was all too much for his co-therapist Cherry who fell asleep, her cheeks flushed with the innocence of her youthful slumber. On the other hand, the lullaby seemed to incense Maurice Pincing. Attacked by so much information about Mrs Rainbow's covers, and not a word about two scratches and a bruise, he fell to strangling the arm of his chair.

Sammy noted the psychiatrist was aware of the reactions he produced and was perhaps sardonically amused by them. He appeared to think that if he must put up with them, they must put up with him.

This was followed by Ron's message of the week. Ted Coveyduck, who sat next to the absent group member, was often the hapless victim of the group's frustrated anger. 'I should have been in Burton-on-Trent today,' and Joan Ridley had fixed Ted on to the scalding prongs of her eyes. 'But I went to the trouble of making alternative arrangements so I could be here.' 'Many people would be glad of a place in this group,' Ted was told by Maurice Pincing. 'People are crying out for this kind of treatment. Crying out.' None of these remarks were ever addressed to Edwina Grimshaw, who sat on the other side of the empty chair. She confused them. They only knew her as a peach nylon knitting machine and though it was known that people talked to machines and even gave them an occasional kick, they had not yet done so.

Sammy was as angry as the others that all Ron Saffia offered them was his absence. 'He doesn't think we're good enough for him? Who does that man think he is?' Two months ago this sense of injury had been personal. 'He doesn't want to know someone like me.' He was aware of this shift in his attitude in much the same way he noticed a change in the weather. He didn't, though, have any feeling that he'd come to belong to the group, or had any loyalty to it.

Sammy had spent many years trying to achieve the status of perfect nobody. Ron Saffia's absence was keenly felt by the group. Sammy's presence was ignored. He was conscientious, he came every Thursday afternoon, but such was his mastery that the group would not bother themselves with the complete nonentity he was. In that he was a member of their society, he was a hole in their fabric. Ron Saffia, who really was absent, was often powerfully present in the circle. How each and every one of them resented that man.

Contrary to the spirit of his vanishing act, Sammy felt warm to the tips of his fingers and toes when the group did notice him. This was in spite of the fact that he felt they knew him for what he was not, a bit on the simple side. He felt safety in what he believed was their falsification of him and yet it was a grief to him, too. Though he really wanted to be known as himself, he was terrified of being found out. There was more too, but just that much made Sammy's belly ache.

Dr Rainbow extracted a cigarette holder from his jacket pocket, fitted a tipped cigarette and lit up. Beaming, he leaned back in his chair, stretching out his long legs in front of him and crossing his ankles. The smoke rose to loop the loop over his head.

They were in full session.

No one was looking at the livid scratches on the doctor's face yet Sammy was sure that everyone knew to a centimetre just how long and deep they were and how the one nearest to his ear curved like a scimitar. No one would look at each other either, for fear of somehow being forced into asking about them.

The longer the tale was untold, the more dreadful it appeared to be. Why had no one mentioned it in passing as they'd entered the attic room? Perhaps made a bit of a joke about it? Well, for a start, thought Sammy grimly, it's no laughing matter when your leader, the man you perhaps hope will be your saviour, has been on the receiving end of a good hiding. What kind of a hero is that? Even I can handle myself well enough to escape being thumped though there's more than one who would happily knock me into the middle of next week.

They were now all stirring, as agitated as a herd who might be catching the scent of a predator.

Joan Ridley suddenly jumped into a litany of her complaints. The group knew them so well they were now little more than a buzz in ears, but today they were a comforting buzz. 'He's always watching me. The way that man watches me all the time! What does he want to do that for? I mean, I've never looked at another man in all the time we've been married.' Joan was tall and this seemed to be an agony to her. She looked as though she'd been stretched out on a rack and resented every added inch. 'He wears those pebbled glasses. You know, the old-fashioned kind. Oh, I'm under his microscope all right. Squashed flat on his little slide. Now what do you make of that?' The group, aware of Joan's fighting prowess – hadn't she stolen that chair from under two members' noses? – were at a loss to know what to make of it.

'Would you say Joan is paranoid?' Maurice Pincing asked Dr Rainbow. They could have been two doctors consulting together. 'Definitely paranoid.' Maurice then looked at Joan and put her firmly under his microscope.

She thrust herself forward so he could get a better view and continued: 'Well, I've always had nerves. I've always been sensitive. I keep thinking he's looking at me. Watching me. You know? In a not very nice way. Is it to do with sex?' she asked Dr Rainbow with a ghost of a bat of an eye.

'I can't stand that. Men undressing you with their eyes,' said Mirry. 'That's how your husband looks at you? O-oh, I hate that kind of thing. It brings me out in goosebumps. Really it does.'

'Many wives might wish they aroused such interest,' said Dr Rainbow.

'Well, he doesn't look at me quite like . . . more suspicious. As if he suspects me. But of what?'

'He's trying to catch you out in something? That's what you mean?' asked Mirry.

'I just keep thinking he's looking at me. That's all. I told you. I'm ever so highly strung.'

'Of course, it could be obsessional.' Maurice Pincing was again in consultation with Dr Rainbow.

Dr Rainbow grinned and shuffled his feet. Sammy thought he looked smug. That man enjoys himself far too much, he thought. And at our expense, too! And he nervously touched his cheek, the left one, as if probing for two scratch marks.

'Perhaps I'm mad,' Joan Ridley said. She sounded hopeful.

'No,' said Dr Rainbow.

'You're lucky,' said Ted Coveyduck. 'Truly. Truly. My wife wouldn't notice me if I dropped dead at her feet. She swims. She goes to a health club and does aerobics and weight-lifting. Forty squats, not to mention flying inclines. She spends hours on a sun bed and in a jacuzzi and on Monday afternoons she does her lotus movements and slips a second or two. Then there's her hair and Housewives' Register and taking Jeremy to his piano lessons after school.' Ted should have had blond hair and eyelashes but they were just colourless. He looked as though he'd been through the wash too often and all the dyes had run and faded.

Maurice Pincing said: 'I'm not too keen on women doing weight-lifting. Call me old-fashioned if you like.'

'I'd hate to have muscles,' said Mirry.

'Oh, I expect I'm being a little hard on Sandra,' said Ted. 'I mean, I'm not much fun to live with, am I? And Sandra has always been a very healthy girl. You bachelors have got the best of it, if you ask me.'

'I think he thinks I'm having an affair and that's why he spies on me all the time,' said Joan.

'If only I could get a decent night's sleep,' said Ted. 'I'd be fine if I wasn't dog tired morning, noon and night. Exhausted. I've had all sorts of tests. They can't find a thing wrong with me. My body scan turned out to be a peach. My stools couldn't be more normal. "It's all in your mind," my GP told me. But what's in my mind? You tell me. If you're dog tired, you're dog tired. No two ways about it. You just can't be as tired as I am and have nothing wrong with you. It's not natural.'

'I've thought about it a lot,' said Maurice Pincing. 'My mother was a whore.'

'I don't think that's a very nice thing to say,' said Mirry.

'Really, that's terrible,' said Joan Ridley.

'I went to bed with her when I was thirteen. Nothing improper, I hasten to add. My aunt had come to stay and Mother slept in my bed. But I think it had an effect. All that scent and black frilly nylon. Such dainty little feet but a trifle thick round the ankles.'

'Actually Maurice, there doesn't seem to be anything wrong with you if you really want to know,' said Mirry. 'You've got a lovely tan for a start.'

'I think you're being too hard on him, I really do. I mean, not everybody makes a great song and dance when they're in agony, do they? If he was well, he wouldn't be here, would he?' said Joan.

'As a matter of fact my own mother was a bit of a goer in her younger days,' said Mirry, adjusting the collar of her cream Jaeger wool jacket. 'Of course, she's dead now. But all the same, our mothers can't all be saints, can they? I mean, they are as human as you or I, aren't they? So to speak. I think you're making too much of it, Maurice. Life's life, though my husband has to have his principles, a man in his position.'

She suddenly sat herself very upright, shoulders back, hands clasped demurely in her lap, ankles crossed. She announced: 'I'm not at all sure I shall be coming in future.' She went on to explain that her husband owned a factory in Birmingham. Then, suddenly aware the two pieces of information didn't fit, she told them that Henry believed her coming to the group was a waste of time.

'But this is ridiculous! You should make your own mind up about it.'

'That's very easy to say but you don't live with Henry. He

expects people to do what he tells them. What's the point in having your own firm if people will go off and follow their own fancies?'

'You're not his employee. You're his wife!'

'You don't understand at all. Henry is a man who prides himself on getting his own way. You can't take away a man's pride, can you? What's he got left? That's what I'd like to know.'

'You mean you always do what he wants?' Ted Coveyduck then put his question in a different way. 'He says something and you do it?'

'Oh no. I wouldn't put it like that.'

'How would you put it?'

'Do you want to carry on coming to the group?' asked Dr Rainbow.

'To be honest ... I mean, it's not as though we do anything, is it? We just sit about and say the same things over and over. We just go round in circles. I can do that at home. I can sit down and do nothing at home.'

'So it's you who doesn't want to come any more? It's nothing to do with your husband,' said Maurice.

'You haven't heard a word I've said! If he won't let me come he won't let me come. I will say one thing for Henry. He's always known his own mind.'

Ted was following his own train of thought. 'Women can be so unfeeling. Talk about finer sensibilities! Hard as nails, matey. As ruthless as old Mother Nature herself.'

The group fell into silence; it crept between them and isolated one from the other. The prospect of Mirry Vesey's desertion seemed to make each of them retreat and seal himself off behind a fortress of skin. They saw no future in the group.

Mirry, aware of the power she was wielding, seemed to have shaken out all the creases and folds in herself. She was new-laundered, crisp and smug.

Sammy, who had never been quite bound into his life, found himself drifting beyond the range of gravity. An interstellar wind seemed to set the very structure of the chairs groaning. Perhaps legs would fall off, heads cave in and crumple to dust.

It was Dr Rainbow who broke the silence. The thump of the temple bell recalling those who had dwelt with the spirits back to this life. 'I should have mentioned this before. It slipped my mind.' He paused to consider this fact before moving on. 'I have a patient, a woman, who would like to join the group. Jenny Bone. What do you think?'

'New blood, eh?' Maurice perked up. 'Why not? Wheel her in. The more the merrier.'

'We could do with another now that Lucy Lessor's left us,' Joan said. 'What do you think, Mirry?'

Mirry, recalled to her duties to the group, said: 'I don't mind.'

'Why not,' said Ted. 'That's if you think she'll fit in, Christopher.'

All the members of the group had been told by Dr Rainbow that they must call him by his first name. "I'm Christopher." Sammy, however, was having nothing to do with this; in his mind the psychiatrist was Dr Rainbow. Christopher implied a willingness to be close, and to be quite frank Sammy had no intention of touching Dr Rainbow with a barge pole. No thank you. But most of the group members said the name carefully and with evident pride. He thought they were fools. Get too close, get Christopher close, and you were done for. The rest of them seemed to have no real conception of who they were dealing with; in Sammy's opinion a man who thought so deeply he thought with his bones was in league with the devil. You could become his thing, his creature, if you weren't careful. Forget selling your soul; this operator would get it for nothing. Perhaps the other group members had decided they didn't add up to much and would amount to more if they became Christopher's creatures but Sammy, who had mastered the art of being nobody, had a thorough appreciation of what it would be like to be somebody: himself.

Dr Rainbow said: 'If we're all agreed, perhaps she could start next week.'

At this point Edwina Grimshaw seemed to recall her function as harbinger of first and last things; she wound up her wool and knitting. While she gathered her work in, the others usually collected their scarves and gloves. Today, they panicked.

'What happened to your face? Someone's had a right go at it,' Joan said as the psychiatrist rose up on the spongy soles of his fawn suede shoes.

Maurice's forefinger was pointing out the doctor's face. As he got up the finger rose precipitously.

'Too long a tale to go into now,' said Dr Rainbow.

Sammy knew they were being punished for not asking sooner. Awkward questions must be tackled, answers you didn't want to hear had to be listened to. Actually, Sammy preferred to be punished, as long as it was in similar ways to this. If someone started carving up his face, well, that was different. He knew he was wicked and he was quite prepared to take his punishment, but not too much punishment. Those scratches looked really angry. And then he was aware both of Maurice Pincing's open mouth, as though, in his frustration, Maurice had lost the power of speech, and the scary white lividness of Ted Coveyduck. Gone was the limp stringy flaccidness. Ted coiled like a bull whip. One flick would sever the doctor's head from his shoulders. Sammy's heartbeat thundered through his body. His skin began to pop with sweat.

'If Henry had come home with a face like that I'd have asked straight away. I'd certainly want to know what he'd been up to,' said Mirry. 'But of course you're not Henry, are you?' she said to Dr Rainbow.

'Or Duncan,' said Joan.

The women's remarks seemed to some extent to mollify the men but Sammy had no intention of waiting around to see what happened next. He made himself scarce. When he got out of the clinic he took one or two deep breaths and then went about the business of trying to start the Escort. It needed a new battery but he couldn't afford one. While he cajoled the engine into life, a process which this time took the best part of five minutes, he found himself thinking again about what had happened. It occurred to him that maybe the group had been giving the doctor a lesson, too. All these stories, like the one today about Mrs Rainbow and her loose covers, were no doubt true but they gave a false impression. They were not in the Rainbows' cosy sitting-room. Even the daftest of them didn't believe that. They were out in Indian country, likely to get themselves scalped, a bunch of dead legs who were as likely to scrap among themselves as fight any enemy. In not asking about the scratches could they, among other things, be pointing out that Dr Rainbow wasn't telling them the score?

The thing that really got up Sammy's nose, and he thought this was down to the psychiatrist and not to him, was the fact that Cherry always fell asleep. The doctor might not worry about being so boring that he had pretty girls snoring in two minutes flat, but it maddened Sammy. Even though he was a nobody, he deserved better than that.

Now he found himself dwelling with satisfaction on the doctor's injuries. He bet that smart arse was really smarting. Practically brought tears to your eyes just to look at him. The psychiatrist's bones might think when he put one foot in front of the other but that hadn't stopped him walking slap bang wallop into some bitch's claws.

He eventually got the car to start. Remembering the roadworks in Bristol Road, he did a detour round the university and five minutes later picked up Pershore Road. He'd eased down the zip of his anorak, turned on the windscreen wipers and was flipping the car radio over to Radio Brum when he saw her. She'd parked her yellow Mazda by the entrance to Cannon Hill Park and was in the process of putting up her umbrella. She did not look round and if she had it would not have been likely she would have noticed Sammy's Escort. If he was beneath Mirry Vesey's notice, it was likely that his car was, too.

What's she about? he wondered. Who goes into a park for a walk in a heavy downpour? His glance was quite admiring. She was the best-looking woman in the group and the youngest. He reckoned her to be no more than thirty-one or two. Of course, he liked brunettes and she was blonde and hoity toity with it, but if push became shove would he say no?

Forget it, he told himself. Her? You've got to be joking. Like putting your dick in a mouldy tin of pilchards.

He sighed. As far as tarts went, this group of Dr Rainbow's was an absolute wash-out. A real house of horrors. Of course, it had been different when Lucy Lessor had been a member. That bint's legs had almost been hinged to her jaw bones.

Fair's fair, though. That Mirry Vesey knew how to grind her bum. He wouldn't be surprised if there was more to her than met the eye.

And then he'd driven past her and was tasting the honeyed words of the Radio Brum presenter. And that voice, as he'd taken the trouble to find out, told no lies. When she'd swung her knockers the whole of Sammy's universe had tilted through ninety degrees.

3

The fireplace in the sitting-room of the flat Mitch was renting was, she discovered on Friday morning, a scaled-down version of the entrance to a Victorian lunatic asylum. Cold Ash, she learned from the man in the flat tweed cap and Harrods green riding mac, was a classic example of the type of hospital built between 1845 and the last war. This one, just beyond the boundaries of Sutton Coldfield, was fairly early. 'Cold Ash is its own parish and has its own church, All Saints. They perhaps felt the inmates were in need of more than one and jolly good luck to them, hey?'

Mitch plugged the microphone into her tape recorder and glumly surveyed the building. Though it was built in brick and not granite, it reminded her of the edifice of more than one Victorian bank in the Wellington Street area of the city. That may have been the sire, she thought, but it's out of pure nineteenth-century workhouse and a very odd mix they make.

John Sargeant, the site services manager at Cold Ash, said: 'There's a water tower, of course, and a cricket pavilion. Around seven hundred thousand square feet of buildings. We housed two thousand-odd people in our heyday. There's two hundred acres of land. The hospital's always been held in high esteem. And we've had some very famous types here in our time. Film stars, politicians, telly personalities.' He touched his nose. 'No names, no pack drill but some jolly good sorts have been here, I can tell you.'

'When was this place built?' He had unlocked huge oak doors and they were walking into a cavernous hall which had a black and white tiled floor with a key pattern border.

'It was started in the 1880s. Around one hundred and thirty institutions like this were built. In the 1950s about a hundred and forty thousand people were housed in 'em.' They began to move down corridors which were glazed to shoulder height with bottle green tiles. Panelled oak doors still bore their labels. Linen. Night kitchen. Showers. The names of the wards were echoes of empire. Clive, Rhodes, Livingstone, Cook. 'Some people virtually lived all their lives on a ward like this.' They had paused at the doorway of Gordon. Even though the ward was empty Mitch saw rows of beds and painted lockers marching into the horizon. Would charts have hung from the bottom end of the iron bedsteads? But what temperatures would there be to plot, what pulse rates to record?

'I suppose I've got prehistoric ideas about madness,' she said. 'I can't equate stepping into Dante's Inferno with service users.'

'Nobody is mad these days, Miss Mitchell. The term is never used. I hope you'll bear that in mind when you make your programme. I won't say that psychiatric disturbance is a piece of cake but we do have some excellent drugs. There are highly effective forms of treatment. At the end of the day, it's our job to educate. I am sure you are in full agreement. We must remove the jolly awful prejudices which we still all too often come across. Only the other day I was speaking to the relative of one of our service users about the closure of Cold Ash. She said they'd been waiting twenty years for it to happen. "He's been so ashamed of being here." Her very words.'

'I appeciate that,' said Mitch. 'I'm afraid I was speaking my thoughts out loud.'

'Actually, I'm sure you'll make a super job of it. Do us proud. I'm a bit of a fan of yours, really. Hope you don't mind me letting on. You're a regular date with me.'

'Thank you. That's nice to know.' Up till then Mitch had thought he reminded her of a country auctioneer she'd once done a story about, a little too fleshy, a little too florid, a shade patronising in the way he always placed her on his notional inside as if they were walking along pavements and not down corridors. Now her mind was stirring with images of old-fashioned black and white films where fighter pilots are eternally at twelve o'clock high or tubbily parachuting into enemy territory.

'In earlier days people, I fear, were placed in Cold Ash and institutions like it simply because they couldn't meet the moral standards of the day. An unmarried mother, for instance. Most became totally dependent on the institution. The better class of schizophrenics were allowed to do the dirty work in the superintendent's house. That kind of thing. Here there were workshops where the lads and lasses made a special kind of rivet which was used in the ship-building industry.'

'In their time these would have been very humane institutions, surely? Better than Bedlam at any rate.'

'Oh, totally with you, totally with you. And, as I'm sure I must have said, some very good therapeutic work has been done here. Particularly since the last war.' He glanced down at his watch. Vigorous golden hairs on his forearm curled over it. 'Colin is due to meet us over at Amy Johnson in fifteen minutes.'

'Colin Parsons? The chief executive of the North-East Birmingham etc. etc.?'

'It does go on a bit, doesn't it? But there you are. People like a good long title these days. Puts a bit more beef into the old shoulders, eh? He – we – thought you would be interested in seeing the last building to be erected on the site. It was built during the 1930s as a small self-contained facility for private patients. Amy Johnson was the female wing, Scott the male. Latterly, both have been used as observation wards. Normally first admissions would go there for assessment. It would give you some idea, Miss Mitchell, of how things have moved this century.

We'll take my car. It's a good ten-minute walk from the main block and the weather remains very uncertain.'

'Could you just hang on a minute? Must get a bit of that door on tape. It almost groans, doesn't it? And a few nice hollow footsteps echoing in the corridor.'

'Into the trade secret stuff, hey? Good job I've got my leather-soled shoes on.'

Five minutes later they were in his small black Toyota and bowling along a tarmac track through parkland. 'Terrific cricket pitch, really terrific. All grown over now, alas, and the pavilion's boarded up. Druggies are the problem. Leave a building empty these days and the rats are in it, my word they are.' He drew up the car in front of a neo-Georgian building nestling in the centre of tattered rose gardens framed with half-bare lilac bushes. 'The site will be bought by a volume builder, I expect. They might preserve the church and the water tower, maybe even the entrance to the main block. For a start there are some rather nice plasterwork ceilings in there. Cost an oil sultan's ransom to build like that these days.'

'I wouldn't mind a stay in Amy Johnson myself,' said Mitch, looking around her as he took out his bunch of keys.

'Nice, isn't it? In fact I'm not telling tales out of school when I say we had a devilish job getting some people out. I've been told, my dear, and keep it under your hat, mum's the word, some of the lads and lasses had spectacular relapses on the day they were due to go out. In my opinion it beats a Forte though I can't quite say we're a challenge to the Savoy. Knew you'd like it.'

'Lord. Parquet floors.' He had stepped aside so she could go in first.

'Meals were taken in the conservatory and there's a fine day room overlooking the countryside, your own occupational therapy room, a very nice room where you can entertain your visitors, nice cosy little wards, handsome private rooms and a jolly good kitchen too for the old night-time brew of cocoa. Let me tell you, Amy Johnson was the place to be.'

'I can see that,' said Mitch. 'What a pity it's going.'

'Gone, my dear, and there you are. The world will move on as indeed it must. Ah. That sounds like Colin. He rather favours these risqué cars and why not? Chief exec perks are what it's all about at the end of the day. Wouldn't you say? Why bother to get to the top, else? New breed these top dogs nowadays but you'll like him. Easy to get on with and he certainly knows a thing or two.'

Colin Parsons was small and dapper, a navy blue chalk-striped suit under his navy blue Crombie, black hair greased back behind ears pink from October chill. Mitch judged him to be around forty, the same age as his site manager, John Sargeant, but in attitudes she guessed they would prove to be a generation apart. He shook hands with her. 'Right. How are we getting on?'

'We've certainly had a good natter. Filled in all the background, wouldn't you say?' John Sargeant asked Mitch. What surprised her was that he didn't make way for his superior but, like some ancient oak, stood there and darkened Colin Parsons's living-room with his abundantly leafy presence.

'To give you a perspective,' Colin Parsons said, opening his overcoat, 'our Trust serves a population of two hundred thousand and every year we have about four thousand service users. As the name implies, the service is not imposed on them, as Cold Ash was, but shaped, each according to his need.'

'This is the conservatory,' said John Sargeant.

'Very pretty.'

'As you will note, it is not a conservatory at all. It has a roof,' said Colin Parsons.

'It was called a conservatory,' said John Sargeant, 'by everyone.'

Mitch managed to smother her yawn. 'Do you have any padded cells?'

'My dear, padded cells went out with the introduction of the major tranquillisers. Must be over thirty years ago,' said John. 'In actual fact Amy has some but they were converted into very pretty little single bedrooms. Absolutely charming, actually.'

'Can I see them? It will be a little peg to hang some information on . . . about how things have changed over the years.' Nothing like the words 'padded cell', Mitch was thinking, to buck up some poor listeners wading through wodges of bureaucratspeak.

'About turn then,' said John Sargeant.

They trotted briskly back the way they had come, sun now beginning to stream through dusty windows which had not yet been boarded up. 'All this gorgeous parquet. What a shame,' said Mitch.

'Parquet needs polishing,' said Colin Parsons. 'It cost nine million a year to keep Cold Ash up and running. Hardly feasible for a hospital taking only two hundred of our service users.'

'Though, of course, we housed well over a thousand lads and lasses at one time.'

'Wooden double doors. Mahogany,' said Mitch.

'You are thinking of general hospitals if you're thinking rubber doors, my dear. Bodies weren't normally trolleyed through Amy, alive or dead. Here we are. Nice little row. We jollied it up with prints. That kind of thing.'

Mitch opened a door and poked her head in. 'I see what you mean, Mr Sargeant, but you can tell they were cells. A bit rum, really. Duck egg blue bars and pink chintz curtains.'

'Of course our new fourteen-bedded unit for acute cases is purpose-built. We opened it just two weeks ago,' said Colin Parsons. 'One or two en suites.'

'My word, are there? Well, there you go,' said John. 'That's the new order of things.'

Mitch found she was sniffing. 'Good heavens,' she said. 'It rather smells like bonfire night.'

'That's it. You're right. I caught a whiff of something when we came through those double doors. Couldn't put a name to it. Not for the life of me,' said John.

'Kids,' said Colin Parsons. 'They must have slipped in between the security patrols.'

In this wing the parquet flooring had given way to grey thermoplastic tiling. The corridor was only dimly lit with high porthole windows each defended by a cross of iron bars. Mitch, her eyes now used to the diminished light, pointed to two cartridges by an open door at the far end. 'Burnt-out fireworks?'

'Oh dear. This is too bad. The place hasn't even been empty a week!' The two men strode off down the corridor in front of her. John Sargeant bent to pick up one of the cartridges. Both men were partially blocking the end wall of the corridor and the opened doorway to a cell. Like a child at a football match, Mitch put her head down and burrowed her way through. Coat buttonholes straining and gasping a little, she arrived in the cell first though later she realised she could not have been first to see the naked corpse.

The woman sprawled belly down, bathed in the jaunty light coming through the baby blue bars of the window. Darker blue cornflowers budded on candy floss pink curtains. These were spotted with charred motes. A smoky frieze, funnelling at some points almost to the ceiling, ran along the bottom of the two long walls of the small room, which measured about eight by eleven. On the thermoplastic tiles at intervals along these two walls were burnt-out Roman candles. The smell of spent fireworks, of ashes, was so strong Mitch seemed to absorb it through her skin as well as her nose, though it was not uncomfortable to be in the room.

The woman, it was reasonably clear from the start, had been tied to the bars and cut down after she'd died. The splat of flesh reached towards the door, pigeon-toed in death. Her arms were splayed out, palms down, in a rough V, each longish fingernail a glittering dab of pink. Her toenails had been painted, too, a darker shade. What Mitch could see of the woman's stomach and thighs were already mottled reddish purple as blood, with death obeying the laws of gravity, laked within her to the lowest points.

Even then, even though each of the three of them knew she was dead, there was something dreadfully frisky about her as though some part of her had not died. Perhaps it was the dark and luxuriant curls which completely obscured her face. They were so thick, so glossy, so springy.

As far as Mitch could see, no blood had been spilled. It was a completely bloodless affair.

4

When Mitch had woken on Monday morning she'd found the fingers of her right hand entangled in her hair. It was only then she realised how like the dead woman's hair was to her own.

As soon as the first freezing sense of shock had worn off Mitch had become aware of how like her own body was to that corpse, the small waist, the rather too chunky thighs.

And now the hair.

Over the weekend she had been rather successful in keeping the image of the body out of her mind; imageless the corpse had somehow seeped into and sickened her flesh. She'd barely eaten. She hadn't been at the gin bottle either. She'd known that even the smell of alcohol would make her sick.

Mitch was now in the production office at Radio Brum, the telephone in one hand and a pencil in the other. She was pretending that nothing out of the ordinary had occurred. She was acting on the principle that if she went on in a completely normal fashion, her world would become normal again, too. She was aware that some would see it as carrying on walking when you've gone over a precipice. 'Say again?'

'Henry Vesey,' said A.J.

'Marzipan comes to mind,' said Mitch, writing the name down.

'So it does,' said A.J. 'The factory you can see as you come out of the underpasses on to Spaghetti Junction. Vesey and Benson. But

I don't know if he's one of those Veseys. You're supposed to be here, Mitch. It's not your day for the radio station.'

'Just dropping off a tape. I'll be right over. When have you fixed the appointment for?'

'Eleven.'

'No idea what it's about?'

'Actually, I handed him over to Tommy. Vesey wanted to know about fees.'

'Why isn't Tommy seeing him, then?'

'He specifically asked for you. Said he'd met you.'

'It must be the marzipan factory Vesey then. I once did a piece on the place. So we don't know what it's about.'

'If Tommy does, he's not told me. At the moment he's out tracking down a lead on a missing husband but he said to tell you he expects to be back around lunchtime.'

'Much else doing?'

'Fairly quiet,' said A.J. 'We need some more coffee. Shall I take the money out of the office petty cash?'

'If there's enough.'

'You haven't been dipping into it again?'

'I went to the bank on the way over to the radio station. I'll stick it back as soon as I get to the bureau.'

'If you remember.'

'You'll remind me.'

As Mitch put the phone down Digger Rooney asked: 'Was that the lovely A.J.? I don't know why she puts up with you and your Chinaman chum.'

'She wants to be a detective.'

'Talk about the blind leading the blind.' Quentin Plunkett was holding open the door with a blue suede boot as he reversed through with a large pile of tapes. 'Mitchell can't even detect the difference between a tuba and a tuber. Have you seen that trail she's written for the news room boys?'

'She's a broadcaster,' said Digger. 'I mean, none of us is going in for the Booker. I'm surprised that lot of big dicks in the news room even know what a tuber is.'

'Well, for a start they know you don't blow down the fucking thing.' Quentin dumped the tapes on his desk.

'I did it in a hurry. And anyway you always get artiste wrong. Performers have an "e", you know.'

'Obsolete usage. If you hadn't been educated before Methuselah was a lad you'd know that.'

'Children, children,' Digger said.

'I'm out of here, I don't need this shit first thing in the morning.' Mitch gathered together a large handbag and an assortment of bulging plastic carriers. 'Oh Digger. If you can come up with someone who has slipped their trolley – but who is a good talker, you know? For my programme . . .'

'Look no further than your own mirror, Mitchell,' said Quentin. 'See yourself coaxing an E sharp out of a fucking dahlia.'

'We'll ignore him,' said Mitch. 'I'm not going to waste my time being side-tracked by that fatso Frankenstein.' She didn't look at him as she marched towards the door.

'OK. If I can fit it in I'll give it a whirl.'

'At least someone in this office is a nice human being,' Mitch said.

'Let's not go for understatement here,' said Digger. 'I'm an angel.'

'Fairy more like.' Quentin Plunkett was unlocking the top drawer of his desk and extracting a whole new box of chinagraphs, a smile on his face, like the kid in the class who has the largest collection of marbles.

'At least he's got something down there,' said Mitch. 'What could you stick up a tuba?' She slammed shut the production office door. Gr-r-r-r. She bared her teeth and wondered how it was that Quentin Plunkett always had his contract renewed. Perhaps Freya Adcock kept employing him because she thought he was the grit that made the pearl? After hearing about some of the management courses the organisation had sent the station manager on, Mitch considered anything possible.

The broadcasting centre was a multi-storey complex built round a courtyard with a small tail at one end. The production office and engineers' rooms at Radio Brum were tucked into the second storey of that tail, the management offices in a section at the front of the building with a suite of studios across the corridor overlooking a courtyard closely planted with ivy and other shade-loving plants. As Mitch walked along this corridor a disembodied voice was telling her: 'Any hope that England might win the first test in Australia . . . ' The station's output, like the lingering smell of fish for lunch, was ever present. The row of framed photographs of the presenters met her eye. She was seventh from the left. As much hair as she'd been able to muster fell in curls over her face. It hid a multitude of sins. Mitch was getting to an age when, on her bad days, she rather regretted veils had so totally gone out of fashion.

She clattered down the stairs, passing the carpeted mouth which led to the national radio stations, and crossed the large foyer studio which was being set up for the day's Sharon and Larry television chat show. Girls in multi-layered clothing and farm labourers' boots were thudding along between portable screens, clipboards clutched to bony chests.

Was I that young once? Sometimes Mitch found herself stopping and staring at these girls in disbelief. 'Actually, I've worked it out. They're aliens,' she'd once told Digger. 'They get them from Mars.'

'Venus, blossom. They come down from Venus. So the news room boys tell me. I wouldn't know, of course. You should not drink gin and hold conversations as morbid as this. If you get paralytic I can't haul you back off the floor. I don't want my slipped disc playing me up.'

'You don't have a slipped disc.'

'I will have if I haul you off the floor.'

'I'm not that heavy!'

'Only dogs are allowed to bury their bones,' said Digger and he'd shaken his head.

Well, at least I've got myself back down to a size ten, Mitch thought now as she passed Radio Brum's reception desk. And if I carry on not eating it will be a size eight – and suddenly her stomach began to rumble. As she passed the security guard on the top step she realised she no longer felt sick. Probably getting mad at Quentin Plunkett got my juices going again, she thought. Am I going to be all right? Jesus. I thought I was going to throw a real wobbly.

Eyes forward. Don't think... but suddenly a vision of the corpse's splayed legs assailed her, both feet turned in.

She hurried across to her car which was parked under trees on the opposite side of the strip of lawn which marked off one side of the dual carriageway from the other. The sky was overcast, the air moist, the world uniformly drab. Even the lichen wetly felting the trunks of the trees seemed more beryl than emerald. Leaves formed treacherous, slippery patches under the soles of her boots.

She checked her make-up in the driver's mirror. The face that stared back at her seemed her normal everyday one; it showed no hint of her early morning vigil when she had sat wrapped up in a duvet in one of the armchairs, cold and clammy, staring at the purple marble fireplace. She focused down on the slither of reflected face. Perhaps, at her age, she should tone down the warpaint a bit? A pinker shade of lipstick? Was she thinking of making herself less visible, less of a target?

Don't be ridiculous, honeypot. You've more chance of winning the National Lottery than getting killed. My lips have always been scarlet and that's the way they'll stay. Pink isn't a colour. It's an apology for being here.

Panic momentarily engulfed her.

I'm getting so old.

I don't want to see dead bodies.

I'm old enough now to realise one day I'll be a corpse, too.

But was it more that she seemed to have run out of certainties? Freya Adcock might or might not renew her contract at the end of the month; a lifetime in broadcasting could be over in little more time than it took to blink. The detective agency she and Tommy Hung were trying to catapult off the ground could crash before it even got one wheel in the air. At this moment she hadn't even a roof she could call her own.

Her stomach rumbled. Well, at least she'd got an appetite again. She'd stop off and buy a packet of digestive biscuits on her way to the bureau.

She put the key in the ignition. Don't look down, she advised herself. Eyes front and keep on moving. Digger's right about the nineties. Half the time you are so scared you're worried about wetting your pants. The engine stuttered, died, stuttered again and then coughed into spluttering life. Putting her foot down, she slammed through the gears. The car leapt forward with a squawk. The flooring rattled and popped under her boots.

The rush-hour traffic was over but there was still a build-up on Bristol Road because of the roadworks at the Middleway Junction. Mitch detoured though the byways of Edgbaston, stopping off to buy biscuits and coffee. She emerged at the interchange at Fiveways, circled into thickening traffic and suddenly found herself humming. What the hell. She was still on the move, wasn't she? Life was still an adventure, wasn't it? She couldn't stop Freya firing her if that's what the station manager wanted to do, but she could do something about the Mitchell and Orient Bureau. With Tommy Hung's help she could make it the best damned detective agency in this city. Right? Right, she told herself, swinging into Broad Street, nosing her way through to Gas Street. She was a city soul. She liked the rhythms of urban life. What wired her were lots of hurrying feet on pavements, grinding gears, neon, distant sirens, big lungfuls of air spiked with carbon monoxide and sulphur trace elements, tarmac, concrete, the great Victorian buildings of Birmingham crowding shoulder to shoulder with the soaring glass cereal boxes of the sixties and seventies. It was not always a well-regulated city, but cared for by its councillors: new concert halls, flower boxes, statuary. Of course, Birmingham was a seriously unsmart place. Mitch liked this, too much the outsider to feel comfortable in what other people considered fashionable milieux. She didn't want to spend her life being laughed at because she couldn't help seeing the emperor had no clothes. She needed to get what she thought of as a proper grip on things, dig her hands into what felt real. Also, seriously unsmart appealed to the remnants of a Puritan conscience she'd inherited from her Nonconformist forebears.

Here's all right, she told herself now as she swung the car up on to a multi-storey and squeezed it into a parking bay. Here you don't have to be anyone but yourself.

Whatever that may be.

Broadcaster?

Detective?

Suddenly she was laughing at herself. That's not what you are. That's what you do. For now. Tomorrow? Who knows?

Leaving most of her bags in the car, she locked up and clattered into the street, sniffing the air. Walking down a side passage into the Gas Street Basin, she paused for a moment on the patterned brick towpath and then turned to her left, away from the bureau's offices. A short walk brought her to what had once been a small Nonconformist chapel. The gable end butted directly on to the towpath. She stood back as far as she could, but the only way to get a proper view of the building was to cross to the other side of the basin and make her way past the pub and the recently built post-modern blocks with their nursery-coloured ironwork and entrances. She had agreed to buy the chapel off Kenny Colville who had used it for his printing business until he went bust. If she couldn't get planning permission to turn it into a house, the deal fell through. She bit her lip and gazed up at the brickwork and boarded-up windows. A down spout had broken away and the funnel of brackish green damp seemed to be fanning further out every day. 'You need rescuing, old pal,' she told the building. 'You and me could do all right together. We started off from the same place.'

She planned to put in another storey under the great pitch pine hammer-beam roof. This would have a deck overlooking the canal, with the lounge, kitchen-dining-room and a cloakroom behind it; below, two bedrooms, bathrooms and a garage giving on to the street behind the basin.

'If we can swing it you and I can sing hymns together when we get up on Sunday mornings. Great roaring ones –

'Oh God our help in ages past
Our hope for years to come –

'as we shove the cholesterol-stuffed roast of old England into the oven...'

She sighed. She was certainly an atheist. There was no doubt about that. But she did miss the thwack, bang, and wallop of an old hymn. She felt at home in chapels, too. She'd spent most of the Sundays of her childhood in places just like this.

She stole another look at the damp-riddled pile. She crossed the fingers on both her hands and then strolled back down to the bureau. Little breezes were fretting the canal waters, chopping up the reflections of buildings. Two seagulls had perched on the bright blue railings. Harbingers of weather to come? The nearest coast was well over a hundred miles away, across the Welsh mountains.

The Mitchell and Orient Bureau was housed in a small row of white-painted terraced houses all of which had now been turned into offices. Tommy Hung had found their premises, he had decided their front door should be Harrods green, and filled the reception area with leather chesterfield settees. Josh Hadley, Mitch's ex-lover and one of the city's biggest antique dealers, had provided the newly born enterprise with its godmother, an oil portrait of a Victorian bitch who had the look of someone pickled in prune juice and self-righteousness. Tommy had arranged the picture so it was the first thing clients saw when they crossed the threshold. 'Detective agencies have a very sleazy image,' he'd told Mitch and their assistant, A.J. 'But anyone can see this lady is respectability personified. Here, my dears, is rectitude, reputation, reliability. My solicitor has four old portraits of the firm's founders on his walls. But she beats the lot of them. She has real class and if you have that you can charge more.'

Mitch had said: 'She looks as if she fries babies,' but softly, so Tommy couldn't hear. He'd put a lot of money into their venture.

Tommy treasured the portrait. If he could have got away with it, A.J. believed, he'd have made obeisances and delivered up votive offerings.

His devotion worried Mitch a bit, it was a little pocket in his Oriental mind which she knew would be forever closed to her. 'I mean, if she weren't frying babies, she'd be castrating Attila the Hun,' she'd told A.J. 'Whatever can he see in her?'

This morning as Mitch blew in, bags dancing in her left hand, A.J. was putting the phone down. 'That was for you,' she said. 'About that body at Cold Ash.'

'Oh no.' Mitch was looking round the office as if the white walls would open up and hide her.

'It's not the newspapers. Not a reporter,' A.J. assured her.

'After the experience I had last time – the awful Johnnie Drake thing – well, I couldn't go through that again. I was hunted, caught and roasted alive.'

'But Mitch, it's likely to come out at some stage that you were one of the people who found the body. There's the inquest for a start, they'll have to open that soon. You're a journalist. You just can't sit on a story and get away with it. Freya will surely fire you.'

'I've thought about that. I'm going to lie. I'm going to say the police asked me to keep silent. I simply won't go through it again. They had me so rattled the last time I turned round and thumped a guy in our own news room.'

'Anyway, it was an Inspector Briggs. He's going to ring you back.'

'Are you still going out with Inspector Pritchard?'

A.J. coloured a little but she said: 'Ian and I aren't serious. You know? Did you hear the news this morning?'

'Bits. I was flying round. Why?'

'They've found out who the dead woman was. I wrote it down . . . ' and she slid her memo pad towards her. 'Lucy Lessor, a thirty-five-year-old divorced primary school teacher. She was on the staff at Sutton Ash. She was last seen leaving the school about four o'clock the day before you found her. The police are appealing for witnesses, particularly anyone who saw her later than that.'

'What was she doing in the loony bin? How did he get her there? I mean, if she was divorced presumably she could entertain any man friend at home.'

'There was her daughter. She had a six-year-old child.'

'I wonder what the child did when Mummy went missing?' The sick feeling in Mitch's stomach was back again.

'Now she's being cared for by relatives. That's what it said in the news bulletin.'

'I really must try to eat something. I feel quite peculiar. I've had no breakfast,' said Mitch. 'I've got some biscuits in one of these bags.'

'I'll put the kettle on.'

'Why the fireworks?' She'd produced digestive biscuits out of a carrier. 'They didn't appear to have anything to do with her death.'

'Some sort of weird ritual? I see we're both assuming it's a man,' said A.J., taking a jar of coffee from Mitch.

'She was naked. There were burn marks on her wrists so it would seem she was shackled to the bars and, probably after death, untied. Her hands would have been over her head, like this . . .' She put her arms up in a bow formation, the packet of biscuits waving aloft.

'Perhaps he's a stalker. I mean, it really does have to be a man, doesn't it? He knocked her out and took her there in his car?'

'Whoever the murderer was, he seemed to know Cold Ash well. Maybe a former patient or a member of staff or someone who used to visit regularly. A relative of a patient.'

'That's an awful lot of people.'

Mitch gave A.J. a couple of ten-pound notes. 'You'd better put these back in the petty cash box.'

'Do you want the post?'

'Anything urgent?'

'No.'

'Give it to Tommy when he comes in.' She re-collected all her bags in one hand and picked up her mug of coffee in the other. 'Send this chap Vesey up when he arrives.'

'And Inspector Briggs?'

'If he rings put him through. But not if I'm with Mr Vesey.'

Mitch's office was on the first floor, overlooking the canal basin. Tommy's idea of respectability had not been allowed to set foot in her door. She'd gone for Italian designed chairs, bleached wood, grey wool carpeting and grey steel filing cabinets. There was a large Washingtonian palm tree in one corner. 'The car salesroom look,' Tommy had called it. She'd told him: 'Better than being buried under a load of mutton chop-whiskered horse shit.'

'I think if one – as it were – sets up shop in Birmingham one has a duty to be extra careful. After all, this city was practically founded on the manufacture of gimmicky rubbish. Brummagem.' He'd slowly surveyed her office again.

'Is this your way of trying to say I'm a bit too flash, Tommy? Well, I don't care. Flash is fun. But, believe me, no one will think this office flash. Just remember how much you paid for my chairs and you'll see I'm right! All I want is to be in the twentieth century when I'm working. Not in some Victorian gentlemen's club. I want to feel free to scratch my bum, launch a few paper planes, even stick a coffee cup on my head if the mood takes me that way.'

The disconcerting thing about Tommy's slitty eyes was that they were as readable as the day's headlines. Looking inscrutable seemed beyond him. What they'd told Mitch on this occasion she decided she'd better disbelieve or her self-respect would walk about on crutches.

And yet, thought Mitch, as she dumped everything on to her desk and took off her coat, the partnership was working. Tommy Hung provided a solid framework which supported the bureau in all its activities.

She opened the biscuit packet and took out a couple before wandering over to her window. Looking through the pane, she determinedly began to chew a digestive. Canal boats were moored opposite one another along the narrow jetty which linked this side of Gas Street Basin with the pub across the water.

The Mitchell and Orient Bureau is going to be more than all right. It's going to be a whopping success.

You do know that?

Do I? She was surprised. Tell that to my bank manager, she thought.

Henry Vesey was exactly on time, a small rotund man in his late fifties. His capacious cheeks were as battered as empty cement bags, his navy blue striped suit as out of shape. Rogue grey hairs in his eyebrows, nostrils and ears projected and curled about his head. Even Mitch, not an enthusiastic gardener, felt a need to weed him.

'Of course, you wouldn't remember me,' he said and she didn't, though she did recall the visit to the Vesey factory, part of a Birmingham at Work series she'd produced and presented a few years ago.

It was a full five minutes before Vesey got round to talking about why he'd come. He was shuffling his feet about like a schoolboy up before the beak. 'Look here, Mirry . . .' He stopped short and then added: 'My wife.'

Mitch at last reached for her pad. 'Do you mind if I take notes as we talk?'

'Not at all sure one would want to be on file.'

She didn't argue with him but waited. Eventually, he said: 'In for a penny, eh? Get out the old pen then and let's get on with it. I married Mirry, that is Mirralees Walker, seven years ago. She's thirty-two now. By the time we got spliced Norma, my first wife, had been dead five years. About a year ago Mirry's mother Rose Walker died. I might as well say from the start my in-laws are a bunch of dead legs. Right? Seem to be thousands of them, my dear, and all kept by the state. Most live around Balsall Heath way. What I'm trying to say is that Mirry originally came from the wrong side of the tracks. You follow? You'd never believe it now if you met her, but there you are. That's the size of it.'

Mitch thought about her partner Tommy Hung who now spoke English like the Duke of Edinburgh, though he'd fallen out of the rear end of Hong Kong around seventy years ago.

Henry Vesey went on: 'When I look back on it, it all seemed to start after Rosie Walker died. Mirry seemed to be a bit off colour – no, that's not it – sort of . . . distant . . . not quite with you, if you see what I mean. I don't notice too much of that sort of stuff usually but even I saw that. Six months later, in May it would be, I got home one night and found Mirry on that damned silly *chaise-longue* affair. The most uncomfortable piece of furniture I've ever sat down on in my life but Mirry would have it. She'd taken the bottle.'

'Bottle of what?'

'Dalmane. It's a sleeping drug. She was sleeping badly. Banged her into hospital and they pumped out her stomach.'

'Was it a serious suicide attempt, would you say?'

'More a silly trick. She knew I'd be home around sixish. But they kept her in hospital for two or three days.'

'Why did she do it?'

'She said she didn't know. She said she wasn't unhappy or anything. Nothing like that. Just tired. I couldn't get any sense out of her and I suspect the psychiatrist chappie who ran the rule over her couldn't, either. Look here, I want to get one thing straight. Absolutely clear. I know there's a big difference in our backgrounds and ages but we have a good marriage. Mirry was married before, too, you know, when she was twenty. It didn't work out and they'd split up by the time she was twenty-three. There's no marital friction. Nothing like that. We've always got on pretty well together. My family and friends thought I was a jolly lucky chap to get her and so did I, let me tell you. Still do. Absolutely. No question.'

'Children?'

'She can't have any. I have a son and daughter by my first marriage, grown up now, of course. There was a little friction between them and their stepmother at first but Mirry handled that very well. The psychiatrist chappie did talk to us about our marriage. I told him we hit it off very successfully and Mirry agreed. Right in front of him. Agreed. "I don't know why I did it." That's what she kept saying. There was nothing wrong. She didn't feel down in the mouth. It was as if she hadn't taken a whole bottle of pills!'

'What did you think of that?'

'What could anyone think? The psychiatrist at the general hospital must have been as puzzled as I was. He sent her along to the Glick Hope to see a consultant who specialises in psychotherapy. A Dr Rainbow. He put her in his Thursday group. A lot of twaddle, if you ask me, but I thought it would give her something to do. She wouldn't be moping at home as much.'

'When and where did you first meet?'

'At Crabtrees, that very posh lingerie shop off Corporation Street. She couldn't have been more than sixteen then. My wife was still alive and I used to pop in there to get her something for her birthday or at Christmas. After a while we got to know each other, you know, the way you do. She used to pick things out for Norma and Norma always liked them. Mirry has very good taste. Of course, after Norma died I didn't see Mirry for quite a while. And then I had another lady friend and started popping in again. Mirry started telling me about her problems with Damian, her first husband, and I gave her the name of a good lawyer. Set her on the right track, so to speak. I had one or two more lady friends before I realised the lady I really wanted was right under my nose.'

'I don't quite understand. Why have you come to a detective agency, Mr Vesey?'

He was silent.

She waited.

'A couple of days ago I had occasion to look at my share portfolio. The certificates of two blue chips were missing. Glaxo and BTR. It was not readily understandable because I keep all my share certificates together in a folder in the bureau in a drawer which is always kept locked. The key is on my key-ring. Of course, no great harm would be done if the certificates had been stolen. The nuisance would be going through the rigmarole of getting them replaced. Hence the precaution. We have been burgled twice, the last time three years ago. Now we have a very efficient alarm system. The point is, I'm a very methodical man, Miss Mitchell. I do not misplace things. I certainly do not sell shares and forget I've done so.'

'You found out the shares had been sold?'

'When I got hold of my broker, David, he told me I'd sold the shares in August! Had all the paperwork to prove it. The whole thing was nonsense. I wouldn't have sold in August anyway. The market was down two hundred points . . .' His hands were spread on his knees. He was looking at Mitch in dismay.

'You think someone sold those holdings and pocketed the cash? How could they do that if they were in your name?'

'Quite simple, really. Forge my signature. When I want to deal, the drill is that I ring David and then send a letter confirming my instructions. That way there's no room for misunderstandings. Occasionally, I will just write and tell him the price I will buy at or sell at. He received such a letter at the beginning of August, purporting to be signed by me. I made it my business to go to his office yesterday. I saw the letter. It was written on a word processor just like mine. It was worded in the way I word such letters. The signature could certainly have passed for mine. But the fact is, Miss Mitchell, I sent no such letter and nor did I sign the document transferring the shares.

'The amount raised, just over ten thousand pounds, was sent direct to my current account, a joint account I hold with my wife. Documentation shows that Mirry drew the money out, in cash, almost immediately.'

'You said you were a methodical man. Didn't you notice the amount on your bank statement?'

'At the time I was in hospital. I have a pacemaker, Miss Mitchell. Mirry was left in charge of such things for a while. One or two documents had gone missing but I thought nothing of it. Mirry had a lot on her plate at the time.'

'From what you tell me it's quite obvious that your wife stole the money. I assume you've tackled her about it?'

'I haven't. That's why I'm here. Of course, having it out with her was my first thought. But I kept seeing her lying on that stupid *chaise-longue* and the empty bottle of pills and that silly little voice saying . . .' He'd opened his small mouth wider and a high twitter of words spat out: ' "I don't know why I did it." ' His hands were twitching.

'You thought she wouldn't tell you . . .' Mitch spoke slowly and calmly. The sudden outburst of rage had shaken her. 'But she must have known you'd find out at some stage. The fact that the certificates were missing had to come to light.'

'I suppose one of those psychiatrist chappies would go on about attention-seeking behaviour. First the bottle of pills and then this. And, by God, she's certainly got my attention! But I don't believe all that malarky. Something's going on and I want to know what it is. When I've got a handle on this, then I'll tackle my wife.'

'Do you know what your wife's diagnosis is?'

'A clinical depression, the chappie said, featuring anxiety.'

'She certainly can't be very confused,' Mitch said. 'It took a lot of clear thought to pull that share scam off.'

'But as you said yourself, she must have known right from the beginning that she would be found out. What the hell is she playing at?'

'Is she extravagant? Would she be likely to be in debt?'

'In all our married life, Mirry's never run up debts. Extravagant? Yes and no. Mirry likes quality. Good clothes, eighteen carat gold in her ears. She would never drink tea out of anything except a china cup. To some extent, I think, it's a reaction against her childhood. What she buys is expensive, no doubt about it. But she's very careful about what she selects and she never buys much. She works to limits she sets herself. I never put my oar in. As I've said, we have a joint bank account. Of course, she can't readily get her hands on ten thousand but I have known her spend five hundred pounds on a suit. But that would then be the only outfit she'd buy that season.'

'What about her family? You said they were an impecunious lot.'

'She's never kept up with any of them. The only relative she saw after her marriage was her mother and she didn't see her very often. That has nothing to do with me, I may add. Mirry simply didn't have any time for them. She felt she'd pulled herself up by the boot straps and they could have done the same if they'd wanted.'

'And you are saying you've seen no visible evidence of her having spent the money.'

'I suppose there could be a fancy man.' Suddenly it was out, the words tumbling over each other. He immediately back-tracked. 'She's given me absolutely no reason to think there is.'

'Blackmail?'

'What kind of hold could anyone have over Mirry? Miss Mitchell, she's a very ordinary sort of woman.'

'She's done some extraordinary things in the last twelve months.'

'There's one other thing I must mention. It has no relevance as far as I can see, but nevertheless . . .'

She waited.

'Perhaps you've heard on the news about this woman whose body was found at Cold Ash? Lucy Lessor used to be a member of this psychotherapy group Dr Rainbow runs. Mirry tells me she left about a month ago.'

Mitch started. She thought about it. 'I really don't see how the two could possibly be connected. For a start, you say the woman who was killed is no longer a member of the group.'

'The worry is that the man who did it must be sick in the head. That goes without saying. The point is, the Glick Hope is full of characters like that. There're four chaps in Mirry's group for a start. In the circumstances, I'd rather she packed the whole thing in. But I know her. She'll say yes, yes, yes and go her own sweet way.'

'She agrees with you and then does what she wants? I don't think you've any need to worry, Mr Vesey. Look, I know I'm no psychiatrist but one would have thought people with such behaviour patterns, a psychopath say or a paranoid schizophrenic, wouldn't be amenable to therapy. If you are worried on that score couldn't you have a word with this . . .' She turned back her notes: 'Dr Rainbow? Honestly, I'd put it out of your mind. The police may not be so hot on solving burglaries but they do catch murderers. I don't expect this one will escape them for long. And really, it seems incredible to me that a psychiatrist would let a potential killer loose in his group.'

'You've got more faith in the johnnies than I have.'

'Coming back to the business of the stolen money, what we could do is put a tail – a very discreet tail – on your wife for a couple of weeks. Put her under the microscope, so to speak. I should be very surprised if what she does won't tell us what we want to know. If we're lucky, it will probably lead to the need for one or two side investigations but, of course, we'll keep you fully informed and, of course, all decisions which might involve extra expense will be yours. What I need is some sort of sketch of her weekly routine, as you know it, friends. When did you say she went to this group?'

'On Thursday afternoons. But I can't tell you much about that because she won't talk about it. I didn't even know this Lucy Lessor had been a member until she heard the news this morning.'

'She never mentions any of them?'

'She's not supposed to, to be fair. Confidentiality and all that. The only thing I know is there's a chap called Ron Saffia who never turns up and a woman called Joan who talks too much.'

'We'll also need a photo.'

'Brought one of those with me.'

'Well, if you could be jotting down one or two details for me, I'll get you our standard contract . . .'

As she opened the door for him five minutes later, he said: 'Look here, Miss Mitchell, it would be wrong to say I don't care about the ten thousand. But the thing I really care about is Mirry. Why is she doing this to me?'

'I don't know.'

'Well, find out. A.s.p.'

As soon as he'd gone A.J. came into the room bearing a leaf from a memo pad. 'An Ann Bateman's been on the phone. Wants to see you urgently. She's out for the rest of the day but wants you to ring her around six. This is her home number. She specifically asked you not to ring her at her office. Do you know her?'

'Bateman? Bateman?' Mitch shook her head. 'Doesn't ring a bell.'

5

Aunt Ada had been the first person to apply for a place in Magnolia House. She'd gone round to view when the workmen were converting the Victorian mansion into a rest home. She'd chosen a first-floor room overlooking the sweep of drive and she'd a very good view of an ancient cedar tree. Three months later, after she'd priced the removal of her bedroom furniture, she'd informed her nephew, Sammy Pink. Neither of them had ever directly spoken about how her move would affect him though Sammy now sometimes woke from sleep with tears on his cheeks. When Aunt Ada's building society account had been emptied, the house in Cherry Park would have to be sold to meet the nursing home fees. Aunt Ada was tearing the roof from over his head as surely as if she were taking off the tiles one by one.

Though it was now six months later, the sense of betrayal was as strong as ever. It haunted their relationship. Sammy bought off his fury by getting his aunt all manner of little gifts which he presented to her when he visited her. Her guilt found more devious expression. She passed most of it along to him by demanding more of him than he could give. He was never able to do quite enough for her. Though both of them knew it was she who had betrayed them, it was he who felt the most guilty.

Today he'd brought her some Stilton cheese. It had cost him more than he could afford. She'd be the ruin of him. The thought quite satisfied him. There. Now look what you've gone and done. She had thanked him and then a little later said she didn't quite know what it was but she'd lost all taste for Stilton. 'Of course, you can't taste things at my age. Everything tastes like foam rubber.' She looked at the cheese as if it were a bit of stuffing from a chair that she was expected to eat.

He turned away from her accusing eyes. Shoving his hands in his pockets, he looked out of the window. He was always feeling mad at her. He was mad at himself for being mad at her all the time.

Trying to regain his temper he focused on Colonel Snoddy roaring down the drive in his motorised wheelchair.

She was saying: 'You know what you ought to do, don't you?' She was propped up on her bed; pretty white hair, pretty baby blue eyes, anyone's idea of a prize-winning grannie. She was certainly fit enough to be pottering about but after a lifetime of haring around looking after other people she was determined not only to put her feet up but keep them up.

'What?'

'You ought to get married, that's what.' She was trying to push him into getting another woman to house and feed him. This was her way of trying to make amends. She went on: 'Men who live alone are noted for getting very odd in their ways. There's nothing like a woman for keeping a chap shipshape and Bristol fashion. The trouble is that men have no idea about a proper way to go on. Left to their own devices, they've gone to the devil in no time at all. I can't be doing for another any more. As I said to the doctor, there comes a time when you can't look after yourself, let alone a man. But doctors aren't what they were. These days they expect you to do your dying not just stood up but jogging round the blinking block. They've no sense of what's decent.'

It was Aunt Ada's sense of what was decent which had brought her to Magnolia House; no one was going to stop her from putting up her feet and meeting her maker in a bit of peace and quiet. 'I'd an idea I'd take to it,' she'd told Sammy triumphantly after she'd been in the rest home a couple of months. 'Just because you're used to running around fagging yourself out doesn't mean you'll be happy doing that till you drop, does it?'

'I'd look after you.'

She'd swept such nonsense aside with a wave of her hand. 'Of course, your Uncle Norman was more of a handful than most. A really particular man. Why, on his death-bed and what does he fret about? A fly on the counterpane. Oh, he took some upkeep did Norman Price. It was a job and a half seeing to him. And then you blew in with the leaves of the storm still sticking to your head. Well, I don't regret giving you that bed in the small room, not one bit. But there's always plenty of work in a man. There's no denying that.

'When they got to doing up this place . . . well, it seemed as if it were meant to happen. There you are, Ada, just the ticket, get your name down quick. They can talk about palaces all they like but you'd go far to beat Magnolia House, my word you would. You hurry up, Ada, get your name down. Those medical blighters won't be jogging round blocks when they're on their last legs. They'll be on their b.t.m.s and so should you be.'

She said now: 'You're not really a bad-looking chap or wouldn't be if you got your hair cut proper. Lots of girls wouldn't say no.'

'It's getting dark before tea now,' he said, trying to change the subject.

'If you could just get proper full-time work instead of this odd-job gardening lark. I mean, Mr Morpargo is never going to pay the proper rate. Solicitors are known for it. Charge the earth but expect people to work for them for nothing. And I don't expect your Miss Cadman could pay much more. You can't keep relying on me being here –' She stopped abruptly; the crepey skin about her neck tinged pink. The trouble, and they both knew it, was that he could rely on that. Since she'd started doing nothing his Aunt Ada had experienced a new lease of life. She persevered. 'What you need is a nice woman with a bit property. After all, you're quite a catch. Of course, it were different when you were younger. A girl can take her pick then. She can afford to be choosy. Come forty she's to lower her sights and that's a fact. There's not many men willing to marry when they reach your age. They've more sense. When a woman's knocking on, Sammy . . . well, it makes them see things in a different light. You're a catch, lad. They say every dog has its day and I reckon yours is about due. You think on. A nice little woman providing she's got a place of her own.'

'I don't know any women,' said Sammy. 'And if I did – which I don't – I don't want to be tied down.'

'Why not?'

'I don't want anyone breathing down my neck, do I?'

'That's silly talk,' said his Aunt Ada. 'You stick your feet under some nice woman's table and as like as not a nice bit of roast beef and Yorkshire pudding'll land up under your nose. You don't want a lonely old age, do you? I should think not.'

Sammy said: 'There's Colonel Snoddy coming in. You ought to go downstairs and mix more.'

'Forever changing the subject. In the end you've got to face facts.'

'I can manage.'

'But for how long, Sammy? You're a real worry, you know that?'

'I said, I'll manage. You really ought to get up and mix more, you know.'

'I like my own company. Though I might go down to lunch tomorrow.'

'But what do you do with yourself all day?'

'I'm not by myself all the time. There's the girls who do the beds and they usually stay for a bit for a chat. Then there's you. And I've got a lot to think about. Today I was thinking about our Norman being away in the war.'

'What on earth do you think about that for?'

'I want to get it all straight in my head. What's the use of having a life if you can't get a proper look back on it? It all needs to be thought about. Look, mark, learn, inwardly digest.'

Sammy wondered what the use of that was when, with a lot of luck, she might be in her grave by Christmas.

She went on: 'Did you know, Sammy, they did their own dhobi in the navy. Still do, for all I know. Kept everything clean and shipshape and not a woman to be seen. HMS *Ark Royal*, he were on, and he said it was ever so big. Decks as long as you please and kept clean enough to eat your dinner off. Men doing all that scrubbing. Makes you think, our Sam. You've got to agree there.'

It didn't make Sammy think. 'Take care anyway,' he said. 'I'll be in again next Friday.'

'No more oranges. The pips work up under my top plate. That can be very trying, that can.'

'What about pears?'

'Not any hard buggers like you got me last time.'

'Right. Pears.'

'Williams. I fancy a Williams. And bring me the little hammer.'

'What for?'

'I've not a hammer to bless myself with. A hammer always comes in. You must agree there. You're always in need of something to knock a nail in.'

'Why on earth should you want to knock a nail in?'

'They're always sticking out,' she said. 'That's been my experience.'

He escaped before she could add to her list. He wasn't wily enough to evade Colonel Snoddy, who had stationed his wheelchair in the hall by the morning-room door.

'Well, my boy, did it come?'

'On Wednesday, as a matter of fact.'

'Zeiss. Sounds German to me. Funny that. You expect everything to be Jap these days. I'd have some myself, but it's not worth it, old boy. Not when you reach my age. I've no use for binoculars any more. Are they any good?'

'I've not had much chance to find out. They seem fine.'

'Ordering from a top quality newspaper does carry some guarantee, d'you see? Those special offers in the tabloids – rubbish, I'd say. Bound to be. Stuff for the other ranks. These Jerries know a thing or two about binoculars. You can take it from me. A blinking good engineer, your Hun, and a very sound fighting man. And you can't say fairer than that.'

'Sorry. I've really got to get a move on –'

'Wouldn't mind a weekend pass myself.' The colonel winked at him. 'Glad the bins came. Jolly good show.'

Magnolia House was set in two acres of lawns and woodland. 'Grounds, not gardens,' Aunt Ada had corrected him on his first visit. The nursing home was covered with Virginia creeper and only two weeks ago the building had been the colour of one of Miss Cadman's clumps of red hot pokers, but now the leaves had gone brownish and were beginning to fall. The place was surrounded by a huge modern housing estate, some of it still being developed. Five minutes' walk away, on the other side of the estate, was Aunt Ada's house in Cherry Park. Sammy always came on foot. He saved the Escort for longer journeys. Petrol was expensive, so expensive he sometimes switched off the engine at the top of a hill and coasted down.

The drive led on to one of the estate's feeder roads and Sammy, coming through the gates, noticed for the first time all the satellite dishes appearing on houses. Most of the estate was already tricked out with barbecue pits, Victorian conservatories, burglar alarms and Spanish-style porch lanterns. Sammy, observing all these things, wasn't at all envious. He could no more imagine being among them than living among the mountains of the moon. What he did need, though, was a roof over his head and Aunt Ada rubbing salt in the wound didn't help.

But where was the money to come from? All he earned at his odd-job gardening was sixty pounds a week, more in the summer months when he sold bedding plants and the produce from the garden to his employers and neighbours. Of course, there was the dole money and that practically bumped him up to a hundred pounds but he hardly ever mentioned that source of income, even to himself, because like as not someone would grass him up with the DHSS. Sammy's life worked, after a fashion, because he had free accommodation. Without Aunt Ada's house where would he be?

It wasn't only the Thursday group sessions which were likely to give him bellyache. Any thought of the fix he was in since Aunt Ada had deserted him was likely to crease him.

Now, as he walked along the feeder road towards Cherry Park, he could feel his anxiety as sharply as if it had crab's pincers on the end of it. He hastily made himself think of other things.

He wondered whether he might try out his binoculars after tea. Just to test them, make sure everything was bang on. They'd cost him almost fifty pounds and that was a lot of money to a man like Sammy.

Why shouldn't I try them out? I've got to use them sometime, he thought. That's what I bought them for. And the idea, like a stiff shot of whisky, warmed him to his toes.

Cherry Park was set on the town side of the new housing estate. The lower end of the road led to a small cul-de-sac of council houses. Sammy lived above them, in an Edwardian semi-detached villa. The villas, some forming a short terrace, some semi-detached, faced primary school playing fields and a day centre for the mentally handicapped. The houses were set close to the road but at the rear the gardens ran for two hundred yards or more. Sammy used all his back garden and much of the land belonging to the old man next door to grow his vegetables. He raised his bedding plants in what had once been Uncle Norman's greenhouse. 'The glass house', his Uncle Norman had christened it, implying enforced detention. In fact this was where he and Sammy had been happiest, pricking out seedlings, rooting twigs of forsythia and redcurrant, feeding tomatoes.

Sammy, as he often did, began to whistle as he heard the welcoming click of the latch as he opened the front gate of Denmark Villa.

His Aunt Ada, who'd always had her eye on fashionable living, had thrown the front and back rooms into one large drawing-room and 'achieved a breakfast kitchen' – as she'd told them at the paper shop – by knocking down scullery and wash-house walls. The house was, as she said, 'the right sort of semi-detached, people like a bit of coving and proper doors, it all adds the right sort of air'. As such, it would fetch over a hundred thousand pounds when sold, enough to finance seven or eight more years of expensive living at Magnolia House.

But he wasn't going to think about that. He was going to plan his tea. Beans on toast, he decided, and the end of the Bakewell tart Miss Cadman, who prided herself on her baking, had given him. He let her think that because she provided him with homemade cakes he let her have her bedding plants at a reduced price. Of course, he did no such thing. She paid the going rate which he always set at fifteen per cent less than that at the local garden centres. 'People always like to think they're getting a bargain,' his Uncle Norman had always said. 'Give 'em a bargain and you've got dogs with two tails. You'd be amazed at what folk'll buy. No one likes to be deprived of a bargain.'

Looking back now, Sammy realised that what he admired about his uncle was that he seemed to have been born with the right ideas. What a man for being in the right. He was right about everything. Above all, he enjoyed being in the right. That was what really put the flesh on his bones.

Sammy, who absolutely knew himself to be in the wrong, had a proper appreciation of rightness, of that magic, unobtainable goal of being 'as right as rain'. In his opinion, that was the pot of gold at the end of the rainbow.

Sammy did his best. He never broke into a house to steal. But if lazy bitches left their milk on their doorsteps, well, it served them right if it vanished. And sometimes opportunity knocked in other ways; Sammy was never one to turn a deaf ear.

Of course, he'd like to be the same as his Uncle Norman, but he knew this was impossible. However hard he tried, he could never be in the right, though he was very often in the wrong. Wrong was about all he could manage. He had a real talent for it.

He wasn't knocking it.

Not really.

There were times when being in the wrong could be magnificent.

There was, of course, the fact that wrong did add up to a wrong 'un in the end and sometimes he wondered whether he was the devil himself. But that, thought Sammy, was pride speaking. Wrong again.

After tea, Sammy tidied everything away, washed up and scoured out the grill pan. He then sat and watched the television.

He didn't go out until shortly after ten o'clock. Before he did, he went down to the greenhouse and took twelve yards of clothes line from under the standing. When he got back in the kitchen he slipped on his anorak and then took the binoculars from the dresser drawer.

He hung the binoculars round his neck and then half zipped up his anorak. He dropped the clothes line in the paunch at the front before closing the zip. From the hall stand he took an old dog lead.

Pulling the hood of the anorak over his head, he turned as he closed the door. A sting of rain hit his cheeks. He fumbled in his pocket for his car keys. His heart was already beginning to beat more quickly, the inside of his elbow joints tingling a little in anticipation. He climbed in his car and met his reflection in the driving mirror. He was grinning. He wriggled, getting comfortable, and then edged the car away from the kerb.

First he paid a visit to Mirry Vesey. The way her hips had swayed as she walked towards Cannon Hill Park had stayed in his mind. Not that he really fancied the hoity toity bitch. Each window of Mirry's late Victorian house was crowded with net curtaining, though sometimes they left the curtains undrawn and when the light was on he could see her and the old man she lived with. Tonight the curtains were shut and he accelerated away, picking up the dual carriageway at the top of the hill. He forked on to the A38 and drove down into Birmingham, pushing it a bit, even though he was trying to curb a growing, bubbling eagerness. He made himself slow down when he reached the city, keeping well within the speed limits as he rode the underpasses and overheads which looped through the commercial and industrial maze. He circled down to Pershore Road and made for the Moseley area.

Many of the gaunt Victorian houses in Ladysmith Road had been turned into flats, the multiple occupancies causing parking problems for the residents. Mitch Mitchell had been forced to leave her red TVR half a block away. After spotting it, Sammy did a three point turn and back-tracked to the milk depot behind the road. He parked his car in a side street.

The buildings at the centre of the depot were floodlit and there were one or two lights seeded in the lawn which surrounded them. Beyond was rough grass which shaded into the darkness of a belt of trees. Somewhere behind it were fences which marked the boundaries of the back gardens of houses in Ladysmith Road. Sammy, after looking quickly to the right and left, hopped over the wall into the end garden and made for a hole in the interwoven fence behind an old lean-to greenhouse which was leaning more than he felt was safe. He thrust himself out into the copse of trees and was just about to make his way through them when he heard a cracking of twigs. He could not make out a figure but he knew someone was fifty yards ahead of him, probably by the chestnuts just beyond the post and chicken wire fence which separated the house Mitch Mitchell lived in from the milk depot's grounds. He drew back into the shadows, for a moment undecided whether to stealthily creep forward or go back. The noise could indicate that he had stumbled on lovers. A short tug of war was won by discretion in the shape of a magistrate's face which looked like it belonged to a blanched tortoise. Sammy had vowed only to let himself look if the chances of him being caught were minimal. He retreated to the car and sat on his hands as he often did when he was frustrated. He didn't want to go breaking anything, did he? Calm down and have a nice think, he told himself. He did and then started the car again, trying not to worry about the petrol he'd wasted in the last hour. He drove back out of the city to Sutton Coldfield and turned off the main road, making his way through streets of pinchy-mouthed fat-bottomed houses, frilly blinds stuck about their windows, all forever done up in their Sunday best. He parked the car at the bottom of a building site and locked it up.

He walked up the rough muddy road, swinging the lead, for all the world a man out walking the dog. Only the foundations of houses were laid at the beginning of the road, but now he was walking past half-completed houses, some with their roofs on. He picked his way over the rubble to the back of one of them and hopped through the back door opening. The distant glow of neon light which had partially illuminated his way was dimmed within the walls and he waited until his eyesight adjusted.

Downstairs floorboards had been laid but on the first floor only joists were in place. Above them rafters supported the newly tiled roof. Sammy took the clothes line out of his anorak, slung it over a joist and caught the end. He wriggled it nearer to the unplastered wall and then walked up, his body balanced between the wall and the two strands of rope in his hands. Panting, he hauled himself on to the joists. He swung the binoculars on to his back, flattened his body across the joists and pulled himself along to the back bedroom window opening.

Now he could see the back gardens of a row of town houses. He fished for the binoculars and trained them on the bedroom window of the house opposite. Ron Saffia may not present himself to the group but he did not escape Sammy's eye. Roller in hand, the absent member was emulsioning the ceiling. A couple of small blobs of paint dented a frizzy halo of hair which doubled the size of a bony head bobbing about on gawky shoulders. Sammy noted that the tray of emulsion balancing at the top of the kitchen steps looked none too secure.

Almost immediately the bedroom door opened and a dark-haired woman came in with a mug of tea. She looked disquieteningly familiar, and Sammy kept waiting for her to turn round so he could see her face. But she didn't.

Suddenly he began to feel excited. He hadn't come out this evening expecting anything to happen. It rarely did. Yet a prickle at the back of his neck was telling him he was in for a good show. And yet not only were the couple yards apart, Ron was still half-way up the kitchen steps. He was coming down them now, the roller in his hand.

The woman still had her back to Sammy. She was wearing a T-shirt and jeans, the material stretched tightly over her buttocks when she bent to put the mug down on the oblongs of chipboard used to make the floor. Ron said something to her. She moved her head slightly, not enough for Sammy to see her face. She appeared to be staring at Ron. He reached up and put the roller in the tray. He turned and looked at her intently as he slowly wiped his hands on his buttocks.

They're off, thought Sammy, his blood a web of honey, and he adjusted the binoculars and bore hard down on them.

She also wiped her hands on the back of her jeans and then unzipped them. She stepped out of them and folded them neatly. Her back arched a little as she straightened after taking off her knickers. She had very long legs and nice chunky rather piggy thighs. Sammy loved them. If only she'd take off her T-shirt but she didn't. Ron smiled at her. The arch of her back grew more pronounced. He said something else to her and she got down on all fours. Her elbows bent as she placed her cheek against the floor. Her bottom reared. She shuffled her knees further apart. Sammy lowered the glasses a little so he could get a better view of her genitals.

Ron unzipped his jeans and with his right hand pulled out his penis. It jumped upright between his fingers. Sammy's jumped too. He hastily unzipped himself and grabbed it with his free hand.

Ron and Sammy studied the woman with a proprietorial eye and then he and Sammy moved behind her and climbed aboard, bracing their arms against the floor, and as one thrust forward and took her, their force almost flattening her. They drew back and she shifted, rebalancing herself on the play of penis they'd given her. She grew more bold, rearing so she sucked them in.

Sammy came sooner than Ron and sat moaning in the spillage of his seed but even as he did so the implacable observing eye observed. The absent member was a stayer, all right; the woman's black curls popped and popped as she bounded up and down like a ball vibrating under a footballer's boot. And then the pounding ceased and he saw Ron's loins twitch and tremble. The pair of them rolled apart, she with her legs awry, scattering shining drops of liquid which became black as they were absorbed by the chipboard. Ron stretched out his hand and patted her bum. It was then that she fully turned towards Sammy and he saw her face for the first time.

His belly rose up off the floor. The plates of his skull lifted.

He was staring into the satiated face of Lucy Lessor. The ghost of a smile was hovering over her prim little lips.

6

'Isn't it a coincidence? I'd no idea she'd married again. Bateman. Bateman. The name doesn't ring a bell. I wonder what he does? Of course, if she'd said Dr Ann Lester . . .' Mitch was holding a coffee cup in her left hand. Her right shoulder was up, cradling the phone against her ear. She'd only put on one side light in an effort to obscure the weevil-patterned wallpaper and fibreglass curtains. The rosy light cast by the red shade made the room look surprisingly pleasant.

'What interests me is that the doctor didn't want you to call her while she was at the Glick Hope Clinic,' said Mitch's partner, Tommy Hung.

'We might find ourselves dealing with something *sub rosa*, you think?'

'It's got to have something to do with that former patient of theirs who was killed. Lucy . . .?'

'Lucy Lessor. But that's hardly hush-hush, is it? It's been in all the papers.'

'However, it's not known the woman attended the Glick Hope Clinic. I've seen no reference to that.'

'They always say things come in threes, don't they? First I hear that Henry Vesey's wife goes to the clinic, next I learn the dead woman did and then, for God's sake, the director of the clinic rings me! Talk about synchronicity. Jung himself would have been seriously impressed.' Mitch wriggled the phone nearer to her ear. 'I don't suppose it would have cut any ice with Freud.'

'When are you going to see her?'

'First thing tomorrow morning. And get this. We're not to meet at the clinic, our office or even chez Bateman in town. No. I've got to trail out to their weekend retreat at Yoxall.'

'Well, if it turns out to be iffy we can always say no,' said Tommy.

'The Mitchell and Orient Bureau can't afford to say no to anyone,' said Mitch. 'Anyway, Ann Bateman just isn't the naughty type. Now if it had been that first husband of hers . . .'

'As far as I know, he's still behind bars.'

'Amen to that,' said Mitch. 'Look, I'll give you a ring as soon as I've seen her. I don't want you expiring with curiosity.'

'When I stop being curious you can be sure that I'm on my death-bed,' said Tommy. 'What is synchronicity?'

'I think it means links between unconnected events. Meaningful coincidences. Jung had a whole theory about it. Honeypot, I wouldn't even begin to think about it unless you're going to make it your life's work.'

'Actually, I always find coincidences cluster around turning points in my life. As though logic develops a hole and lets a new world in.'

'Tommy, I've enough on my plate without you going philosophical on me.' Mitch slammed down the phone.

She thought of the dead woman's hair.

She thought of the size and shape of her body.

It had to be entirely coincidental that she and Lucy Lessor were physically like each other.

But she didn't want any holes in logic letting in a nightmare world of smoke-funnelled walls, burnt-out Roman candles and bars of baby blue.

That world is already here, she suddenly realised, staring at the shadows cast by the purple marble mantelpiece. It started to become real as soon as the site services manager met me before the entrance to Cold Ash.

Actually, the only thing all this comes down to is pre-menstrual tension, she told herself. Have a gin.

She did.

From that point things began to look up. The next morning she even discovered that her landlord had not lied about everything. Her bedroom did catch the morning sun. She had a cup of coffee and took some time over her wardrobe. She wanted Dr Bateman to see a very much toned-down Mitch Mitchell; someone sober, a reliable lady who would never break a confidence, someone competent, discreet, effective. What we need to portray is a woman who is the exact opposite of all that you are, she told herself, but being what she was there was no grey in her wardrobe. There was black but by the time she'd whittled down the garments to what she thought of as 'respectable black' this came to one suit and somehow, on her, the skirt looked as if at any moment it might develop a thigh-high slit.

The trouble is, God made you all wrong, she thought as she walked half a block to collect her car. All the ancestral Puritan genes inexplicably hitched up their skirts and did the can-can at the critical moment.

She dumped her handbag on the back ledge of her bright red but ancient TVR and lowered herself in. Her knee joints creaked. She pretended the noise came from springs in the mock racing driver's seat. It was already almost nine o'clock and the rush-hour traffic had thinned. She bowled over roads which looped above the roofs of the city. Eventually dropping down on to the Tyburn Road, she drove north towards Stafford. She picked up the A515 beyond Lichfield and planed down to the river flats in the Trent Valley, the cloudless sky becoming bigger as hills fell away. She crossed the single lane bridge and began the gentle climb into Yoxall. Just before the village she picked up the B5016 to Barton-under-Needwood. She came to Barley Moe Cottage as soon as she nosed her way from under the overhanging branches of trees growing by a river bank. The gable end of the old part of the house faced the road, a new wing jutted eastwards. Thatched, latticed-windowed with an oak-studded door – the only thing that was missing, Mitch thought, was Mrs Tiggy-Winkle and Tom Kitten.

She'd no sooner clicked open the gate than she saw the front door open. Dr Bateman waited for her quietly, arms laced over her chest, a cardigan with a Clarice Cliff puffy cloud and tree-top design slung over her shoulders. She was, Mitch saw, plumper, her skin moist, almost dewy-looking though she was in late middle age. 'So good of you to come. Come in. Come in.' The doctor led the way into a soft green and pink drawing-room in the new wing. Mitch found herself looking round as she waited for her to make coffee. There was a Victorian bride's quilt thrown over the back of a settee covered in softly faded linen union, an imitation decoupage wall clock above the faux marble fireplace, a pair of rose and pansy plates flanking it. Mitch, who liked to think domestic interiors reflected the quality of someone's mind, was confounded. This cosy once-upon-a-time atmosphere seemed in no way to reflect the doctor she knew, the woman who had the reputation of being a very good psychiatrist as well as the exceptionally able director of a famous psychiatric institution. Perhaps this late romance had opened up an unsuspected seam in her character.

'Congratulations. I hope I'm not too incredibly late. I didn't know you'd married again,' Mitch said as the doctor came back in the room with a tray of coffee.

The doctor blushed, suddenly looking ridiculously girlish. 'He's in the States at the moment.' Almost immediately her professional mask was in place again. 'You've heard of the murder of the primary school teacher? Lucy Lessor was a patient of ours until a month ago. Black? Sugar? I hope you will excuse me if during our talk I put aside my – our – feelings of horror. As director it is necessary for me to look at how this tragedy may affect the clinic and the patients still in our care. After five years of negotiations, Miss Mitchell, we are on the brink of receiving a one million pound donation from a delightful but wholly eccentric benefactor. It will be used to build a special children's unit in the grounds of the clinic. Anything ...' and she spent some time searching for what seemed to her to be an appropriate word, 'untoward could prejudice that donation. The link between Lucy and the clinic is not general knowledge yet but one must suppose it will become so. The fact of the matter is that I and the chairman of our trustees would like forewarning of any ... any trouble ... which may be heading in our direction in the hope that we can deal with it before it is blown up out of all true proportion ... We do not expect, you must understand, that Lucy's death is in any way connected with the clinic ...' She stopped and then said: 'All this must sound quite awful when the coroner has not even released that poor woman's remains for burial ... If it weren't for our children ... we have no in-patient facilities for them at all, Miss Mitchell.'

'I can see that an awkward situation could develop ...'

'Lucy was in our in-patient facility for six months and then transferred to an out-patient group run by Dr Christopher Rainbow, an excellent doctor. You may take my word for that. She felt she might need support when she first came out of the clinic but she had only attended the out-patient group for about two months before deciding that she was well enough to make it on her own.'

'You are worried that a patient at the hospital or in this group Lucy attended is her murderer?'

'That is highly unlikely. All our patients are screened by psychiatrists before being offered treatment . . . I think the chairman of the trustees and I . . .' She paused and thought. 'What comes to mind is the look-out in the crow's nest . . . a precaution, you might say, against any possible reefs ahead. Naturally, we don't want to interfere in any way with police enquiries. We merely wish to keep a weather eye open for any possible situations which may arise and affect the well-being of the clinic . . . I mean . . . Oh Lord, one finds oneself at a bit of a loss . . . It all sounds so cold-blooded when one thinks of what happened to poor Lucy . . . yet we do have to think of our other patients, we do have to keep in mind the fact that much of our money comes from outside donations and that source of income could dry up if we were to be subjected to a bad press. I'm sure you understand that, Miss Mitchell. We have come to you because I know from past experience we can rely on you to be both extremely competent and completely discreet.' She smiled briefly. 'A rare combination in my experience.'

'What exactly would you like us to do?'

'Three things. We only know Lucy from a patient point of view. We would like to have information about Lucy's life in the outside world, so to speak. Secondly, we would like you to run a check on the members of Dr Rainbow's group – I am sure you will realise this goes against all medical ethics but the brutal truth is that if our income goes down our ability to provide even rudimentary mental heath care is at risk. Thirdly, I'd like you to take a look at any friends or acquaintances from her in-patient days. I realise this will involve your agency in a lot of work, especially as speed is of the essence. We are prepared to pay very generously for your help.'

'How much background information can you actually give me? Can I see case histories, for example?'

'Absolutely not. In fact I have pulled the files and brought them out here for safe-keeping.' She smiled, though this, Mitch realised, was a nervous reaction to the unpleasant situation she found herself in. 'Quite against my own very firm rules, I have to say. As you may imagine, all staff at the clinic have easy access to the patients' files. We didn't want the group members to become the focus of idle curiosity or, even worse, find ourselves bolting doors after horses had fled. No doubt we are being ridiculously over-cautious. Even paranoid?' She was putting the question to herself. 'Anyway, what you will have is access to all the information that will pretty soon be in the hands of the police, the names and addresses of members of the group and friends, that is to say one particular friend, Lucy made while she was an in-patient.

Naturally I shall deny giving this information to you. One of the most distressing things about becoming an administrator, Miss Mitchell, is the number of lies one is bound to tell if one wishes to protect the institution. However, I am sure you know we are not villains. We would never in any way impede the capture of Lucy's killer, even if this led to the most unfortunate repercussions for the clinic. Our position is that we wish to protect our interests as best we may without in any way jeopardising the course of justice.'

'I do fully understand, Dr Bateman.'

'I'm sure you do. If I thought you would not, we wouldn't even be holding this conversation.'

'Can you tell me something about Lucy? The dead, I've always understood, have no rights to privacy.'

'Yes. It has been agreed that I should.' She paused, marshalling her thoughts. 'Lucy was a thirty-five-year-old divorced schoolteacher with a six-year-old child, a girl. The child was only three when Lucy's husband left home to find work in the south. He not only got himself a job, he got a new partner as well. Mrs Lessor's divorce was made absolute while she was still in our in-patient facility.

'Lucy, as I understand it, coped admirably at first with what became very acrimonious divorce proceedings. And then she began to cry and she simply couldn't stop. She couldn't work, of course, and soon she became exhausted. Crying is a very strenuous activity.'

'I'm not sure I quite follow. You mean she never stopped crying for days?'

'She cried virtually without cease. She even cried in her sleep. The child naturally became very distressed, too. Soon Lucy was quite unable to cope as a mother. She forgot to take the child to school, to wash her, to feed her. Lucy's mother begged to be allowed to look after her but Lucy became quite hysterical and barricaded herself in her house. The child managed to get out, determined to go to her grandmother's house, which was not far away. She got lost and landed up in the middle of a dual carriageway. A woman motorist stopped and took her to the police station. It was at this point the social services were called in. Lucy agreed to come into the clinic and her mother took the child.'

'What was the diagnosis?'

'A reactive depression. Lucy was not psychotic, she was responding to adverse circumstances. In fact, she was given no medication, no anti-depressants, no tranquillisers. The doctor who took care of her at the clinic, Eva Dainty, has a policy of only giving medication to psychotics. Lucy did however get a lot of attention and support and though progress was rather slow at first she began to improve very rapidly in the end.'

'What form did her treatment take?'

'Some one-to-one, that is to say doctor–patient sessions, and then she was placed in an in-patient group. Later I believe she joined the meditation classes and she also did art therapy. Her work there aroused some interest. We have a doctor who is researching what you would know as shell-shock, how it affects people who have never been near a battleground – its prevalence or otherwise following domestic crises, for instance – and he found in Lucy's case a degree of depersonalisation in her drawings which would indicate quite severe shell-shock. What I am trying to convey to you is that Lucy was a very vulnerable woman who, though much improved when she left us, still had quite a long way to go.'

'She would be more likely to make wrong decisions? Might get herself in an awkward, even dangerous situation and not know how to get herself out of it?'

'Quite possibly. Normally when a patient leaves us you are thinking of a year, or even two, before the individual could truthfully say: "I feel myself again." '

'And you feel that there is virtually no possibility at all that Lucy's killer was an in-patient with her or a member of the outpatients' group she attended?'

'Absolutely. From the few details which have been released about Lucy's killing I think we can be pretty certain the individual who did this is either a paranoid schizophrenic or a psychopath with sadistic tendencies. They would present with a certain cluster of symptoms. A paranoid schizophrenic, for instance, may hear God telling him to kill prostitutes, have hallucinations about his body, believe that he is being touched or experience electrical sensations or feelings deep in his stomach or chest. The Yorkshire Ripper, for instance, felt a hand gripping his heart. Such a person might feel his thoughts are being tampered with or he could read the thoughts of others; he could also suffer from delusions of perception, and then there is passivity. The research on sadistic killers indicates they hardly ever relate to an adult woman. Most of them are unmarried. A psychopath has a rich sexual fantasy life, dreams about sex and is usually very anxious, given the opportunity, to discuss his fantasies. You may find such an individual interested in whips, torture, female underwear. A psychopath is quite different from a paranoid schizophrenic. Someone like the Yorkshire Ripper mutilated his victims after their deaths but a psychopath mutilates first and so on and so on. We do see such individuals at the clinic from time to time, of course, often because they have come before the court and magistrates decide to obtain a psychiatric report. Naturally, such people would never become part of our community or placed in one of our groups. It would be like putting a wolf in a chicken pen.'

'Could one of your staff have been hoodwinked?'

'The people who are referred to us are usually those who can't function any more. Lucy, for instance, cried so much that it was impossible for her to work and she ceased to be a mother to her child.' She paused and then said: 'Look at it this way. It is not usual for a desperately ill man to deceive his doctors. He knows he needs help, he wants to be cured. Actually, we see our job at the clinic as helping people to help themselves . . . but nevertheless, I'm sure you see my point. Of course, not all our patients are in such desperate straits as Lucy . . . but I would not see the point of anyone entering a consulting room with the intention of deceiving his doctor.'

'Nevertheless, it is surely conceivable that it could happen. And then, of course, there is the medical staff.'

Dr Bateman smiled. 'Quite. But all our therapists will have undergone analysis, you know. It is one of the ways of learning the trade. The kind of killer who is likely to have murdered Lucy would not have been able to survive such intense scrutiny. The odds are that we will find this to have been a stranger killing. That is what this type of murder usually is. The killer's eye has lit on Lucy almost at random, he has perhaps fantasised about the way he will kill her for some weeks, maybe even months, before carrying out his plan.'

Mitch was aware of a minuscule shifting of her bones, a slight rattling in her skeleton.

'If you are right it might take the police some time to find him.'

'That is what I and the chairman of our trustees thought. There might even be, God forbid, other killings. In the meantime the spotlight may fall on the clinic, we might even find the tabloids chasing our patients in the process of concocting their stories. What we want to do is strengthen our position and one of the ways we hope to do this is by employing your agency as our intelligence-gathering service. Will you take the job?'

'Certainly,' said Mitch. 'But one problem immediately occurs to me. Given the need for absolute discretion, how are we to communicate with you?'

'Well, I don't think we need to go as far as a dead letter box.' Dr Bateman's smile was grim. 'I thought you could ring me here each weekend and brief me. If something urgent crops up I think it perhaps is best if we borrow from the spy thriller. Your secretary could get in touch with mine and say that the books Dr Bateman ordered from the library have arrived and could she collect them. I will then make it my business to get in contact with you. Agreed?'

'Agreed.'

'Now we must talk about the financial arrangements.'

7

Jenny Bone had thought she wouldn't see Dr Rainbow again after the first six meetings, which were held in his gloomy consulting room on the ground floor of the Glick Hope. He'd let her talk herself out and eventually she'd thought: What more is there to say? She'd also thought: It hasn't really helped. I still feel so awful.

It was at this point that Dr Rainbow had told her about the Thursday afternoon group he ran. It had been formed about three months ago, he said. He then said it was not the high-flying Wednesday evening group he might have wished her to join. She'd a feeling she'd been relegated to the 'B' stream, but he said brains weren't important when it came to psychotherapy groups. Just as long as a patient wasn't too dim. 'Not below average. Not as thick as two short planks. I once had a stripper who was too dim.' He sounded wistful. He'd added: 'I'll have a word with the group. See if they've no objection to you joining them.'

She'd read the stapled papers he'd given her, notes on what to expect. It caused her to think about what she might be seeking. Redemption, she realised, and was shocked.

She checked the stapled papers to see if redemption was on the agenda.

'Our groups are secular and can accommodate people of any religious persuasion but cannot be counted on to provide answers to questions of a purely religious nature.'

Was redemption a purely religious matter? she wondered.

She read on. 'Nevertheless problems of a philosophical nature, particularly those concerned with the many dilemmas surrounding human existence, are sometimes processed in the group.

'Help may be found in answering questions connected with personal identity, moral values and what might be the best path for you to follow in life . . .'

She was doubtful. That didn't seem to cover redemption. And then she realised she didn't quite know what she meant.

She looked up redemption in the dictionary. 'To recover possession or ownership by payment of a price or service; to regain . . .'

But I can never be as I was before, she realised, for that would be to discount all that has happened. Not redemption then; regeneration? But was redemption a prerequisite of regeneration?

She read the stapled papers again. She saw no reason to hope. Though she was sure they were written with the best intentions, they read like a recipe for blancmange.

She'd go to the group though, for the very good reason that she'd fallen in love with Dr Rainbow. She knew the books on the subject called this transference but all the same she judged it indistinguishable from love.

On the whole she found she was furious with him for getting her in such a mess. Her experience of love was that it hurt.

It's as though I'm taking part in a dance, she thought. The music starts and willy-nilly you begin to fall in with the steps. I'm already dancing to that man's tune. And what's more, he knows it. The smug bastard.

I'd like to kick his teeth in.

But he also stirred other feelings. Some of them would have been more suited to a star turn in a brothel.

She thought perhaps it was as well he'd put her in his Thursday afternoon group for it had become very difficult to be alone with him. Maybe, in the presence of others, she'd be able to control her more outrageous feelings.

She arrived at the clinic early for her first group meeting and, too nervous to sit, walked about in the Turkish bath atmosphere of that soaring tiled hall. Just after two o'clock Dr Rainbow appeared from his dug-out and stood about looking for her. 'I'm here,' she said from behind him.

He turned and beamed down at her. 'We'll go up now and meet the others.'

She noticed at once the two scratches, tiny filaments of new pink skin showing through cracks and breaks in bumpy scabbing. 'What on earth happened to you?' It was only now she spotted the bruise on his cheek. It was yellow and fading out.

'Rescuing a kitten. It had got caught in a neighbour's wire netting. I had to practically lie down to extricate it. Bumped my cheek on a post when it went for me.'

'Rescuing things seems a dangerous occupation.' Jenny found herself studying his hands. They hung down his sides but, because he was so tall, they were level with her waist. They were unscratched.

She followed him. He stooped a little as if trying to shrink his exceptional height. When he did straighten up, his blockish head with its schoolboy haircut sat so well back that two small diagonal indentations, one above the other, appeared towards the bottom of the hair-line. Jenny had realised she'd fallen in love with him when she'd found herself dwelling on these indentations one day, full of the smugness and indulgence a mother has for the oddities of her child.

Like an usher or an undertaker, he supervised her journey up two flights of stairs and showed her into the attic room the others were gathering in. He then casually abandoned her.

The room was large and seemed almost insubstantial in the shadowless grey of northern light. All was bathed in a ghostly uniform chill. Jenny could not think of the illumination as light at all, but an absence of dark. Her heart sank. She sat as near to the door as she could.

Settling, the group took no notice of her but remarked on the absence of two of its members.

'Well, I haven't heard from Ron Saffia or Mirry Vesey,' Dr Rainbow said and then introduced each of the members present to Jenny. As she'd been ignored collectively, she was now ignored separately.

Maurice Pincing said: 'It's odd that Ron's sent no message. Ron always lets us know why he can't come. He's very reliable.'

'Yes,' said Joan Ridley. 'We always know why he's not here.'

'Though it's never a good enough excuse,' Maurice said severely to Ted Coveyduck who was next to Ron's empty chair.

'It certainly isn't.' Joan Ridley, equally severe, lectured Ted.

'I think we ought to do something about it,' said Ted. 'Get someone to take his place.' He turned to glare at the empty chair.

'Give him the sack?'

'Well, he's never here anyway. Is he?'

At first it had seemed to Jenny that the group was coldly indifferent to her, but now she detected an anxiety in it, as if they wanted to tell each other secrets but there was a stranger in their midst. Those present had now shuffled their chairs in such a way that she was already half out of the circle. They seemed intent on leaving her stranded nearer and nearer the door. Hey! she wanted to shout. It's Ron Saffia you want to get rid of, not me!

'I've quite forgotten what Ron looks like,' said Joan. 'Mind you, he's only put in two appearances, or is it three?'

'He's got mad professor hair,' said Ted.

'Well, he is a professor. Or lecturer, is it?' said Maurice.

'It's all frizzy. His hair,' Joan remembered. 'And he always wore that jacket which was three sizes too big for him. You know. Like the fashionable do. What do you think, Edwina? Shall we give him the sack?'

Edwina's strange single knitting needle was arrested mid-air. A silence fell on the group and Jenny, even though she was a newcomer, realised something momentous was happening.

'I don't mind.' Edwina shrugged her huge shoulders and the rest of them seized on her words and wondered at them.

'There!' Joan Ridley was triumphant and with a tug the group joyfully bundled Edwina into its bosom, an act which seemed to leave Jenny even further out in the cold.

If they go on like this, she thought, somehow or other my chair will land on the other side of the door.

'After all,' said Maurice Pincing, 'Ron only has himself to blame. He's already made himself redundant. We're just making it official. What do you think, Sammy?'

Jenny turned to Sammy and was alarmed. My God, he's every man in a dirty raincoat rolled into one. What a little runt.

Sammy's lips had disappeared into his mouth. He was plugging up any word which might try to escape. Anxiety began to flush his skin pink.

'I mean, we never see the man. So what's the difference?' Maurice asked.

Sammy's head moved. The group appeared to decide Sammy was disagreeing with Maurice.

'You're too kind, Sammy. I can't agree with that,' said Joan.

United in the aim of making the absence of Ron absolute, most of the group had now almost succeeded in pushing Jenny out of their circle. She knew now for certain that they wanted to get rid of her, not Ron, but they couldn't work against her directly because she'd been afforded entry by their leader. In consequence it looked as if Ron – by proxy – had got the order of the boot.

'Well, if the group wishes, I'll write to Ron,' said Dr Rainbow. 'Tell him our feelings about his non-appearance. Ask him if he ever intends to come.'

'Yes. That's a good idea.'

'You do that,' said Maurice.

The group, now reviewing its collective effort, saw that the alien was still there and was silent. It was an uncanny quiet. Jenny felt the atmospheric pressure about her abruptly rise so that she was being forced upwards and out of her chair like a cork from a bottle.

Desperately, she looked towards Dr Rainbow. He was a study in lack of concern. Sitting pretty.

'I think I'll just go and get a drink from the vending machine downstairs,' she said. She stooped and took her purse from her bag, but left the bag in their circle. 'I'll be back in a minute.'

On the other side of their door, she began to shiver with rage. Who are they anyway? She'd never met such a bunch of nobodies.

Her hand was still shaking when she drew her plastic cup of cocoa from the vending machine. She became grim as she marched back up the two flights of stairs.

When she entered the attic again, she was aware of the group's hostile eye. If she weren't careful, they'd turn her to stone.

Dr Rainbow now offered her the warmth of his attention. He asked about her journey to the clinic and what she thought of the weather and he mentioned, too, that all the members of the group had said they were very happy to have a newcomer joining them.

The group dissociated themselves from this. They remained mutinously silent. There was a restlessness about them, too. Frustration? If she'd only just clear off they could get on with it. On with what?

She understood from all this that Dr Rainbow's approval of her was not enough; to gain admittance she had to force the others into accepting her.

And a poor lot they are, she thought. If she'd chanced on them in a railway carriage she'd have moved on in the hope of finding more congenial company.

Her attention began to focus on Sammy Pink. Though he was a relatively young man, he nevertheless seemed corrupt in flesh in the way the very old are; the fishy smell of dissolution haunted his figure. Jenny noticed that in spite of the fact that he'd drawn his chair towards the circle, he was not fully of it. He was only tolerated at all, she suspected, because the group had a future role for him to play. That of scapegoat?

Jenny knew she was no Napoleon; she was not about to storm gates, set light to powder kegs, blow trumpets, beat drums. No, she'd get Sammy to let her into the group through the back door.

She observed a little more closely the man she was going to make her accomplice. She would certainly warn friends' daughters against such a fellow.

And yet she recognised him; there was no doubt at all in her mind that Sammy was her inside man.

Sammy Pink, startled at being so closely observed, turned to her. In that moment a spark of recognition flew. She felt her bones jolt. But she was content. Events were set in motion. She was already anticipating the key to the group being pressed into her hand.

Meanwhile, Dr Rainbow was telling them the story of how he came to get his scratches. There was a lot more detail and the delivery became more and more singsong. It's almost as if he's hypnotising us, Jenny thought, as she saw Cherry sink slowly into slumber.

Ted Coveyduck, like Jenny had done earlier, was studying Dr Rainbow's unscratched hands. Though the fingers were long and slender, the base of each hand was broad and powerful. They were good workmanlike hands, though Jenny knew that some slight defect in wiring, or maybe inner tension, could intermittently jam his responses and make him clumsy.

Ted, perhaps thinking about how the psychiatrist had rescued the kitten, began to tell the doctor how ill he was. Things had been very dicey indeed yesterday evening. He'd been walking across the lounge to turn the volume down on the television when suddenly everything went blurred. He was sure he was going to collapse only he didn't. These incidents had been getting more and more frequent, particularly over the past week.

Maurice Pincing yawned.

Joan Ridley studied the ceiling.

Cherry, the cherubic co-therapist, slept on.

Truly, truly. It was awful, Ted was saying. He was so ill he could no longer make love to Sandra, as a matter of fact.

Maurice Pincing straightened in his chair. 'You can't do it?'

Joan Ridley's lips had moved back to reveal her teeth. 'And what does wifey say to that?'

'I must say Sandra has been quite wonderful about it. Very understanding.'

'How long have you been impotent? Weeks? Months?'

'I've been falling off for some time now but the real crunch came Friday week.'

'I must say my Duncan's always been all right in that department,' said Joan.

'I can't manage a thing.'

There was silence.

'I'm sure that sort of thing comes back to you. Like riding a bike.' Joan had turned to Dr Rainbow. Her gaze was slipping down from his face. 'Won't it, don't you think? When he's better? I mean, being as ill as he is . . . it's bound to be off-putting.' She was now staring at the psychiatrist's crotch.

'I'm not ill!' screamed Ted Coveyduck.

They looked about them, stunned.

Ted said: 'I've told you. I've had all the tests. No one can find a thing wrong with me.'

'Men are often impotent at some time in their lives,' said Dr Rainbow.

Ted said: 'Sandra's being really sweet to me. She's real sweet about it.'

'I'm not so sure I like the sound of that,' said Joan.

'What do you mean?'

'Well . . . it could be, couldn't it? . . . that Sandra herself isn't too keen on the sexual side of things,' said Joan.

'Perhaps you don't go a bundle yourself?' said Maurice.

'Duncan's ever so thoughtful, as a matter of fact. I will say that about my hubby.'

'You didn't answer my question.'

'Well, it's not very nice, is it? Talking like this. You men. You've no shame.'

'Dirty talk? Is that how you see it?'

'Men. They can only talk about one thing.'

'It's all right for women. Nothing has to happen. If it doesn't, they can fake it, can't they?' said Ted.

Turning away from Dr Rainbow, Maurice suddenly asked Ted: 'Aren't we going to talk about Lucy? Aren't we going to say one word about her?' His hair flared across his eyes. He forked it back.

Joan went on as if the interruption hadn't happened: 'Always on about it, you lot. The way Duncan looks at me. Looking and looking. What's he looking for, I'd like to know? What does he think I'm capable of doing? Oh, I can read his mind all right. He thinks I'm nothing more than a common tart. He thinks I'm up to no good. I swear I've never given that man the least grounds for suspicion. He's a bit weird, if you ask me. I tell you straight. He should be coming here. He's the one in need of treatment.'

Jenny was studying Sammy Pink again. He's revolting. I bet he pinches panties from lines. But she remained open to him, tolerating all his curiosity. Blushing, he ducked back.

Oh my God, she thought. I know what it is. He does nasty things to boys in loos. Did I have to choose a little pervert as my ally?

She knew why she'd chosen him, though; he was the least. He was the man who had nothing to lose because he was already a complete nobody. The weakest point in the group's structure; the one most likely to admit a foreign body.

'Do you think all men are always on about it?' Dr Rainbow was asking Joan. He wore his suede shoes, the ones with spongy soles, the kind known to Jenny in her childhood as brothel creepers. He was extracting a black cigarette holder from his breast pocket. When he'd fitted it with a cigarette, he looked almost a caricature of raffish maleness.

Joan's teeth were chopping blades. 'I'm sure some men are very respectable. Though you do read such terrible things.'

They stared at her as if egging her on, wanting her to say more. Jenny was once more aware of her isolation. It was as if she'd been plunged into a game without being told the rules.

'I didn't mean . . . oh, poor Lucy . . .'

The door was flung back.

'Mirry!' Ted's little prim mouth was swinging loose.

Jenny saw a fluffy blonde with red rims round her eyes desperately trying to clutch herself together. Her silk scarf was slipping off, she was losing a glove, her handbag was half open.

Mirry, controlling herself sufficiently to shut the door, faced them and was about to say something when she noticed Jenny.

Dr Rainbow formally introduced them.

Mirry disregarded her and told the others: 'I'm sorry I'm late.'

'But what's happened?' asked Joan.

Mirry looked at Jenny, pointing her out to them; they could not expect her to reveal intimacies in the presence of a stranger. The group, almost feverish in their frustration, glared at Jenny. Mirry had hardly sat down before they were assuring her of their efforts to get rid of the alien, but as Mirry observed: 'You mean Ron Saffia.'

Regretfully they admitted they did. Mirry's lips remained sealed.

Perhaps they'll come right out in the open and simply chuck me out of the window, Jenny thought, nervously moving her chair a little nearer the door. It was then that Sammy Pink caught her eye. His smile was shy but reassuring.

The others, intent on Mirry, had not noticed this small act of betrayal.

'But you must tell us why you're late.' Maurice Pincing was

almost menacing. At any moment his bristling muscles might burst out of the confines of his too-tight suit. He might get up and with his bare hands tear the truth out of her.

'I got held up,' Mirry said and turned the subject. 'You're really going to get rid of Ron?'

'Well, I wouldn't put it quite as strongly as that,' said Ted Coveyduck. 'Dr Rainbow's writing him a letter.'

'You mean Christopher. We're supposed to call him Christopher,' Joan reminded them.

'Christopher,' Ted corrected himself.

'I don't think we can really be said to be getting rid of him. I mean, he's never here to be got rid of,' said Maurice. 'Anyway, I believe Sammy thinks he should be given another chance.'

'Saa*aammy*?'

Who-does-he-think-he-is-Sammy stared down his nose as if he, like Mirry, wouldn't give that man credence either.

But Jenny, who wasn't of the group, didn't have to play their games. She knew Sammy and looked him out. Now they were silently laughing together at the group's silliness.

No one brought Mirry up to date on Ted Coveyduck's impotence. Ted's fingers had mounted a shield which rested on top of his lap and this more than adequately covered his shame. The others, mindful of Mirry's 'Saa*aammy*', that lash of scorn, felt the need to protect a man who had now become a wounded comrade. Besides, why should they tell her? She wasn't telling them anything.

Joan Ridley, talking very quickly, began to describe a row she'd had with her husband Duncan. She kept glancing at Mirry, afraid Mirry would change her mind, leap out from the wings, and take the centre stage from her. But Mirry was rigidly upright and tightly stoppered.

Maurice's yawn became wider and wider. Now Jenny could see his tonsils.

At this point Cherry, the co-therapist, stirred out of sleep. Jenny was startled. She'd forgotten the sleeping figure. She noted Cherry had been woken by Maurice's yawns after sleeping through Mirry's dramatic entry.

Joan wound up her story, in which she admitted to throwing a book at her husband, by saying: 'Now he's going to ring Christopher.'

'He rang me on Tuesday.'

'He wants to see you.'

'I told him I wouldn't see him without you being present,' said Dr Rainbow.

'Duncan never told me that. You'll have to see him alone. He wants to talk to you about my behaviour. Discuss the case.'

'Do you want to talk about your behaviour?'

'Well, you know, I can be quite violent when I get my dander up. I quite see his point. I could have put his eye out.'

'I thought you said Duncan wears glasses,' Maurice said.

'Well, yes. Just like pebbles they are.'

'Was he wearing them when you threw... what did you throw?'

'My library book. It's a very nice story. Nothing sordid. You know?'

'If he was wearing his glasses, how could you have put his eyes out? Wouldn't you just knock his glasses off?'

'They could have shattered, couldn't they?'

'Did they?'

'Actually, no. Actually, they are shatter-proof if you really want to know. He worries about some of his clients, you see. Being in probation. I mean, he gets all sorts and lots of them are violent.'

'So you didn't hit him in the eye, then.'

'Did I say I did?'

'You said you caught him in the eye.'

'I did not, Maurice! Anyway, it's the principle of the thing. I could have done him a serious injury.'

'What, you? Can't weigh nine stone.'

'It's rum, do you see?' said Ted, taking over from Maurice. 'I shouldn't like Christopher and Sandra talking about me behind my back.'

'Joan will be here if he comes to see me,' said Dr Rainbow.

'Oh no,' said Joan. 'Duncan won't talk freely if I'm there. You'll get nothing out of that man. Not if I'm there. He likes to do things properly. He knows all about this kind of thing, after all. In case conferences everyone talks about you behind your back. I mean, he is probation.'

'We're all on file,' said Ted. 'My GP's got a hell of a fat file on me. More than one, actually. Of course, I've never seen what he's written about me though I know he must put down terrible things. I mean, the tests I've had. And there's never anything wrong with me. You can bet your bottom dollar on that. I always come up trumps. Every test. In the clear. Fit as a flea. Well, it gives a doctor a bad impression, doesn't it? People are bound to get on their high horse about that kind of thing.'

'I think you're daft, Joan, to let Duncan come on his own. What is the point of people talking about you if you don't know what they're saying? There's not much you can do about anything if you're kept in the dark,' said Maurice.

'Well, you have your idea and I have mine,' said Joan.

'But what exactly is your idea?' asked Dr Rainbow. 'You said I'd get nothing out of your husband if you were there. What do you want me to get out of him?'

'I never said any such thing,' said Joan. 'You're twisting my words.'

'She's always saying that he's the one who needs treatment, not her,' Maurice remembered.

'Women are so devious,' said Ted. 'They tie you up in knots and then complain you're not straight with them.'

'Men are good at that too and what's more they hold the purse strings,' said Mirry.

The group now remained silent, giving Mirry a chance to come forward and tell them why she'd arrived late and in such a state. But Mirry contrived to take herself off to a moral eyrie, high above the snow line, from where she looked down on them from a great distance. It was as if holding her tongue about what distressed her had acquired an angelic virtue. Silence was the stuff saints were made of.

'I'll write to your husband, Joan, and invite you both along,' Dr Rainbow decided.

Now the others had turned to Edwina who was looking at her strange knitting needle as if it were a watch. They glanced anxiously at one another. Mirry's hand flapped in panic. Jenny suddenly realised they were seeking a spokesman.

Maurice cleared his throat and then said: 'What about Lucy? We still haven't said one word.'

There was a restless rustling, almost like a whine of distress.

'We've talked about everything but her,' Maurice said.

'Lucy used to be a group member,' Cherry told Jenny. 'But she felt she was well again and so she left.'

'They found her body at Cold Ash,' said Maurice. 'It was in all the papers. Someone killed her.'

'I wonder if that's why I felt so awful yesterday,' said Ted. 'Why everything's kept going blurred practically all week. But I didn't feel upset when I read about it in the *Birmingham Sentinel*. What I felt was guilty about not being upset. I mean, seeing her name . . . I couldn't seem to get it through my head that she was our Lucy Lessor.'

'Have the police been to see you?' Joan asked Dr Rainbow.

'Yes.'

'Well, they would, wouldn't they,' said Maurice.

'Henry doesn't think it at all right that we should be dragged into it,' said Mirry.

'Have you been dragged into it?' asked Dr Rainbow.

'Well, no. Not yet. But we will be, won't we? Everyone's questioned, aren't they?'

'I think they do want to question everyone in the group. I said I'd ask you if you'd have any objection to me giving them your names and addresses.'

'Do you have to?' asked Ted.

'No,' said Dr Rainbow.

'Of course you must. We've nothing to hide. At least I haven't. I'm sure none of us has anything to hide,' said Maurice.

'I mean, her killer must be found as quickly as possible and anything we can do to help. We all agree, don't we? Does anyone disagree?' asked Joan. She was looking at Sammy Pink.

'She's not dead,' he said.

'We are all finding it difficult to believe,' said Joan.

'Why do you say she's not dead?' Dr Rainbow asked Sammy.

'The police wouldn't go to see Christopher if she wasn't dead, would they?' said Mirry.

Sammy's lips had got stuck together again.

'I could never agree with her skirts,' said Joan.

'What do you mean?' asked Cherry, the co-therapist.

Mirry, though her skirt was over her knees, began pulling down the hem.

'Practically up to her bum.'

'Lots of girls wear short skirts. They don't all get killed.'

'You know what I mean, Maurice.'

'No, I don't.'

'The way she used to eye Ron Saffia. It wasn't right. We're not here for that kind of thing.'

Jenny, recovered from her initial sense of shock, found herself looking at each man in the group. Her eye didn't quite light on Sammy, but slid away.

For the first time she was addressed: 'Actually, you're sitting in Lucy Lessor's chair,' said Maurice.

Edwina wrapped up her knitting and they began to shuffle to their feet. The session was over. As Jenny made her way back down the flights of stairs she wondered if the extreme hostility she'd encountered at the beginning of the group meeting was because she'd frustrated their desire to talk about the dead woman.

She suddenly heard Sammy's voice. He was telling group members who were coming down the stairs behind her: 'Lucy's not dead. I've seen that tasty tart, her knockers practically flying from one end of the room to the other.'

'It's not nice, talk like that,' Mirry said. 'Where would we be without respect for the dead?'

There was the clatter of feet on stairs and then Jenny could hear Ted Coveyduck whispering: 'I didn't think they put schizophrenics in groups like ours, Maurice.'

'What do you mean?'

'You know. Hallucinations and all that.'

'Hush. He'll hear you.'

'Well, you've got to admit it's a bit much.'

Jenny would have liked to linger, to hear more, but she was sure she would be excluded from any circle which might form to gossip in the entrance hall of the Glick Hope. How untimely my entry into this group has proved to be, she thought as she hurried across the car-park to her old blue Volvo. After climbing into the driving seat she found herself just sitting there, staring ahead.

Why hadn't Dr Rainbow started the ball rolling? Why hadn't he brought up Lucy's death earlier in their session?

A frisson lifted the hair at the nape of her neck.

In her mind's eye he was there, selecting a cigarette from his pack and putting it into that black holder. The cigarette smoke was looping the loop over his head. Through it she could see shiny pink baby skin peeping through the scabs on his face. The grey-green eyes she'd thought were impudently bright now glowed, phosphorescent, like the sheen on the side of a fish.

He was laughing at her.

She jumped when she heard a knock on the driver's window. Sammy Pink was there, holding an envelope. As she wound down the window he said: 'Must have come out of your bag when you went for that drink. OK?' He posted it through the widening slit and it fell on her lap. He immediately jogged off. She shouted her thanks to his rapidly retreating back.

8

Mitch looked again at the photograph on her desk. She already knew from the note on the back that it had been taken in Key

West, Florida, last year. Henry and Mirry Vesey were on a narrow jetty made out of thin cross-planks of wood, a pelican on a mooring post behind Mirry's left shoulder and a very green sea beyond them.

At first glance, Mitch thought, Mirry looked strait-laced, a rather glamorous head girl from some ladies' college. Not at all the sort of woman who would pull a little share scam on her own husband.

There was always the possibility she'd been put up to it but in that case it would have to be someone who knew how stockbrokers worked.

Mitch stared at the photograph again. But then this woman doesn't at all look the sort who'd try to commit suicide, she thought. She appears too hard-bitten for that.

She sighed, got up and gazed through her office window at the Mitchell and Orient Bureau. Though it was now getting on for eight in the morning, the day seemed to be in the throes of some kind of breech birth. It couldn't push itself out into the light. I hate this time of year, she thought. Winter coming. Everything so dark. The dark is already here.

She began to think of Mirry Vesey again. Perhaps she looked hard because she'd had to be hard on herself. Wouldn't you have to be very determined to pull yourself up by your boot straps? And when you'd got all that money and status, what happened if you found out that was not what you wanted? She thought of Mirry drinking tea out of a china cup and taking one pill after the other. Did she really not know why she was doing it?

That's incredible. Isn't it?

Had she looked in the mirror one day and not known this woman she'd become?

Did Henry Vesey sometimes now study the woman in his bed and see a stranger?

A.J. breezed into the room. 'Tommy's just on his way up,' she said. Mitch, coming out of this tangle of dark thoughts, smiled at Mitchell and Orient's young assistant. She was a black-haired, blue-eyed Celt with a thick, rich creamy complexion, the texture of a delicious dish, one you'd stick a surreptitious finger in and lick it off. A pair of silver Indian ear-rings flew as she swung her head. The pony tail she was regrowing flew, too. 'I think we ought to have a little sign when we're in conference. Hang it on the door.'

Mitch laughed. She remembered the time when she was a youngster and wanted everything to sound important. 'I'm off home for dinner,' she'd told friends when she was going back to her flat for what her mother would certainly have called 'tea'.

Tommy arrived with the coffee, white china on a black tray. Like Mirry Vesey, he would never have drunk from a pottery mug. He, too, was an awful snob but also, Mitch knew, very fastidious. He kept the chaos of the world at bay by ritual use of both silver spoons and polite habits and yet, she guessed, the chaos was a source of endless fascination to him. Why else would he plunge among it in the guise of detective?

'Right, my dears . . .' he said and the exchange of information began.

'Very little up to now on the Mirry Vesey case,' said A.J. 'I did obs yesterday until five o'clock when Tommy took over. The cleaner came at ten in the morning, nets came down and were washed and on the line by lunchtime. Mirry never ventured out of the house. I was cold, miserable and read half my book.'

'I picked up at five,' said Tommy. 'Henry Vesey arrived after six, and went out about eight. He was back by around ten. I was just about to pack up and go when a red Escort slowed down outside the house, practically stopped and then shot off. I hadn't anything better to do so I decided to follow it. Now this is really weird, Mitch. The car came right through the suburbs into the city and landed up very near your place. I thought that was its destination but then the car reversed just near the place where your TVR was parked. And then, damn it, I lost it. I got jammed behind a single-decker bus. God knows what that was doing in those streets.'

'He stops outside Mirry's house but then goes on and lands up very near Mitch's flat . . .'

'Got to be a coincidence,' Mitch told A.J. 'Probably got lost. That's why he reversed.'

'We don't know it's a he,' said Tommy. 'I never got a proper look at the driver.'

'I'll see if I can sweet-talk Ian into running the car number through the police computer,' said A.J. 'I don't like to ask him too many favours because he gets shirty and thinks I'm only going out with him because he's in the police force. But I think this is something we have to get to the bottom of.'

'I keep wondering if the two Glick Hope investigations we're running will link up at some stage,' said Mitch. 'The whole thing gives me a very funny feeling.'

'There's absolutely nothing on the surface to connect the two. I'd forget your uneasiness and concentrate on the positive aspects. Like in some instances getting paid twice for investigating the same characters. I made a start on the male members of the group by taking a look at this Maurice Pincing. He doesn't add up for a start. The old woman who lives across the street from him told me he was a porter at the North-East Birmingham Accident Hospital. He doesn't appear to be living on a porter's wage. He's got an upmarket maisonette in Sutton Coldfield. Most of his near neighbours appear to be smart young professionals,' said Tommy. 'According to my informant he's well dressed, polite. The old lady didn't exactly say he was middle class but she did say he fitted in very well with the area.'

'So why is he working as a porter? Easier access to drugs maybe? Altruism? He's not as well off as he appears and this is the only job he can get?' Mitch wondered.

'There's something else, too. Before I got chatting to the old woman I rang the bell at his place once or twice and looked in one or two windows as if I couldn't believe he was out.' Tommy grinned. 'You know? Well, on the mantelpiece were three photos, taken abroad, I thought the Continent . . . but I only got the briefest glimpse of what was in the background . . . They were photographs of the same two men, one, judging from the description I managed to get, Maurice Pincing, the other a very good-looking blond man . . . Now, I may be way off beam here, but I got the impression that the blond chap was gay.' He thought about it. 'No, I can't quite pin it down. But the impression is there. And if Maurice's companion actually is a homosexual . . .'

'Well, I don't think it could be a member of his family. Most people don't put three photos of their brother on the mantelpiece,' said Mitch.

'The chap, whoever he is, doesn't appear to be around any more. The old lady hadn't seen him and, believe me, not much happens in that street without her knowing about it. Pincing gets, I was told, very few visitors. No girlfriends as far as she knows.'

'Well, he wouldn't have, would he, if he is gay,' said A.J.

'If he is I think we can rule him out as our murderer,' said Mitch. 'From what I saw Lucy was a sexual thrill killing. His victim would surely have been a pretty boy, not a pretty woman.'

'All I'm going on is the fact that his companion in the photograph gave me the impression of being gay,' Tommy reminded them.

'I've got contacts at the North-East Birmingham,' said A.J. 'A friend of my sister's works there. I think I could find out more about him without showing our hand.'

'Wonderful, my dear. Do that,' said Tommy.

'Mitch and I have divided the women between us,' A.J. told him. 'I drew Joan Ridley and Edwina Grimshaw. Because of the Vesey investigation, I've only taken a look at the Ridley woman so far. I spent a couple of hours digging around and all I came up with was that she lives with her husband who is a probation officer and that she works as a secretary in an estate agent's office in the mornings. And then I had a bit of luck. I ran into this woman who had had a blazing row with the Ridleys. She was more than willing to tell a few tales out of school. According to her, Ridley's husband Duncan was investigated a year or two back when a woman client of his made a formal complaint. She accused him of making suggestive remarks, following her, spying on her.'

'I think at this stage we've got to presume your informant is reliable and take a closer look at the pair of them,' said Tommy. 'But how are we to do that? Have you any contacts in the probation service, Mitch?'

'No. But someone in the Radio Brum news room must have. I'll see what I can come up with.'

'It's struck me that we could do with photos of our subjects,' said Tommy. 'I think we should do that as quickly as possible.'

'Good idea. Nothing like a photo for jogging people's memories,' said Mitch. 'Actually, I'm afraid I've not much to contribute at the moment. On my list is Carole Carmichael, the woman who was friends with Lucy when she was an in-patient at the Glick Hope. But she's moved and I spent the best part of three hours tracking down her new address. I thought I'd go there round about teatime tonight. Most people are in then. I'm not at Radio Brum tomorrow so I can take over the Mirry Vesey observation. That will free you two for the Dr Bateman enquiry.'

'I expect the picture will start to become a bit clearer by the end of the week,' said Tommy. 'And then we can make some policy decisions.'

'Something has been bugging me. Not about the Mirry Vesey investigation. The reason Henry Vesey is employing us is straightforward enough. But Dr Bateman...' Mitch paused, trying to tease out her worries. 'I mean, it's all a bit nebulous...'

'It seems perfectly reasonable to me that a foundation like the Glick Hope would try to avert any bad publicity which might be on its way. Much of their funding does come from donations. And to exhume that old cliché – to be forewarned is to be forearmed.'

'Lots of big institutions employ detective agencies these days for all sorts of tasks,' said A.J.

'Perhaps I've been a journalist too long,' said Mitch. 'I've started to smell the reek of fish in bare cupboards. Well, must love you and leave you. I'm doing an interview for the radio station at nine. I'll ring the bureau before I leave the studios. Check up on the latest.'

But Mitch was so busy she forgot to put in the call, though she did manage to find time to go up to Radio Brum's news room and shake out a couple of social services contacts. She stuck the names in her bag. She wanted time to work out the best way to go about getting the information she needed.

By the time she left the studios a small inverted V of an ache hung from the knob at the top of her spine and there was a heaviness behind her eyes, as if small weights had been attached to her optical nerves. What she wanted to do was go home, undress, and have a gin and tonic handy by her toothbrush as she showered. But at the moment she hadn't got a home, only this couple of rooms, ridiculously dignified by the name of flat, where Count Dracula was likely to rear his death's head and ask to have a G and T with her. If she was ever going to raise the wind to get herself a decent pad she'd better hoist her shoulders back into position and do a bit of yomping over to Carole Carmichael's place.

Though it was only just after six, it had already been dark for an hour. Spray rose rhythmically from under wheels as cars reversed through light-streaked puddles, then circled towards the exit gates of the car-park. Mitch chucked her bag and an unedited tape on to the ledge at the back of the TVR and fished her keys out of her jacket pocket. She settled herself into the driving seat, switched on the interior light, and took a look at the A–Z. Carole Carmichael lived in Kings Heath. Mitch turned right when she emerged through the security barrier. She turned right again at Pershore Road. She wriggled her shoulder blades, trying to ease the ache.

The large terraced houses in Great Wire Street had been built at the turn of the century. Many of the short front gardens retained the privet hedges which had been so popular before the war. Some bore strange fruit: an empty crisp packet, a polystyrene box which had held a takeaway meal, an empty Coke can, a child's lost yellow mitten. They hung between the moist leaves Mitch glimpsed between parked cars as she looked for a place to leave the TVR. She drew into the kerb at the top of the street. It had begun raining again. She fished in the back for an umbrella.

Number sixteen had been turned into flats. Three names were in slots beside bells arranged on a wooden board mounted on the old grass green tiles in the porch. Mitch rang the middle bell and looked around her, shaking and closing her umbrella. Above her head was an embossed tiled border of acanthus leaves and above that the plasterwork had been painted toffee pink. Mitch rang the bell again.

The girl who opened the door was not far short of six feet and the colour of crystallised dates. There was a musky hint of purple blue where her flesh shadowed, enhanced by the peacock blue scarf plaited through her glossy jet locks. Mitch had seen these extraordinary skin tones before; they usually occurred in people of mixed African, Indian and white parentage. Feasting on the vision before her, she forgot to introduce herself.

'Yes?'

'Sorry. I'm Mitch Mitchell and I hope you're Carole Carmichael. I work for Radio Brum and I'm hoping you'll help me with some research I'm doing for a programme.'

'I saw you once when you were doing an outside broadcast in Chamberlain Square. Come on in. I don't know how I'll be able to help but I'll do what I can. I'm on the top floor. I warn you, it's a bit of a dump. Beggars can't be choosers.'

Carole Carmichael was no conventional beauty; she had the large beaky face of a Plantagenet and rather hooded eyes which made her appear to be looking inwards rather than at her surroundings. Even though she could be no more than nineteen, there was already an authority about her, partly due, Mitch thought, to her height and the craggy boniness of her head.

There was very little trace of her personal possession of the flat, rented fully furnished, Mitch guessed. A Monet print hung over the fireplace, and there were a couple of postcards propped up on the pink-painted cast-iron mantelpiece. Books were lined up along the back of a fifties teak sideboard with splay legs. Folders and more books were stacked under it.

'I am told that you were recently in the Glick Hope and while you were there formed a friendship with Lucy Lessor. I'm trying to get a programme together on women as victims, looking to see if anything marks those women out as being more vulnerable than their sisters. At this stage I am simply trying to gather background information. Your impressions would be very helpful.'

'I'm not sure I can help you much. Do sit down, please. Lucy was sixteen years older than me. People would have said I was the vulnerable one. Lucy was my big sister. Look, it's a bit soon, isn't it? I mean, her family . . .'

'I'm sorry, Carole. I realise you must have been fond of her. But

I really need to ask the questions now. I mean, while your impressions of her are vivid. The programme itself won't go out until next year.'

'I see. Yes. I do see. Actually, I don't feel a thing. Someone took a photo of us together while we were in the Glick Hope and I dug it out last night and looked at it. Not a thing. That's one of my problems, of course. Inappropriate affect. I might have frozen up somewhere along the way. I might have been born like that.'

'Do you mind telling me how you came to be friends?'

She didn't immediately answer. Then she said: 'You know, she had a feeling something dreadful would happen to her. I suppose you might call it a premonition. She'd been in the Glick Hope a month when I was admitted. She was the one asked to show me around, teach me the ropes. We were in the dining-room when she burst into tears and I suddenly found myself crying. A bit of a first for me. Lucy's tears were somehow catching. And then she put her arms round me and apologised and told me she was much better than she had been. We found we both had the same shrink, Eva Dainty. I mean, we became buddies, comparing notes, looking out for each other. I seem to gravitate to older women. Eva would say I'm always on the look-out for a surrogate mother.'

'Did Lucy have any other friends while she was in the hospital? Any male friends who visited?'

'Her mum and dad visited her and Becky, her daughter. But nobody else as far as I know. All the patients got along pretty well. I mean, that's the idea. A therapeutic community, lots of positive feedback. We were a pretty mixed bunch, of course. You get to look at your problems through many different eyes, problems you often don't even know you have. Another of mine, for instance, is I'm an over-achiever. Quite literally too clever for my own good. With all this feedback going on you get to learn how to handle the things other people find difficult about you. I don't say this kind of thing works for everybody but it worked for Lucy and me. She left perhaps a bit too early because she wanted to be with her daughter. It was arranged she should go in an out-patient group so she would have some support for the first few months she was out.'

'Did you see her after she left?'

'She used to pop down to see me after she'd been to her out-patient group. That was on Thursday afternoons. I told her I was leaving Birmingham when I was discharged.'

'Why did you do that?'

'Some friendships only work in exceptional circumstances. Back in ordinary life they can become a bit of a chore. I didn't want our friendship to end on a sour note. I wanted to remember it as the good thing it was.'

'So you haven't seen her now for quite a while?'

'Actually, I bumped into her about ten days ago. She was sitting up to the counter in the sandwich bar in the underground foot subway near Rackhams. It was quite a shock to see her. She looked so different.'

'In what way?'

'Well, terrifically attractive. Being in tears a lot, being depressed generally, does nothing for your looks. I mean, this was a new Lucy. She was a knock-out. New hairdo, good make-up, showing a lot of leg. I made some excuse about coming back to Birmingham to pick up some stuff but I think she understood. I think she guessed I'd never left the city. She gave me a real old-fashioned look. You know? She told me she'd left the group because she'd fallen for one of the members. Group members aren't supposed to meet outside the clinic. Generally people want to follow the rules. It's like being in church. You want to perform all the rituals properly. Anyway, Lucy left the group so she could see him. It didn't work out, though. That was one of Lucy's problems. She always managed to do something to men that in the end turned them off.'

'Do you know the name of the man from the group she fancied?'

'No. She didn't say and I didn't ask. After all, it hadn't really got off the ground, had it? Just before I split she seemed to get alarmed and started looking around. She said she thought someone was watching her. She said it had happened before. I thought that was a bit of a joke. I mean, she had dolled herself up, hadn't she? She was looking terrific. What did she expect? I told her to forget this man in the group. She could take her pick.' She thought about it. 'Maybe she needed a man but didn't really like men. Maybe I'm speaking for myself. Maybe I don't really like men. I mean, none of this is set in concrete. These are just my impressions of Lucy. I'm talking off the top of my head. You know?'

'You mentioned she had a premonition. She had a feeling something dreadful would happen to her.'

'Perhaps not really a premonition. She told me she wouldn't live to see forty. She told everyone that. She was really bothered about what would happen to her little girl. Of course, Lucy was being treated for depression at the time. Quite often depressives think they are going to die. Some commit suicide. Some believe they are already dead. It is so dark down there that one or two disappear altogether. They don't even inhabit a corpse. They become see-through. Invisible.'

Mitch found herself staring at Carole. There was a ghost of a smile round the girl's lips. 'Dante only told the half of it,' she said.

'Well, thank you for your help.' Mitch stood up, gathering her umbrella and bag.

'Want to see a photo of us taken while we were in the clinic?'

'Please. If I could.'

Carole sorted through a pile of envelopes on the mantelpiece. She handed Mitch two snaps. 'Both graduation pictures in a way. This was taken of me and her the day before she left the clinic.'

Carole was standing behind a chair, bending towards a small, dark woman who was sitting cross-legged. There was something childlike about Lucy Lessor. Her sweater and leggings were too big. Mitch was reminded of her schoolgirl days, when her mother bought gymslips and blazers a size too large. 'You need room for growth,' she always said. But perhaps Lucy had lost weight while she was ill? The way she was holding Carole's hand made her think that if anyone was playing big sister or mother it was the young kid.

'Second graduation,' said Carole, showing her the other photograph. 'I took this one of her and the out-patients' group after her last session. She asked me to, God knows why. The group agreed so I did it but in actual fact Lucy and I lost touch almost immediately afterwards. I'd forgotten all about the pictures to be honest. It wasn't until I saw this photo of her in the newspaper . . .'

The group photograph had been taken in the summertime. The men were in T-shirts or shirt-sleeves, the women in dresses or skirts and short-sleeved tops. 'Would you mind if I kept these for a day or two? I promise I'll post them back.'

'Why?'

'You know. Body language. What it might tell us.' The lie was so bald that Mitch had an almost irresistible urge to elaborate. She controlled it.

Carole Carmichael did not think her explanation too improbable. 'Sure,' she said.

There was a feeling of relief when the door of number sixteen closed behind her and she found herself out on the pavement, the rain already beginning to dampen her hair. Now she could knock off, go home and put her feet up.

She was just about to close the curtains in the sitting-room of her flat when a movement attracted her attention. Something there in the shrubbery under the trees at the bottom of the garden.

'She said she thought someone was watching her,' Carole Carmichael had said.

A sudden noise made her feet stand proud. It's the telephone, you fool, she told herself crossly.

'You can be really difficult to get hold of. You know that? One minute you're in the studio, the next you've left,' said Radio Brum's station manager. 'I heard you were after someone for your community care programme. You know, a nut. Or whatever they call them. Client, service user or whatever.'

'I suppose Digger's been talking.'

'Well, I think I've got one for you. Do you know that woman in the flat next to mine? Adelaide Perkins?' asked Freya Adcock.

Mitch sighed and reached for her pen.

9

Sammy Pink was sitting on an upturned crate in Miss Cadman's garden shed eating his lunch and reading his employer's Sunday newspaper. She had given him a Bakewell tart and the paper before he started work that morning and then gone off to her upholstery class at the local college of further education. Munching his cheese sandwich and drinking coffee from the flask, he glanced at the naughty vicar story again and then reread the juicier bits. He was about to turn the page when he glimpsed the words 'was there to witness everything' and quite unbidden there came into his head a picture of Juicy Lucy, down on all fours, head neatly tucked in and bottom rearing enticingly.

He heard himself telling Ted Coveyduck and Maurice Pincing: 'Lucy's not dead. I've seen that tasty tart, her knockers flying from one end of the room to the other.'

He came out in a sweat at the thought of it. What he needed was his tongue cut out, his dick too, for that matter. They'd tell the fuzz, wouldn't they? And then the pigs would know Sammy Pink was still up to his old tricks.

Anyway, Ron Saffia couldn't have been giving Juicy Lucy one. The tart was dead.

I'll say I dreamed it, decided Sammy. They're always talking about their dreams in the group, just as if dreams were real, like frying a bit of bread or rooting a geranium cutting.

And suddenly he found himself reading the words 'was there to witness everything' again and Juicy Lucy's mop of luscious curls swung as the rutting corpse looked at him from over her shoulder. Roots of his hair jigged as he found himself staring into the eyes of Jenny Bone. Her face was thrust towards him and then swayed away as she danced on a penis as long as a pike. Her inky eyes were somnolent and half shut, her eyelids smiling at him.

His loins fluttered. The image and his erection disappeared. Still quivering, he leaned back against the wall of the garden shed. Agitated fingers pushed his hair from his forehead.

You'd better watch it, Sammy, he told himself. That pecker of yours was always big trouble. It was bad enough last time you were caught and that was just for looking.

'Don't you like to touch?' Dr Rainbow had asked him.

'Just look,' Sammy had mumbled. 'Only a bit of a look.'

'Why don't you like to touch?'

'They're women, aren't they?'

'Don't you like to touch women?'

'They don't like it. Nothing to do with me. Nothing wrong with me. They don't like it.'

'You've tried?'

'Fat chance,' said Sammy. 'I just look. No harm in looking, I'd have thought.'

'Have you ever been out with a girl?'

But at this point Sammy had got mulish. 'Piss off,' he'd wanted to say but he didn't know if that would land him back in court.

Anyway, it's quite all right, he told himself now. That Jenny's no more than a stick, she is. I like a bit of flesh on them myself, something to grab and swing with. Pathetic, she is.

I like tits.

That bird Jenny gives pancakes a bad name, she does.

Brushing crumbs away, he stood up. He packed the remains of his lunch in the haversack which had once been used by his Uncle Norman, then went to finish off digging over the back end of Miss Cadman's vegetable plot. Before he left Poppy Cottage he posted her Sunday paper through the letter box.

Miss Cadman's cottage was quite close to Cherry Park, so Sammy walked there and back. He didn't mind at all. He even liked walking in the rain. The world smelled so different when it was wet. Tarter. Nothing wrong in walking, what got him was having to deny himself use of the car because money was so tight all the time. All because his Aunt Ada wanted to swan about queening it in Magnolia House.

Making a detour through the new housing estate, he selected a bottle of milk on the steps of a dormer bungalow. He pretended to ring the bell, then bent to retie the lace on his boot. As he did so he scooped up the bottle and secreted it in the inside pocket of his anorak. Whistling triumphantly, he made off down the path.

Teach the lazy cow a lesson, he thought as the bottle bumped up against his heart. She won't leave her milk out all day again.

Reaching the edge of the estate, he saw Magnolia House through the trees. Fury spurted. It's not even as if she was anyone once, he thought. Her father was a brickie. Who does she think she's kidding? The plain fact is she was never brought up to be waited on hand and foot just as if she was somebody.

The last of the leaves were beginning to fall from the trees in Cherry Park, well-pruned branches emerging liked maimed warriors. Now when he came home he was always aware of how dear Denmark Villa was to him; the shape of the bay window, the shiny brick used to form the ornamental arch above the door, the tile mosaic surrounding the mat well in the porch. When he opened the gate and walked up the short blue brick path sometimes his stomach tightened on a great babyish howl of protest.

In spite of the fact that he couldn't afford to, he'd taken to giving himself little treats, biscuits coated on both sides with chocolate, plastic pots of jelly from the Co-op, ice-cream with rum and raisins in.

I'll have one of those jellies with my tea, he thought now as he took off his boots in the porch. Holding them in his hand, he walked down the chill hall.

After tea he'd give his binoculars a good polish. His heart jumped again, this time in excitement. At one time he'd used the binoculars his Uncle Norman had brought back from the navy. But, on a fairly recent occasion, he'd been surprised and in his haste to get away he'd left them behind him.

That wasn't the story he'd told Dr Rainbow. 'I'm never, never going to look again. The dustman took my binoculars away Tuesday week. Chucked them out I did. Swear to God.'

All the same, Dr Rainbow had said: 'I think you ought to join the group.'

'I'm no good at that sort of thing.' Sammy was twisting in his misery.

'You don't have to join,' Dr Rainbow had said. 'But I think you'll find it very helpful.'

Still haunted by the chilling image of the chairman of the magistrates, he'd caved in. 'If you think so. But I'll never look again. That's for sure. And I'll tell you another thing. They won't like me being there pretending to be a member of their group. People really don't like that kind of thing.'

He began toasting bread and then opened a tin of sardines. Anyway, I never do nothing wrong. And I wouldn't even have got some new bins if it wasn't for that Colonel Snoddy. What did he have to go and mention that readers' offer for? It's all his fault. People like that are forever getting people like me in trouble. I suppose if they didn't put temptation in other people's way they could never do their magistrating or coloneling. They'd have no one to get uppity with. It just shows you. People like that will stop at nothing and all because they want to look down their nose at you and think how much better they are. He was getting righteously angry.

And now look where they've landed me. They've got me seeing a psychiatrist. What's potty about wanting to see a tart getting a good poking from a chap? Why, every night of the week people are hiring films to see those sort of carryings-on and no one sends them to get their heads examined.

'What's the difference?' Sammy asked a headless sardine.

He began to wonder what Jenny had done wrong to get herself put in a group. Actually, she wasn't a patch on that Mitch Mitchell, but then when you go and hunt down a star and take a peek at the boobies and bum you expect something a bit special, don't you? But when he thought of that now, when he thought of Jenny's boobies, flatter than pancakes even, he came all over tender and protective. Jenn-eee . . . oh, Jenn-ee . . . And the bitch looked over her shoulder at him with those inky asking eyes and she spread herself a little wider.

He groaned. Look what Dr Rainbow had gone and done. Oh, he'd known that man was as dangerous as a barrel-load of monkeys from day one. Why, you'd only to see the way that man moved. He'd never known anyone's bones think like the psychiatrist's and Sammy could bloody well see why now. He's saving himself from plunging head first down the pitfalls he's engineering for everyone else, he told the sardine. You can bet your tail, fishy, that the doctor isn't being tormented by a pair of inky asking-for-it peepers.

But maybe the doctor was. Maybe those scratches weren't made by a kitten of the four-legged variety. There was no reason why a psychiatrist shouldn't take his trousers off like someone normal, was there?

He now spoke his thoughts aloud. 'Thank God I don't like skinny women. If she'd been built, the fat would really have been in the fire.'

But even when he was free of the image of her eyes, her name seemed to whisper about his ears causing the hairs at the nape of his neck to waft to and fro, like palm fronds in southern breezes.

It's women who do for a man. No doubt about it. In no time at all the poor sod's up before the beak or having his head examined or catching something very nasty.

He turned on the six o'clock news in the hope this would distract him. He saw Mrs Thatcher, plant pot hat and one string of pearls, telling the people of America what was what. Well, she's not skinny, he thought, you've got to give her that.

Later he cleaned his binoculars. After all, fifty pounds was a fortune. He couldn't afford not to clean his bins.

As soon as he'd taken them out of the dresser drawer, he knew he was going out 'on a recce'. He used his Uncle Norman's military slang to try and make his enterprise sound more respectable. The price of all the petrol he found himself using now was really beginning to worry him. Perhaps he could suggest taking his aunt on an outing and get her to fill up the tank?

He was pretending to himself that he had a choice, that he didn't have to go and sniff round Jenny Bone. He was thinking of Mitch Mitchell and how clever he'd been at hunting her down, following the bitch home from the studios one evening. Of course, she was the oldest of the lot of them but some women, he reckoned, were like pheasants. They were tastiest of all when they'd gone off, when they weren't too high, mind, but high enough. Ms Mitchell was well-hung meat in every respect. He picked up his rope and length of dog lead. It was going to be a cracker of a night. He knew it.

It had been raining and it was windy. The night had been scoured and was sparkling. It was then Sammy realised that it wasn't the night that had changed, but him. Everything was clearer in his vision, as though that which had always been blurred had pulled into sharp focus.

He knew this new way of seeing had to do with just one woman.

Jenny looked at me, and even though it's night, I can see better. Sammy, though he was frightened, marvelled.

Jenn-eee . . .

Suddenly it was as if she were entering every pore of him, flooding him out, washing him clean.

Nonsense. She was just a bitch like all the rest of them. Just a bag of bones. Catch him going to see her when he didn't have to. When there were better fish to fry.

He didn't have to see nobody he didn't want to.

He'd go and see Mirry Vesey.

As he got into his car he told Jenny Bone to sling her hook.

She'd be bloody sorry if she didn't.

He put his foot down and roared along as if doing so would leave that inky-eyed bitch far behind him. The houses on the opposite side of the road gave way to fields. Cabbages, carrots, swedes, in their season they'd all flourish on this rich market gardening land. On his side of the road he could now glimpse more fields in the gaps between the houses; sometimes he saw the wires which ran along the main railway line to Euston. On a still night he could even hear the rattle of the trains in Denmark Villa. Sammy had acute hearing; sometimes he believed he heard the noise of the planet turning through space.

The straggle of building ended with a large Victorian house set close to the road. But as he slowed down he could see that curtains were drawn against the rosy glow of the lamps within. So much for Mirry Vesey, he thought. Just like that hoity toity bitch to spoil a man's fun.

His heart had begun to sing like a budgie in its cage.

Satisfied now that he needn't see Jenny Bone if he didn't want to, that he could eye up any tart he wanted to, thank you very much, he put his foot right down on the accelerator and shot off to his love.

Now he felt free enough to sing the praises of his lady. For a start, he'd bet Jenny's background was a lot classier than Mirry's for all Mirry's scented handkerchiefs and soft kid gloves. A smart woman, Jenny. Full of her own ideas of herself and none of them cheap, he reckoned. A classy lady with a brain or two in her head.

And that lady had not looked at that big dick Maurice Pincing, nor Ted; she'd not looked at Dr Rainbow. She'd chosen him. Sammy almost crowed.

And then he found himself asking why? Nobody looked at Sammy Pink. He was always overlooked.

He began wondering if she got her kicks from rough trade – was that the reason she'd been put in the group? Sammy knew all about rough trade from reading Miss Cadman's Sunday papers. Even royal blood managed to get itself up the spout with Mr A.N. Other.

There isn't really anything wrong with having a skinny little body. Very fashionable that, after all, though if you fancied a juicy pair of knockers you were well out of luck.

But I've always liked plenty swinging about up top.

What's the matter with me?

Those inky eyes again. Sammy found himself licking his lips.

Suddenly the land began to vibrate. A hum became a roar. The sound of the hooter was left in the air after the deafening rattle of steel wheel on track had died away. The Intercity bound for London, he reckoned. He'd only been to the capital a handful of times; he found it dirty and smelly, too many people fouling too little land.

Much better here, in this fecund place, where a man could sniff out the lair of the dark Jenny Bone. In his mind he was perfecting her. He was rounding her out, growing her short hair down her back. He made her skin as waxy as a cherry petal. He rather overdid her breasts and had to take off half a foot. He went too far altogether when he gave her a Venus mount as large as Vesuvius. He almost drove into a hedge when it erupted. He did a redesign job. Sometimes it was better to start again from scratch.

As he approached, the poles which barred the level crossing were lifting, inserting themselves snugly into the night. He put the car back into top gear.

Five minutes later he was on the outskirts of Sutton Coldfield. He took a left turn into Tamworth Road and then left again at Whitehouse Common. He looped St George's Barracks and took a third left by St Catherine's Close. He nosed down Withy Bottom Lane.

He pulled the car into a grass verge, got out and locked it. As he straightened he saw to the north a rocket burst in the brownish neon wash of the night sky. Another went up and there was a huge cascade of twinkling silver lights. He sniffed, almost expecting to inhale a gunpowdery smell. But the fireworks were far too far away. He waited but there were no more lights in the sky. Well, you've got to keep most of your powder dry for Bonfire Night, he thought. 'Couldn't wait, won't have,' his Aunt Ada had always said. Now she was in Magnolia House he'd bet she'd forgotten November the fifth altogether and if she hadn't she'd be too idle to get off her b.t.m. and see the show.

He walked down a road which rapidly became a single lane track. There was a short row of cottages on the right-hand side. He counted up the numbers. Almost there. Two houses to go. The cottages ended but a little further on were two bungalows. Hers was set in a triangle of land which shelved down towards a stream. The light was on in one of the two box bays which flanked the front door. The curtains were drawn but against the glow he could see a shadow. The breath sighed out of him.

Did he have a heart?

If he did, it had stopped beating.

And then it fluttered like a bird trapped in a chimney.

The palms of his hands were sweating. His vision blurred.

The fuzziness became the shadow in the window and then was the inky darkness of her eyes; friendly eyes. He was astonished all over again. When she'd looked at him she'd seen – like the chairman of the magistrates – a pervert. But she'd judged him worth knowing. She'd seen something in him.

Bewildered, he shook his head.

'Sphinx, that's your woman,' his Uncle Norman had told him once when they were heeling in geranium cuttings. 'All riddle and no reason. They're like cats, my boy. Did you ever hear of a man and his cat? Dogs yes, but cats, there's no fathoming them.'

Even as he was remembering this and seeing his Uncle Norman's beaky nose and ginger moustache he was also observing that the bungalow was hedged in by holly and that there were one or two gaps.

Without making a conscious decision he was over fencing and his shoes were sinking into the newly ploughed field which surrounded the bungalow. He chose a gap in the hedge near the very end of the long back garden.

In the untended nettle and bramble wilderness of Jenny's garden, his heart performed such a huge somersault he seemed to have to wait forever for it to plunge earthwards again into his ribcage. When it did, it rocked dizzyingly.

What she needed, it was obvious, was a man like himself to clear her land of weeds and replant it. He saw rows of carrots and celery. Artichokes, root ginger, asparagus. Only the best, only the most succulent, only the tenderest, should ever pass her lips.

My Jenn-ee. Oh, Jenn-eeee!

As he crept nearer the back of the bungalow he could see a small line of her underwear slapping jauntily about in the stiff night breeze. His finger reached out to poke the gusset of her knickers. Like sticking your finger up the trumpet of a lily, he thought, only there wouldn't be a sticky yellow of pollen to lick off. And then he noticed the gap on the line, between the pair of knickers he had touched and the next pair. Just enough space for another pair of knickers and a bra.

He rounded the coal bunker and moved nearer the kitchen window. Flitting towards her nest he was revelling in his skills as a master of his craft; he was an art form in the adoration of his dark lady. He was so much a part of the night he was invisible; a breath of a brownish shadow.

The kitchen light snapped on. The curtains were undrawn. His eyes and mouth rounded. When he saw his love he didn't recognise her. She'd not got long hair at all, it was short. What was more, her breasts had practically vanished. He couldn't see her hips but guessed that there was nothing in that region which would recall Vesuvius.

But instead of being disappointed he now loved her, oh so tenderly, for all that she lacked. I don't mind, he wanted to shout. In all that was lacking he saw the most perfect vision of all. The vision of his love.

Sheee-eeee . . . and it was as if the sharp, unfriendly wind of the night held this soft thread of sound like the carapace of some sea creature.

It was while he saw her making herself a cup of coffee that he became angry.

What was she doing in this isolated place out in the middle of nowhere?

Didn't she realise how dangerous it was?

Anyone could break in and seize her. Any Tom, Dick or Sammy could grab her from behind and force her to her knees.

Didn't the silly bitch know she was in mortal danger?

The light snapped off.

His love vanished. In the blink of an eye.

He selected the flimsiest knickers on the line and a matching bra. He popped the pegs in his mouth as he unpinned them and then pocketed the pegs and the underwear.

He was short of pegs.

And then the thought occurred to him.

Had someone been there before him?

His foot felt around.

He picked up one dolly peg. He picked up another.

10

In her own home Mirry was beginning to feel like a spy in occupied territory. And she wasn't at all sure Henry wasn't on to her. The way he looked at her sometimes! Of course, she'd not told the group about Henry and the way he had of staring at her, as if he didn't know her at all. After all, Joan Ridley had cornered the market in husbands who looked.

Henry couldn't be on to her, could he? He'd have said something.

What am I going to do? She sat down on the *chaise-longue*. Sometimes, and this was one of them, she saw the Mirry who had stopped counting the sleeping pills she was popping into her mouth, then saw her lying down and folding her hands neatly across her chest, tidying herself away. What had worried her the most was the fact she hadn't collected the dry cleaning and now never would.

As it was she got it three weeks later because Henry had needed his pin-stripe suit and she her cream three-quarter length jacket.

Once or twice she'd felt a little envious of Lucy Lessor. It was obviously much easier if someone else did the killing. Of course, he might have hurt her first. The prospect of pain terrified Mirry. If it could be quick and no pain, well, that wasn't so bad, was it? She was sick of gazing in her mirror and seeing a normal face look back at her. How could all her terrible wounds have been magicked away by a piece of bevelled glass? Where were the crushed bones, the bleeding flesh, the torn sinews of her being?

All in your mind.

That's where Henry would say they were if she gave him the chance, something she'd no intention of doing.

She got off the *chaise-longue*. She walked up her drawing-room and then down it. It had originally been two rooms, a drawing-room and a morning room. Now the two were connected by an elegant archway and the whole area covered in thick soft grey-green carpet. The walls were pale pink and Henry's small collection of Victorian oil paintings were lit by elongated brass lamps. It was not a room you could see out of unless you lifted the net at one of the bay windows, which Mirry did now. The bright late October sun winked at her.

I'll buy a new dress, she thought. That will cheer me up. Oh, if only we were out to dinner tonight. She was thinking that Henry would get on to her again about going to the group and they would have another row.

She dropped the freshly laundered net. She didn't really think anyone in the group had killed Lucy Lessor, though fear had once or twice surprised her. She did have to admit to studying the male members very carefully after hearing the news. The one who really stuck in her mind was Dr Rainbow with that absurd cigarette holder of his; what could be more villainous than the picture he created?

Or could it be that, among the men in the group, Dr Rainbow frightened her the most?

And yet something about him thrilled her, just as it had about Henry when they'd first gone out together. She responded to power, opening her petals like an ice plant when the sun comes out.

She was smiling a little. Oh, Henry and her in the old days. The way they'd eyed each other then.

Looking back, it seemed a fairy tale. He'd rescued the beautiful Cinders from the wickedness of a life of drudgery. He'd swept her off her feet in old-fashioned style: flowers, expensive meals, detailed attention to her comfort.

And she'd not just fallen in love with his money, his position, the life he could offer her. She delighted in his flesh. They had hardly been able to keep their hands off each other.

When she'd miscarried twice it was he who had decided that she'd been through enough. He wouldn't risk her trying for another child.

He truly loved her in his way.

She viewed this early part of their marriage in wonderfully bright colours; she heard it in majestic surges of music.

And yet, she saw now, the flaws had been there even before she'd had her miscarriages. He must wipe his feet on the woman he put on a pedestal and worshipped, this sweet mistress of his dreams. He must see a worm in the apple of his eye. This vision of his love must be forever at fault in order to reassure him of his faultlessness. Imperfect, she perfected him.

When they no longer lusted for each other, the flaws became gapingly apparent; holes through which sniping winds blew. She'd grown colder and colder. Slowly the flesh of her life had become embalmed in permafrost.

Had she become frozen stiff in an effort to stop him sucking out any more of her goodness? All the same, she'd become good for nothing. Not even good enough to live.

The worm had digested the apple.

Perhaps all those years ago I already felt that I was not good enough to have his babies and murdered them before I tried to murder myself.

All in the name of love; to be bad enough for him to feel really good.

Even so, she'd put down this being out of sorts all the time to the dampness. Fogg House was a devil for dampness.

'I get so tired,' she tried, aware of how feeble she sounded. 'I'm bone weary. Drained.' She'd always tarted herself up before these expeditions to the Health Centre; after all, she told herself, one can't be entirely without pride. She had to think of Henry and his position. One couldn't let the side down. 'I'm having periods all the time or I'm never having one,' she said and wondered what in the world it must be like not to spout blood regularly, like a cracked teapot. 'I never get a wink, really, but of course there are difficulties. Henry can't stand a duvet and I don't do well with blankets.' She tried harder. 'I feel so faint. As though there's nothing in me. Perhaps I'm on the change but surely it's too early for that? Well, I'd have thought so. Is it diabetes? My grandmother had that. I simply can't keep up with him at all. Henry. You know? And, of course, it's not right. I'm so much younger than he is. It should be me who has all the energy. Of course, he's always on the go. That man never stops. The council, fund-raising for the roof of St Mary Martha, Good Samaritans, the hospice. But I'm only thirty-two, after all. I'm not an old woman. I shouldn't be as tired as this. It's not natural. I feel like death.' She was aware she was boring her doctor. The back of his bald head rested in clasped palms and he was rocking his chair up and down. One day he'll topple over and break his neck, she thought. You'd think a medical man would have enough sense to realise you don't mess about like that with a chair.

She persisted. 'Perhaps it's iron? Have I any iron, I wonder?' And the more fidgety he got the wider her mouth got; words flapped and scurried round the starkness of the consulting room. They fell in desperate heaps on the thermo-tiled floor, obliterated the examination couch, beat with tiny fists on his shining head and finally stopped up his ears.

He had tried in his way. 'Have you thought of the WVS?' he had asked her last November. 'They are always short of really good people.'

Last December he had ventured: 'Well, you're in a splendid position to get a job, aren't you? Not many wives are married to a chap with his own company.'

'Henry wouldn't care for that. Not family. No. Never. You don't mix your social life with business, do you? That could spoil a very good relationship.'

Last February: 'Take my advice. Get out and about. Get interested in something. It will all follow on from there. If I may say so, I have a lot of ladies in my waiting-room with problems like yours. Valium isn't an answer. You've got to roll up your sleeves and get stuck into something. Stop thinking of yourself. If I may say so, it doesn't do.'

One chill afternoon in May, Mirry drew the net curtains back from the window in the master bedroom and watched the Euston-bound train hurdle over the level crossing in the valley. As always the driver sounded his horn and she wondered why British Rail didn't cheer things up a bit by giving their horns a pretty voice. They are so mournful, she thought, not at all like ice-cream vans.

She went downstairs and made herself coffee in a china cup. There was some weariness in her limbs but most of it was in her head. Sometimes her skull was so heavy she thought it would crash right through her shoulders or maybe the awful weight would just snap off and her head would roll across the biscuit-coloured ceramic tiles of the kitchen floor and bash against the built-in electric cooker.

She never knew how many pills she took because she stopped counting.

Was she glad or sorry it hadn't proved to be enough?

She had never thought of taking more pills, but sometimes now she did find herself almost guiltily envious of Lucy Lessor. If only there was no pain, if it could be like a light switch snapping off. Sometimes when she looked in her mirror what she saw was the murderer staring back at her. Terror forced her mouth open but she never screamed out loud.

While she had been in hospital Henry had sent her one red rose. 'My heart,' he'd written on the card.

But she hadn't wanted Henry; like a young child she'd wanted her mother. She'd needed to be properly cared for.

Of course, that was ridiculous. She'd not even liked her mother when she was alive and all the nurses had thought Henry's rose-shaped heart very romantic.

Perhaps I'll get myself a red dress, she thought now. After all, Christmas is coming. And red is so jolly.

It was an effort to get herself ready though today was one of her better days. Her legs often seemed like boneless worms and she wanted to slither away and hide in some dark place. But today it was OK and that was a good thing. She had to get going. There was this afternoon, for instance. No, no, she wouldn't think of that. Not now.

Mirry parked her car at Tesco's and did her grocery shopping. When she'd put the bags in the boot and slammed down the lid, she looked about her, sniffing the air. There was a whiff of burning. From a nearby garden bonfire? She went down the hill towards the shopping precinct.

As she crossed the street, she saw a man with his back to her looking in a shop window. He seemed wholly familiar and yet quite strange, strangely exciting, she thought. He was dressed in jeans and a green anorak with yellow and blue insets on the sleeves. His fair hair curled alluringly over comic ears. Her eyes began to bat enticingly as he turned round. He moved as neatly and as nicely as a cat.

She found herself dumbfounded. Across a few feet of pavement was Sammy Pink. Blue eyes met, matching in shade and the shock of recognition.

'Good heavens!'

He was blushing, tongue-tied. He thrust none-too-clean hands into his jeans pockets.

'It's an absolutely super day, isn't it?' She was aware of a sudden girlish gaiety in her voice.

He turned and dived off down the street.

Mirry remained where she was, feeling very confused. He must live somewhere round here, she was thinking, fancy that. What shocked her, though, was he hadn't looked like a dirty old man. But when I first met him, he did. He most certainly did. I'm sure he did.

Almost sure.

She'd thought for some time that very bewildering things were happening in the group; they might talk about Lucy Lessor, as they had last time, but what was happening wasn't really about her. For instance, how had such a slippery creature as Jenny Bone fooled Dr Rainbow so completely? Oh, he might think he knew what he was doing, but did he know what Jenny was up to? Had he even realised she'd become his favourite? And that's not fair for the rest of us, she thought. After all, he's supposed to be treating us all. It's not as if she's good-looking. Sometimes she looks quite the death's head. The man's a ghoul.

Mirry, who had become a serious student of status, having spent a lifetime improving her own, laid her indignation to one side as she tried to see why Sammy had improved beyond recognition.

In her mind's eye a triangle formed. She saw the alliance between Dr Rainbow and Jenny and the alliance between Jenny and Sammy Pink. Was it because Jenny was the doctor's favourite – giving her, Mirry thought, a quite undeserved prestige in the group – that how Jenny looked at Sammy influenced the views of the other members of the group?

As always, it comes down to having the right connections, Mirry thought. What you are is who you're connected to. As if I didn't know!

But were the right connections in the group proper connections?

There were times when being in that circle was like standing in a fairground surrounded by mirrors which so distorted the correct view of things that you lost track of what that was.

At least I usually know where I am with Henry, she thought. Count your blessings, lady, she told herself. Many women would give their eye teeth for a man like her darling Henry.

She was a very, very lucky woman.

Thinking about Henry and how good he was to her began to make her so nervous that her hands and feet started to prickle. Perhaps I really am on the change, she thought, as a sweat began to engulf her.

Could Henry have found out about the money? He'd said nothing to her.

Play it by ear, she told herself. Nothing's happened up to now and that probably means nothing will.

She looked in the window of Alison and Maye and then pushed open the door to the shop.

'Good morning, Mrs Vesey. Seaside weather and we're practically in November.'

Mirry moved over to the racks. The assistant, who knew Mirry Vesey liked to concentrate while she viewed possibilities for her wardrobe, wandered over to the plate glass door and looked out over the precinct.

Mirry saw at once that red wasn't being worn that year. In the end she chose a fine black wool three-piece. There was a straight skirt, a sleeveless hip-length tunic which skimmed over it and a jacket curved to swing in cloak-like style at the back.

The assistant said: 'It could have been made for you.'

Mirry viewed herself in the mirror and saw that she was right. She handed over her debit card. Henry felt that only an astute businessman like himself knew how to handle credit. 'One must never forget credit is debt,' he told her, though he only said that when he talked to her about it. When he chatted to men he called it gearing.

A clever morning's shopping, she told herself as she triumphantly bore her purchases back to the car. And what's more I needn't worry about what Henry may say. No one can object to black.

When she got back to Fogg House, she put away her groceries and took her outfit upstairs. In the master bedroom she tried on the suit again, twirling experimentally so she could get used to the feel of the jacket, letting the wool and silk folds ripple through the air.

Perfect, she thought and tried looping a bone silk scarf round her neck and studying the effect. Sometimes, as now, when she dressed in a new outfit she got a little sexual frisson. She discarded the scarf altogether and turned this way and that, then swung to fully face herself in the mirror.

She was still smiling when she suddenly felt a twinge of dismay. I'm dressed for a funeral, she thought.

She had an image of herself lying on the couch in the drawing-room below. All those pills inside her and so warm and content and happy. Yes, happy.

She found herself touching her ash blonde hair. It was straight and parted in the middle. Nothing could be further from Lucy Lessor's dark curls, burnished copper on black when the sun caught them. Too wild, she'd thought them. In her opinion Lucy Lessor had had too much hair altogether.

Mirry remembered the box of tissues Lucy used to bring to the group 'just in case, you know?' But she'd never used them. 'And now she'll never cry again,' Mirry said, looking at the reflection and seeing her pale blue eyes. Eyes which were too frozen to cry.

I've got to get out of this house!

Well, she would and in less than an hour if she were to get to Birmingham and back before Henry came home.

Shall we have a little bit of salmon for dinner? she now began thinking. A potato or two and some carrots. Henry's a man whose heart you've got to watch. She was already planning treats for him as if this would make up for what she was about to do.

After hanging up her new suit, she changed into clothes she normally wore for gardening, jeans and a navy blue fisherman's jumper. She always avoided the word sweater because of its connotations with sweating. 'If you choose nice words and use them properly, you will think correctly. That's the secret of living a good life,' her old elocution teacher had told her. 'Always, always, use well-mannered words.' At the time she'd had her lessons no one in her world had used well-mannered words; she wanted to be nothing like any of the people she knew so she'd followed the old woman's advice. She'd not regretted it, though even the words she heard on the television now made a mockery of her vocabulary.

After lunch she cleaned the make-up from her face, emptied her handbag and put her debit cards in her dressing-table drawer and locked it. She took the handbag downstairs to the kitchen, put it on the worktop, opened the cupboard underneath and lifted up a large flour bin. Sticking a plastic bag over her hand, she searched through the flour and came up with two bundles of ten-pound notes which had been wrapped in clingfilm. She put the bin back, washed her hands and dropped the money into the handbag. Hiding her hair under a green silk scarf, she put on an old navy blue jacket. As she got into the driver's seat of her car she wondered if she could keep just going on as if nothing had happened or was happening.

But now, driving down to Birmingham, she stopped thinking. What was the good of it? It got her nowhere. She concentrated on the road. In actual fact, she was a good driver, had never been in a serious crash. A well-mannered vocabulary had enlarged; she was a well-mannered road user, too.

She drove through the suburbs on the south-east side of the city and parked her car just off Pershore Road at the entrance to Cannon Hill Park. She felt that the vehicle would be safe here. Henry had told her that thieves and vandals were lazy, usually never straying far from their own territory. This was an unexceptional area, the broadcasting centre just across the road and the police training college not more than five minutes' walk away.

When she crossed the park she always stopped and watched the kiddies bounce down the little aluminium slide in front of the orange, yellow and blue play area. The way they stretched out for everything; it was as if they thought they could grab the world and swallow it whole.

She didn't linger long, she never did, though once or twice, in her imagination, one of the children followed her and poked its hand into hers.

She came out of the park at Edgbaston Road, looking to make sure the flag was flying over the cricket ground. This told her she was still in safe territory. It was like a Union Jack flying over a frontier fort. Behind it was Balsall Heath. Even before she'd quite skirted the cricket ground, her heart rate quickened.

And yet, as she'd told herself more than once, it was a really nice place for a red light district. It was shot through with greenery. There was Calthorpe Park and the recreational ground off Tindall Street, the sports ground and on its rim the county cricket ground and Cannon Hill Park. There were plenty of good solid Victorian terraced houses and pebbledash semis and gardens filled with shrubs. And she'd never seen so many churches in her life.

At the heart of Balsall Heath was the Church of God's Prophecy. The building vied with a Baptist chapel with twin minarets, a newly spruced-up Catholic church and the Church of the Bible Way. Good taste, she had noted, prevented the Church of England competing with equally large signs and bright paint. Only the Day Care notice was prominent.

There were other signs of faith: new workshops, new planting in raised beds, new houses, though the windows of one or two of them were blocked with chipboard. The brewery, however, had installed glass sandwiched with wire mesh and not a little non-decorative wrought-ironwork in the pub opposite the betting shop. Mirry was amazed that anyone, male or female, would dare enter it.

Outside the betting shop, black males gathered, bigger, bolder, more full of chutzpah than the predominantly Asian population. But she'd been told it was from these smaller, quieter people that the legendary Jasmine sprang. It was said she was so prized by Asian businessmen that she could command two hundred and fifty pounds, fifteen times more than the black and white girls who plied their trade in this district.

There was one other legendary whore, though Mirry was not sure if her leg was being pulled about her. She was a window girl who sat in one of the Victorian terraced houses whose privet hedges had been chopped down and net curtains raised so the goodies could be properly displayed. Unlike most of the others, this girl was fully dressed, did not sign her price with her fingers and was too young at over fifty. Queenie, they called her, the spitting image of Elizabeth the Second.

Mirry knew she'd never be able to find nice words for what happened in this district. Like the man who had changed the War Ministry into the Defence Department, all she could do was make the best of a bad job.

Concentrating on some of the physical attractions of the area helped her do this, even though she knew that the raised planting which narrowed the mouths of the more notorious streets was there for a purpose. It slowed traffic so the Vice Squad could record number plates. She'd read in the *Birmingham Sentinel* that almost twenty thousand vehicles a day nosed their way past the planting and strategically placed bollards.

Of course, even a stranger would know he was in the city's red light district and not some garden suburb. Look at this one and it was still early afternoon. What never failed to surprise Mirry was how terrifically attractive some of the girls were. This one was at least six feet and wonderfully slender. Hair a dark and vibrant curly halo, skin the colour of new-laid tarmac, the tops of her fishnet stockings rubbing against her micro-skirt. Almost November and in a woolly halter top with her midriff bare. Brass, they called them, Birmingham brass, the price of a Chinese takeaway and a bottle of beer. She'd already attracted the driver of a white Rover and Mirry had to be truthful and say she lowered herself into the passenger seat very prettily, legs nicely together, skirt patted into place.

Mirry turned the corner and walked into Ada Road. At this time of day, the nets in the window were down. She walked up to the door of number eighteen and rang the bell. No one in a garden suburb would have chosen quite this shade of purple paint. But at least, thought Mirry, it's not red.

11

'I've been given some clamato juice by an American friend, my dears. So I'm going to make us some Bloody Marys.'

'What's a Bloody Mary?' asked A.J.

'What's her name, this American woman?' asked Mitch.

They were in the lounge of Tommy Hung's flat. The pancake-roofed block was off Sir Harry's Road, Edgbaston. Tommy was pulling thick faded plush curtains against the intermittent glare of floodlights which seeded lawns surrounding the block. Half-dressed beech and chestnut trees swayed on the rim of the grounds, beaded by limelight, tossing grotesque shadowy heads. A final tug and the curtains were closed. In this room Tommy played out fantasies of being a patrician English gentleman in his club. Well-worn hide and frowstiness, laking shadows and the laking shine on old mahogany. Had he ever set foot in such a club? Mitch had always thought that improbable but he had so conjured up the atmosphere she was always looking round for an ancient waiter, the greenish sheen of years impregnating the fabric of his black suit.

'A Bloody Mary is a classic vodka-based drink,' Tommy was telling A.J. 'I'll pop out and get the vodka now,' and he disappeared into a kitchen which Mitch knew to resemble a miniature operating theatre. She'd have been incapable of cooking in it. Every time she took out a joint of beef for roasting she'd see in her mind's eye the leg it had been cut from and then, if she were not careful, the whole creature, including large and velvety eyes. Why she'd see this in an operating theatre setting and not in her kind of kitchen, which was full of pictures and plates and clutter, she couldn't really say. She suspected herself of smothering her flesh-eating activities under a veneer of homely jollity.

Tommy came back in with a tray bearing glasses, various bottles of sauces, celery and a vodka bottle in an overcoat of ice. He was no longer the patrician English gentleman, nor the surgeon in his operating theatre, but the consummate transatlantic barman. 'What's she called? This American friend of yours?' Mitch asked again.

'Bonnie, actually. Bonnie Fairweather. Americans are so refreshing, don't you find?' Tommy obviously did. He was so full of his oats that his shiny little shoes were pip-popping along the Turkish rug. He had almost broken into a caper.

'How did you get that covering of ice on the vodka bottle?' A.J. was fascinated. She might have been watching a conjuror.

'*Bain marie* principle. One puts the bottle in a can of water which comes up to its neck and then pops it into the freezer. Later one removes the can by running hot water over it.' He was gazing at the iced bottle of vodka. 'Isn't it . . . why, it's beautiful.'

'Why doesn't it explode?' A.J. wanted to know.

'Vodka doesn't freeze, my dears. The glasses have been in the freezer too, just so their rims get frosted. Now, you run salt round them. One measure of vodka – see, it's like syrup now! – three shakes of Tabasco, three of Worcester sauce, now we squeeze a quarter of lemon into it, salt, pepper, top up with clam-a-t-o . . .' He strung the word out and pronounced it to rhyme with the American way of saying tomato. 'Actually, it's a Betty and Frank Bloody Mary, that's what she calls it.' He was using a knife on a stick of celery and suddenly it had turned into a flower. He popped it in one of the glasses. 'There you have it. Elixir.'

'What the devil is this clam stuff, Tommy? I thought you were supposed to fill up with tomato juice.' Mitch, glass in hand, was viewing the elixir doubtfully. 'Looks more likely to burst you out of your boots than give you everlasting life.'

'Juice from clams mixed with tomato juice,' he said, answering her doubt by sipping from his glass.

A.J. was holding her glass as if it were a hand grenade.

'It's not half bad,' said Mitch, 'though more like eating than drinking. Yes, it does do something to the cockles of the heart. Like roast them. I have to tell you I've spent most of my day feeling like that bottle of vodka. My blood turned to syrup, too and I'm not at all sure it's thinned out yet.'

'But it's been a lovely day,' said A.J.

'What you really need when you are doing obs,' said Mitch, 'is an adult-sized baby-gro electric blanket, something with feet in and a hood. Still, it was worth it all. After doing her shopping and buying an outfit this morning, Mirry Vesey drove down into Birmingham, parked her car off Pershore Road and walked across Cannon Hill Park. I thought we were into some tryst with a lover, but no. She trots into Balsall Heath and homes in on perhaps the most notorious street in the city. She goes into 18 Ada Road.'

'The red light district? You're kidding?'

'That's a turn-up for the book,' said Tommy.

'Quite,' said Mitch.

'Quite what?' A.J., having thought about it, was bewildered.

'Absolutely. What on earth is a respectable matron doing visiting Birmingham brass?'

'Kinky sex?' A.J. wondered. 'Surely not. You can't even imagine a hoity toity piece like that doing it.'

'Can't you?' Mitch was amused. 'As far as I know shopping at Harrods never stopped anyone having sex.'

A.J. was obviously viewing Mirry Vesey in a different light. 'Hey, she could be bisexual. She goes there to have it off with this dyke. Or maybe a stoker-type toy boy? She's seriously into rough?'

'Honestly, the young of today. Is there anything they don't know about?' Mitch asked Tommy.

'Spelling,' said Tommy.

Mitch, remembering her run-in with a tuba, didn't take that any further. 'I don't think she'd be after sex. I mean, she was so depressed she tried to kill herself not long ago. As I understand it a severe dose of the glums plays havoc with your sex life. That lady probably couldn't pop her juice for all the tea in China.' She paused. 'Though, I suppose, there are exceptions to every rule.'

'Anyway, it wouldn't cost her ten thousand pounds, would it?' Tommy said. 'More like twenty. The nineties are the era for negotiating downwards.'

'There could be blackmail involved,' said A.J.

'We certainly need to know who is operating from that house and what goes on there.' Mitch thought about it. 'Not long ago I did a story about the anti-brass pickets in Balsall Heath. A bunch of mostly Muslim chaps out on the streets twenty hours a day, seven days a week. They are supposed to have all but killed off vice round the Ada Road area but we're talking about a ten-million-pound-a-year business. Something like that doesn't die easily... There was a woman I interviewed, an old-time prostitute the girls elected as their spokeswoman. She gave me their side of the story... We seemed to get on OK. For a bit of cash, she might come across with some info.'

'We could get hold of Henry Vesey and see if he'll spring it?'

'I'll contact him tomorrow morning if you like, my dears. Discreetly give him the run-down and put it to him.'

'Right,' said Mitch and then told them about her interview with Carole Carmichael and showed them the two photographs. 'I don't quite know why I asked her to lend them me. They don't help. Do they?'

'Lucy has rather a look of you. The hair-do, something about the eyes. Thinner, though,' said A.J.

Mitch felt her skin prickle. Even though she'd noticed the similarities herself, the fact that someone else had remarked on them had given her a jolt. 'Brunettes are hardly an endangered species,' she said.

'I must say the doctor and Maurice Pincing look quite smart in their shirt-sleeves. T-shirts always look scruffy to me.'

'Let's have a gander,' said A.J., craning forward. 'God. Look at Maurice's pants. They must have come out of the ark. Flares. Well, almost. God . . . I mean . . . you know . . .' and she wrinkled up her nose. 'Funny thing is his clobber looks bang up to date on the pictures Tommy took of him. Have you seen them yet, Mitch?'

Tommy handed Mitch a pile of prints. 'Still one or two faces missing from this lot. The thing that really strikes me is that they look so ordinary,' she said after she'd gone through them, noting the names neatly printed on the backs.

A.J. had been thinking. 'Lucy'd been dropped from a great height by two men in a row, her husband and this male member of the group she fell for, so she was a lady with something to prove. She ups the ante, slaps on the warpaint and starts cruising for talent.'

'You make her sound like a whore,' said Tommy.

'You don't get anywhere these days by hiding your light under a bushel,' said A.J. 'There's a lot of competition out there. You've got to admit it sounds like she was really going for it. But I think Lucy must have been right when she said she thought she was being watched. Admiring glances are one thing and if you're lucky you get some. What you don't do is confuse it with being watched.'

Tommy said: 'I'm afraid I haven't yet got very far with Ted Coveyduck.' His face was on top of the pile of prints Mitch was handing back to him. 'He lives in a semi in Solihull with his wife Sandra. They've got a ten-year-old called Jeremy. He lost his job as middle manager with a big engineering firm six months back and now works the ten to six shift at an all-night garage in the town. He was quite possibly working the night Lucy was murdered but I haven't yet managed to check it out. I'm going to pop over to the garage tomorrow night. Ted Coveyduck was a lot of hard work for not much reward and I didn't get over to Rainbow's place until after seven last night. At that point the angels took a hand. I've hardly arrived and am wondering how and where to begin when the doctor comes out of his house and gets into this red VW Golf. I decided to follow him. I tailed him to Yoxall and Dr Bateman's cottage. He went in and I got very itchy. The top and bottom of it is, my dears, I sneaked over the garden wall. It wasn't as risky as it sounds. There are no houses nearby and a convenient belt of trees running by a river that one could melt into. The curtains were undrawn and I could see they were in Ann Bateman's study. There were some files on this big table she appeared to use as a desk. She left the room and he quickly went through them. He opened one file, glanced through the papers, took one out and stuffed it into his pocket. He quickly shuffled the files back into place and was sitting in an armchair when Dr Bateman reappeared with a tray of coffee.'

'It's got to be the group members' files on that desk,' said Mitch. 'Had he remembered something, spotted something? But if he is legit, why would he steal a page?'

'I dropped everything else today to see what else I could get on him. I got on to Dr Maidley, the chap who helped us in the knight's death case. Christopher Rainbow, as far as I've been able to discover, is Mr Squeaky Clean. He's a psychiatrist who got the job as consultant psychotherapist at the clinic a number of years ago after doing a few stints in local mental hospitals. Written some well-regarded papers, does some lecturing at the university. He lives with his wife, another academic. There are two grown-up children. What is this pillar of the establishment doing stealing from a file almost under the nose of the director of the clinic he works for?'

'I wonder if he's on file, too. I wonder if Dr Bateman pulled his file as well as those of the members of his group,' said A.J. 'There could be something on his record that could be seen in a different light after the murder of Lucy Lessor.'

'Psychiatrists aren't a wonderfully stable bunch. Don't they have one of the highest suicide rates of all the professions?' Mitch finished her drink and put it down. 'Psychotherapists are supposed to go through a training analysis but on the other hand no one would be in a better position to know what bits of himself to keep quiet. Or it could be he's let someone into his group he shouldn't have because he's researching material for a paper. It might be helpful to take a look at the stuff he has published and see what his line is.'

'Well, there's one thing for sure. There are some pretty scratch marks on the good doctor's face. Haven't managed to get a shot of him yet. It was dark, of course, and I daren't risk the flash. But when I get one in you'll see what I mean. Now how about that?'

'Wow-www . . .' and A.J. rounded her lips and let out a low whistle.

'When did I last see a man with scratch marks on his face?' wondered Mitch. 'Did I ever? He's certainly been up to something.'

'I've got one or two contacts at the university,' said Tommy. 'Maybe they can tell me more about him. I've invited one of them out to dinner. All this means I haven't got round to the last two on my list yet, Sammy Pink and Ron Saffia. I start on them first thing tomorrow.'

'Do you think we should now suspend observation work on Mirry Vesey? I mean, this Bateman enquiry needs all we can give it and we do have an angle to follow on the Mirry thing now. This Ada Road business.'

'OK, Mitch.'

'Which reminds me,' said A.J. 'Do you remember the red Escort, Tommy, that you said stopped outside Mirry's house and then went down to Birmingham landing up near Mitch's pad? Ian put the number plate through the police computer. It belongs to Sammy Pink.'

'Right. He has to take priority,' said Tommy.

'Do you think that Mirry could have once been a prostitute?' asked A.J.

'Anything's possible. But she's been married to Vesey for ages. Why would she go back?'

'We can speculate all we like but what we need are some facts. And now, my dears, I really must shoo you out.'

'Bonnie's coming? Where did you meet her, Tommy?'

'At a CBSO concert. The new Russian virtuoso was playing. This fellow Kissin. When he unleashed Chopin's scherzo in B flat the audience practically rose off its seats. I looked round to see if everyone else was totally astonished, too, and Bonnie was sitting next to me and she was.'

'What a lovely way to meet,' said A.J.

'You mustn't read too much into it. We're just good friends.'

'Really?'

'Shoo, shoo . . .'

Minutes later, as she was driving her TVR back to her flat, Mitch found herself becoming more and more depressed. A.J. had her policeman and now even Tommy had found a partner. She sighed. Her last amorous adventures had been with the programme assistant Marco Rice, a lad who had ditched her for an eighteen-stone cook.

Not the best of recommendations, honeypot, she told herself.

She sighed again.

Come on-n-n, she told herself. She thought perhaps that this was not the moment to make for Count Dracula's flat, not when she had at least two hours to mope in before she could decently go to bed. She decided to take back Carole Carmichael's snaps, perhaps have a few more words with the girl. She made the short detour to Great Wire Street.

She had just located Carole Carmichael's bell on the wooden board when she heard footsteps and the gate grate open. A black woman trailing a shopping trolley which appeared to be bulging with laundry bumped into her. 'Is Carole in, do you know?' Mitch asked her.

'Tony's out so Carole's in, babs. It's the only time that girl gets peace and quiet for all the studying she does.' Her teeth gleamed in the darkness as her smile stretched wider. 'That boy likes to whack the sound out. He'll blast the roof off one day soon. He's in the middle, see. I'm on the bottom, she's up top. I'm used to a bit of noise myself. My ex was into heavy metal, you know?' She took out her key and Mitch followed her into the hall. 'Be sure you don't keep her too long. Carole's going places. That never did leave much time for small talk.'

'I won't.' Mitch began to climb the linoleum-tiled stairs, her heels ringing once or twice on the metal strips protecting the edges. When she reached Carole's door she saw, surprised, that it was open. She called to the girl and pushed the door further back.

She advanced into the room. The Monet print above the pink-painted fireplace lurched slightly. Other than that, everything appeared much as it had done when she'd first entered the flat. She then noticed an opened notebook by the phone. 'Hey there!' she called again as she went over to the splay-legged teak sideboard. She picked up the notebook. No names or numbers, just a lot of doodles, one more carefully executed than the rest. It was a staff with two entwining winged serpents. It was a moment before Mitch realised it was a caduceus, an emblem used by the medical profession. In ancient times, she remembered, it had been carried by Mercury, the messenger of the gods.

She opened the door off Carole's sitting-room and found herself in a spartan bedroom overlooking the back of the house. There was a curtained-off recess, probably used as a wardrobe, a futon, a side lamp by the pillows and a half-read upturned paperback on the floor. It was Christopher Isherwood's *Mr Norris Changes Trains*.

Mitch, feeling a draught, only then noticed that the sash window, which almost came to the floor, was open a crack. Something was caught on the old-fashioned brass-levered window lock. Going nearer to investigate she saw it was a little piece of peacock blue silk and she remembered the scarf woven into Carole's hair. Beyond the window was a fire escape which led down to a backyard filled with junk. The high, close-boarded back gate, which looked almost new, was wide open.

Hearing footsteps behind her, Mitch spun.

'That Carole. She thinks I don't know she uses the fire escape as a short cut to the chippie.' The black woman was shaking her head. 'If the landlord knew he'd have her out, but quick. Why, he's just put that new gate on to try and keep out the vermin we got round here. I told him. Get rid of that fire escape, I said. If you don't we'll all be murdered in our beds long before we get caught in a fucking fire. You can stay with me till the stupid cow gets back. Can't have you up here and her not in.'

'That's all right. I only dropped in to give these two photographs back. Perhaps you could do that for me?' and Mitch fished them out of her pocket.

'Sure thing. Shall I tell her who's been?'

'No need. She'll know.'

When she reached her own, not dissimilar, doorstep ten minutes later Mitch found someone ringing her bell. He was big and burly and butch, just the way Digger Rooney liked them. But he can't have this one, she decided, as she gazed into eyes which she described to herself later as Nordic blue.

'Are you Mitch Mitchell?' Nice timbre, a voice which would broadcast well. But men's voices nearly always did. On air, it was only women who squawked. She suspected the engineers. They tweaked something in the transmitter which responded better to the male tone of voice, or didn't untweak it.

'Who are you?' Two inches of hair stood all over the top of his head; so sexy, she thought. It brought to mind well-developed muscles, thighs packing plenty of fire power.

'Detective Inspector Briggs.' He showed her his warrant card. 'Can I come in?'

She instinctively felt her back arching a little, her breasts tilting, nipples hardening. 'Do,' she said, producing her key. She was very conscious of putting it in the lock and turning it.

She snapped on the hall light and walked in front of him. Their feet made music on the blue, claret and brown Victorian floor tiles, hers a fluttery tapping, his carrying the rhythm, clop, clop, clop. She was cocking an ear to listen to it. One of those horses in the Trooping of the Colour. Oh, how she would love a military ride.

Must be good, she warned herself.

If I'm not careful he might shy. Bolt.

Opening the door to her flat, looking over her shoulder, noting his rather bony nose. There was a lot of bone about him altogether. He was a big man. Perhaps in his late forties?

She turned on the central heating and the gas fire. Let's get warmed up, she thought, though she realised she must not mean that in the literal sense because she was now taking off her coat. She was wearing her Jeeves outfit, silk shirt, black jacket, pinstripe trousers. Unlike Jeeves she was aware, since her last stint of dieting, she went in and out at all the right places. 'Perhaps you'd like a drink? Gin? Whisky?'

His eyes had not once, but twice, done the Grand Tour; bits of her anatomy were still glowing.

'Whisky. With water.' He was now looking at the weevil wallpaper, the liverish-coloured marble fireplace, the fibreglass curtains which she'd drawn before she'd left to see Tommy and A.J. She refrained from apologising for the place, from telling him this was a temporary address.

'Of course, we're now in the thick of it.' He smiled. 'There's not a lot we don't know now about Lucy Lessor's life. But we've done a bit of back-tracking, too. What I want to know is if you've still got the tape you recorded the morning the body was found. Has it been edited? Used?'

'Pick a pew,' she said. 'I've not even listened to it yet. Normally I would have, but if we put to one side everything else that happened that day, I get a sinking feeling about the tape. It's full of bureauspeak. It won't do as a programme. I'm going to have to go out and find more people, get some personal stories. I'll use some of that tape, of course. I'll need the official point of view. In fact, I'm off to see Colin Parsons again – you know, the chief exec – tomorrow afternoon to finish the interview. I'm going to listen to the tape again tomorrow morning, find out what I'd not asked him, and then get the rest of the stuff I need. I'll dub off a copy for you, if you like.' She gave him two measures of whisky and a small jug of water.

'You were conducting the interview as you walked round with the two of them. How did that work?'

She sat down in the chair opposite him, nursing her gin and tonic. 'We'd stop at various places and talk. Maybe I'd put in a little background description. You know. Now we are in Amy Johnson House, built in . . . or whatever. That sort of thing.'

'The tape was running all the time?'

'No. Switched on and off. You can have it by all means, but I don't see how it will help. I'll leave a copy with reception and you can send someone by to pick it up. Make it late afternoon.'

'Thanks. You never know. Just to recap, you are absolutely sure it was you who suggested going to that part of Amy Johnson? You wanted to see the rooms which had once been padded cells?'

'Correct.'

'First you smell the spent fireworks and then see the remains of the cartridges at the end of the corridor. The men go before you to investigate and partially block the end of the corridor. The door to the room at the bottom is open.'

'Sargeant, the chap who's site services manager at Cold Ash, was nearest the doorway. He was looking in. If I thought anything I supposed some kids had been in letting off fireworks and making a mess in the room. He didn't say anything. At that point, nobody said anything. If you're small like me and want to see what's going on you just stick your head down and barge through. I was actually the first in the room though I'm pretty sure John Sargeant was the first to see Lucy's body.' She was going to ask if the dead woman had been mutilated before she died but then realised she didn't want to know. If she hadn't seen the body she wouldn't have hesitated. But now Lucy was real and if Mitch weren't careful her agony would haunt her. It's because I'm getting older, she thought. When I was young my flesh knew it was immortal. Nothing could touch me.

'Tell me again what happened then.'

'John Sargeant pushed me aside, quite roughly, and knelt. As you know, Lucy was belly down on the floor and her head faced towards the far wall. Her face and the tops of her arms were covered by her hair. He pushed some of the hair away from her neck and he had to dig down a little before he placed two fingers against what I assume was an artery. After a short while he got up. He just said: "No." '

'Colin Parsons was already taking off his coat by this time. "We can't be absolutely sure. Not till the medics come." He covered her up. I remember the rope burn marks on Lucy's wrists. I've the impression of more rope burn marks on her neck when John Sargeant moved her hair. Of course, I read in the paper that she'd been strangled, so I might think I saw them because I ought to have done. There was the smell of fireworks, of course, burnt-out fireworks.'

'And you're quite sure the body wasn't moved?'

'Not while I was there. It was amazing, really. It was all very calm, all very ordinary. Colin Parsons went out to use his car phone and John Sargeant said: "There's nothing we can do. We'd better wait for Colin in the corridor." I said something like: "She's dead, isn't she." He said something totally ridiculous like: "It's a nasty business." '

'Is that all?'

'More or less. I mean, we hardly talked at all. What could we say? It was quite clear, whatever Colin Parsons said, that Lucy was dead. Rigor mortis had set in. I mean, John Sargeant's feeling for a pulse was just a ritual. You know? John Sargeant asked if I was all right and he kept looking at me to make sure I was. Afterwards I felt rather guilty about not fainting, or screaming or anything. It was all ridiculously low key as if we didn't believe it. It reminds me of those hoary old black and white war films, all British and stiff upper lip and somebody bringing Jack Hawkins a cup of cocoa while depth charges fall all round his submarine.'

'And now?'

'I find I don't want to know precisely what happened. I'm being a bit careful with myself, nursing myself through, trying not to land in a God Almighty soggy heap of . . .' but she didn't finish the sentence. She drained her glass.

'You're doing fine, it seems to me.'

'Am I?' she asked herself.

'Well, sorry to keep you out of bed.'

'If I can help with anything more . . .'

'I'll be in touch.'

Mitch stayed up for a while after he'd gone. She made herself coffee and found herself studying the architect's plans pinned up on the wall. She felt sad. Isn't Digger Rooney right? Shouldn't I be buying a flat? Why do I want to convert this chapel into a house? I've no one to share it with. There's only me.

She quite literally tried to shake herself back into a jollier mood. This is going to be a terrific pad, she told herself. It's going to be great to come back to after the kind of stinking day I've had today.

Suddenly she was striding across to the windows. Her fingers grasped the fibreglass curtain.

She peeked out. A knife of light cut through the shrubbery, highlighting a drizzle of detaching leaves.

She let the curtain drop.

She fetched her coffee and sat down facing the purple marble fireplace. The regulated flames of the gas fire made the kind of sound you'd have to retune your brain to even hear, like white noise in a studio.

But if you were ever to hear him coming closer you'd need to do that.

A hand reached up to her face. A finger hovered a hair's breadth from her cheek.

What had Lucy Lessor's face been like before he strangled her?

But then she remembered something she'd once heard in a courtroom. Psychopaths never touch a face. A face is personal, breasts and genitalia are every woman.

There is nothing personal about lighting a firework and using it to set fire to the mount of Venus. Even the person in the mount loses all identity in the explosion of pain.

She woke before dawn with a jolt. She was clammy with horror.

Had he got Carole Carmichael?

12

As soon as she saw Ron Saffia Jenny knew the group would have a lot more fun. She was not sure she approved of this. She was here to be redeemed. Wasn't that a dreadful matter? Surely not something for laughter.

But, looking at Ron Saffia again, she couldn't regret his coming. He was the complete intellectual, down to the scruffy proof copy of a book in his regulation two-sizes-too-large Oxfam jacket. When he leaned forward on the plastic seat of the chair more of the book was exposed and she saw it was Oliver Sacks's *The Man who Mistook his Wife for a Hat*. Wonderful, she thought, and surveyed him further. Lemon and cream striped Indian cotton shirt, buttoned to the neck but no tie, grandfather's navy blue pin-striped waistcoat, mole-coloured corduroy pants and black plimsolls with an elastic gusset instead of laces. The man himself was slim and there was a lot of wild curling ginger hair. His skin was freckled and he had a beaky face.

He's a wow, she decided, and he's going to be quite splendidly awful. See how he stares at Mirry Vesey. He looks like an initiate of the Thuggee who has stepped into a Mothers' Union meeting.

All this assessing was going on while she and the rest of the group were studiously ignoring the man. He was worse than a stranger; he was the fellow who always absented himself because he had better things to do with his time. No. They weren't going to know Mr Ron Saffia. They pointedly mistook him for his habitually empty chair.

The painful silence – enjoyed, it seemed, only by Dr Rainbow who beamed now his group was complete – was eventually broken by Joan. She wanted to know why the psychiatrist hadn't told them their story. 'You always do at the beginning of our meetings. You know. Something to start the ball rolling.'

Dr Rainbow did. The usual singsong way he told his stories had been abandoned. He harrowed them with a tale of a bird trapped in the Rainbow chimney and the attempts of the family to rescue it. Everything they did seemed to worsen the creature's chances. He even held Cherry Bye Byes's attention for the first five minutes but eventually the co-therapist slid into slumber.

The bird was still up the chimney.

Dr Rainbow hadn't heard it cheeping for a day.

Joan was almost in tears. Jenny was surprised to find she was very angry. If the idiot couldn't even rescue a bird, what chance did she have?

'I have a faux fireplace. I don't have a chimney,' said Maurice, who clearly thought psychiatrists shouldn't be allowed one either.

Ted Coveyduck decided that Dr Rainbow was coming down with a virus. 'It's a known fact that this is a very dangerous time of the year . . .' and he looked anxiously round the rest of them, seeking confirmation of his theory.

And then, as one man, they turned on Ron Saffia. This was the cause; he stared them in the face. The newcomer had upset their leader and little wonder when he went around boasting about thinking his wife a hat. Ron, the magnet of such collective ill will, began to shrivel. However, and Jenny admired him for this, he didn't push his chair further from theirs. Now he'd at last decided to come he was going to stick it out.

The silence grew so heavy that even Dr Rainbow looked uncomfortable. If they weren't careful the weight of all this quiet would crack the floorboards and send them tumbling down.

'I expect the bird's dead.' It was Mirry who actually cracked.

The group stirred. The dead bird brought Lucy to mind. No one had rescued her, either. The force of their thought seemed to almost make her materialise in their circle. Jenny found she was thankful she'd never seen her.

The moment passed and Jenny became aware that Cherry was now becoming the focus of attention. She slept prettily in her bright red tracksuit, curling her knees towards her chin. Though she couldn't see the fluorescent lettering from her seat, Jenny knew Cherry's sweatshirt was printed across the chest with the words: 'If Nobody's Perfect, I'm A Perfect Nobody'. Jenny found the message disturbing in the light of Cherry's frequent lapses into unconsciousness.

At first Jenny had been indignant – as they all had – with the co-therapist's inability to keep awake in their presence. But she'd now joined in one of the group's unspoken conspiracies; they conspired to see worth in Cherry's snoozes. They were the guardian angels of a sleeping beauty. It was their duty to protect and cherish this innocent in their midst.

And what the group now scented was danger. But, as if they were the sleeping courtiers in the fairy tale, not one of them moved when Ron Saffia got up. He marched across their circle. His bony fingers seemed to elongate. Claws spanned the carotid arteries on either side of Cherry Bye Byes's neck. A snipe of icy air found fissures in Jenny's being as her skin lifted and tried to resettle on rattled bone. The span widened. Ron shook the girl vigorously.

Cherry's head bounced up. One hand forked her hair. She thought the session was over and only slowly realised it was not.

'You shouldn't have!' Joan squeaked. 'You should never wake someone abruptly. It's dangerous.'

'Tell that to the sergeant major,' said Ron.

'I've wanted to do that. For weeks I've wanted to do that,' Maurice discovered. He was full of admiration.

'Why didn't you do it then?' Ron turned to look at each and every one of them before going back to his chair.

'It's not our place,' said Ted.

'After all, she's Christopher's co-therapist,' said Mirry.

'It's our group,' said Dr Rainbow. 'Why should I do what you're not prepared to do?'

'I was not asleep. I always concentrate better when my eyes are closed.'

'We get used to Cherry sleeping. She's a youngster after all,' said Joan. 'All that going out and boyfriends.'

'Really, it's quite normal. She always goes to sleep,' Ted told Ron.

'What do we do to send you to sleep?' Maurice asked Cherry.

'More what we don't do surely,' said Jenny.

'I expect we just bore her dreadfully,' said Ted. 'Really, it's all our own fault. We're hardly John Waynes, are we?'

'He's dead.'

'She's paid to be bored,' said Ron. 'Christ, the sentries at Buckingham Palace don't fall asleep and they must be bored out of their bearskins. What's the matter with you all? How can she do her job if she's unconscious?'

Jenny suddenly realised that they were now all talking to Ron. By this one act of violence he'd not only gained admission to the group but looked set to become their revolutionary leader.

She was thoroughly annoyed with herself. Why hadn't she thought of doing that when she was trying to get into the group? Instead she'd formed an unholy alliance with a very shady character. She found herself glancing at Sammy and brooding on the error of her ways. Sammy, startled by her hostile stare, bent his head in shame. They both knew it was all his fault; but what had he done?

Meanwhile, the revolutionary leader was staring sternly about him. No one dared blink in case it could be construed as falling asleep. At this rate, Jenny thought, men are shortly going to be burned at the stake for not regarding their wives as hats.

She found herself looking anxiously towards Dr Rainbow. He seemed quite unperturbed by this new leader who had erupted in their midst. The smoke from his cigarette was making a pattern of eight over his head. In the tarot cards, she recalled, it was the configuration over the head of the magician. There were still traces of the scratches on his face but now they were very much faded. Soon they'd be altogether gone. She was comforted. If only he were more adept at rescuing birds, she thought, I'd feel easier in my mind. Even magicians are far from perfect these days.

Ron, wanting to consolidate his position, was looking round for possible recruits. A leader had to have his troops. He turned to Maurice, who had admired his action, and began to interview him. 'Why are you here?' The abruptness of the question made one or two of the others gasp.

'My nose.'

'It looks all right to me.'

'Actually, it's a very nice nose, don't you think?' Joan asked the others. 'Nice and neat and none of that horrid hair growing out of the nostrils. Some men's noses are absolutely disgusting.'

'Perhaps he has difficulty in breathing,' said Ted. 'That can be very nasty. One can get in a frightful stew about keeping on breathing.'

'If there was something physically wrong with his nose he wouldn't be here, would he?' asked Ron.

As Maurice's head bent his hair swung across his face; he could be a wounded predator tumbling down its burrow. 'I keep seeing it,' said Maurice.

The others stared at him. 'Do you mean in the mirror?' Mirry asked.

'No. I look at a tin of baked beans and I actually see part of my nose as well. In my dreams it is growing. In my dreams I'm being taken over by this monstrous nose. I'm trapped in it.'

'I don't believe any of this,' said Ron. 'Are you some kind of nut or something?'

'But if you squint down a bit you can see your nose – or at least the end of it – as well as what you're looking at,' Jenny discovered.

'Perhaps there's something wrong with his eyes,' said Ted. 'I expect they wander about. Swivel round a bit.'

'My eyes are fine. My nose is fine. And I know it's not becoming monstrous really. It just feels as if it is. It's no joke. Really. I wake up drenched with sweat. Anxiety. That's what Christopher puts it down to.'

'Christ, you've got to be a contortionist to keep seeing the end of your nose.' Ron's face was horribly screwed up with the effort of seeing his.

'Well, I can't stop seeing the end of mine,' said Maurice. 'And that's about the size of it.'

'Hmmmp...' Ron had unscrewed his face and was giving Maurice a very hard look. Did he want a lieutenant who had difficulty seeing beyond the end of his nose? 'Yes...' and he turned to see if he could discover more promising candidates. He began to size up Sammy Pink.

Jenny was both alarmed for Sammy and annoyed that anyone should try and poach her man. She jumped in first. 'Why are you here?' Her voice was much sharper than she intended.

Sammy leapt so far out of his skin that it seemed he'd be lost forever. Jenny had a horrific vision of him dropping off the rim of the planet. 'Sammy!' she wanted to cry. 'Come back!' She found herself concentrating her forces of gravity.

He slowly returned into her orbit. There was a jolting feeling of fusion when he said: 'I'm a peeping Tom, actually,' and she said: 'Well, then.' But two into one wouldn't go and she had a sensation of being forced to grow in order to accommodate him.

Sammy was suddenly back in his own skin and sitting across from her as large as life, which was larger than he had ever been. Jenny's straining muscles relaxed. What a weight that man had proved to be. She was weak with relief.

'I used to do that kind of thing when I was twelve. Me and this other kid. We used to creep up on courting couples and once we actually caught two at it. It didn't seem like much to us. Afterwards, I remember feeling there should be a lot more to it than this,' said Ted. 'I'd expected it to be . . . somehow . . . well, extraordinary. Not like dogs. You know?'

Sammy began to study the ceiling.

Mirry seemed thrilled. 'You mean you creep up on courting couples, Sammy?'

'There's a chap in the next avenue who has always got his binoculars at the ready,' said Joan. 'There have been one or two things said. He knows we know. He certainly does.'

'Well, I don't see it as dreadfully bad,' said Ted. 'I mean hundreds and thousands lug home porn videos. And they don't land up in psychotherapy groups, do they?'

'I don't know why they bother. They'd see more if they switched on the telly and watched one of the serials. Randy as rabbits on the box. I'll tell you that for nothing.'

During these exchanges, none of the group members looked at Sammy. It was as if, in acknowledging him, they must acknowledge some shady part of themselves. Knowing what had happened to Lucy, one or two were on the brink of being frightened.

Eventually Jenny did venture to glance out of the corner of her eye. There was an almost dreadful liveliness about Sammy. It was as if a glass case containing a stuffed animal had been broken apart and the animal – not stuffed at all – had sprung to life.

Admit it, Jenny told herself. He scares you.

She turned to Dr Rainbow for reassurance. The figure of eight no longer crowned his head. Has he noticed anything? she wondered. But what was there to notice? She'd simply asked Sammy a question to which the psychiatrist already knew the answer.

'Woman. That's the cause of mankind's troubles. You always know where you are with another chap. Am I right or am I right?' said Maurice.

'When she left me she took the roof over my head,' grieved

Sammy. 'I'll be out on the pavement in two shakes of a lamb's tail. I'll have nowhere to go. Nowhere.' His voice was rising in panic.

'Irinia only went to two lectures on applying structuralism,' said Ron. 'That's what I managed to find out later. When it really comes down to it a woman likes to drop her knickers. An academic woman drops them twice as often as her fucking sisters. That's what she thinks being intellectual means.'

'Who is Irinia?'

'My ex. She slung her hook. Took off with the Chair in English.'

'They come on like spring chickens,' said Maurice. 'But at heart women are all bloody old boilers!'

In the silence that followed Jenny noted that Ron had stopped sizing up the male members of the circle. He'd given up his hunt for henchmen. He studied his nails. Dr Rainbow grinned at him, stretched his legs out in front of him and contemplated the toecaps of his suede shoes.

'Men aren't much cop,' Joan said eventually. 'Don't go thinking they are. I had to have Duncan up in front of Christopher. Looking and looking like that. What's he looking for?'

'I thought Duncan wanted to see Christopher to discuss your behaviour. Not the other way round,' said Ted.

'Well, it is crazy. The way that man keeps staring at me.'

'But is he really staring at her? Isn't paranoia a sign of schizophrenia?' Maurice asked Ron.

'Why don't you ask Dr Rainbow? He's the psychiatrist,' Jenny said.

'Joan isn't schizophrenic,' said Dr Rainbow.

'I keep telling you. It's not me that's mad, it's Duncan. Don't you listen? But I don't suppose you can expect Duncan to undergo psychiatric treatment. I mean, he'd lose his job, wouldn't he? Probation officers are expected to be normal. They've got to be very stable types.'

'You mean you think you're having the treatment you think your husband should have?' Jenny was astonished.

'I wouldn't go quite as far as that.'

'But you have,' said Maurice.

'That's like putting a pacemaker in me rather than in Henry who needs it,' said Mirry.

'Not quite,' said Ron. 'I think the theory goes that if you change the behaviour of one person in the family the others will have to react in a different way, and when they do their behaviour changes, doesn't it? Isn't that so?' Ron asked Dr Rainbow.

'That can happen, yes,' said Dr Rainbow. 'But in my opinion Joan's husband isn't mad.'

'According to you no one's mad,' snapped Joan. 'The whole world is in its right mind.'

'I think that's a very nice attitude for a psychiatrist to have,' said Mirry.

'Oh, I expect Christopher has committed lots of people in his time,' said Maurice. 'After all, that's part of his job. You don't get paid if you don't do your job properly. Not these days.'

'All I know is no one on our side of the family is doolally. But I will tell you this. Duncan has a very funny cousin. Fair gives you the creeps, he does.'

Mirry said suddenly: 'Actually, I think Joan sent Duncan to see Dr Rainbow because she was afraid he might be the maniac who killed Lucy. Being stared at like that. Well, I should think that dreadfully frightening. I'd be scared anyway. I expect she wanted to be on the safe side.'

'How can you say a thing like that? Oh, that's terrible,' said Ted. 'You can't really think Joan's being frightened out of her wits by her own husband. That's not on. Really it isn't.'

Ron leaned forward. 'Have the police been to see you?' he asked Ted.

'And Maurice. And I can tell you, it didn't worry Sandra one tiny teeny bit,' said Ted. 'I mean, this is really funny. It seemed to make her, well, excited.'

'In what way?'

'Well, she stroked me.' Ted thought about it again. 'You'll laugh at me. This sounds way out. It was as though I was a wild beast and she was taming me.'

'You're telling us you cracked it,' said Maurice. 'You are. Aren't you? Jesus. Good old Ted. He's got it up again.'

'Well, I wasn't going to let on. It's private, isn't it? Really it's between her and me.' And then his grin widened.

'Will anyone let me get a word in edgeways? I never thought what Mirry said. Never ever.' Joan turned to Mirry. 'How could you say such a thing? I'd never be so nasty to you. Not ever. Good God. It's maniacs like Lucy's killer that are Duncan's clients. He's on the side of law and order. He's probation, isn't he? I don't go saying horrible things to you, Mirry. Have I ever just once?'

'Perhaps Mirry has her doubts about her husband,' said Ron. 'I wouldn't like to be a woman. Not with this killer on the loose.'

'Don't be ridiculous. I know Henry as well as I know myself and I certainly didn't kill Lucy.'

'Know him? Pull the other one. You're kidding yourself, babs.'

In her agitation Mirry almost rose off her chair. Her fists had clenched.

'It's not the secrets which we keep from others which worry me,' said Jenny. 'It's the secrets I keep from myself.'

Joan said: 'My Duncan doesn't even squash spiders. He sticks a bit of paper under them and puts them out of the back door. I'll tell you one thing. I wasn't going to mention this but I saw Carole Carmichael the other day in town. You know, that kid who took a picture of us on the day Lucy left the group? Well, Carole said the real reason Lucy left was because she started going out with one of the chaps in this group. It's not Duncan at all. So there.'

'Lucy went out with one of us?' said Maurice. 'Christ.'

'You never said before because you don't believe it. It's a damned lie,' said Ted. 'Anyway, I'm not well enough for that kind of malarky. Really I'm not.'

'I bet Lucy's been telling porkies,' said Maurice. 'Or Carole is.'

'Why should either of them lie about it?' asked Dr Rainbow. 'Really, Joan, why didn't you tell us this earlier?'

'I don't go about causing a lot of trouble for other folk, that's why. Not like some.' Joan was glaring at Mirry.

'Is it true?' asked Jenny.

'Don't look at me like that,' shouted Sammy. 'It wasn't me!'

13

'I tracked down the name of the woman downstairs and then phoned her. Thought it was safer. No names, no comeback. I said I couldn't get through to Carole. There must be a fault on her line. Well, let's be honest, I bullshitted like mad and in the end she did go up and take a look.'

'And?'

'The place was empty. The bed not slept in. I couldn't seem to make her understand the urgency . . . Let's be honest, most girls round there often don't sleep in their own beds, do they? Sometimes I don't.'

'I should have stayed and waited for her. I never thought anything of it when I was told Carole used the fire escape as a short cut to the chippie.'

'Oh, come on, Mitch. Carole slipped out to a boyfriend's as like as not.'

'We can't just leave it there!'

'I told the woman that Carole was a friend of Lucy Lessor. She was a witness, I said, and maybe knew something she shouldn't. What if the same bloke had grabbed her? I frightened the bitch enough to ring the police, I'm sure I did. After all, we can't get in touch with them, can we? They'd want to know what we were doing interviewing their witnesses.'

'You're an angel, A.J.'

'Stop worrying. She's OK. I mean, why would the killer go for her? You interviewed Carole. Remember? She knew nothing. Will you be over at the bureau later?'

'Much later. I've just finished dubbing off a tape for Inspector Briggs. He wanted to listen to the stuff I recorded that day at Cold Ash. In a moment I'm off to see the chief exec of the Hospital Trust. Freya Adcock is screaming for this programme on community care. Oh God. I do hope Carole's all right. She had all the makings of a good kid. You know?'

'You worry too much.'

'If anything happens to her that's got to mean this is down to someone at that clinic. OK, OK. I'll hold my horses. See you later, honeypot.' She put the phone down.

Bang, bang, bang, scuffing the toe of her boot, her face screwed with anxiety.

'That's the sort of look that would make a gargoyle look like a happy little angel,' said Digger Rooney. 'What's the matter, Medusa?'

Mitch, caught on the hop, found herself pointing a finger at the tape machine.

'Crap? So what's new?'

'Oh God,' she said.

He stood in front of her, blocking her view, bent his sturdy legs, lowered his hands to his knees and cupped his podgy fingers. 'Up, up, up,' he urged. 'Oh spirit, I call you. Rise up. Take wing and in yonder heaven sport.' He saw mind over matter was not working. He tried matter over mind. 'Up, up, up. Think of a fuck. A jolly good fuck. Up, up, up –'

Outraged, she pitched to her feet. 'Digger –'

'Ooh. Ooh. She's after me. Help! Save me!'

'What on earth's going on?' Freya Adcock was at the production office door. 'This is not a kindergarten. Digger, have you a mo? One would like a little word. Now. My office.'

Oh, poor devil, Mitch thought. He's in for a bollocking.

'Did you hear his show yesterday?' asked Quentin Plunkett.

'No.'

'He said AOK. She'll hang him. And quite rightly too, in my opinion. It isn't even a modern Americanism. He used party as though it were a verb, too. Partying.'

'Well, at least his listeners would understand him. What Brummie knows what palimpsest means?'

'You mean you don't know. You can't even pronounce it properly. Don't suppose your average Brummie is as ignorant as you are.'

'I know too.'

'And I seem to remember you used crepuscular on your show,' Quentin said.

'There was a very good reason. It was part of that arts quiz. And anyway it's a knockout word. All articulated crocodile... Palimpsest is poncy.'

'The Queen's English.'

'It's not hers. It's mine.'

'Oh, if you're going to persist in being childish...'

'And two fingers to you,' she said, collecting the original and dubbed tapes and marching over to her desk, picking up her phone as it began ringing.

'Hi there,' said A.J. 'It's me again. Just got some information from my contact about Maurice Pincing. He'd been travelling on the Continent for about five years with a friend of his called Eddie. Eddie was killed in a car crash in Greece and Pincing came back. If he's gay, he's keeping pretty quiet about it. My contact never mentioned that. Before he left England he apparently worked in insurance but couldn't stand the boredom. It must have cost a lot of money to jaunt about the Continent for all that time. I don't know where it came from. Perhaps this Eddie. Pincing's good with the patients apparently, gets on with the other porters, particularly one called Brian. Brian's a doctor of philosophy but can't get a job in his field. But no talk about them.'

'Just good friends.'

'You've got it. Tommy's now gone off to dig up what he can about Sammy Pink and I'm off to the university to see if I can take a look at some of the stuff this Dr Rainbow has published. Earlier I did have another go at Joan and Duncan Ridley but the only other thing I've come up with is that he organises a fireworks display every year for mentally handicapped kids. After going to the university I'm going to move on to Edwina Grimshaw.'

'And I'm hoping to do Jenny Bone later this afternoon. After the

Trust man,' said Mitch. 'Apparently she used to work here, but in television. I've got a ready-made excuse. This care in the community programme I'm trying to get off the ground.'

'Didn't Dr Bateman tell you Jenny had joined the group after Lucy Lessor left?'

'We were instructed to do reports on all the group members. Listen, A.J. . . .' She hesitated. 'Well, you know . . . I am all right. There's no need to ring up every five minutes. Look, you did a great job in coming up with the name of the woman downstairs. I'm sure Carole's OK. You know how it is. You wake up in the middle of the night . . . But honestly. Hysterics over. I'm OK. Right?'

'You weren't hysterical, Mitch.'

'Wasn't I? Oh, good.'

'More tired and emotional.'

'And balls to you too. Tell Tommy what I'm up to when he rings in. I'll be in touch later.' Mitch put the phone down again, looked at her post which still remained unopened though it was by now early afternoon, and decided it could wait. She went to collect her Uher, which was on charge. She put on her bright red coat, hefted the tape machine over her shoulder, gathered her handbag and Inspector Briggs's dubbed tape. Heavily laden like this, she always thought of herself as floundering forward like some cargo boat in stormy waters. She made the reception desk without sinking and handed over the tape. She had to return through the building to get to the car-park.

She dumped her gear in the passenger seat of her TVR and lowered herself in. Her feelings for her red sports car had recently started to grow tender, like an owner of an old dog who knew it would die soon.

Apart from the fact it was not at all the sort of vehicle to use for incognito detective work, she had to practically lie down to drive the thing. Mitch's bones had not seen twenty for a very long time. How much longer could she ignore their grumbles as she got in? She had a feeling that if she didn't change her ride soon (ride, she thought, what would Quentin Plunkett say about that Americanism?) one or two of her bones would spring out of their parcel of skin and bat her about her numbskull head.

As the engine spluttered into life, the tender thoughts the sports car engendered began to drift towards other bodywork. What is Inspector Briggs's first name? she wondered. Oh, how I like big men with lots of muscle and bone mass. Lots of material to work with. I haven't had any proper fun for ages. And ages.

She passed the security guard on the gate and nosed on to the road.

Yes, I think I might enjoy fucking with that policeman, she thought. It really is peculiar. I've never been keen on the law before.

I'd be safe in his arms.

She began to think of other things than safety, to the detriment of her driving. Well, she thought, it's better than tying yourself in knots wondering what's happened to Carole Carmichael.

She turned into Bristol Road, driving west towards Selly Oak. Passing Edgbaston Park Road, she glanced to her right. In the distance on the incline was the brick tower which marked Birmingham University's campus. The buildings were Victorian institutional and mid-twentieth-century brutalism collected together in ill-conceived spaces. She'd never gone to university. One May she'd discussed *Persuasion* with the rest of the A level set, the following December she'd been recording how much the magistrates had fined a man for an act of sodomy. After working for a year on a local newspaper she'd certainly known more than perhaps was comfortable about the way society worked.

She had met lots of Colin Parsons in her time. This one, the chief executive of the North-East Birmingham Learning Disability and Mental Health Services NHS Trust, was on holiday and she'd arranged to see him at his home. He lived in a pre-war detached house with curved bays and steel window frames, hints of art deco in the stained glass door panels. Rose bushes flourished under the bays on each side of the porch, but they felt winter's coming. The new flowers stayed in bud and would never open. Only a few leaves had dropped as yet, but their grip was more tenuous.

Mrs Parsons showed Mitch into her lounge. 'He won't be a moment. He's been jogging. He's having a quick shower and towel down.' The carpet was grey, the walls a light grey-green. Black and white prints were on the wall. 'You'll take coffee? Good.'

Left alone, Mitch approached one of the neat rows of books on the sills of small stained glass windows set on either side of a mottled grey tiled fireplace. Here were National Trust publications, catalogues from travelling exhibitions of the works of Marc Chagall and Henry Moore. W.H. Auden and Ted Hughes were in paperback, W. Keble Martin contributed his *Sketches for the Flora*.

'Right, Miss Mitchell . . .' Colin Parsons, in cashmere sweater and slacks, glowed from the door. Mitch had noticed before how, after exercise, flesh recaptured something of a childlike innocence. 'By the way, has an Inspector Briggs been to see you?'

'Last night.'

'That's something of a relief. He came to see me yesterday afternoon. We both made very full statements at the time. Why do you suppose he needed to go over the ground again?'

'I really don't know, Mr Parsons. Thank you . . .' she said to his wife who had come in and was pouring coffee. She set up her tape recorder next to the tray. 'Testing, testing, one, two, three . . .' She ran the tape back to listen. 'Right. We're at the starting gate.'

'I'll leave you two to it then,' said Mrs Parsons. 'Call if you need anything.'

Colin Parsons leaned forward. 'The patient model of mental health –'

'Mental illness, don't you mean?'

'Mental illness' – he cut straight through her – 'assumes sickness. Here is someone who needs taking care of by others. This isn't at all what it's about. These are people with problems or difficulties using services our staff provides. What people want now is the necessary support revolving round them in their own home, in the community –'

'Don't statistics show that sixty per cent of the homeless are mentally ill? Haven't these people fallen right through your net?'

'Even when all the old systems were in place a large proportion of the homeless had mental health problems. That is not to say we must not strive to bring what services we can offer to everyone in need of us. And we have a wide spectrum of help people can choose from, including long-term care provision housed in a fifteen-bed facility, sheltered workshops, support accommodation, special needs housing schemes, day hospitals, places where people can go in the evenings or at weekends, a thirty-bed acute hospital unit –'

'But there was a case only the other day where a severely disturbed man strangled his own daughter even though his wife told her GP he had become deranged and violent. Her doctor could not find a bed for this man anywhere, either in the region or out of it. In fact, is it not true that in Britain one hundred murders a year are committed by mentally ill people?'

'No system, alas, can be completely foolproof. But I am here to tell you that we do provide the best possible set of options – choices – for our service users.'

'Can mad people make an informed choice? Won't, in practice, other people make a choice for them?'

'Madness is not a helpful construct. I really feel, Miss Mitchell, we should all be out there fighting for better understanding, better services. I see our job in the Trust as empowering our service users to help themselves.'

'We are not talking here about saving money, about withdrawing both help and protection from very vulnerable people?'

'Absolutely not. We are talking about targeting the money available so that it is used as effectively as possible.'

Mitch switched off the tape machine. 'Well, thank you very much, Mr Parsons. That about covers it. I'm going to talk to one or two people who have been through the system or are going through it. I may at some stage come back to you for further comment. I hope you won't mind.'

'Not at all. Not at all. Anything I can do to help. Only too willing. Absolutely.'

When she had packed up and they were on the front doorstep, he said: 'Odd the police coming back to us like that. Did they tell you about the silver cuff link? It was in the form of a caduceus. You know, a staff with entwined serpents.'

'The medical profession's emblem.' Mitch's skin shrank against her bones. In her mind's eye she saw the doodle on Carole's telephone pad. 'No, the police haven't mentioned it to me.'

'Of course, I did spot it. Just by the front wheel of my car.'

'Did you get your coat back?'

He shook his head. 'It doesn't matter. I'll never wear it again. Wendy wouldn't like me to.'

'Well, goodbye. Thank you.' Mitch, embarrassed she'd asked him about his coat, dived for the car.

I wonder why Inspector Briggs never mentioned the cuff link?

Right, Jenny Bone, she thought as she turned the ignition. She glanced at her watch. Too early if she'd made that Thursday's group session, she decided and went back to the station to open her post.

In her mind's eye she again saw the doodling on Carole's notepad. The sign of the messenger from the gods. A killer with a calling card? Or could Carole have been killed, if she had been killed, because the caduceus meant something to her? She'd drawn it instead of that person's name when he'd called her. After all, thought Mitch, I've only got her word for it that she didn't know a lot more about Lucy Lessor's love life than she's letting on. But Lucy had been murdered. Wouldn't Carole have told the police everything she'd known? Everything she knows, Mitch firmly corrected herself. Something might have spooked the kid.

She might have flown the coop. Until her corpse turns up she must be presumed to be alive.

Having cleared her desk at the station, Mitch set off to see Jenny Bone two hours later. Pulling her car over, she got out Jenny's address and looked it up in her A–Z. She had to switch on the interior light. Dusk was already creeping across the city.

Jenny lived on the east side of Sutton Coldfield, not far from Cold Ash. It took her half an hour to drive through Birmingham's suburbs and what she found at the end of her journey was an unprepossessing rural landscape getting darker by the second. Jenny's home was one of two 1920s bungalows at the end of a row of what had once been agricultural labourers' cottages.

Like its neighbour, Jenny's bungalow had a large garden, hers mostly overgrown, though it must have been richly productive at one time. The nettles in places were practically six feet high. As Mitch walked up the concrete driveway she saw that duck egg blue paint was peeling from window frames and that the windows had not been cleaned for some months. The front door was blue and egg yolk yellow. Ringing the door bell, Mitch was beginning to wonder if she'd come to the wrong place.

There was a click, silence, another click as the door was opened. A beam of electric light, at first wavering, became wider. At first Mitch had the impression of a small birdlike youngster. Looking again, she judged Jenny Bone to be in her thirties. Under a cap of spiky black hair a pair of luminous black eyes stared from a very pale face. There was something haunting about her; a casting director's perfect ghost.

'Sorry to call unexpectedly but I happened to find myself in the area . . .' and then Mitch began her pitch which was much longer than usual because the woman didn't say anything. Jenny Bone had retreated a step.

Suddenly, as if following the orders of some distant commander, she straightened. 'I don't think I'll be any help at all but you can come in. We'll talk it over and then you can decide.'

The wood chip paper on the hall walls was painted candy floss pink and a pinkish oval mirror with a pearl border of roses hung over a half-moon wrought-iron table piled with directories and a phone. The heavily patterned red carpet extended into the lounge. A lot of unpolished brass stood about a tiled fireplace. An oak sideboard with a machine-carved cherry pattern on the lips of the drawers took up most of the wall opposite the window. There was a jug of dying yellow chrysanthemums on the sill.

Jenny said: 'A woman called Jeanie Black may interest you. I'll get some coffee and her number. Make yourself comfortable.'

Mitch went over to the window and looked out. The scene was forked with blocks of light cast by two side lamps behind her. To her left was a shadowing creosoted garden shed and a concrete coal bunker with a wooden lid. Weeds were encroaching into the crazy paving under the lounge window. Above the central garden path was a long washing line, spaced pegs blowing about in the twilight. No washing hung there.

Coming back with the tray, Jenny said: 'This was my grandmother's house. She left it to me. I was brought up in it.' She looked round. 'I don't know where to start. It's nine months since she died and I haven't done a thing. I'd like to sell it but the market's so bad at the moment. Here's Jeanie's number. I think you'll find her much more suitable for your programme than me. Do sit down.'

Mitch chose the armchair furthest from the gas fire. She did it without thinking but then she realised it was because Jenny was so chilly. It was nothing in her manner. It was as if her roots had turned to ice.

'Jeanie's mother was taken into Cold Ash a year ago. She suffers from Alzheimer's. The point is, four psychogeriatric wards were closed when the hospital shut down. The patients have been moved to private nursing homes and those who had assets over eight thousand pounds have to pay for their own care. I think that figure was doubled in the last Budget. In any event the nursing home bill for Jeanie's mother is almost three hundred and fifty pounds a week. Jeanie is having to sell her mother's house to meet the bills – and she isn't the only one. The relatives have banded together into an action group. Their case is that as their parents paid their NHS contributions all their lives they are entitled to free care and, of course, they were getting free care when Cold Ash was open.'

'Right. Thanks. I'll certainly follow that up.'

'Jeanie got hold of me because she knew I'd worked in television and thought I might still have some connections.'

Mitch, slipping the telephone number into her pocket, was wondering if she was being manipulated. It was obvious Jenny didn't want to be interviewed, but thought the issues should be aired. To appease her conscience was she giving her another story? For all her lack of substance, Mitch was beginning to perceive in Jenny a very formidable woman. And yet on the surface she was noncombative, pliable, seemingly anxious to please.

Jenny was saying: 'The trouble is I don't suppose there's enough money in the national kitty any more. I heard the other day that nurses at a psychiatric Trust hospital down south were nipping off at lunchtime to buy food for their patients. The management had run out of money and not paid its bills so the local traders wouldn't supply them with groceries. I believe Birmingham's debt alone is three times more than that of Albania after forty years of Communist rule.'

'Could we now talk about you?'

'Ah, yes. Me. I'm afraid I don't make a very good story at all.'

'Tell me anyway.'

'Four years ago I was one of the youngest television producers in the country and I was engaged to be married to a very nice guy. One day I went off into Birmingham shopping and suddenly – out of the blue – my heart went weird. I thought I was having a heart attack. But I didn't collapse though the weird frantic beating went on. I couldn't eat so the doctor gave me some stomach medicine. Eventually I was sent to a heart clinic and a doctor there prescribed a beta-blocker. It regularises the heartbeat. When I took it my heart slowed down and I went into an acute depression. I couldn't seem to feel alive, feel anything at all. Logically I knew I wasn't dead but it seemed to me I was. I once looked in the mirror in a shoe shop and didn't recognise myself. I didn't know me any more. As I wasn't there I saw this stranger, I suppose. Eventually I couldn't get out of bed because there was no me to get out of bed. The dead really don't put their slippers on and go for a shower, do they? It was at that stage they took me into Cold Ash.'

'The Amy Johnson Ward? I was there the other day.'

'Very civilised,' said Jenny. 'The whole ambience is 1930s parquet and roses with Joan Crawford being insane in elegant lingerie. Didn't you find? They were going to give me ECT but tried anti-depressants first. I never did have ECT. I improved and I came out. I didn't realise how frightening it was for other people to live with someone in an acutely depressed state. At that stage I was living with Mark, my fiancé. He was wonderful about it all for quite a long time but in the end he couldn't cope. I came back here to live with my grandmother.'

'What's happened to Mark?'

'I don't know. We seem to have lost touch. But after a bit of foot-slogging around I managed to get a researcher's job with the Sharon and Larry show.'

'You had to start all over again at the bottom?'

Jenny shrugged. 'It's a very competitive market place, as you know. You have to be fit to survive. But I actually did quite well until my grandmother died and I got pretty ill again. My contract with the Sharon and Larry show wasn't renewed. This time my GP sent me to see a psychiatrist called Dr Rainbow and after a few sessions he suggested I join his therapy group.'

'Group therapy? Will it help?'

'It's too early to say. But you do see my point? No great tragedy occurred, nothing like that. I just went out for a day's shopping. At that time I was feeling really good, I was going great guns at work. It was a bolt from the blue.'

'There must have been a reason. What about your parents? You did say your grandmother brought you up.'

'My father was never in the picture much and my mother died of cancer when I was nine.'

'What happened to him?'

'I see him occasionally. He married again about ten years ago.'

I can't use stuff like this. People want reasons. It's all too airy-fairy. Does she know I won't use it? Of course she does. I don't doubt that she is telling me the truth but what she is really doing is editing herself out of my programme. God, she is sharper than I am, much cleverer altogether. Why did she walk slap bang into a breakdown? There is something so cold about the way she tells her story, as though it happened to someone else. A disturbingly lurid cartoon jumped into Mitch's mind. The luminosity had vanished from Jenny Bone's eyes. All Mitch saw were a pair of black holes in a sheet doing duty as a shroud. She was unnerved but she tried again: 'What do you hope to get out of group work?'

Jenny was deciding, Mitch could see, whether to tell her. A small smile played round her lips. 'Redemption.'

Mitch stared at her.

'I've startled you.'

'I don't think . . . well, you express it in religious terms.'

'Why not?'

'I don't know,' Mitch said unhappily. At the moment her story seemed to be squeezing into all sorts of unmanageable shapes. Those old folks chucked out of their psychogeriatric wards, she could control that, shape the material into a decent programme. Recognising defeat as far as Jenny was concerned, she was horrified to find she was putting the boot in. 'Thinking of what the NHS management has in mind for its service users . . . aren't you being a little ambitious?'

'When nothing else will do you go for it, don't you?' Jenny said. 'And the people one has to work with . . . Take the psychiatrist himself. I'm sure he'd be horrified if he knew the role I'd earmarked him for. He'll try to skive off. I know it. He'll jolly well wriggle off the hook if I'm not careful.'

'Shouldn't you go to a priest?'

'I don't know any. He's what turned up. Anyway, he's set himself up as some sort of brain doctor – some kind of shaman – so he must expect to do this kind of work. He's just going to have to get cracking. It does take two, you see. This kind of work. I'm rapidly coming to the conclusion there's no such thing as man alone. That's a myth. We are in and through each other . . . I think. How could a hermit be a hermit if no one saw him as a hermit?'

'Yes. I see,' said Mitch though she knew she didn't see at all. She cast around for something to say. She now had the feeling she ought to be encouraging in some way though she wasn't sure whether this was at all a good thing. Was she colluding in some sort of dangerous delusion? A question seemed safer. 'And you really think you'll pull it off?'

'I tell myself it is only a matter of concentration.'

'But how will you know? I mean, if it works?'

'Not for a long time, I suppose. Perhaps many years. Not until it becomes apparent.'

'I don't think you're playing the same game as the rest of your team, Jenny. It seems to me you aren't even speaking the same language.'

'Oh, I'm not going to worry about that. I don't have the luxury of considering that. I just intend to get on with it.' She smiled. 'I really am no good to you, am I? I'm not the right kind of stuff at all. Besides, it's a bit tricky, this group I'm in. That girl who was murdered, Lucy Lessor, used to be a member. In fact, I'm sitting in her chair. Don't you find that coincidences, when they come, well, they seem to arrive in little clusters.'

'Coincidences, Jenny?' She was aware of using Jenny's first name again, like a kindly grown-up addressing a small child.

'Actually, mine is spelt with an "ie", but I'm really a Lucie too. Jenny's my middle name.'

Mitch suddenly felt as if she were spinning, part of the mechanism in a fruit machine. She knew that though it operated by chance she was going to hit the jackpot. She saw an endless row of fruit clicking up. 'Bananas.' She just managed to refrain from speaking aloud. 'Everything's bananas.'

Jenny got up. 'I'm sorry I've not been much help.'

The trouble was that as far as her detective work went nobody was being much help, thought Mitch gloomily as she drove back through the suburbs to the city centre. It wasn't the fact that there was so much information to process which was worrying her, more that it felt like chaos rather than shape which was emerging from the Mirry Vesey and Ann Bateman enquiries.

14

It was a hot afternoon in late August and all the windows in the attic room at the Glick Hope had been open. It had all begun then. When Sammy had told the chairman of the magistrates that he would never, never, ever take another peep he'd meant it. Just a load of grief. That's what slags were. Always getting him into trouble. Stuff that for a game of soldiers.

Flies were buzzing and Ted Coveyduck was buzzing too, on and on about all these tests he'd had to find out why he felt like death and how these tests had made a liar of him. They all showed he was as fit as a flea. 'I might not be able to walk to the pub without feeling faint but, believe me, according to the quacks I'm A1. I read that if you play them up they put nasty things on your notes. PBM or NFN. Awful things like that. Worse than that.'

'What do the letters stand for?' asked Joan.

'NFN is Normal For Norfolk. Everyone is hopeless in Norfolk. They say it's all the inbreeding that went on down there. And PBM is Poor Biological Material. I've never even been on holiday to Norfolk so I suppose I'm PBM.'

'Do they really do that?' Joan asked Dr Rainbow.

Dr Rainbow was grinning and saying nothing.

'I don't call that very nice,' said Joan.

'You should worry,' said Maurice, laughing, 'I was born in Norfolk.'

'I bet, Ron, you and me were the only ones born in Brum.' Lucy Lessor had leaned forward in her orange plastic chair. She was smiling, tucking in the wings of her shoulders, lifting her chin. As her body rocked back, Sammy, who had a side view, could see which two knobs in her bobbly knit cotton top were nipples. Their rosy pinkiness was almost poking through the loosely knitted stitches. The bitch's got no bra on. The knowledge slightly unhinged his jaw. Her stretch Lycra skirt began to ride up as her pelvis tilted, giving everyone a good eyeful of the pawlike shape of the pad of flesh which surmounted the junction of her pubic bone. Dr Rainbow coughed. Sammy felt a dreadful prickling which might be the beginning of an erection. Lucy lifted her legs, folded them to the side and neatly tucked her heels under her bottom, lowering her head demurely.

What chance had a chap got?

It didn't take him long to track that hot little bitch down and stake out the ground-floor housing association flat she lived in with her daughter. The block lay between a main road and a high railway embankment. On the other side of the line was a chapel which, according to the faded sign, was now an old folk's sun-shine club, though Sammy had never seen any sign of activity. The only time he felt vulnerable was when he crossed the railway lines. On the other side he was camouflaged by a rampant growth of buddleia which had self-seeded and now thrived in the dry gravel of the embankment. From here he could look down on Lucy's sitting-room and master bedroom, rooms which in the late afternoons were dappled with shadows from a siver birch tree.

Through many hot hours he saw Lucy hoover and build Lego brick houses with her blonde-haired daughter. He saw her spray polish the television set before sitting down to watch it. And then one early afternoon in September he saw her coming into the sitting-room in a blue cotton dressing-gown, rubbing her wet hair with a towel. She dropped the towel on the bamboo-framed settee, took off the gown and dropped that on top of it. A small, piping whistle blew like a kiss through Sammy's teeth.

He noticed that even though her hair was black, her skin was a bluey white and, marvel of marvels, her pussy was ginger. He didn't think much of her nipples. They were much smaller than he'd imagined they would be. He'd seen better jugs, too, if he was honest.

She raised both arms over her head and bent to touch her toes; up, down, up, down and the slow rhythm of her movements became his breathing.

She sat down.

He unzipped himself.

She spread her legs. Her torso swayed over her right leg and her hands travelled down to her toes. She touched her foot with her nose. She moved to her left leg. She rested, elbows propping up her head, her legs drawn up but still apart. Through her pelt he could see the folds of her labia. A hooded little antler of flesh pouted under the pubic bone and then a stalk four inches long rooted itself between her thighs. He felt rather confused, for it etched out the shape of a stamen and this was the male reproductive organ of a plant. He looked down at his erect cock. That, too, had similarities with a stamen.

He observed her again. She'd walked over to the windowsill and pressed her face and breasts into the pane and what he saw now were monstrous distortions. His prick jumped a little. Shock, he reckoned. As she moved back she picked up a cut glass vase shaped like a champagne flute. She plucked out the roses and then tilted the vase and he and she watched the water trickle over the many lips of a furry-leaved African violet.

Suddenly she was spinning on her toes, tossing the roses in the air. One caught in her hair. She sank down to her knees, her back towards him. Her buttocks relaxed into her heels. She spread her thighs.

What was the crazy bitch up to now?

He was biting his lips in a fury of frustration.

She slowly rose back up on to her knees and he saw this great cut glass cock between them, the round foot presented to her cunt. She tippy-tiptoed round the carpet on her knees as she repositioned herself. She carefully brought herself down to the glinting disc of light. Very gently she dusted the top with her furry brush and then began to work it through the soft folds of her labia. Her thighs widened, her buttocks danced back and forth, back and forth, the cock dancing too but it only advanced. Suddenly her thighs split apart; her arms were akimbo, hands hanging on to her hip bones. Her buttocks began to judder. Two quick spasms jolted her tail bone off the floor.

Sammy's joints were springing out of their sockets. He knew he was whimpering.

She slowly arched back, her wild wet hair splashing about her as her shoulders touched the floor. Her ankles moved out from under her thighs, the soles of her feet tilting to their inner rims. She pushed up so her buttocks rose off the floor. He saw the great glittering cock had been transformed into a cut glass cunt which rode in triumph above her ginger pussy. She teasingly turned her new diamond-polished labia into the sun and blinded him. When he opened his eyes the witch had magicked the cunt into a cock. She was holding it over her head. Her arm jerked back. She hurled it against the wall. Shards of stars powdered her hair.

He never went back.

No fear.

And no. He hadn't come. But that was hardly surprising, he told himself. How could any man perform when he didn't know which way up was what?

Mind you, Ron Saffia didn't seem to have his problems. Under his tutelage Sammy had got there all right.

That Lucy had been dead for a week when all their corks had been popped was unsettling.

He didn't want to put it any higher than that.

If he did, he might faint with anxiety.

Sammy was proud that these events hadn't put him off. It showed you he was a proper peeping Tom and not one of these small-time amateur wankers. No, Sammy was your hardened veteran.

It seemed a shame that having proved himself under fire, so to speak, he'd a feeling he might soon be posted.

The problem was that he'd fallen in love with his Jenny.

He didn't want to watch anyone doing anything to her and that included observing any action with cut glass vases.

What he wanted was to do it all himself.

Well, he thought, no one could say he hadn't learned the theory over the years, could they? All he needed was a bit of practice. The more practice the better. The thought of all that practice was making his lips do the splits.

But how would he get his Jenny to lie down with him?

The only thing he knew about courting was what the adverts on television told him. Sammy now had a shower and shampooed his hair before he went on his adventures. He changed his underwear and socks and wore a new light blue jumper over a well-pressed shirt. He thought the colour of the jumper brought out the blue in his eyes. He put on his new shoes, the ones with the crepe soles which were just like Dr Rainbow's. Yesterday he'd bought a bottle of Brut and he now squirted this over every fold he could find. Having never used it before, he didn't realise he should put it on his skin and not his clothes.

Viewing himself in his Aunt Ada's cheval mirror he thought he didn't look half bad. Any girl could do worse than Mr Sammy Pink.

Mr Sammy Pink, the landscape gardener, he thought, inspired, as he closed the front door behind him and stepped jauntily down the garden path.

Home produce consultant?

He should have seen his Aunt Ada tonight but hadn't because he knew she was working herself up to tell him something. He'd no doubt what that was. But if he didn't hear the words, the roof would stay over his head. Sometimes now when he saw that white-haired old lady with the big baby blue eyes he also saw his fist ramming her teeth into her brains and bits of her skull exploding through her skin. She was aware of his rage and waited until it had soured into guilt. Her eyes would sparkle. 'I could do with a chocolate éclair. You never bring me anything really nice, Sammy, like a chocolate éclair.'

Still, he was jaunty enough to get into his old Ford Escort the way they do in American films, hand on the top of the door, dropping into the driving seat with a big swing of the buttocks, like an ape settling on its tree branch. After he switched her on, his hand slipped all over and between the knobs and shiny bits. He gunned her, taking off so fast he practically left his bumper behind.

But he knew he'd be canny, too. He must find more out about Jenny's bungalow. 'A nice little woman providing she's got her own place,' his Aunt Ada had counselled. Sammy, head over heels in love as he was, saw the wisdom of the old woman's advice. That's a good stretch of land she's got, he was thinking. Why, I could almost turn it into a market garden. I'll even grow her herbs, basil in the summer, thyme, pot marigold. That kind of bird will like stuff like that. And any poncy veggie she sets her mind to.

Oh, oh, here we go. Flying off to my love. He could feel the wind rushing to fill his unfurling wings.

Proper lovers, he realised, don't go hiding behind bushes waiting to catch glimpses of their ladies' tits and bum. Dirty old men do that. His heart jumped on to his tongue and lay bleating.

I should have a bunch of flowers in my hand. Or a box of chocolates. I should knock on her front door and she should invite me in. She will have cooked me a fancy meal or I will take her to a restaurant.

What would happen if she caught me behind the bushes peering in at her?

Well, he thought truculently, she knows I'm a peeping Tom. After all, she asked. And I told the bitch, all right? Anyway she'd never come out with me. I'm not good enough for the likes of her.

I was quite good at technical drawing, he told himself, rallying his defences. I'd lay odds she's clueless about that. Woodwork, too, and metalwork.

The only thing I'm really good at is making things grow. And everybody knows gardeners have no brains.

He began to despair. The floor of the car shifted and sidled under his crepe soles; he might have been perched on the back of a snake.

'Well now . . .' Jenny said to him as he restored himself to himself. She could have done many things when he told her the shaming truth but she'd taken him in as he was. And he called her a bitch. Why did he do that? Using her as though she wasn't his Jenny but a twopenny bit tart.

She's certainly no saint, he told himself angrily. The way she makes up to that creep with the cigarette holder. She's out for it if she can get it. And the way that doctor treats her. All flirty eyes and come on. And that's what the taxpayer foots the bill for!

Listen here, stop this. She's been good to you. Before she came into the group you were Mr Nobody. People didn't even look down at you. You weren't worth that much notice. She not only noticed you, she chose you. Why did she do such a thing?

She's got to like you. Stands to reason.

Fancies you, I daresay. So put that in your pipe and smoke it. And now his wings were really becoming unstuck, right to their furthermost tip, and all the winds of heaven billowed beneath them until he planed through the air and was deposited softly near Jenny Wren's door.

He had to back up a little because he didn't want any nosy parker spying on him. He parked the car neatly, so its bonnet faced the way he'd come, just before the lane narrowed into a single track.

There was no moon but here, on the rim of a million souls, the dirty wash of neon was draining into an outer darkness, the kind of darkness Sammy liked. Here you could peek at the stars if the cloud cover dispersed, you could get an eyeful.

He turned down the single track towards her lair, smelling the cost of all that Brut. Still, what did it matter when it all added up to him smelling good. He was still sniffing himself as he trotted by the row of cottages and the bungalow which wasn't Jenny's. He was only a few feet from the concrete driveway which led to her.

Now he began to sniff her out. Into his mind jumped a pair of juicy steak and kidney puddings. His lips moistened. He knew he was bewitched, that her breasts were no more than griddle scones. If he bit into her he'd be spitting out splinters of bone. It didn't stop her bum appearing, dangling from its twig like twin ripe pears and his hand moving up to feel under the ripe roundness, pads of his fingers sinking into soft flesh.

She's got no bum.

Sammy, have some sense.

The whore's a bag of bones.

But the inky eyes were hooked into him and the tug of her relentless. He hardly stopped to note that the front of the bungalow was in darkness. He was into the next-door field, padding back down along the hedge to the gap. He inserted himself through it and came into her garden.

What an overgrown mess.

He could see straight away that she really needed him.

And I could tickle her ears with my forefinger, he thought.

I've had a shower, haven't I? I smell nice.

It was at this point he noticed the back of the bungalow was in darkness, too.

The truth almost drowned him; a clear, chill, crystal font of knowledge.

My love's not in.

When he bobbed up again he found that outside his rage was something else, circling round the rim. He was glad.

You don't go spying on your bird, just as if she's a tart.

I'll pop by casual like, with some veggies, those late tomatoes in the greenhouse and that lot of lettuces, I can pick her one or two of those.

But frustration had so agitated him that his limbs were practically dancing.

There's always that radio show tart. You can go and see her, he told himself. Now she has got some knockers and a really bouncy bum into the bargain.

But he realised he was fagged out. Better call it a night, he thought, remembering to cover his wide yawn with a hand. If Aunt Ada had taught him nothing else, she'd taught him what was proper in that respect.

It was then he made out a shape, someone wearing an anorak very like the one he used to wear before he'd bought his new one. It was the movement which had caught his eye, he realised. This shadowy figure was making its way stealthily through the gap between the two bungalows to the front garden.

Sammy eased back on to his heels and was perfectly still. In his mind's eye he saw himself unpegging Jenny's bra and knickers from her line, observed again the gap where more of Jenny's underwear should have been.

He remembered retreating through the grounds of the milk depot when he'd heard someone prowling at the back of Mitch Mitchell's garden.

It was as if his shadow had broken free and jauntily gone off on its own to get an eyeful of Sammy's collection of hot little bitches.

But what if those dark fingers stretched out and touched?

What if the biggest, darkest finger of all was intent on impaling Sammy's pussies?

Perhaps this thing had concealed itself behind the buddleia bushes on the embankment above Lucy Lessor's house. Waiting for an opportunity to pounce?

The figure was gone.

I'm seeing things, thought Sammy. It's this way. I've seen so much I'm now seeing what's not there.

Was that a footfall he heard? Footfalls on the concrete driveway, a gate clicking?

Three shadows rose up in his mind. They were called Ted Coveyduck, Maurice Pincing, Ron Saffia.

But they didn't know I was a peeping Tom. No one in the group knew that until I told Jenny.

Dr Rainbow did.

Sammy was aware of a rattling. His teeth.

He's trying to pinch my Jenny. Why wouldn't he have a go at the rest of my birds too?

That little slag they found dead will be down to me.

It'll all be my fault.

After all, that's what Aunt Ada did, isn't it? She dropped me right in it and now makes out I'm the guilty party.

He was recalling the way the doctor walked. The way his bones thought before he made his move, before he put one of his brothel creepers in front of the other.

And then Sammy stopped thinking because he felt himself being tugged towards a well of terror.

Back in Cherry Park he parked his car in the usual place and crossed the street. He turned when another car door slammed.

'Hello, Sammy . . .' and the warrant card was already out of one of the detective's pockets.

'One of the big cheeses wants a word. He's come up to the local nick specially to see you,' said his partner.

Sammy's hand fumbled to find the right place because his stomach had drained into Dr Rainbow's crepe shoes. When he did feel the pouch at the front of his anorak he found it was empty. He'd been so befuddled by love he'd forgotten to take his binoculars with him.

'I don't know what you want me for. If it's about that Lucy you're well out of luck. I've told you all I know already.'

'You haven't told Inspector Briggs.'

15

'It was on the early morning news?'

'If only I'd waited, Tommy . . .'

'That's ridiculous. Apart from anything else, if he'd got her it was already too late. But they haven't found Carole's body. Until they do, there's hope . . .'

Mitch shook her head. 'As soon as Colin Parsons told me about this cuff link – shaped like a caduceus – something in me has known for sure.' She told Tommy about that and the doodle in the flat. 'Forget stranger killing. This maniac is someone we know. I think he's a member of the psychotherapy group. I don't care what Dr Bateman says about their checks and all that stuff. A wolf's in the chicken coup. Everyone makes mistakes, including psychiatrists. Well, at least the police have hauled someone in. A guy in our news room said they nabbed him yesterday. He's been held overnight. That looks promising.'

'Did you tell Dr Bateman about me seeing Dr Rainbow steal that page from a file?'

'She's going to front him with it. Pretend she saw him do it and has been waiting ever since for his explanation.'

'Sounds a bit weak.'

'Best we can come up with.'

'I wonder if he's the one being detained? After all, a caduceus is the sign of the medical profession.'

'The man appears to have been in charge of psychotherapy groups for years. Why would he suddenly start killing off patients?'

'I don't think psychiatrists are a wonderfully stable bunch. Don't they have one of the highest suicide rates of any group?'

'That's still a far cry from stringing patients up and doing God knows what, including letting off fireworks. Then strangling them. There's something so weirdly schoolboy prankish about the fireworks. As if the Marquis de Sade had jumped into the skin of an eleven-year-old Just William.'

'There are certainly some rum customers in that group,' said Tommy. 'Did A.J. bring you up to date on the Sammy Pink thing?'

'About him being a peeping Tom? Yes.'

'She's gone down to the central library. See if she can come up with the press reports of the court case. I'm moving on to Ron Saffia. What's worrying me is while we're doing all this we're not moving ahead with the Mirry Vesey investigation.'

'I might have some news for you there later today,' said Mitch. 'Look, I'm going to have to go. I want to nip up to the canteen and have some breakfast. I'll give you another bell before I leave the studios tonight. Tommy . . .'

'What?'

'I hope you're being very, very careful. It's not impossible this maniac will switch from girls to chaps.'

'If I weren't a careful fellow I would have been dead years ago. As a youth I lived in adventurous times.'

Mitch dropped the phone back on the hook and silently sat at her desk. She shrugged off her anxieties and went up to the canteen to treat herself to some eggs and bacon. When she came down fifteen minutes later she felt like a new woman. There was nothing like unhealthy food for perking up your blood sugar, she thought. Putting some fizz back into you.

Passing Digger Rooney's desk in the production office, she picked up one of his fireworks brochures. 'Blossom after spring thunder ninety shot multi-effect Roman candle cake,' she read aloud. Digger was sitting behind his desk, staring at his pudgy forefinger which he'd placed two feet from his nose. 'Why are you doing that?'

'It's an exercise in emptying my mind,' he said.

'Aren't you afraid to go pop? Like a balloon?'

'Ha, ha and up yours. I'm controlling my stress levels.'

'Hey! This one really has my vote. Battling Ninjas Jumbo Fountain. Silver effects, whistles and then thunderous crackling sounds.'

'We're not having that. If I've got to organise this ghastly Radio Brum fireworks display I get to pick. What we're going to have is a lot of Shrieking Eagles.'

'What do they do? Do put your finger down, Digger. There's something latently obscene about it. I keep looking for the other one.'

Digger sighed and lowered his finger. 'Absolutely horrid ear-splitting things Freya Adcock will loathe. I also plan to stick some rockets under her arse.'

Mitch spotted the Eagles on the list. 'Silver tail whistles howl in their high flight and explode as bright stars in the sky. Sounds rather good. I'm sorry I won't be coming.'

'Oh, but you will, blossom. The whole of Radio Brum will fall in. Including our music maestro. Even Quentin Plunkett won't be able to fiddle his way out of this one. I've decided Quentin's going to be in charge of handing out sparklers to the smaller kiddiewinkies.'

'Does he know yet?'

'Look up and tell me what you see.'

'The ceiling?'

'If the roof's still on he can't know. Can he?'

'What have you put me in charge of? Gorgeous, darling, glamorous hunkie-punk, can't I field a substitute? I really don't like fireworks.'

'It's meeting listeners you don't like.'

'That's quite untrue. Mine are extremely bright and lovely with it. It's everybody else's I can't stand.'

'The only people who listen to you, Mitchell, are the ones you've interviewed for your show. They want to hear what they sound like coming out of a radio.'

'Will you just stop your squabbling, you two. I can't hear!' Trish, the production office secretary, was waving a phone receiver about.

'I might forgive you for that shitty remark. But only if you put me on something at this yukky firework night of yours that I can slope off from after ten minutes,' Mitch hissed, sotto voce. 'I don't know, Digger. You're becoming bitter and twisted in your old age.'

'I did use to be nice, didn't I? I can remember when I was nice.' Digger gloomily reviewed his character. 'Radio Brum hasn't improved me for a start. But it goes deeper than that.' He sighed. 'The trouble is, however hard I try not to, I keep on growing up. It's a withering experience. All one's illusions falling away. It's more horrid than a game of strip poker. And when you're not losing your nether garments to life and love there's this.' He looked round the production office. 'Toytown radio, blossom, is not something really grown-up people do. Not really really. But what do I want to be?'

'Honeypot, try a bit harder and you'll be world champion wanker.' Mitch dodged back into the storeroom as she said this, banging the door behind her. And yet she did feel a little sorry for Digger. She hoped he wasn't going to go into an early mid-life crisis. She unplugged her tape recorder from the charger. Poor old sod, she thought. I shouldn't be so nasty to him. No, you shouldn't, common sense told her. If you're not careful he'll put you in charge of doling out sparklers.

She was all smiles when she re-emerged into the production office. 'Someone will recognise your talent one day, Digger. You just see.'

'No they won't. You get a feeling about these things after a while. You know?' Digger had been drawing on a piece of paper. He now bit off a piece of sellotape and stuck the paper to his brow. Guy Fawkes, tears dribbling on to the firewood at his feet, was begging: 'Don't burn me up.'

Mitch went round his desk and kissed him on the ear. 'I'll bring us back two vanilla slices. You can have the biggest one.'

'Don't you mean bigger?' Quentin Plunkett had come into the room. He flicked his golden hair back, stretched out a hand and scratched the back of his neck as he considered the notice hanging from Digger's brow. 'At least Fawkes took a lot of faggots with him when he went up in smoke. Good man, that.'

'You shouldn't read other people's private correspondence,' said Mitch. She bent to tenderly ease the paper off Digger's brow. 'Such an uncouth man.'

'Very uncouth,' Digger agreed.

'A very, very uncouth man,' said Mitch. 'Aren't you in need of an i.c. latrines, Digger? For this big do you're organising?'

'Blossom! That's inspired.'

'Well, chaps, I'm off. The skin trade calls. If you can't be good don't even try to be bad. That takes real talent.' Mitch began rounding up handbag, notepads, shopping bag and her jacket. She tucked a crooked forefinger into the chain hanger at the back of the jacket and swung it over her shoulder. 'I'll be back around lunchtime,' she called to the production office secretary.

'If you're going down to Balsall Heath I'd wear a hat,' Digger said.

'Why?'

'It's a good idea, that's why. You know.'

'No. I don't know.'

'You might get accosted.'

'Talk about pigs flying,' said Quentin. One hand on hip he turned and surveyed Mitch's open black jacket, the scarlet silk lining brushing against the pink braces which secured her black and white herringbone patterned pants. 'Unless she's mistaken for a geriatric rent boy.'

'Don't listen to him. Take my advice.'

'But how would it help?'

'Have you ever seen a bit of Birmingham brass in a hat?'

Mitch considered. 'Have you looked down one of our mean streets lately? Hats generally are as rare as palm trees.'

'You take my word for it. Tarts and titfers don't go together. That's all I'm saying. For what it's worth.'

'Oh, right.'

'And don't forget the vanilla slice you promised me. I'll hate you if you do. You're always breaking promises. It's not fair.'

Mitch, tape recorder and bags swinging, played a few notes on an imaginary sobbing violin before disappearing round the door. Men, she thought. Could Digger really be old enough to have a mid-life crisis? When he's my age, she thought, he'll have gone through so many crises he won't call them that any more. They'll just be times he or the world went arse over tit. She found herself hurrying down the corridor, trying to leave behind her all the banana skins lying in wait in her life at the moment, possible loss of her Radio Brum job, possible failure of the detective agency, no permanent roof over her head and this awful programme about care in the community still to be made.

'Mitch.' Freya Adcock was emerging out of the lavatories. She was wearing a turquoise polo-neck sweater, a lot of bright red plastic beads and a maroon pleated skirt. Her belly was bulging pregnantly over the waistband. Mitch was sceptical. Even the Almighty wouldn't have dared. 'Been to see Adelaide yet?'

Mitch racked her brains. No Adelaide came to mind.

'Of course, she shouldn't be out at all.'

'Your next-door neighbour. The loony one,' Mitch recalled. 'You phoned. Material for the care in the community programme.'

'It's all very well this service user lark and I'm for it. All the way. But that woman's now up half the night moving furniture. Shoving it against doors and so forth. No one at our end of the block can get any sleep. The man in the flat below hers is really up in arms about it. He's even collared her psychiatric social worker but the bitch won't even try to get her taken away.'

'I don't think they've got the money to do that any more.'

'Well, what are they spending it all on? You might like to ask someone that. Get one or two MPs in. Get that fellow from the regional board. Nail some of those bastards to the wall. I'll tell you one thing. If that woman doesn't stop moving furniture at two in the morning someone's going to do her a mischief.'

'Isn't there some by-law about too much noise at night? Noise pollution or something? Can't you get on to someone at the council? I think they can prosecute people for that.'

'Do you know, I think you're right . . . They've got things that record the noise level. I remember something about that.'

'Worth a shot, I'd say. Look, I really must fly . . .'

'What we really need to do is highlight the awful plight of people like Adelaide, d'you see? Maybe giving it a bit of publicity will get something done about her. Well, not just her, you understand. Don't get me wrong. We're all for her. People have their probs. Still, that noise pollution angle of yours might fix it . . .'

Freya Adcock's words were winging after Mitch as she broke into a gallop; the voice of the Fury pursued her to the bottom of the corridor.

Guilt, too, was making her run. Although this was her day for working at the radio station she was, judiciously camouflaged, going about detective agency business.

It was what she thought of as a seaside day, dancing ripples on puddles, the organisation's flags flapping at stem and stern of the building, wind walloping past her ears, the tangy chill prickle of coming winter in her nostrils, wool and silk plastering against her bones as she tacked across the car-park.

She dumped her gear on the back ledge of the TVR and immediately began worrying that it might be nicked if she parked the car in Balsall Heath. They might take her wheels, too. She told herself that the place was full of parked cars. Why should anyone half-inch her clapped-out ride? For a start the holes in the floor were going to join up soon. Any joy rider might find his bum touching the tarmac. All the same, it was still red, still a sports car, still had very tasty lines. OK, OK, OK, she told herself. I'll park it by the cricket ground and let the wind blow me down Cannon Hill Road.

She turned off Edgbaston Road by the police training college and decided to leave it in full view of parading cadets. It would really take some nerve to steal it from here, she thought, but she tucked the tape recorder out of sight before she locked up.

When a prostitute and a client kicked off in Balsall Heath, Mitch always wondered whether they appreciated the fact that they were surrounded by Betjeman's middle England: the thunk of buxom lasses' tennis balls from Calthorpe Park, the sound of cricket ball on willow and shouts of 'Well played, sir!' and 'Shot!' as applause rippled round Warwickshire's county cricket ground. Hot and sweaty and getting his ten quid's worth, did a chap ever pause to wonder about other scores?

She had always thought it rather bizarre, the way the city's red light district butted into Edgbaston, which many regarded as the best address in Birmingham. Within a street or two net curtains, that hallmark of respectability, had been suborned to become props in a peep-show, opened at night to reveal whores striking their poses and signing their prices. It put Mitch in mind of the

Victorians who had raised vast amounts by public subscription to erect statues to Victoria and Albert and other national figures only to subvert them by constructing public latrines under their pedestals. As a child Mitch had often waited, penny in hand, to pee under the skirts of Queen Victoria.

In some of the most notorious streets trade went on in well-founded late Victorian and Edwardian terraces, small gardens leading to their front doors, old-fashioned street lighting pacing the pavements, the silver helmets of the lamps nodding under a curve of iron, the branches of mature trees forming umbrellas over red-tiled roof-tops. It seemed to Mitch that much of this city's vice was covered in old-fashioned antimacassars; even the anti-whore pickets, composed mostly of Muslim men, followed very traditional English rules. They were non-violent, very rarely even talking to the punters; they noted clients' car numbers.

But the picture under this veneer of provincial cosiness told a different story; the mostly immigrant population was afraid to wear sandals for fear of their feet being punctured by discarded needles, bushes sometimes fruited condoms. Five hundred girls were said to ply their trade here. They earned up to a thousand pounds a week. Mitch thought that this figure must be overstated. At a tenner a time that was a hundred fucks a week. Wouldn't it lead to tender flesh tanning like leather?

She'd never found the courage to ask. Anyway, she told herself, Freya wouldn't have allowed her to broadcast such stuff. Too sleazy.

As she left the cricket ground behind her, she found herself looking for condoms and needles. She couldn't see any.

It took a female with a special sort of nerve, she thought, to become a brass. At ten in the morning Sharon Quickly didn't look the part. She stood at the front door of her house just off Ada Road in baby blue jogging gear, a tall, rangy forty-year-old blonde. Mitch recalled describing her to her partner Tommy and A.J. as an old prostitute and compared to most of the girls she was. Like athletics, this was a young person's game. 'Windy,' Sharon said. 'I've only just got back. Had to take our Karen to the dentist. Come in, babs. Fancy a coffee? I've got kettle on.'

'Thanks,' said Mitch.

She was shown into the bay-windowed front lounge. The nets discreetly screened off the street outside though Sharon, she thought, couldn't be a window girl because this was her own home. Usually the brass rented a room by the hour, though many plied the streets in the old way.

'Park your bum,' Sharon said as she brought in a tray of coffee.

'It's really nice,' said Mitch, looking round the room again. Mix and match chintz curtains and chair covers toned in with colour-sponged walls and side lamps. It was like a hotel bedroom in one of the best chains, she thought, and then wondered if that was where Sharon had first got a taste for designer interiors.

'Cost a bomb,' said Sharon. 'But you've got to treat yourself right, haven't you? No other bugger's going to. Sugar? I don't either. Got to watch the poundage. Fat hits the old pay packet like you wouldn't believe.' She looked round the room again. 'Of course you've got to be a bit careful. Can't dolly up a place too much. Never know if a DHSS snooper will come knocking on your door. As if anyone could bring up two kiddies on income support. Got to do a bit of business, haven't you? People think it's easy. They think all you do is shovel on the make-up and pull up the fishnet stockings...' She changed the subject abruptly. 'What's this then about 18 Ada Road? Who's asking?'

'The agency has got a client, a husband, whose wife siphoned off a large amount of money from the family pot. He wants to know where it went and for certain reasons thinks it would be a dead loss tackling her about it directly.'

'Certain reasons. Christ. What kind of talk's that? I mean, come on...'

'His wife is undergoing psychiatric treatment at the moment.'

'And this nutter's been visiting 18 Ada Road? Posh, is she? Must be if her old man can afford you lot! What you are wondering is why a bint like that would mix with the likes of us lot?'

Mitch laughed. 'I wouldn't quite put it like that.'

'Only because it's not polite. Would you pay for information?'

'If it's good. If we can use it. As long as the price isn't a silly one.'

'This girl I'm thinking of shared that house with another two kids until she slung her hook. That would be about a month ago. Moved over Chelmsley Wood way. Had enough, I hear. This feller, a Maltese chap, runs the show. Me, I don't do kinky. Well, not so's you'd notice. The word is that is all they do at 18 Ada Road. Lot of money in it. Geoff calls it the value-added end of the market. He used to be in plastic coatings, did Geoff. The more fancy the coating, the more the price went up! But Pagan, she got scared and took off. The kid'll want paying for opening her mouth...' and as Mitch made a move for her handbag Sharon laughed. 'No, no. I don't want nothing, babs. What do you think I am? Give us a break.'

'Do you know the names of the other girls in the house? And this Maltese?'

'The guy's called Lino. Good-looker, I'll give him that. Wears a diamond in his nose. Just got a real fancy car he usually keeps well locked up in a garage by the cricket ground. Maybe a present from your rich bit? None of the girls he runs are out of their teens. They're all druggies, of course, including Pagan. But though she was as high as a kite much of the time she had enough sense to get shit scared and clear off.' She shook her head. 'Bad for the business, places like that. Too high a profile and the Vice Squad's crawling out of the woodwork.'

'And the other girls?'

'There's a kid called Shelley. Don't know the name of the other. Dark girl, Shelley is. Stunning looker. I hear that the council went and served an enforcement notice on the place. That bastard Lino got his shoulder tapped because he'd not applied for planning permission to turn the premises into what they called "a business used for prostitution". Got to laugh, haven't you?'

'Really?'

'Had to move his girls around for a while. To tell you the truth, I've got to get out of here sooner rather than later. It's not just these so-called pickets infesting the place. I've our Karen and Marnie to consider. I thought maybe the seaside...' She shrugged. 'The trouble is, all my muckers are here. I mean, what would I do for a bloody good laugh? Still, it's not the same as it was. Me and Geoff, we've been talking. But you don't want to know about that. Look, give me a day or two to track down Pagan's address. I'll be in touch.'

'That's terrific of you, Sharon. Thanks.'

'Someone should warn that rich bit off. You know? She do drugs maybe? Into rough trade? If you ask me, Mitch, your client's wife is neck deep in serious shit.'

16

Tomorrow Jenny Bone had an interview for a job as researcher for the new current affairs series *Rights and Rip Offs* which was going to be produced in Birmingham for the television network. She was in Sutton Coldfield gathering the *Guardian*, *The Times*, *The Economist* and any other publication she felt might yield useful information. But she wasn't telling herself how much she needed the job for fear of getting too nervous and blowing the whole thing. If she landed it, she'd be lucky if her contract lasted more than three months but she had to try and start somewhere and God forbid it would again be with anything like the Sharon and Larry lunchtime special. Still, if I had to go chasing geriatric pop stars and Edwina Currie again I'd do it, she told herself. Though it's about time God bucked up. It's about time he was kinder to me.

That morning she'd had her hair done. At lunchtime she'd gone through her wardrobe, deciding what she would wear. It was a tricky one. If she were in her conventional smart black dress, the producer would be in frayed jeans, collarless Indian shirt and sleeveless duffel coat. If she wore jeans he'd be all braces and butch city banker. Bang went the job before she'd opened her mouth. She decided on a vaguely artistic look; not too artistic, of course, because artists were perceived as all dead sheep and ego.

And then there was the very tricky problem of political correctness. Another minefield which could condemn her almost as fast as wearing the wrong clothes. We'll have to play that one by ear, she thought. But if I sense he's one of those I'll give him the correctest answers he's ever heard.

Jenny, recovering from her illness, was determined to get back in control of her life. A job would not only bring money in, but start to build her confidence again and also put structure into the shapelessness of her days. At the moment she was living off the capital her grandmother had left her. She'd too much in the bank to claim dole money. A job under her belt, she'd start thinking of selling the bungalow and furniture. Being surrounded by all her grandmother's bric-à-brac was irritating her more and more. A good sign, she thought; she was really coming back into the world. Once or twice in the last few days she'd even started to visualise rooms, her rooms. They'd be large and full of empty spaces, varnished floorboards, white walls, windows which looked out on to the tops of trees. She thought perhaps the very act of applying for the researcher's job had caused something to click back into place.

She was aware that underpinning the growing practical plans she had was a project many would think crazier than anything in the Mad Hatter's tea party: her plan to get Dr Rainbow to redeem her. It was odd, she knew, but she didn't feel anxious about this at all. If you really had to shift a mountain you just stuck your spade in and started shovelling.

She picked up a *Birmingham Sentinel* to add to her growing bundle. A stop press item caught her eye.

The man held overnight and questioned at Lichfield in connection with the murder at Cold Ash of the Birmingham primary school teacher Lucy Lessor was released earlier today . . .

She read the item again.

She suddenly thought: Do I really suspect Sammy?

She found she did, or a little bit of her did.

And yet she wanted to deny it. Astonished, she found she'd become rather fond of him. But how could there be anything endearing about a man who always seemed dressed in a dirty raincoat whatever he wore?

She found herself looking at some of the faces of the women shopping in the W.H. Smith store. Her focus narrowed to a pretty young woman not long out of her teens. She suddenly saw Sammy with a piece of her bright blue washing line stretched between his hands, saw him loop it over her head, tighten it round her neck until her eyes started to bulge.

No, no, Sammy couldn't do that.

The image took her breath away.

The scene dizzily dissolved before her and then, as her anxiety diminished, slowly built into focus. The palm of the hand which held the newspapers was sticky.

I chose him, she thought.

I discarded all the others in the group and teamed up with Sammy.

'I'm a peeping Tom, actually,' he'd said.

Does my peeping Tom spy on me? Cooler now and getting colder, she remembered him handing back the envelope which had fallen out of her handbag when she'd first gone to the group. She saw the gap in the clothes line where the two new sets of bras and pants she'd bought had hung.

'That's be eight pounds twenty,' said the girl at the check-out. Startled, Jenny looked at her. She hadn't even realised she'd joined the queue. She fumbled in her handbag for her purse.

Why hadn't I worked out all this before?

You were too concerned with your own agenda. You never gave Sammy's thought.

She picked up her change and put away her purse.

If Sammy had spied on her, wouldn't he have taken the trouble to find out where the other women lived? Had he spied on Lucy?

But I don't even know Lucy was strangled with a bit of washing line. She certainly wasn't strangled with some of mine. I don't even know if she was strangled. Do I? Perhaps she'd read that somewhere. She only realised she was immobile when a woman pushed past her. She began to walk quickly through the Grace Church Street Shopping Centre concourse, making for the elevator which would take her up to the multi-storey car-park.

You don't know that it was Sammy who stole your underwear. It might even have been blown off the line. You've got to put it all out of your mind. You've a job interview. What you should be worrying about is the questions you'll be asked tomorrow. Do you know the name of every minister in this present government, for instance?

And yet when she reached Level Three of the car-park and threaded through the vehicles she found herself listening for footsteps, looking into shadows. Suddenly she was hurrying.

This is ridiculous, she told herself as she settled behind the wheel of her car. Sammy might be a peeping Tom but he wouldn't be in Dr Rainbow's group if he wasn't harmless.

As she drove down through the levels to the exit, she forced herself to think of other things. What if I just clear everything out of the bungalow and start again there? Maybe open it up, sand the floors, get a few dozen tins of white paint?

Too near, she thought. Into her mind's eye came a picture of the ward at night. It had never been in complete darkness. There had always been a light shining through the glass panes of the sister's office and another lit the way to the washroom. For the most part the women lay in drugged sleep, but though she had sleeping pills with her nightly cup of cocoa which she made in the kitchen the patients were allowed to use in the evening, she nevertheless always woke at three in the morning. Among the snores was a whimpering sound; little Tracey, who never cried when she was awake.

She paid the car-park attendant and drove towards Rectory Road through the neon-washed dusk. She turned right down the hill. The real trouble with her grandmother's bungalow was that it was too near Cold Ash. It didn't matter that the hospital was closed now, that soon the acres of roof would be torn off the main block, that the Amy Johnson ward would be reduced to rubble. To her it would always be there, three fields away beyond the stand of birch trees.

I don't even need to stay in or around Birmingham after the group finishes, she thought. If she could get back into the job market, build up a reliable track record again, she could maybe go to Manchester or down to London.

She was aware that planning to move was in some way a reflection of her need to distance herself from madness. The next time I think I'm dead, she promised herself, I'm going to have a coffin to prove it.

First I must get a job, she told herself, then a new place to live, perhaps rent for a while. Eventually I'll move out of Birmingham. I'll make up an entirely new life for myself. 'You can't make a habit of madness,' she'd told Dr Rainbow. 'Too unnerving.' He'd laughed. He thought she was making a joke. She'd laughed, too. But like all the most appalling jokes, it was true.

Suddenly it occurred to her that Lucy Lessor was coffin dead.

Why didn't you move when someone pointed out to you that you were sitting in her chair? Was it Maurice Pincing who had been prepared to change places?

Perhaps it would have been better if she had known Lucy. At least she'd then be able to put a face to all the anxieties she realised now had been growing for days. Slippery dark fears, not readily nameable. Or was she afraid to name some of them?

I'm a Lucie, too.

Lucy's flesh will already be starting to liquify.

Her own skin lifted and sighed as it settled back on her bones.

As soon as she parked her car on the concrete driveway she could smell it. The stench of rotting cabbages. It came from an adjoining field. The crop must have been killed by the frost three or four nights ago. She hurried up to the front door, dumped her shopping on the step and opened it.

The place was cold for her grandmother had never installed central heating. Jenny put on the light and looked round the hall. She had loved her grandmother and yet the cheap pettifogging fussiness of the decorations had had its reflection in the old woman's character. And, of course, there was the passage of years; the thirties sideboard in the lounge, the half-moon wrought-iron hall table from the sixties. There was even a utility wardrobe from the war years.

Suddenly she surprised herself by realising she'd long ago escaped from the imprisoning restrictions of her upbringing. She'd been grateful she'd been able to come back to her grandmother and her childhood home when her life had blown up but now she was ready to move on again and this time, whatever happened, there would be no coming back.

She went to turn on the electric fire. Somehow or other the stink of the cabbages had crept into the house. She took an air freshener and sprayed the hall, sitting-room and kitchen, then put her shopping away. After making herself a cup of coffee she began reading and marking stories that she might find useful to talk about. She was about to make her evening meal when the phone rang.

'Is that you, Jenny? Someone called Mitch Mitchell has been to see me. She's from Radio Brum, a wee little thing with eyes like a monkey. She's doing something about our campaign for the folk they tipped out of the psychogeriatric wards at Cold Ash. You'll be knowing her then,' Jean Black said.

'I did mention your action group to her but I wasn't sure she'd follow it up. She used to present a consumer show on television before she started doing stuff for local radio.'

'So the lassie is serious. All that hair and bounce. I thought we might end up as the talk between discs in some kind of pop show. Of course, she's a bit old for that kind of thing. But you never know these days, do you?'

'She's got a reputation as a good journalist.'

'Well, I'm happy to hear that. Hilda Braithewaite worried me a wee bit.'

'I'm sorry. Do I know her?'

'I'm surprised you don't. Hilda used to work for the BBC before she retired. She thinks she once came across your Miss Mitchell when she was working for Radio Four. She's not quite sure because the Mitchell woman had a proper Christian name then. This is going back some twenty or more years, you understand? Miss Mitchell would be at the start of her career then. Well, Hilda remembers her so clearly because she got fired for climbing on a desk and pouring a pint of milk over the producer's head. Actually, Hilda says, it was the language she used which upset *her*. In those days no lassie used barrack-room language. In all fairness I can't say that she was other than polite to me and if you say –'

'Really, I only know her by reputation. She is supposed to be a very professional operator.'

'Then I shall disregard the fishnet stockings. And anyway there is no saying that this Lucy Mitchell Hilda knew is our Miss Mitchell, is there?'

'I shouldn't worry about it.'

'Oh, but I do. It's not for myself so much, you understand? I don't want to let the others down. Everyone's been working so hard. However, you have eased my mind, Jenny. I feel much better about it all now I've talked to you. I hope I didn't interrupt anything.'

'That's all right. Talk about coincidence . . .'

'What's that, hen?'

'Nothing, except that my life seems suddenly full of Lucys.'

'It's hardly an uncommon name,' said Jean Black.

After she'd rung off, Jenny got a bottle of white wine out of the fridge and poured herself a glass. Is that what's in store for me? she wondered. Ending my broadcasting career running round interviewing the Jeanie Blacks of this world?

She saw Mitch Mitchell sitting in the armchair, her Uher on the splay-legged coffee table. Were those stick-on false nails? she wondered now. Definitely false eyelashes. Mitch was enjoying it all, Jenny realised, trying to find her story, wondering if she could do anything with the material Jenny was giving her. She's still full of enthusiasm. Why shouldn't I be?

She got out a half-empty packet of smoked salmon and the rest of the salad and cut herself some brown bread. She added a banana to her tray and another glass of wine and carried it through to the lounge.

I must try to be more truthful with myself, she thought, holding skinny arms to the warmth of the electric fire and then rubbing her hands. Admirable though community radio is, I don't want to end up there. I've too much ambition. The scope's not large enough. Producing on television. That's my first target. And after that, well, who knows?

But you were not only a producer, you were engaged to a man you loved when you walked into a nervous breakdown. You thought your life was splendid but none of it could have been working, could it? It must have all been horribly wrong.

Bewildered, Jenny stared unseeingly at the wall in front of her.

None of it made sense. But was that because it was senseless?

It was always at this point in her thinking that she could almost hear a slither as if she were sloughing off the real world, like a snake shedding a skin; not hidebound, she saw herself as a negative waiting for her picture to be printed. And yet she never had the impression of standing still. Through it all, though often intermittently, was a sense of journey.

It would be nice to know what I'm heading for. I might not be so frightened all the time if I had an inkling as to what I was getting into.

She finished her meal, looked at the papers again, but decided she'd had enough. She bandaged herself in television and within this warm cocoon of speech, of bangs and pops and long and short shots, eventually found herself lulled towards the borders of sleep.

She needed a bath and to lay out her things for her early morning interview. She went to switch on the wall-mounted electric fire in the bathroom and then turned on the electric blanket in her bedroom. The bungalow was of very simple design. The two bedrooms, separated by a central hallway, were at the front, the bay windows overlooking the lane and a wedge of woodland beyond. Jenny's was the smaller bedroom because between it and the kitchen the builder had shoe-horned a bathroom. Behind what had been her grandmother's bedroom was the lounge which projected out some eight feet from the building line at the back. During the years she'd lived here as a child, Jenny remembered her bedroom having bright yellow curtains which had blown out in summer breezes, a smell of meat and potato pies cooking in the gas oven, washing steaming round a coal fire on a maiden during rainy winter Mondays. The whole place had had an air of brightness, of bustle and purpose; now it was sunk in an old woman's decrepitude, cold, damp, an aching grimy feel to the place which seemed to point up the tawdriness of the pleated nylon lampshades with their gold bobble trim, the clock face in the helmsman's wheel.

It's like the left-over shell of a nut, she thought. You feel that if you prod it with your foot a bit more it will disintegrate. She pulled out her long blue and white striped nightshirt from under the pillow. She took it back into the lounge, dragged an oak-legged pouffe across the carpet and set the nightshirt on that to warm before the fire. She was not long in the bath for the water cooled quickly. Jenny had grown so thin that for much of the time she felt chilled, the blood leaving the tips of her fingers so they turned a greyish yellow.

She undressed in the lounge, switched off the fire and carried her clothes with her into the bedroom. When she turned off her bedside lamp the only illumination in the room came from the fluorescent hands of her alarm clock.

A wind had got up. She could hear it whine in the branches of the trees across the lane; a chill, bone-picking wind, she thought, a clean wind. Headlights filled and drained from the room. Mr Hamer, who lived at the bungalow next door, coming home from the pub. She could hear the metal clank as he opened the doors of his corrugated iron garage. Later she heard his footsteps on the crazy paving of his drive.

Will I ever be able to get away from here? Suddenly she was panicky, feeling suffocated in the small, suburban sounds, but gradually she controlled her fright and, as she got warmer, stretched out her limbs. She switched off the electric blanket just before she fell asleep.

When she opened her eyes she thought it was the stinking smell of cabbages which had woken her. She lay there with legs drawn into her belly for warmth, hazy with sleep, not yet alert. She turned her head and lifted it a little. It was just gone two o'clock. She dropped back on the pillow and her eyes half closed.

A small scraping sound.

Had she imagined it? Was it mice, leaving the fields now most of the crops had been lifted and creeping in, their bellies contracted, their snouts sniffing for food?

I'll have to get some stuff from the council, she thought, and yawned. She turned over on to her belly, head to one side.

Cracking. One short, one long.

The smell of stinking cabbages was sourer.

Jenny sat up. She blinked in the shaft of new moon. An edge of rayon unlined curtain eddied. There was a draught from somewhere. The stink of cabbages was so tart her throat contracted a little. I must have left a window open somewhere, she thought. The only room she hadn't been into since she'd got back from Sutton Coldfield was her grandmother's bedroom.

She swung her legs from under the duvet. Her toes wriggled out, feeling for her slippers. Her hand reached out to click the bedside light on. As she rose she felt goosepimples swill along her skin. Her teeth jarred together as if she had bitten on ice. She pulled on the lined kimono she used as a dressing-gown and opened her bedroom door. The narrow hall was bathed in moonlight. She heard the small engine in the fridge start up. The house was creaking, her grandmother's house always creaked, its arthritic joints forever looking for some ease. Still not fully emerged from sleep, she found herself looking down at her slippers, almost expecting the floor to swell up and down, as if she were on some small ocean-going craft.

She saw her grandmother's door was slightly ajar. A diagonal shadow sliced through the oblong panel at the top, draping the three long bottom panels in darkness. Icy undercurrents were seeping between the edge of the door and the jamb. She seemed to note the stink of cabbage more in the tightness of her throat than in her nose.

The pads of her fingertips braced themselves against the wood. She pushed the door back.

She realised at once that someone was sleeping in her grandmother's moonlit bed, a giant child, she thought, for the figure under the duvet was curved in the foetal position. The child had burrowed itself deep into the warmth. Just two small splats of hair spilled out, inkily staining the pillow.

'Who's that sleeping in my bed?' The little bear's voice sifting through the years to reach her, the story book open on her mother's knee.

Her hand reached up to her face, fingers hovering just over her eyes. She blinked. The giant child remained. 'Who are you?' she wanted to ask but she didn't because to do so would have been ridiculous. Nothing could be there, certainly not a giant's child. Her hand was now reaching out, looking for something to grasp hold of. She blinked again.

The child was moving. First she realised that because of a slithery sound, a limb shifting against covers. Her heels lifted off the carpet as a penguin plopped out and swung against the valance. In an instant she realised it was a hand, the palm grey-white, the back black.

There was a noise coming from the back of the house, the sound of the lavatory being flushed. A fragment of whistling. A door opening. She spun round, hands rising to her cheekbones, protectively caging her face. Her mouth opened. An empty pop like a bell button pressed against defective equipment. She opened her mouth wider. Total silence and then footsteps in the hall. She threw herself against her grandmother's door. She slid the lock into place, then backed away. She bumped into the bed post.

Her eyes widened as she heard the gentle tapping on the door. 'May I come in?'

She swayed.

'Whose bed will you end up in?'

A pause.

'Cat got your tongue?'

Suddenly, as if waking from a nightmare, she found herself looking at the moon-filled windows. She raced across to her grandmother's dressing-table and felt around for the key to the window locks. A cut glass jar toppled as she swept it up. She heard the front door bang. Holding the key in sweating fingers, she scrambled to the window. A splutter of cracks and leaping lights filled the front garden. Eddies of smoke. Dark shapes emerging, born in thrashing noises. For a moment she thought it was a sea creature, some monstrous octopus, inking the window panes. She heard an unearthly wail and only slowly did she recognise this as her own voice. The octopus's head had come into sharper focus. It was a black motor-cycle helmet. A series of neon flashes, one after the other, blinded her. She could still hear the wailing. It seemed to have taken on a life of its own. Beneath it something warmer. Something hot-blooded.

Rage. He's taking photographs, she realised. Her fingers turned into claws.

Hitching the kimono, she ran to the bedroom door, shooting the lock back. She raced through to the kitchen. She tugged open the cutlery drawer and took out the carving knife. Jerking open the back door, she bounded out on to the concrete path. 'Mr Hamer!' she shouted. 'Hey! Somebody!'

She hauled herself up on to the concrete roof of the coal bunker. He had come round the front of the house and was running down the path towards her. She jumped over the fence on to the path next door. Pain seared through her foot. 'Mr Hamer!' she screamed. As she staggered up she banged on the frosted glass of his bathroom window. 'Hey! Somebody!'

The octopus head rose above the interwoven garden fence. She backed against the wall of the bungalow. Two hands were clasped round the knife. She held it in front of her, waist high. Lip was beginning to curl back from her teeth. Black leather hands crawled over the fence. 'You've become a pest.' Though they were muffled, she heard each word.

Damaged foot in the air, she hurled herself towards the front of Mr Hamer's bungalow. She was not moving fast enough. She grunted with pain as her injured foot took its share of her weight. She was past the garage and half-way along the wide drive when light from the bungalow jumped over azaleas to the left of her. 'Mr Hamer! she screamed, turning her head, seeing a curtain twitch open. The curtain fell back. Dogs began to bark.

She looked back again as she turned into the lane.

The light in Mr Hamer's bungalow snapped off. The crashing black figure had reached her garden gate. Gravel flew up from her pounding naked feet. She was no longer aware of pain, only the thump of her blood, the feel of the knife handle squeezed by the pads of her fingers. She sprinted towards the row of terraced houses at the bottom of the lane.

Suddenly, above the sound of barking dogs, she heard the engine of a car gunning. Headlights bounced across the puddled, gritted lane.

He's going to cut me off.

He's going to run me down.

Air rushing past her ears, mouth wide open but not screaming, needing all her breath. Arms coming down in furious hammer blows as naked feet squealed and bled on the drifts of stone and gravel.

Panic blind, hearing the screech of car tyres, reaching the gable end of the terrace.

'You've become a pest.'
He's going to plaster me against the wall.
Picking a plant pot up from the windowsill, bashing through a glass pane, fumbling for the catch on the door. Haloed in headlights, white blind, hair on end, she was caught in a down blast of air funnelling between squealing rubber, steel and brick. Turning into the noise, her arms flew up to protect her face. She stumbled back on to sisal matting. She collapsed, the whole of her skin sobbing in fright.

17

Mitch was making a cup of coffee in the cubby hole. Unlike her landlord, she would not call it a kitchen; that would be to collude with him. She'd left Tommy Hung admiring the great marble fireplace. 'I say-y-y . . .' he'd said and Mitch had realised, with a pang of nostalgia, that it was years since she'd heard the phrase. Tommy, who had learned his English from a ship's chaplain, still sometimes exactly parodied his master.

As she took the tray of coffee into her lounge, she looked around for him. She saw the double doors to her bedroom were open. She dumped the tray and walked through. Tommy was staring out of the big bay window, hands in pockets. 'He's got enough electrical stuff to start a shop. I haven't seen any furniture come out.'

'That belongs to the landlord. The electrical stuff's his own.' Together they watched a thin sandy-haired man stagger down the front garden path with an overgrown computer. He put it into the back of a small van.

'That's the second,' Tommy said. What in the world would anyone want with two computers? Why is the fellow moving out?'

'I don't know.'

'He's got a vacuum cleaner and a carpet sweeper. Three buckets. If he uses one for the waste, he shouldn't. He should get one with a lid. It's not as though they cost much.'

'Come away from the window. He'll see you. He'll think we're terribly nosy.'

'I am nosy,' said Tommy. 'I mean, it's interesting. Wouldn't you say?'

'No. He's looking at us.'

'My dear. Why shouldn't he? We're looking at him.'

'Your coffee's going cold.'

'I expect he has a very fancy record player. That girl who is helping him brought out four speakers. You must have been deafened.'

'Actually, no. He lived on the top floor. The flat on the middle floor is vacant. Do come away. It's not polite.'

'Don't be silly. People are always staring at me. Amazing, really. You'd think they'd be used to an Oriental chap by now. They never look at Asians like they look at me and those chaps really are odd. I don't think it at all fair.'

'I never knew that. Really? Perhaps it's because you sometimes walk with one hand clenched behind your back like the Duke of Edinburgh. Now that is odd. The coffee will be stone cold.'

'Oh. All right.' Reluctantly he withdrew from the window. 'So you'll be living here on your own now.'

'Suits me,' said Mitch. 'I can't say I'm keen on bumping into total strangers in the hallway. I suppose you'd like that. If they dropped their shopping you could poke your nose in it.'

'The brigadier in the flat next to me eats oven chips which he washes down with cheap sherry. Lets the side down rather, don't you think?' He picked up his coffee cup and wandered over to Mitch's armchairs. He plucked at the uncut moquette and clucked disapprovingly before settling into one. 'You'll have heard, of course, that they've found Carole Carmichael's body. In this house near Sutton Coldfield.'

'What amazes me is they haven't arrested anyone yet. He takes her to his house, does her in there . . . at least one presumes so . . . and they still haven't arrested him!'

'He might have done a runner. It might be an empty house or a derelict place . . . we don't know the circumstances, Mitch.'

'No. Sorry.' Mitch paused. 'I mean, she seems – seemed – a nice kid. You know?'

'They will get the bastard.'

'But when? How many did the Yorkshire Ripper kill? Sorry, sorry . . . Let's get down to our business . . .'

'Right. A.J.'s been hot on the Vesey trail. She's a persistent little thing. I'm so glad I employed her.'

'For the record, Tommy, she was my idea. You wanted to give the job to a Miss Sloane Ranger. Thought it would raise the tone of the establishment. Don't you remember?'

'Nonsense. Where on earth did you get that idea? I only hope this Inspector Pritchard of hers won't make an honest woman of her. One can't care for that man. My dear, the sleeked-back hair. He's only one step away from wearing sun-glasses in the pouring rain. One would think he was a greasy little dago.'

'Oh, if only God would send me one. Plenty of shoulder and thin at the hips. I'd let him wear sun-glasses in bed if he wanted to. How is your Yankee lady?'

'Bonnie? My dear. A breath of fresh air. They're so enthusiastic, the Americans, don't you find? Terrific vim and vigour . . .'

Mitch gave him a sidelong look. 'I'm all for vigour.'

'She admires you, you know.'

'We haven't met!'

'She never misses your programme. She thinks you've got a sexy voice.' Tommy laughed.

'I've been told that before, you know. You might not believe it, but some people do think that. Rather a compliment, really, when you're knee deep in such topics as plans for a new city tramway or urban renewal. Anyway, what's A.J. been up to?'

'She found out from Henry Vesey where Mirry's mother used to live and went down there. Eventually, she traced an old school chum of his wife's, Mrs Shirley Platt. Well, my dear, it seems that in her very young days Mirry was a shocker. Not turning up for lessons. Bunking off, I think Mrs Platt called it. From the age of twelve always hanging round the boys. She had an awful reputation locally.'

'You're telling me she was one of the town's bicycles?'

'Hardly how I'd phrase it. But rather better than Mrs P. puts it.' He took a yellow notebook from his pocket and fingered through the pages. 'Ah. Here we are. "She shagged anything that moved." She got into drugs and started breaking into houses according to Mrs Platt. In no time she was having sex for money. And this little lady was not yet fourteen.'

'It doesn't at all sound like the Mirry we know. But, of course, we have tracked her down to a brothel in Ada Road.'

'Suddenly Mirry and her mother vanish, leaving father in charge of the other two kids. The rumour is that the couple have split up and Mirry's mum has gone off with her fancy man. Anyway, it looks like they patched it up for they both came back and Mrs Platt says you've never seen anyone so changed as Mirry. The girl was as thin as a stick and sickly. Later Mrs Platt heard they'd been living on a caravan site in Blackpool. Mrs Platt only seems to remember all this because the change in Mirry was so startling. Everyone talked about it.' He read back the notes. ' "It just wasn't the Mirry we knew. She was ever so quiet. Didn't bunk off no more. Didn't want nothing to do with drugs or lads. It was like a different person come back. Unnatural, if you really want to know. People thought she was dying. True. But she never did." After leaving school, Mrs Platt didn't see Mirry until three years later.' Tommy read: ' "She were working in some posh shop and looked ever so different and when she opened her trap you could have knocked us down with a feather. All la-di-da." Apparently she'd turned into an extremely smart young woman and had acquired some sort of middle-class accent.'

'It certainly looks as if there's a possibility of blackmail then. Wow. There's more to that woman than meets the eye. I suppose we'd better trace one of the other kids in the family. They must have known what went on.'

'That could lead to difficulties. Henry doesn't want his wife to know about us.'

'Oh, we can bullshit our way through. We could even be detectives, say searching for a woman named in a will.'

'You're always so alarmingly inventive . . .'

'I like it when you admire me, Tommy. I find it so much nicer than when you admire my fireplace.'

'All I meant was that you're a jolly good liar.'

'I see. Not a compliment.'

'I mean, when it comes to porkies you're never stumped.'

'As long as you don't lie to yourself I suppose it's all right . . .' Mitch could not help being dubious and then remembered: 'But I do always lie to myself about my weight. Anyway, fascinating as all this is, Tommy, it still doesn't tell us why Mirry Vesey visited a brothel. Hardly her past catching up with her. That's got to be unlikely. It's over fifteen years since she was junior challenger in the best bicycle stakes.'

'It's hard to believe that anyone could change so radically.'

'Well, you must have done. If you met the Chinese laundry boy you once were I'd lay odds you wouldn't even recognise him.'

Tommy smiled. He could have been an old woman looking back to the time she rocked her first-born. Then he said: 'I've been ploughing ahead with the Bateman enquiry. Sammy Pink certainly is a peeping Tom. That's all true. I managed to dig out a report about him in the *Birmingham Sentinel*. May 18th. He was caught by a woman's husband. He was making a run for it when his trousers fell down. He hadn't had time to fasten them up properly. Pink was remanded by magistrates for reports.'

'And it was his car outside Mirry Vesey's that evening. At least he's the owner of the car with that registration. Are you getting the feeling that our two investigations are going to tie up at some point?'

'The really startling turn-up, actually, is Ron Saffia. I got photos of all the group eventually. It's certainly paid and how. Ron Saffia has been seen sniffing round Lucy Lessor's parents' house. How about that?'

Mitch groaned. 'As soon as you think all this is about to make some kind of sense another bit of new information throws everything into confusion. How the hell does Ron Saffia even come to know where Lucy's parents live?'

'Was he the group member Carole told us about? The one Lucy fancied?'

'Could be. I'm back on the Vesey trail. I told you I'd got a line on a girl who has just left 18 Ada Road. I've fixed an interview for later this morning but it's going to cost a hundred pounds. It's twice what we bargained for. A.J. had to clear out the petty cash for me,' said Mitch.

'How will you know what this woman tells you is true? She could come up with any old thing.'

'I haven't been a journalist for thirty years for nothing. It's my belief that only politicians lie convincingly. That's because one, they've usually learnt their lines properly and stick to them and two, some of the best brains in the country have checked out all the angles for them. While you know that some minister or other is telling you a load of old crap at least he himself doesn't convict himself of lying out of his own mouth. Not usually. But this Pagan? Forget it. She'll be amateur night out, Tommy. Believe me, if that's the way of it she won't get paid.'

'I hope so. I mean, Pagan. What kind of a name is that? It sounds made up before you begin!'

'If I'm going to see her before lunch, I'm going to have to kick you out.'

'Heavens! Bonnie's taking me to Stratford. She's rather into Shakespeare and sitting in the Dirty Duck. And the roses at New Place.'

'The miracle of love. What roses? It's now almost November, Tommy.'

He tapped the side of his head. 'Roses need never stop blooming.'

In Sidney Gardens they had, Mitch discovered half an hour later as she looked at the tarmac and concrete wilderness where only plastic bags and paper rustled round four five-storey blocks of council flats. The long oblongs, each stepped back at a slant from its neighbours, were wrapped by concrete walkways which rose storey by storey to flat roofs. Graffiti covered walls and doors of a garage block and spilled over on to concrete lamp posts and around communal entrance halls.

There must have been gardens once, she thought. Perhaps they fell to council cutbacks or were destroyed by vandals. Mitch had parked her car among others some distance away, near a row of shops and the main road. She was walking down a street cutting through wasteland. Acres of it surrounded the blocks, though relics of one or two of the streets which had been there intersected weeds and rubble. Beyond were factory sites, barrels of barbed wire topping mesh fences. Half a mile away, like a lazy, looping river, Spaghetti Junction hung in the sky, bubbles of light exploding as fitful sunlight caught windscreens.

Almost as soon as she crossed the street to the flats she felt uncomfortable. Birmingham was not a specially violent place but all the same Mitch didn't like being alone in some inner city areas. One or two, like Balsall Heath or Handsworth, had cosy rather than sordid townscapes but all the same hair was apt to prickle at the nape of her neck. She would hate to be poor, she knew it. As a kid reporter on the breadline she'd had a marvellous time but even then she'd yearned for really good soap, decent wine, a frisky car.

What if I had only that much money now, but all my future was behind me? How do you cope if you're a mother on a sink estate, walled in alive among graffiti and drugs, cringing and propitiating every time a gang of adolescent males comes round the corner?

She couldn't help thinking of all the projects she had in hand. What if they all went wrong? What if she magicked herself into this?

She shook her head. People who lived here had never even got down to basics, like learning how to swim. They just drifted downstream until they found themselves washed up in fouled shallows. She hoped.

The truth was, though, that death frightened Mitch less than poverty. She could never see it as a lack of money; it was as if all the goodness in life was in discarded tins and discolouring plastic bottles and she'd been dumped on the council tip with them among the fluorescent-eyed rodents and the pong.

Of course, she knew that this was ridiculous, that there were as many kinds of living in poverty as there were life styles among the more comfortably off.

But it was hard to believe that faced with Sidney Gardens. Already she could see there had been a fire in one of the flats. There were scorch marks round the door and window which had been blocked in by chipboard. She was looking for Clare House. She only realised the blocks were named for poets when she passed Shelley. John Clare. Didn't he write 'The Shepherd's Calendar' and 'The Rural Muse'? No care in the community for him. He'd ended up in a lunatic asylum. She looked up at Clare before entering. What she found really scary, she decided, was the greyness of it all; futility was part of the atomic structure of the concrete and glass.

As she climbed the stairs Mitch began to hope that Pagan had invented her name. It seemed to show a spark. Perhaps if she changed it again, she could get out of here?

Number forty-five was on the fourth floor. On the way up she saw no one though as she passed doors she could sometimes hear snatches from televisions and the rumble of spinning washers. Once she heard a kid bawling. As she rose higher the wind began to snipe and rattle, bits of paper and plastic wrapping whirred.

Mitch found the flat she was looking for. The grey concrete walkway in front of the yellow door was spattered with white. Above the letter box was the kind of sticker sometimes plastered on empty shop windows. She realised now she hadn't seen one for some years. Post No Bills.

She rang the bell. By now she was chilled. She began to rub her hands together. Deciding that the bell probably didn't work, she knocked.

'Keep your wig on.' Startled, Mitch looked up to a bald six- foot female with a ring in her nose. She was wearing a pink T-shirt which came down to her knees. Across the chest a fluorescent Minnie Mouse was holding a blazing shot-gun over her head. Mickey had no head.

'Are you Pagan Neville?'

'What's it to you?' The woman planted her unlaced Doc Marten's boots further apart.

'I'm Mitch Mitchell. You know? We arranged to meet.'

'Come in, Sherlock. Brought any opium with you, then?'

Mitch almost found herself saying, 'I beg your pardon?' Aware of the danger of being made to feel absurd, she closed her mouth.

'Joke,' the woman said. 'I'll get the little cow out of bed. Hey! Bug-a-lugs! Shift that carcase!' and as she passed a stained white door she smacked it hard with an open palm.

'Who are you?' Mitch asked as she followed the woman into a kitchen-diner festooned with partially dry washing and piles of unwashed crockery.

'What's it to you then?' The bald woman was clearing cassettes and newspapers off a kitchen chair.

'I only asked.'

'I only asked,' mimicked the woman. 'Bootsie. If it's any business of yours. You got a fag?'

'I don't smoke.'

'Well, go on.'

'Go on what?'

'Think the chair'll bite or what?'

Mitch sat down. Bootsie reached into the pocket of a pair of jeans hung over one of the other kitchen chairs. She pulled out a flick knife. 'Belonged to my grandad,' she said. 'He was a Teddy boy. Had a DA myself once. Before I became a slap head.' The blade sprang out and she began paring her nails. 'You're no spring chicken.'

Mitch said nothing. She was aware of how ridiculous she must look. She was perched on the edge of the chair, very upright, fingers on the top of her handbag, like some 1930s maiden aunt on an omnibus.

'My mam's a bloody sight younger than you.'

'Is she? How old are you?'

'Twenty-four.' Bootsie was still staring at her. 'You don't look like my nan. Christ. You're a real bloody funny-looking grannie.'

'I'm not a grannie.'

'When I think about it my nan's not a grannie either. She's a great grannie. My mam's the grannie. My sister's got a kid now. Our Lorraine dropped one at Easter. Well. Where is it then?'

'What?'

'Are you daft or what? The cash.'

Mitch's heart had begun to race. She felt completely helpless. This Amazon could beat the shit out of me. She probably will. 'The money I have is for Pagan Neville. And she gets it only if she tells me something worthwhile.'

'Says you.'

'That's how it is.'

'Who'll stop me whipping that bag? You? And whose army?'

'You're going to beat me up and steal Pagan's money? Is that it? Or do you think I've been crazy enough to come here festooned with credit cards?'

'Just testing.' Bootsie was grinning. 'Can't you take a joke? Some people. What you doing being a detective anyhow? I thought you did some crap radio show.'

'It's a job.'

'Not the kind you get at any Jobcentre I've been to. Bet you've never been down the Labour. Not in your entire life.'

'I wasn't born in your era.'

'Too right.'

'She's come then, has she?' A slight child in a white collarless Indian shirt and fluffy slippers shaped like rabbits stood at the kitchen door. Her blonde straight hair fell to her waist, her very pale skin was slightly freckled. Her eyes were large, pale blue and fringed with white lashes. It was the wondering childlike look in them that had made Mitch think she was no more than ten. On closer inspection she realised the kid was fifteen or sixteen years old. 'Kettle on?'

'We got business to attend to first. She's all yours, Sherlock.'

'Pagan?'

The kid looked at Bootsie and then at her. A hand ruffled through her hair and then she began to nervously tug a lock.

'I want you to tell me about 18 Ada Road. I believe it belongs to a chap called Lino and there were two other girls there besides you. Who were they?'

'You mean Shelley and Chrissie? Well, they're nothing special. Just like me really.'

'Do you know their second names?'

'Chrissie Hill. That's the one that got me there. I was working the street, see, but these fucking Muslims –'

'The pickets?'

'Yeah, well, the punters don't like them, do they? Anyway, Chrissie were in my sister's class at school, see and she tells me about Lino's place. And he supplies the rubbers and . . . well, just everything, see? You have to monkey around a bit with the punters and that but Lino, he's there. He makes sure nothing goes too far. Shelley turned up a few days later. I never knew her second name but she's all right, you know? All this monkeying around didn't bother Chrissie and Shelley. But it scared me. Just because you're on a bit of stuff doesn't mean you can't get scared. There was one bloke used to come . . . talk about a nutter. I'd be tied up in all this weird gear with these Roman candles burning all about the bloody place choking up the atmosphere. Well, that was it. I come to live with Bootsie. Nobody fucks about with Bootsie. She saw Lino off and double quick.'

'When that clown comes banging on the door I'm ready for him. He thinks it's acid I'm chucking at him through the frigging window.'

'You told him that, that's why!' Pagan turned to Mitch. 'The things she does. She's a real mad bugger. It was bleach. Nobody fucks about with Bootsie, not many. I mean, what Lino and them were into, well, it's not my scene. I just didn't find it funny. I couldn't laugh about it. Not like Chrissie. She thinks it's one big joke, she does.'

Mitch, shocked into silence, found herself staring intently at the girl.

'Yeah, well . . .' said Pagan. Her voice sounded defensive.

Making an effort to control herself, to make the question sound casual, Mitch asked: 'Did he have a name? This man who liked fireworks?'

'Guy Fawkes? Are you kidding?' Bootsie was laughing at her.

'Doc. That's what Chrissie called him. She usually did the business. He liked them white-skinned but with dark hair, see. Shelley's black and I'm a blonde.' She shook her head. 'It's not for me. Right? That kind of thing.'

'What did this Doc look like?'

'What fucking business is it of yours? What's going on here?' Bootsie wanted to know. 'I thought you come here to talk about some stupid cunt.'

Mitch looked from Pagan to Bootsie and then pulled a photograph of Mirry Vesey out of her handbag and handed it to her. 'Did you see this woman while you were there?'

'Oh, sure. She used to come to see Chrissie.'

Mitch felt her eyes widening.

'Don't be daft,' said Pagan. 'She was some kind of relative. Right? Chrissie was always talking about her. Said how she'd got pots of money and they were screwing it out of her. Said she was a right daft cow, fell for any old line they fed her.'

'They fed her?'

'Her and Lino. They're an item. Right? It all sounded crap to me but he has got a new car. Keeps it locked up in a garage by the cricket ground. But I don't know this woman paid for it. I mean, that place of his in Ada Road. Well, it's a gold mine.'

'What kind of relative was this woman?'

'Chrissie called her Mummy Dearest. After some American movie, I think.'

18

'Your foot isn't a balloon. You can't go bursting it with impunity. It's amazing there are no bones broken.'

Jenny, possessed of a colossal rage after her adventures that night, stuck the houseman on the prongs of her eyes and nailed him to an eggshell-finish wall. 'I'm in agony. Do something, you little shit.'

'So-r-r-e-e-e,' he sang and did. Later, Jenny had to admit he'd made a reasonable job of putting three stiches in her flesh. Though her foot and ankle had swollen to twice the size of their fellows she was surprisingly mobile with the aid of her grandmother's favourite stick and, as one of the walking wounded, had cut a great dash at her interview. A secretary had rung her back the same day 'for your details'. She'd landed the job.

It was surprising, thought Jenny, what rage did for you.

At the moment it was certainly making a new woman of her.

If she'd been asked to visualise how she'd have felt after someone had tried to kill her she'd have supposed she'd have been scared, afraid to go out, maybe weepy. She'd never have imagined this rage of hers.

How dared he?

When she shook, she shook with fury.

She sensed the police were less than happy when they interviewed her. A detective had asked her if she was 'into fireworks'.

'In what way?'

'Have you bought any recently?'

She stared at him. 'Are you crazy?'

'Well, November the fifth is coming up.'

'I'm not a little kid.'

'There were burnt-out rip-raps in your front garden.'

'I know. I told you. That crazy bastard set them off.'

'You've seen no kids larking around?'

'No.'

'Oh.' Then he asked: 'Did you recognise it? The voice?'

'He sounded like my dad.'

'Your dad!'

'I don't mean it was my father. I mean that was the kind of voice. Middle-class.' She paused. 'Not just any kind of middle-class. Authority, you know? Headmaster say, or bank manager . . .'

'A doctor?'

She stared at him. 'That kind of thing.'

'But you're saying that you couldn't identify him from his voice?'

She shook her head. 'It was probably a bit distorted. First there was the door between us and then he might have had the motorcycle visor down. He certainly did when he said I was becoming a pest.' She paused. 'Anyone would have thought I was a kid who was breaking the school rules!'

They had suggested she went and stayed with friends for a few days.

'In case he comes back?'

'We think that is highly unlikely, Jenny.' It was the policewoman speaking; Jenny didn't know her first name and it seemed strange that, though they hadn't been introduced, the policewoman was using hers. It made her feel like a little kid. And yet she wasn't sure she'd like to be called Miss Bone either. That somehow seemed too impersonal after the highly personal things she'd been telling them.

'I'll have to go back to the bungalow some time.' But at the moment her rage was protecting her from worrying about that. She went to stay with friends because she didn't want that creep attacking her while she was unconscious. She intended to be fully awake so she could bust his balls. See how he liked having three stitches in.

All this, and much more, she told the group. She'd had to come by taxi because she couldn't risk driving with her injured foot. That was another thing she had against the intruder. It all fuelled her rage. It was as though her blood had been exchanged for rocket fuel.

No one asked a question, no one commented. There was something stoical about them; she had to search back through a rag-bag of phrases to define it more exactly. Stiff upper lips, that's what I'm dealing in here. She was reminded of the time she'd been in London when a series of IRA bombs were being let off. She'd been on the Tube when the rattling train had suddenly vibrated in a different way. It had then stopped, started and stopped before limping into a deserted Underground station. 'There must have been an explosion,' someone said to the black man next to her. 'Looks like,' he'd said. The doors of the train opened but only one or two got off, perhaps those whose station it was. Everyone else remained, apparently stubbornly determined to complete their journey if they could. When the public address system told them to disembark they did so without bad temper but they would not be hurried. Some stopped to admire posters. Stuff the IRA. Stuff their rotten bombs.

On that occasion Jenny had read in the paper that the 'incident on the line' had been an explosion which had gone off at the next station along the route. On this occasion she realised she was regarded as the bomb. What had triggered the group, apparently not under the leadership of anyone, into dealing with the incident in the same way?

The silence lengthened.

I'm this awful disaster in their midst which could engulf them at any moment. Are they really saying up yours?

She said: 'Even though at the time it felt unreal, it would be untrue to say I didn't realise it was really happening. I think what I mean is that there seemed to be a parallel reality in operation. I've thought, too, that I suddenly became trapped in someone else's fantasy. That this fantasy had somehow escaped, splashed into real life. In a split second before I turned to run from the bedroom somehow I got the impression of his astonishment. I wasn't supposed to escape. That wasn't part of what was fantasised. And yet it was quite obvious I wasn't inanimate, I wasn't a doll which could be completely manipulated to his satisfaction. He acted as though I really was all in his mind when he was astonished and as though I wasn't when he took the pictures of me screaming my head off.'

'I think I see what you're getting at,' said Dr Rainbow. 'I remember a patient who thought he was Napoleon telling me the water he was scrubbing the steps with was too cold. When I told him Napoleon wouldn't be cleaning the steps, whether the water was too cold or not, all he said was that didn't make his water any hotter!'

'None of us thinks we are Napoleon,' snapped Joan Ridley.

It seemed to Jenny that though the group as a whole had known how to react to her story, individually most were at a loss. Mirry was the only one who tackled it head on. 'I'll never be able to close my eyes again.' Her hands had begun to shake. She clamped them together. The others, after noting this, looked away.

Sammy Pink ostentatiously stuck his legs straight out in front of him. He was wearing suede shoes which were such an exact replica of Dr Rainbow's that Jenny thought if you only looked at feet you wouldn't know who was who. He pointed the soft toecaps heavenwards and stared at the ceiling. His hands were in his pocket and at any moment he might start whistling.

Maurice was gazing at her as if she were a bowl of olives just out of the reach of his hand; he'd like a nibble.

Dr Rainbow wasn't quite radiating concern; his curiosity, it seemed to Jenny, was always getting the better of him.

At least Edwina had stopped knitting.

At least Cherry was awake, but that might have more to do with the presence of Ron Saffia. He wasn't interested in Cherry, though. He was trying to disguise the fact that he was weighing her up; Jenny thought he'd discovered she was growing another head or, like those doughty Indian gods, six arms.

Mirry pointed them back firmly towards normality, the world of water rates, car insurance and the weather.

Ted admired Jenny's dressing. 'It's very well bandaged up. You can see that was done in a hospital. It's so neat.'

Joan said: 'The police are more interested in charging speeding motorists. That's the problem. They only go after people who are easy to catch.'

'You're so brave.' Edwina's single knitting needle, which always looked to Jenny like a snake swallowing its own tail, was still stationary.

'Brave?' Jenny was astonished. 'No one could have run faster than I did.'

'On an injured foot, mind,' said Ted. 'Oh, the pain. I don't think I've ever injured my foot. If I did they'd find nothing wrong with it. They never find anything wrong with me.'

'I didn't feel any pain. When you're as scared as I was all you feel is terror.'

'You imply he was going to kill you. How do you know that? This may be nit picking, I know,' said Ron. 'But would a killer go outside a house and start taking snaps?'

'He had killed Lucy Lessor and, though Jenny didn't know it, that was the body of Carole Carmichael under the duvet, wasn't it? I think it's a miracle she's alive,' said Cherry. 'Really I do.'

'It makes you wonder what will happen next,' said Joan.

'Well, I'd rather not, thank you very much,' said Mirry.

'It's not because it's crazy that I want to laugh. It's because it's so awful,' said Ron. 'Nerves, I expect.'

'I just feel rage,' said Jenny. 'I can't tell you how much rage I feel.'

'Well, he does have an awful cheek. Thinking he can just do anything. Thinking he can do things like that and get away with it.'

'Men think they can get away with anything. That's been my experience,' said Joan.

'Well, all I can say is my best friend worked in a life office before he saw the light and I can tell you his firm wouldn't insure any of the women in this group,' said Maurice.

There was a long silence which began to be broken by little rustling noises. It was as though Joan had a mouse under her skirt. People in acute distress look absolutely ridiculous, thought Jenny, who in her rage had discovered she possessed a very cold eye. What has Joan to be distressed about anyway? It happened to me.

'What do you mean, Maurice? Saw the light?' asked Dr Rainbow.

'Took off,' said Maurice.

Ted asked Jenny: 'Who else knows your real name is Lucie?'

'My real name isn't Lucie. It's Jenny. Lucie is my first name, that's all.'

'I didn't know she was really called Lucie,' said Ted.

'None of us did,' said Mirry.

'There's Christopher. He must have done, mustn't he?' said Maurice.

'I suppose I must have,' said Dr Rainbow.

'And she is sitting in Lucy's chair,' said Maurice, as though this explained everything.

'Well, I'm not called Lucy,' said Mirry. 'Mirralee Jean and that's a fact. And I'm sitting in my chair. Actually Henry always says Mirralees. He won't be told.'

'And Carole was called Carole and she never was a member of the group. All she did was take that picture. Remember? Oh, this is awful,' said Ted.' I can't stop looking at women's throats.'

'I'm a boob man myself,' said Ron.

'I think he means because Lucy was strangled. He's worried he might be tempted,' said Maurice, who was stretching out his own hands.

'Where would he find the strength?' asked Ron. 'He's always telling us how unwell he is.'

'Have you ever imagined it, Sammy? Putting your hands round a woman's throat?' asked Maurice.

'No, I never,' said Sammy. 'And don't you look at me like that. I kept telling them that it's nothing to do with me. If I could get my hands on him I'd ... I'd ... well, he'd know about it, that's all I can say. I'd smash his head in. Anyway, the police knew I didn't do it. They let me go.'

'You were the suspect they were holding?' Ted was amazed.

'Well, I know it's daft. They could see it was daft. That's why they let me go.'

'If they picked you up you must have form,' said Ron.

But Sammy was saying no more. He had turned to Jenny. He was making odd little movements with his hands. He's pleading with me, Jenny realised. And Jenny found herself taking him in; like a mother with a kid she was lumbered with him, as

Dr Rainbow was lumbered with her. Sometimes when you have no trust you simply have to find it from somewhere.

'This is beyond my experience,' said Dr Rainbow. 'If you want to disband I'm sure I could find places for you in other groups.'

'I can't see that would help much,' said Mirry. 'I mean, Lucy Lessor was killed after she left us and Carole Carmichael never had anything to do with us in the first place. She was just Lucy's friend. And anyway, I don't believe it is one of us.' She paused. 'I'm really scared. I wish I hadn't joined. But it's too late now. Anyway, that's what I think.'

'I wouldn't like to start all over again,' said Ted. 'Telling people ... it's sort of tricky, isn't it? Everyone knows quite a bit about everyone else now. You know? We're sort of starting to get there.'

'Where?' asked Maurice.

'Well, I don't know. But we've started. And as Mirry said, Lucy Lessor had already left the group when she was killed and we didn't know Carole at all.'

'We do know Jenny, though, and she hasn't said anything,' said Maurice.

Jenny looked at Sammy and then turned to Dr Rainbow. 'Oh, you can count me in.'

'You don't think anyone in this group did it either,' Mirry said.

'All I said was I'm staying,' said Jenny.

'You're all so brave,' said Edwina. She'd stopped knitting again. 'What are you going to do?'

Her face was already screwed in thought. 'I've got the buses properly worked out now. There's two connections each way.'

'You're going to carry on coming?'

'If it's all right. Yes. I will.'

'Perhaps you're the really brave one among us, Edwina,' said Ron.

'Why do you say that?' Maurice asked. 'They're all being terrific. Really. And if the girls can do it, well, we chaps should be here, shouldn't we?'

'We don't know about Joan,' Ted reminded them.

'It's Duncan,' said Joan.

'Your husband? He wouldn't like it?' asked Maurice.

'I shan't tell Henry about Jenny. He'd certainly put his foot down. He'd never let me near this place again,' said Mirry. 'Don't tell him. That's what I'd do.'

'He's gone.'

They stared at her.

'There's this solicitor he met when he took a client to the Legal

Advice Centre. Apparently it's been going on for over a year. I really thought there was something wrong with me. I mean, wouldn't you? The doctor gave me pills for depression and sent me to see Christopher. I knew things weren't right, but I thought it was me. I've always been highly strung. Some people are, aren't they?'

'You mean you thought you were a mental case when in fact it was your marriage that had cracked up? But what about this way Duncan had of staring at you? You kept feeling you'd done something awful only you knew you hadn't.'

'It was him all along. Pretending it was me when he was the guilty one. Letting on it was all my fault. I was doing something terribly wrong. You'd think he was being martyred, all these case conferences he had to go to. Half the time they were taking place in that tart's bed. Oh, I've been hearing about her. Always after the men. Talk about a zip yanker. There he was giving out about the rights and wrongs of that hedge in our front garden and all the time he was at it with this tart. Her head's done over in bristles and she's got the muckiest fingernails. I can't believe it of him.'

'He's going to divorce you?'

'I don't know.'

'When Irinia left me I got this horrible nagging sensation in my chest all the time. I thought heartache was just fancy words but it's not, it's so bad you double up. I cried like a baby for that bitch,' said Ron. 'Christ. I used to write her love poems. Can you believe it?'

'I'd say she's well rid of him. She got him up before Dr Rainbow, didn't she, and all to make sure he wasn't Lucy's killer because he was acting so funny with her. You can't go on like that, can you?' Mirry asked. 'It would never even enter my head that Henry would kill someone.'

'I'm ashamed to go out,' said Joan. 'Everyone in the street knows he's left me. He's shamed me, that's what he's done.'

'But it's not your fault,' said Ted.

'You've got to take no notice of the buggers,' said Sammy. 'That's what I do. There's been some things said about me but I take no notice. They stop soon enough if they see there's no fun in it.'

'I told one old biddy the other day just where to get off,' said Cherry.

They turned to stare at her.

'Well, my boyfriend, he's quite a lot older than me, see? But it's no one's business but mine, is it?'

Jenny noticed that the men in the group, who were also quite a bit older than Cherry Bye Byes, began looking at her with renewed interest.

'How are you managing for money?' Mirry asked Joan.

'Well, I've got my part-time job down at this estate agency's office, haven't I? And he did say in the note asking for his clothes he'd see me right. He's never been too bad about money, has Duncan.'

'I'm really sorry, Joan,' Ron said. 'God. Have I been there. Worn the T-shirt. At the time I could have finished off that bitch. I could have swung for her.'

'We're back to killing again,' said Maurice.

'Bet it was her husband that did Lucy in. Her ex. Bet he decided to give her what for,' said Sammy.

'The police must have covered that one the very first day,' said Ron.

Dr Rainbow was looking at the men in the group and they were looking at him. Jenny thought there was a sudden thrill of electricity binding them. They were excited by their physical powerfulness. Any bitch who messed around with them, well, they could do her in if they wanted to. And now they were looking at each other in a different way. Who, among them, would actually commit murder?

Which one of them had choked the life out of Lucy Lessor?

Which one of them finished off Carole Carmichael?

Not to mention me. Jenny felt her rage rise so high it nearly choked her.

Joan Ridley's rage joined Jenny's. Suddenly all the women were lit with fury.

The two groups confronted each other.

The ghost of Sammy's hand came to rest in hers. Jenny felt it as distinctly as if he'd really placed his flesh in hers. He wanted to be comforted and like it or not she found herself comforting him, doing some of the work that Dr Rainbow couldn't do because she loved the doctor. However, and this was a terrible thing, she did not believe Dr Rainbow incapable of murder.

'Which reminds me,' said Ron. 'I won't be here next Thursday afternoon.'

'Go on. What wonderful excuse have you dreamed up this time?' asked Maurice.

'Actually, I'm going to Lucy's funeral. They opened the inquest on Wednesday and the coroner has released the body. Louise wants me to be there. As you can imagine they're very cut up. I can do a bit of running about. At least I can do something.'

'What is going on here?' asked Maurice. 'Who is Louise? How come you know Lucy Lessor's family?'

'I went out with Lucy a couple of times. Now don't any of you go getting any wrong ideas. It was Lucy who was doing the chasing. She just turned up in my evening class one night and made out it was a big coincidence. Surprise. Surprise. I took her out a couple of times. That's all. By then, she'd introduced me to her sister. And well, there you are. Me and Louise didn't plan anything. It just happened.'

'You are going out with Lucy's sister and you never said anything?' Joan was astonished.

'Well, I might have but the way everyone is around here . . . I mean, somehow or other I can't actually bring myself to believe any of you lot killed poor Lucy. And I certainly wasn't going to let you get any crazy ideas about me. What are you staring at? What kind of a monster do you think I am?'

'You tell us,' said Jenny.

'Look here, I might at one time have thought of having a go at Irinia but that is a hell of a sight different from doing anything. As for Lucy, I only went out with her twice. Never even slept with her, for Christ's sake. Do you really think her family would have asked me to help with the funeral if they believed I'd done that terrible thing? God, it's horrible. The way you are looking at me. Making me wonder if I'm a monster. But I'm not. I'm all right. And that's the truth.'

'Well, Jenny's bound to be upset after what happened to her. I bet she's in a lot of pain, too,' said Ted. 'I wouldn't like to see her foot. I'll tell you that for nothing.'

'We just can't seem to get past Lucy, can we? We're stuck on her. My husband's left me. You know? I'm sorry and all that but we just keep nattering and nattering about Lucy and getting nowhere. Anyway, we can't do the police's job, can we?' said Joan.

'I think we should all go to the funeral,' said Maurice.

'Bury her, you mean?' asked Jenny.

'Well, she was one of us, wasn't she?' said Maurice.

'That's right. We couldn't go to Carole's funeral, could we? But we can go to Lucy's. It says in the Bible that you should honour the dead,' said Joan. 'I used to wonder when someone had died in a horrible way in the street and the next night on telly you'd see all these people laying flowers on the spot . . . you must have seen it, too . . . well, it's right, isn't it? You've got to do something, after all.'

'I wouldn't go so far as to do anything for a stranger but I do think we could do something for Lucy,' said Mirry.

'When is it?' asked Jenny.

'The crem at Sutton Coldfield at two thirty next Thursday afternoon. Apparently they've shut down a crem in the city for maintenance work so things are a bit difficult at the moment. You can't just pick a day or a time. You've got to fit in with them.'

'We're not supposed to meet outside the group,' said Ted. 'That's the rules.'

'Christopher has said already that all this goes beyond his experience,' said Joan. 'Attending the funeral of a dead group member, well, that can't be a bad thing to do. Can it?'

'I want to go. People have said some very bad things about me and it makes me feel so rotten.' In his eagerness Sammy had almost interrupted her. 'Like I'm dirty all the time even though it's nothing to do with me. I did nothing.'

'You want to hold your head up high and show them?' asked Joan.

'I want things to be proper,' said Sammy. 'As they should be. I want to do . . . like someone said. That . . .'

'Honour her? That's in the Bible, Sammy.'

'Nothing wrong with that. Lots of people have a lot they need forgiving for. Everyone has, really, I shouldn't wonder. This is one way of doing it, isn't it?'

'You want to lay her to rest.'

'Does this Louise look like our Lucy?' asked Sammy.

'A lot younger, of course. But yes. Yes, I'd say so,' said Ron.

'Doesn't that bother you a bit?' Maurice asked Ron.

'I suppose she would really look like a dead ringer, wouldn't she? Being her sister,' Sammy was saying. He sucked his cheeks in as if he were rooting about in his tongue for the words to express what he felt. 'It would be nice if things were proper, you know? A funeral is the right way to go about it when you've got someone dead, isn't it?'

'Jenny needn't come,' said Mirry. 'She never knew her.'

'Either I'm a member of this group or I'm not. Besides, I didn't know Carole Carmichael but that didn't stop her landing up under my duvet.'

'How can you say things like that? Have you no feelings at all?'

'I was terrified and then I was terrified and mad at the same time. That started when he started photographing me while I was screaming –'

'Why did you get angry then?' asked Dr Rainbow.

'Well, I know I was in my dressing-gown and howling my head off but it felt sexual. It felt obscenely dirty. As if I was just casually walking down the street and someone had pulled his dick out. I was scared stiff but wanted to whack him one at the same time. I tell you. I'd have used that knife if I could. And now sometimes I just steam with fury. I went to see a producer the other day about a job and I'll tell you straight. If he hadn't given it me I'd have castrated him.' Jenny grinned. 'There was no need. He took one look at my claws and decided to employ me.'

'You've got a nice job? That's very good, dear. I wouldn't be without my little job,' said Joan.

'Good for you,' said Maurice.

'Really, well done. It's not easy these days,' said Ted.

'Anyway, she's coming with us,' said Sammy.

'I'll come too,' said Cherry. 'I'd like to. If Christopher doesn't mind.'

'All those who want to are perfectly free to go. She was my patient. I'd like to pay my last respects, too.'

Suddenly they were smiling triumphantly, even Joan. There are moments in life, Jenny thought, when virtue really is its own reward. Perhaps when chaos breaks out, a community, if not impeded, feels driven to try and stabilise the situation by whatever means are to hand.

'I've got a hat,' said Ted. 'Do you keep it on in church?'

'Men must take their hats off. It's a sign of respect. It's women who keep them on,' said Joan.

'I'll borrow my sister's coat,' said Edwina. 'She's about the same size as me. She got it when we buried our dad. I always regretted not going to the expense. A black arm-band didn't seem enough somehow.'

'I'll see Louise. I'll arrange for the group to have a pew among the colleagues and friends. That would be right, wouldn't it?' asked Ron.

They fell silent, one or two of them having second thoughts. Mirry voiced the unease. 'Going to a funeral isn't very pleasant. It'll make me think of her. You know. As she was. She'd got lovely hair, hadn't she? Even if it could sometimes do with a comb.'

'We've got a super flower shop near us. She does them beautifully. I'll order white lilies,' said Joan. 'They're just gorgeous. When I got married I had a chaplet of them in my hair. They held the veil in place. Everyone remarked on them.'

Later Jenny was the last to leave. Though she could walk well with the aid of her grandmother's stick, she was slow. She didn't want to hold up the others. She stood for a moment at the door, looking back into the attic room. Unlike any other hospital clinic walls she'd seen, these were wallpapered, a rather repellent design of brownish roses but faded now and silvery-looking in the cold grey light of the winter afternoon. A place without grace, where nothing she looked at pleased her eye, but full now of the rustling sound of the high trees which surrounded the institution. She sometimes heard the rustle when the group fell silent. It made her think of wind filling canvas, of boats leaving the harbour.

By the time she'd negotiated the stairs she was late but her taxi was only just pulling up at the clinic's doors.

'Where to then, babs?'

She gave him the address of her friends and settled back. Suddenly an extraordinary feeling came over her; even when she began to weep she could not at first make it out. She only knew she was mourning when her shoulders began to shake. She knew she couldn't be mourning Lucy or Carole Carmichael. She'd never known them.

The glass door between her and the taxi driver opened. He was holding out a couple of paper handkerchiefs. 'Always keep some in the glove compartment,' he said cheerfully. 'They come in handy more often than you'd think.'

19

They had had the most terrible row about it. Tommy, forefinger stabbing the air under Mitch's nose, had risen to his toes. She had placed her legs apart, keeping her limbs loose, riding it out. Sometimes she'd felt her feet move under her, as if his rage was about to blast her out of the water.

When he realised he couldn't move her, he'd become silent. 'If it backfires on me, I'll pay Henry Vesey's bill. The firm will get it's money,' Mitch told him.

'You most certainly will, my dear.' Each syllable frozen in its own ice cube.

'I know that by your standards what I'm going to do seems unethical –'

'It is unethical.'

'But it is the decent thing.'

'If you want to play fast and loose with the probity of this firm it seems nothing I can say will stop you.'

'But can't you see –'

'Ethics are not elastic. If we make a contract we abide by it. I should say I abide by it. You appear to be completely unprincipled.'

'I'm sorry, Tommy. I really am. I simply have to do what I feel is right.'

'In that case I'm going to have to consider my position. We are supposed to be partners and yet it would appear we cannot agree on the principles on which we will do business. I believe client confidentiality is sacrosanct. You apparently are willing to run around blabbing your mouth off to all and sundry.'

'Not all and sundry, Tommy.'

A.J., who had been in Mitch's office at the start of the row, had made herself scarce. Mitch didn't blame her. Tommy's wrath had practically scoured the paint off the walls. She'd been far more shaken than she'd been prepared to admit and as she pointedly walked across the office to get her coat she hoped he wouldn't notice that her knees were shaking.

'So you are going ahead?'

'Yes.'

His chest heaved up. 'Right-ho!' The word exploded. He turned, showing her a back as stiff as a railing; his measured march through the door was precise enough for a state funeral. Mitch hoped this wasn't going to be the funeral of the Mitchell and Orient Bureau. She put on her coat and collected her handbag. When she went through the door two minutes later she was as stiff as he'd been. She didn't march so well. It was more difficult in high-heeled grannie boots. She wanted to leave one or two messages with A.J. but the kid was still nowhere to be seen. She was probably hiding in the loo. Mitch thought it a very sensible thing to do. She would too, if she didn't have to be grown-up and run this damn detective agency and do what she thought had to be done. Even if it meant running into a typhoon which shook her to her foundations. She felt so frangible. If she weren't glued stiff she was pretty sure bits of her would drop off.

Was Mirry Vesey worth it?

Probably not.

Did that matter?

Yes. It did. Mitch had always thought it ridiculous to do something just for the principle of the thing. When you did something you wanted it to work.

She wondered if it was a man/woman thing. If she'd had a woman partner, would she have sided with her? Probably not, thought Mitch. She slammed the office door behind her, just to show him that there was no way she was ever going to back down from doing what she considered to be the decent thing.

What a start to a long day, she thought, looking up into a blue and bowling winter sky. Tonight they'd be lighting the Radio Brum bonfire; the wood was certainly going to go up with a whoosh. The wind was already lifting the tail of her scarlet coat.

He's a formidable man, she suddenly thought. I never realised that about Tommy before. Did I have him down as a bit of a joke? Well, he is a bit of a joke with his Duke of Edinburgh accent and his old maidish a place for everything and everything in its place. Even though he's put most money into our venture, I've always regarded myself as the senior partner. Haven't I? It's usually me rolling up sleeves and wading in. I think I'm going to have to realise this is an equal partnership. She reflected further. I think he's going to have to realise it's an equal partnership.

Her car was stacked in the multi-storey. She only realised she was still a bit shaky when her foot trembled on the clutch.

Am I out of my mind? Is this really the right thing to do?

Too late to worry about it now, honeypot. Though it would be a bit much if, having come through a typhoon to see her, Mirry told you not today, thank you, and shut the door in your face.

She was up on Spaghetti Junction now, looking at the glitter of sun on roofs and feeling glum. If you were a proper detective you wouldn't be doing what you are about to. You do know that? You do realise you've put fifty thousand pounds into the bureau. How can it work if you're not prepared to be a proper detective? Do shut up, she told herself. Whinge, whinge, whinge. You're getting as bad as Tommy. Well, not as bad as that. Who could have thought the rage of such a little man could be so big? Mitch's mouth was forming into an O. O for awesome, she thought and checked. It would appear she'd stopped shaking. At least that was something.

As she drove out through the city's suburbs, passing long rows of semi-detached houses served by short rows of shops, she found herself crossing her forefinger over her middle finger. I do hope I get planning permission for my chapel on the canal. I simply can't see myself living here. I'm not a suburban type of person. It's not my sort of thing at all, any more than fields full of cows and turnips are. Give me a bit of life, a nice mix of neon and sulphur dioxide, a statue or two gungy with pigeon droppings, the whiff of a hot bus engine, oh joy.

The Vesey house was practically surrounded by turnip fields, oblongs and squares of dirt now the crops had been pulled, bisected by grubby-looking hawthorn hedges which were losing their yellowish brown leaves. In the distance railway lines were edged for a stretch by electricity pylons; along the road cables were threaded through the tops of twenty-foot wooden poles. Mitch thought that there could not be many days in the year when the wind didn't saw and pluck the wires, making sour tunes.

She parked the car and pushed open the white-painted farm-style gate. The house, set near to the road with a coach house built ten feet beyond the gable end, presented a blank face to the visitor. Every window had its net. The elevations were tall and narrow. Like a Victorian child who must sit straight in her chair, shoulders back, chin up, hands folded neatly in her lap, this house sat in its garden of blue-black rhododendron leaves. One pinched-looking white rose belatedly nodded by the doorway.

The brass bell push sprayed refracting sunlight. Mitch rang it. She found herself squaring her shoulders.

Mirry Vesey opened the door no more than six inches. She had to peer to see who was on her doorstep. Even so her head was back a little, like a woman reading a newspaper at arm's length. 'Yes?'

'I'm Mitch Mitchell from the detective agency Mitchell and Orient. I'm not looking for clients or selling anything. I have something to tell you, Mrs Vesey. Something you should know. It's very important or I wouldn't be here.'

'Yes?'

Mitch had to explain a second time though it was quite obvious Mirry Vesey had understood her straight away because her face seemed to thin down to bone. 'You had better come in,' she said. 'I've just had to phone the engineer. My washer's broken down. Isn't it a pest? I expect my husband employed you. Did he think I was having an affair? Well, I'm not.'

'I know you're not.'

'Would you like some coffee?'

'That would be nice.'

Mirry Vesey left her in the lounge. Mitch looked at the small collection of Victorian oils arranged on the pale pink walls. Pictures of dead pheasants and about to be dead deer, an unlikely eagle with a lot of Queen Victoria's Scotland behind it. She turned away and sat on the edge of a pink Dralon-covered *chaise-longue*.

'Oh, that's not very comfortable. I'd sit in one of the chairs,' Mirry said when she came back with the tray. Though it was only ten o'clock in the morning and she'd apparently been doing her washing, Mirry was fully made up and wearing a very smartly tailored black jacket over an electric blue wool skirt. Small diamonds were in her ears. A long heavy gold chain with a large articulated gold fish hanging from it swung outwards as she put down the tray. 'At least it's not raining,' she said. 'We do seem to have been having a lot of rain. Do you take sugar?'

Mitch moved to one of the chintz-covered chairs. The air seemed chilly though the central heating was on. Perhaps, she thought, it is a visual thing. The room is so preternaturally neat it doesn't seem quite real, more like an exhibit in some marble-floored museum.

'I'd never have thought it of Henry. Having me watched.' Mirry was being very careful about not looking at Mitch. 'It's not very nice.'

'I should not be here, Mrs Vesey. In fact in coming to see you I've broken all the rules in the book. You may find this strange, but I've come here because I've grown to admire you. Perhaps I should say, I admire the determination you showed in making a new life for yourself after what happened when you were a little kid. The way you turned yourself round and went for it.'

'Admire me?' Mirry Vesey repeated the words to herself. Astonished, for the first time since she'd come into the room she looked at Mitch. 'Why did my husband hire you?'

'I think you know why. You forged documents and stole ten thousand pounds from him. He wanted to know why you'd done it and where the money had gone to. I think it went to this Chrissie Hill who gave it to her Maltese boyfriend – or at least some of it.'

'She's my daughter.'

'Your father's sister is named as her mother on her birth certificate.'

'I didn't even know I had a daughter until last year. My mother told me just before she died. When I was a little kid, round about the age of twelve, I went completely off the rails. I got in with a very bad lot. I started doing drugs and in the end to pay for them I was out on the street picking up men. But you've found all that out, haven't you? You can guess what happened. I'd not long turned thirteen when I found out I was pregnant. My mother was hardly an angel herself but she did what she could for me. She took me to Blackpool and we stayed on this caravan site. The baby was born in hospital there. It was awful. A breech birth and I was scared out of my wits. Looking back now, I don't think they gave me anything to help with the pain. Wanted to teach me to be a good girl in future. Maybe. Or maybe it was so awful because I was so frightened. Anyway, I was out of the hospital in no time but they kept the baby in. My mother said it was very ill and then two or three days later she said it had died and I was glad. I was so relieved. We went back home and that was that.'

'But why didn't you have an abortion?'

'Well, it's obvious, isn't it? My aunt was childless. She wanted a baby. Of course, I knew nothing about all this at the time. If you really want to know, Miss Mitchell, I guess my mother and my aunt struck up some financial arrangement. We were always in debt, you see. I'll never forget Mr Byrd. He was always chasing after us. Always wore these gloves with no fingers in them. He could count the money better, I suppose. Gloves make you butter-fingered, don't they?

'After the baby I couldn't seem to get well. I felt dreadful all the time. So tired it was an effort to walk down the street some days. Looking back now, I think I'd become severely depressed but no one ever expects little kids to be depressed, do they? I remember this funny feeling of not being in the same world as everyone else. As though there was a glass pane between me and life. In a way it might have been a very good thing in the long run.'

'How do you mean?'

'Well, it distanced me from what I'd been like before. Boyfriends? Drugs?' She shook her head. 'I was a little old lady of ninety going on fourteen. I was distanced from everything, including my own mum. It must alter the way you see things, mustn't it? I got better so gradually I hardly noticed it at the time. When I did I knew I was going to – do you know, Miss Mitchell, I've never put this in words and they do sound so terribly old-fashioned – I knew I was going to better myself. I had a plan.'

'Did you never suspect your aunt's baby was your daughter?'

'No. I can say absolutely truthfully that it never crossed my mind. Perhaps I didn't want it to cross my mind. I don't know. All I know is that when my mother told me about Chrissie I was knocked for six. However, I'm not entirely stupid. I could see that now Chrissie was no more my daughter than Princess Di. I made no effort to contact her. I just kept her inside me. Hugged her to me. After my mother died I suppose I got very depressed, pretty much like after the birth of Chrissie. In the end I took a bottle of pills and landed up in hospital.'

'You tried to kill yourself?'

'If I'd really tried I wouldn't be here now, would I? After that, I thought what the hell . . . I'm at least going to see her. I won't talk to Chrissie, but I'll see her . . . I vaguely remembered this little dark-haired child, quite sweet really, but my mother and father got divorced when I was about sixteen and we didn't see his side of the family after that really. We didn't even see him. It was all a bit of a formality anyway. He was always more absent than there. I tracked Chrissie down through a cousin.'

'Was she already living at 18 Ada Road?'

'I was so silly I didn't know what was going on there. When I did I had it out with Chrissie. She said she'd always wanted a little dress shop, you know? But there was no money. You can guess the rest. Soon they'd found a place but they had to act quickly . . . I took the money for her. You'll hardly believe this. At the time I wasn't scared about what Henry would do when he found out. I was scared they were taking me for a ride. And, of course, that's exactly what they did. They're already after more. They haven't said so, not in so many words, but I think they think they'll be able to blackmail me.'

'They're threatening to tell Henry everything?'

'So, you see, pretty soon I'd have had to tell Henry anyway.'

'My partner has an appointment with him this morning. In all the circumstances I felt it only decent to tell you, give you some warning. It wasn't hard to guess that Chrissie Hill is, in fact, your daughter.'

'I just wanted her to have her chance,' said Mirry. 'I'd had mine, you see. I was devastated at the time but in many ways it turned out a good thing. I realise now, in fact I did at the time, that Chrissie isn't even looking for a way out. I hadn't quite decided not to see her again.'

'Why didn't you tell Henry? Why didn't you ask him for the money?'

'Henry sees things his way, Miss Mitchell. He knows his way is right so you must see things his way, too. But however right they are, you can't always see things the way another person does, can you?'

'No,' said Mitch, remembering her row with Tommy that morning.

'Henry certainly wouldn't have given Chrissie any money, not even her taxi fare if you want the truth. I knew that so I took it. I also knew he'd find out sooner or later. Most people will say it was an extremely silly thing to do. It wasn't sensible. But you can't always force yourself to be sensible, can you? Oh, I was mad, I really was. He'll never forgive me.'

'Do you want him to?'

'Lots of people see our age difference and think I married Henry for his money. I suppose in a way you could say I did because I've always been attracted by – well, powerful men, I suppose you'd call them. I really fell for him.'

'Lots of women fall for dominant men.'

'He's not going to let me get away with what I did, is he? He's going to divorce me.'

'Do you want him to?'

'No. Of course not. We've always got on so well together.'

'But you said yourself. You tried to kill yourself not long ago.'

'Oh, that's just me. I mean, depression's just chemical, isn't it? That's why they give you pills.'

'Well, I must be going, Mrs Vesey. What I've done this morning in coming to see you is very unethical, as my partner told me in no uncertain words. Please say nothing to your husband.'

'I'm grateful. Really I am. You can rely on me.' But already Mirry was looking beyond Mitch to her future. The door bell rang. 'That'll be the service engineer.'

'What'll you do?'

'It's a relief in a way it's all out. It's so awful. Fancy putting detectives on to me. That must show he cares? I don't expect you come cheap.'

'No, we don't,' said Mitch, getting up. 'By the way, when you were at 18 Ada Road did Chrissie ever mention a man called Doc?'

'Doc? No, never. But I was usually there in the daytime. That's why I didn't tumble straight away. I did see one or two, of course and I cottoned on soon enough.' A few seconds later Mirry was greeting the service engineer with a bright smile, just as if this were a very ordinary day and she had been having coffee with a woman friend. There's one thing for sure, thought Mitch, as she walked down the drive, there's no way that man will guess Mirry wasn't born a Miss Toffee Nose.

Did she regret coming out to see her?

No, she discovered.

When you're going into battle, as Mirry surely is, you perform better if you know someone's in your corner. It doesn't matter if it's the cat, the dustman or me, Mitch thought. There's someone rooting for you. It could make all the difference.

All the difference to what?

That's a lousy marriage she's in and she wants to stay in it. They don't even talk to each other, for God's sake.

Well, that's her business, not yours. You did the decent thing,

Mitchell. I'll let you have a nice big gin before you go out on bonfire duty tonight.

She felt good but not quite good enough to go back to the agency and face Tommy. She decided she'd return to the flat, have some lunch, then drop in to Radio Brum and edit the stuff Jean Black had given her for the care in the community package.

I'll give Tommy a day to get over it, she thought. That's the most sensible thing to do. He needs time to cool down.

She'd opened the front door to the flat and was taking off her coat when the phone rang. 'Inspector Jack Briggs here.'

So that was his first name. She rather liked it. 'You got my message?' she asked.

'I did and I'm ringing to thank you. It's proving a very useful lead. Your Doc exists, all right.'

'Pity about your first suspect. I saw from the paper you've let him go.'

'He had all the right antecedents. But when we got down to it there was never going to be enough to make a case. For an hour or two I really thought we had the killer. Sometimes the feeling in your bones is wrong. You can never trust anything in this game.'

'What about Pagan Neville?'

'Sandra Wilkinson you mean? The Social Services have taken over there. Not that it'll do much good.'

'How old is she?'

'Sixteen at Christmas apparently. The Vice Squad won't be able to nail the Maltese guy. It's just Sandra Wilkinson's word against his. Chrissie Hill is eighteen. She and this Lino have been pulled in. It's going to be a long day but in the end I've a feeling we won't get much out of them because they've not much to tell us. Most of their punters value their anonymity. Listen, I was . . . well, I was wondering if we could have dinner tonight?'

'I'd love to, Jack.' There. Using his Christian name for the first time and lingering over it perhaps just a little too long. 'But we've got this listeners' bonfire at Radio Brum. We're all on parade, dishing out the treacle toffee, chatting to listeners. It's a be-nice-to-the-customers night. I don't suppose you have many of those.'

'You'd be surprised. Well, sorry about that.'

'So am I.'

'Some other time.'

When she put down the phone she gave the wall a kick. Wasn't it always the way? Then she wondered what she fancied most about him. Those clear blue Nordic eyes, she decided. Well, that's a change, Mitchell, she thought. It's usually thunderous thighs which get you going. There's hope for you yet.

She picked up the phone and rang Digger Rooney and told him what she thought of his bonfire night.

'Feeling better now you've got it off your chest?'

'No,' she discovered.

'God, I hope I'm still as rampant when I reach my half-century.'

'I wish you wouldn't keep mentioning my age. It's boring.'

'Petal, I was only admiring your staying power.'

'Not much use having it, is there? Not if you can't even have dinner with a man you've got a real itch for. Not if you're letting off fucking sparklers instead.'

'You could always write a memo to management about it. I wonder when I last felt unbridled passion?' He thought about it and then asked: 'Do you think there's something wrong with me?'

'Of course there is. There's something wrong with all of us. Why else are we working for Freya Adcock?'

'Oh, I don't know. Most people will do most things for money. By the way, an interesting parcel has come for you. It's not in a jiffy bag so it can't be boring like a book. It's a proper parcel. Me and the receptionist have had a poke.'

'I don't get proper parcels. They only address those to the publicity assistant.'

'Well, you've got one now and I know it's not your birthday because that's in March.'

'Nothing else's happened this morning?'

'You don't want to know about Quentin Plunkett and buckets of sand.'

'Don't I?'

'He swears they had them in the war to put out fires though how he knows that I don't know. He's appointed himself safety officer and it seems it's no use me telling him we've got a chap coming along from the fire brigade to see to all that. Am I boring you?'

'Yes,' said Mitch and put the phone down.

The parcel, the shape of a much elongated shoe box, was sitting on her desk when she arrived at Radio Brum after lunch. Digger Rooney must have brought it up from reception for her. He'd pushed his chair to the far end of his desk. He was sitting sideways, sturdy legs up, ankles crossed, heels resting on the desk top. 'Oh, oh, I'm with you,' he was saying into the phone. She opened up the palm of her hand and blew him a kiss. He blew one back. Jarvis Johnson, the new black presenter, put his long bony hand on his slim hip and blew kisses to everyone else in the production office. Digger raised two fingers. 'I do see that,' he said down the phone. 'Terrific. Got it in one.'

Mitch pinched some scissors from the secretary's desk, put them on top of the parcel and carried it over to Digger's desk. 'You may do the honours,' she said when he put down the phone.

Digger picked up the scissors. 'It's got to be boring. It's too big to be splendid. Anyway, listeners never send nice presents.'

'I got a *gâteau ganache* the other week,' said Quentin Plunkett. 'It had the most fabulous chocolate icing.'

'Nickie Nolan got some rock cakes,' said Trish, the production office secretary.

They were all looking at the parcel now. 'Eclairs would go down very well,' said Digger. 'Do I like vanilla slices better?'

'One really can't expect too much of Mitchell's listeners, you know,' said Quentin. 'People who choose to tune in to *More Maestro Please* are in a different class.'

'Roman candles,' said Digger. He read the note. 'Enjoy.'

'That's all it says?' A shroud of goosepimples lightly stirred the flesh beneath Mitch's skin. She picked up the phone and got through to reception. 'Lily, it's Mitch here. Do you remember who brought my parcel in?'

'Chap in motor-cycle gear, I think. Couldn't be too sure. It's been quite busy. Is something the matter?'

'Nothing at all. Thanks, Lily.'

'I suppose they're for our bonfire do tonight. It really is jolly decent of him. Or her,' said Digger. 'This little lot must have cost a small fortune.' He held a red-nosed rocket aloft. 'Top series special FX. Has a mega bang and serpents, whistles et cetera,' he read. 'I'd say this lot beats *gâteau ganache* any day of the week.'

'Isn't this something else.' Jarvis Johnson had dipped into the box. 'Lucky dragon ninety shot multi Roman candle cake. Wow-e-e-e. Get this. Battling Ninjas jumbo fountain. This really is classy. Listen. "... a sedate but impressive cascade of silver effects and whistles builds and transforms to a battle of thunderous crackling sound." I buy that. I really do.' He turned to Mitch. 'This is some listener you've got, babs.'

'Quiet, everybody,' Trish, the production office secretary, shouted. 'There's a staff meeting in Freya's office in three minutes from now about tonight.'

'Lord, I thought it was all sorted out. What's La Adcock up to now?' asked Digger.

'She says she wants to review the disposal of her troops,' said Trish.

'As a rule generals tend to go in for the disposition of troops. They don't normally wish to dispose of them,' said Quentin.

'Freya is not normal,' said Mitch.

'Put that Battling Ninjas back, Jarvis, or Mummy will slap your wrists,' ordered Digger. He was looking worried. 'Perhaps she's found a novel way of firing us.'

20

It was a perfect early November day. Sun doused the tops of the stately procession of cypress trees, dripped in broad streams over the blue-black scaliness of glaucous leaves, spotted the fat cones which hid beneath shrouding branches. Jenny had paid off the minicab and walked through the gates. She'd brought her grandmother's stick with her even though she didn't really need it now. The swelling on her injured foot was much reduced and it itched rather than hurt. In the end she had obeyed some flesh-bred caution. It was as well, her corporeal self said, to be extra cautious at funerals.

Jenny's rage had died, the storm of weeping which had so unexpectedly shaken her when she'd returned by taxi to her friends' house from the clinic had not been repeated, but she found herself taking the most tender care of her body. She had had her own revelation on her road to Damascus; she had suddenly seen this conglomeration of arms, legs, fingers, liver and heart as beyond price. Since then her flesh had occasionally glowed, as if basking in her admiration.

She rounded the bend. She spotted Edwina on the pink gravel apron in front of the rather Egyptian-looking doors of the crematorium. On each side of her, like the folded wings of a raven, were Maurice and Ted. Dr Rainbow was a little apart and in front of them. Probably, thought Jenny, his curiosity is getting the better of him again and he can't wait to see who or what turns up next. They and the family mourners were casting dwarf-sized shadows which were nevertheless long enough to mesh most of them together.

Ron was detaching himself from the side of a slender darkhaired girl and both he and Jenny reached the other members of their group at the same time. 'Black really does something for you,' Ron told her. 'Christ. You look terrific.'

'It's a lovely hat. Isn't it a cloche? Those little brimless shapes don't suit my face at all,' said Edwina. 'I've only got a scarf. Still, I expect that'll do.'

'It makes you look impish, that hat,' said Dr Rainbow.

'Oh dear. That's hardly right for a funeral.'

'Joan's here,' said Maurice.

Joan's body was so straight that walking seemed almost an unnatural activity, as if she were being propelled on ratchets. 'Hello, folks,' she said. 'Isn't it a wonderful day?' She was in deeper mourning than the rest of them. Even her blouse was black, though as it was made of a shiny material it was sheened with light. Her hat was so large that practically the only thing visible beneath its brim was a pair of scarlet lips.

Ted looked up into the sun, squinting.

'I think the cortège is coming,' said Dr Rainbow. Jenny noticed for the first time that he was carrying a rolled umbrella. Light splintered from a ring of steel set in the wooden handle. The group had been fanning out and now stood a little apart from the other mourners, a thin black soldierly line. Maurice straightened his tie and smoothed back his hair with the palm of his hand.

Suddenly there was a flurry of anorak arms and focusing cameras as the wheels of the hearse rolled to a stop in a hiss of rising gravel. 'It seems the press are with us,' said Ted. 'Look, there's Mirry.' He raised his arm and semaphored their position in the growing mêlée. New patterns were being formed as mourners, with as much dignity as they could muster, made way for the cameramen. 'I do hope it's not going to turn into some kind of bun fight.' In retreating Ted had wobbled and almost tripped.

The priest, hands clasped in front of his surplice, arrived through the doors and stood waiting on the steps. Suddenly there was a dash and now the cameramen were lining up behind him so they could take photographs of the coffin and mourners head on as the procession entered the chapel. One had scrambled up on a wooden bench which had been placed near the door in memory of a dear departed.

Cherry Bye Byes, hatless, her burnished ginger curls riding through a gentle tingling of cooling down draughts, was sprinting round the bend. She pulled herself up immediately she saw the hearse. Thumbs riding on hips, fingers splayed across her stomach she bent and panted.

The coffin slid out into a cradle of hands and then was expertly manoeuvred on to shoulders. The hearse pulled away along the second arm of the U drive. A middle-aged couple, their arms wrapped round each other, stationed themselves at the rear of the coffin. The dark girl moved in behind them. Was this Louise? Jenny wondered if Lucy Lessor had been as pretty as her sister.

The priest turned to the doorway of the chapel.

'Jesus said, I am the resurrection and I am the life; he who believes in me, though he die, yet he shall live, and whoever lives and believes in me shall never die.'

The shock of the words brought the murmuring gathering to silence. It was broken by the ping of camera shutters and the thump of feet as another photographer jumped on to the wooden bench. The remains of Lucy Lessor swayed on the shoulders of her bearers. Their arms were laced and locked about their black-suited partners, but they didn't shuffle. She was no burden to them.

Joan clawed out for Jenny's fingers, did not entirely miss but caught the ends of them. She was shaking. 'Duncan took his clothes,' she whispered.

Ron took charge, ushering them into the well of the chapel and seating them on the opposite side of the aisle to the family. During the general movement Joan, much to Jenny's relief, had removed her fingers. Restraining an impulse to plunge her hands into the safety of her pockets, she turned to find herself in the seat next to the aisle. Dr Rainbow, with Cherry Bye Byes at his side, was at the wall end. Maurice had managed to bag the seat next to Cherry, though Jenny didn't suppose he thought he'd get away with any thigh-brushing or hand-holding.

'Those dreadful photographers.' Mirry was sitting next to her and Jenny noticed for the first time that Mirry's eyes were rather swollen and bruised-looking, as if she had been doing a lot of weeping. Even though it was well powdered, the bottom of her nose was red and rather raw. 'It is rather nice, isn't it, just having one wreath on the coffin. Usually it's all the most fearful jumble and one worries that something's going to slide off though it never does.' She studied Lucy's coffin again. It now rested on the catafalque and the priest was positioning himself at the side of it. 'White roses. One needs something a little darker than that fern, don't you think? Too bridal.'

The priest began to raise his hands.

'We brought nothing into the world and we take nothing out. The Lord gives, the Lord takes away; blessed be the name of the Lord.'

The words caused a sigh to sidle through part of the congregation, a sound like a breeze bending a large wedge of corn.

'We'll now sing "The Lord is My Shepherd". Page forty. The green books.' It was at this point that Jenny, perhaps unconsciously responding to Mirry's observation of detail, noticed that the curtains behind the coffin were made of Dralon. Men simply have no idea, she was thinking. A woman would have made sure those curtains were cotton velvet. And a colour with depth in it. A good blue.

She turned with others as the chapel door opened. Sammy Pink, his face blotched red and screwed in distress, almost stumbled as he came in. His black suit was slightly too big for him and so old it had a greenish tinge. The trouser bottoms creased over the crepe-soled beige suede shoes which were a replica of Dr Rainbow's. He began to almost hop down the aisle. In his anxiety he couldn't see them, though they were in his direct line of vision. As he blundered towards the altar Jenny shot out an arm and barred his way. 'We're here,' she hissed, shuffling her bottom along the pew, making room for him.

'I'm never late,' Sammy told her. 'Honestly. It was the car. I had to get a new battery. I can't fucking afford one but what could I do? Not to mention Uncle Norman's fucking braces. It took me half the morning to find those.'

'Sssh . . .' hissed Jenny. She thrust an opened hymn book into his sweating palms. She started to sing and soon Sammy was spluttering out notes. Slowly they began to form more perfectly. His pure tenor found Edwina's sweet soprano. Their voices slowly rose above the congregation, began to play on air currents like planing larks. One or two heads turned in the direction of the group's pew. Dr Rainbow had also turned a startled head.

'. . . do not let your hearts be troubled . . .' intoned the priest, as the service moved on. 'Trust in God still and trust in me. There are many rooms in my father's house . . .'

At first the sobbing was no more than a murmur beneath the priest's words but then it became louder. It welled up from somewhere in the heart of the congregation. The noise softened, there was a hiccup. Silence. The priest's words moved on alone.

'. . . this wonderful young woman, cut down so cruelly . . .' the priest was now saying and Jenny suddenly remembered that Lucy Lessor had a child. Was it a little girl? Jenny knew without looking she wasn't among the congregation. No child was.

To avoid her growing distress she made herself concentrate on the black and white tiled floor of the chapel. It was strange how flesh seemed to float off bone when emotion swelled, almost as if engorged with sorrow. The constriction in her throat eased; she looked down the aisle to the coffin. After all, she told herself, I never knew this Lucy Lessor. I'm only here because as a member of the group I feel I should be with them when they bury her.

They went down on their knees again.

'Merciful Father and Lord of all life, we praise you that men are made in your image and reflect your truth and light. We thank you for the life of your daughter, for the love and mercy she received from you and showed among us . . .'

Sammy let out a sound which fell outside Jenny's ability to categorise. His fingers were easing the collar of his white shirt. Is he sick? she wondered.

'. . . deal graciously, we pray, with those who mourn . . .'

Perhaps it's the words. After all, Lucy Lessor received precious little love and mercy when she died. And now there is a motherless child.

But Jenny wouldn't think of it. Again she reminded herself that she had not known the dead group member. It was, she told herself, a matter of manners. It was proper to show her respect; beyond that mourning was the work of Lucy's family and friends. It would be a gross impropriety to intrude her remembrances of past losses into their grief. She realised that it had never before occurred to her that grief was a privilege, perhaps because its pains were so savage.

As they rose she felt Joan's hand seeking hers again. Her nails were sharp and she didn't mind digging them in.

> 'Hear us crying from the deep
> For the faithful ones departed,
> For the souls of all that sleep . . .'

Singing, Joan's nails eased their grip. The hymn was unfamiliar to Jenny. She became aware of Sammy's voice again, faltering at first but then becoming stronger as it rose up towards Edwina's. One or two of the mourners glanced at each other. It was as if the congregation were being haunted by the sound of angels. It put others out of tune.

The memory of angel notes lingered in the shuffling and coughing which followed. Jenny looked towards the catafalque. The coffin itself was isolated in white light though a shimmering of rainbow colours played about it; behind it the stained glass window, of an odd and rather abrupt design, appeared to Jenny to represent feet being washed. If she was right, it seemed a strange choice and yet the rays thrown through these stub toe shapes formed a richly satisfying pattern, like a mandala she thought.

'Let us commend our sister Lucy to the mercy of God our Maker and Redeemer...'

The priest turned.

Joan bent her head. She made a little snorting, popping noise as she tried to imprison her sorrow. She withdrew her hand from Jenny's, wrapping both her arms across her chest. Her bowing head burrowed in her shoulder blades and she began to rock herself gently, legs very neatly together but drawn rather to one side.

'I heard a voice from heaven saying, Write this. Happy are the dead who die in the faith of Christ! Henceforth, says the spirit, they may rest from their labours; for they take with them the record of their deeds.'

At last, when she began to hear the words of committal, Jenny bowed her head and then – like most of the congregation – she peeped and saw Lucy Lessor's coffin jolt into life. It jumped in cranky dance towards the Dralon curtains and vanished through them.

There was a sigh of hundreds of muscles relaxing as mourners waited patiently in their pews while the family was led out into bright sunshine. Very gradually the quietly whispering pews at the front of the chapel emptied.

'I'm sorry I made such a fearful fool of myself,' Joan said in a low voice to Jenny. 'I can't think what came over me. I mean, I didn't know her all that well. And everyone else is bearing up so splendidly.'

'They really ought to do something about that whatjamathing... conveyor belt? Get it oiled or something,' said Maurice.

'It really does bring a lump to your throat when you see the family being so frightfully plucky,' said Ted.

'Full marks,' said Mirry.

'I've a feeling you've all been invited to the do,' said Ron. 'It's at the Golden Plough down the road. I'll check. Now...' and their master of ceremonies steered them out of the chapel and lined them up to shake hands with the priest. In his orchestration, Maurice was first, Christopher Rainbow last. The doctor was still carrying his hymn book. Mirry had to pry it from his fingers and take it back, which made her the tail end of their queue.

'You would never believe it was November,' the priest told Jenny, paper handkerchief in his left hand as he mopped up behind his ears. He had a very bright eye. Black pumps vented with an elasticated gusset peeped beneath his surplice.

Jenny joined the others who stood blinking in the weighty golden light. The apron of gravel was now almost deserted.

'Did you notice? He's carrying an umbrella,' Mirry whispered to her.

'Dr Rainbow, you mean?'

'Perhaps he knows something we don't,' said Ted.

'What's that pin doing in your lapel?' Mirry asked.

Ted turned the lapel of his short overcoat back. They saw a little round badge. 'I took Jeremy to Radio Brum's fireworks do last night and we were given them. But badges don't seem appropriate for a funeral somehow. Sandra said that was nonsense but, well . . . so I pinned it back to front for now.'

'You look lovely in that outfit. You really do,' Joan said to Mirry.

Mirry twirled for them, sending out billows of fine black wool material. 'The jacket is almost a cloak.'

'Very smart.'

'I only bought the outfit a couple of weeks ago. I'm dressed for a funeral, I thought, when I tried it on at home. I was a bit peeved with myself really. I'd wanted something cheerful. Red. But of course black always comes in handy. It does for most things.'

But now they were staring at Dr Rainbow, who was strolling over to them. They all found they were gazing at his rolled brolly. He took not the slightest bit of notice. 'Those press chaps all seem to have gone,' he said to Ron.

'I sorted all that out for the family. I rang round the news editors. Asked them to do all their stuff before the service so the family could get that all over with and then have privacy for the rest of the day.'

'You struck a bargain?' Mirry was amazed.

'Well, they're human just like the rest of us,' said Joan.

'We go round the side now,' Ron informed them. 'We need to leave this area clear for the next funeral. Come on.'

A swathe of grass ran parallel to the long side wall of the crematorium. On it a carpet of flowers had been laid out – well over a hundred wreaths, Jenny calculated. Scents impregnated the glittering air. It's such a sharp warmth, she thought; she almost expected the breeze to make a tinkling sound, like a draught blowing through chandeliers.

'I didn't know you could sing.' She had turned to Edwina.

'Sing? What gave you such a funny idea?'

'You and Sammy.'

'We were all singing,' said Edwina.

'The flowers really are wonderful. They do make a funeral, don't you think? I really can't be doing with donations and that kind of thing,' said Joan. They were beginning to realise that here, too, there was an order of doing things. Mourners circled the tapestry of flowers, bending now and then to read a card attached to a wreath. Afterwards they went to talk to Lucy Lessor's mother and father. They stood a little apart from the rest of the gathering and no longer supported each other but turned to face the other mourners. Lucy's mother's back was very straight. She firmly shook the hands of all those who came up to her. Her husband stood a little behind her, a short, rather tubby pillar and yet so fragile that Jenny saw none dared touch him.

'I never thought of flowers.' Sammy's nose quivered as his nostrils dipped into the eddies of scent.

'It was arranged I should send a wreath from all of us. Don't you remember?' Joan asked.

'Naturally, we'll chip in,' said Maurice.

'The words knock you about no end,' said Edwina.

They turned to her.

'You know. The words of the service. It's like God breathing down your neck. I don't mind telling you it makes me go cold all over. I wonder what I've done wrong. Makes me think I must pull up my socks. You never know, do you? My mum got took very sudden.'

'Funerals always give me an appetite,' said Maurice. 'I could eat a horse.'

Ron was looking up at the crematorium chimney.

'Sobering when you think of it,' Ted told him. 'Even Sandra will go up in smoke.'

They began to move forward. 'Do keep a sharp eye,' said Joan. 'Lilies. That's what I ordered. More appropriate than those roses in my opinion.'

Ron found their wreath, a bar of green-veined flowers paradoxically giving the impression of the purest white. 'I couldn't think what to put on the card,' said Joan. 'I mean, it isn't as if we're family . . . In the end I settled for: "In Our Thoughts. The Thursday Afternoon Group."'

'That's true enough,' said Maurice. 'Perhaps she's been too much in our thoughts. We can't seem to get past her. But I won't mind dipping in my pocket. I do like things to be kept simple and that's a very nice wreath in my opinion.'

'The petals are perfect,' Jenny said. There was not a hint of corruption apparent in the waxy blooms.

'The smell always makes me want to sneeze,' said Edwina.

Ron was orchestrating them again; it became apparent that Dr Rainbow was to lead them to Lucy's mother and father.

They were no more than a few steps away when they turned as one to the crematorium. Jenny was later to think that they did this before they heard anything. Perhaps their feet had felt the earth tremble. The sound when it came was not loud or even sharp. But now the vibrations were in Jenny's spine. Suddenly she feared that all the small bones in her body would splinter.

A black puff of smoke came out of the crematorium's chimney. It was so theatrical that bemused mourners found themselves looking round for a magician, for emerging doves or rabbits.

'Lord.' Maurice began to gag.

Joan Ridley's fingertips wavered about her throat.

The earth drummed. Hot air began to spew out of the chimney.

'Lucy!'

The hairs at the back of Jenny's neck fanned as she turned to see Lucy's father. His head was so far back the crown almost touched his neck. His mouth was spread all over his face. 'Lu-c-eee!' The name thinned to an animal squeal as a blast of hot air plastered their clothes to their limbs.

'Trust in God and trust in me . . .' Joan said as her hat rose off her head and stood on air ten feet above her flying hair.

'The lot's coming down,' said Maurice.

'I think you're right,' said Dr Rainbow. His voice was calm; he seemed not to believe it.

Ted Coveyduck's head was leaping out of his shoulder blades.

Tiles and bricks began to shift at the junction of roof and chimney. A puff of whitish dust billowed through lead flashing. The explosion was long and grumbling, a small lick of flame appeared. Suddenly swirling pink fountains swinging on parachutes burst above them. The crown of every skull teetered on shoulder blades. 'That is a spinning parachute battery,' said Ted. 'Jeremy and I saw one last night.'

Every hair on Ron's head was upright.

The chimney slid downwards very slowly at first. Bricks abruptly began to ricochet out of clouds of dust and debris.

Jenny was in the air. She seemed to be suspended for a very long time. She was quite calm about it but her eyes were tight shut and her face screwed up against stinging dust. Bigger debris was biting her flesh as she hit the ground. Later, as she came round, she was aware of noisy coughing. She struggled to a sitting position, rubbing eyes streaming with gritty tears.

'I've broken my arm.' Ted's voice came from somewhere behind her. Not astonished, not pained, triumphant. 'Blow me.'

Still blinking and rubbing her eyes, she turned to him. She realised they had been pitched into the carpet of flowers. She could not see him through the smoke at first but she did see a pair of brothel creeper shoes, six inches apart and pointing upright. One trouser leg had been split from knee to shin bone. 'Sammy?'

'Christopher. I hope he's not dead,' said Ted and began coughing.

'I'm not dead.' Smoke was clearing and Jenny saw a carnage of torn flowers heave as the doctor pulled himself out of the debris.

'I've broken my arm,' Ted told him through spasms of coughing. 'Bust. Oh definitely. Unless I'm a Dutchman. Neck a bit dicey, too, as a matter of fact.'

'I think I'm all right,' Jenny discovered.

'They won't be able to put this down to nerves. This arm'll certainly come up on the fucking X-ray. Jes-uussss!'

Jenny, wiping her eyes on the back of her sleeve, looked beyond him. Through the thinning dust cloud she saw most of the chimney had fallen to the other side of the crematorium though chunks of masonry were scattered about the grass. One large chunk was no more than three feet from her. One or two mourners were dazedly wandering about. One woman, between bouts of coughing, kept asking for her handbag.

'Was it you who said we shouldn't come?' Maurice asked Ted. His shape emerged further out of the dust. 'I keep thinking I'm missing some of my bits. But I seem to work. Where the hell is Ron?' Maurice's arms were hovering about him like the wings of a fledgling bird; he knew he could do something with them but he wasn't sure what. He appeared to have lost his jacket. A large black mark ringed his clerical grey shirt. He spotted Dr Rainbow who was very slowly lumbering to his feet. 'Did you clock those pink efforts? Did you? Unbelievable.'

'I've lost my hat,' said Joan. 'My hand looks a bit rum.'

'Does it hurt?'

'I don't know. Rum though.'

Dr Rainbow shook himself. Bits of his clothing slapped about him causing puffs of dust to rise and envelop him. 'That's better,' he said.

'There's Sammy . . .' Jenny said.

'He kept shouting Lucy's name. Did you hear?' asked Mirry.

'That was Lucy's father,' said Jenny. 'Before the chimney went.'

'Just where is Ron? He organised all this after all,' Maurice was saying.

'Ron?'

'Never was anything but absent if you recall,' said Maurice. 'The times he never came.'

Ron, the priest in tow, appeared through a group to their left. 'Why is Mirry carrying that stick?'

'I think it's our wreath,' said Jenny.

'All the flowers were blown off,' said Mirry. 'All those lovely roses.'

'Lilies,' said Joan.

'Back everyone, please,' the priest shouted. He was briskly flapping wings of his surplice.

Dr Rainbow would not move without his umbrella. He hooked the handle out of the debris.

'The wall is unsafe. Aren't I right?' Ron had turned to consult the priest.

'You might as well leave it,' Jenny said to Dr Rainbow. 'It's got a hole in it. I wonder what happened to my walking stick?'

'More than one hole. Anyway, the shaft has gone,' and Dr Rainbow reluctantly dropped his brolly.

'What's happened?' Joan asked the priest.

'The bloody place's exploded.' Ron again turned to the priest. 'Wouldn't you say?'

In the distance was the sound of sirens.

Each member of the group now looked at the crematorium.

'Only the chimney really,' said Maurice. 'And the bottom of that is still left.'

Whistling howled out of the remains. The silver-tailed notes flew skywards and exploded against puffing adders of blackness. Cascades of stars haunted the smoking heavens.

'The devil's got her,' said Joan.

Ron crossed himself.

21

'Well, he's talking to me. I suppose that's a start,' said Mitch. She was standing at the window of her office in the Mitchell and Orient Bureau. Below her the waters in the canal basin glistened; winter was arriving on golden beams. The city was buttery with light. 'And we have been paid by Henry Vesey. So it must be all right. Oh, Tommy will get over it. What do you think about it all?'

'I agree with Tommy on this one,' said A.J. She'd brought up the lunchtime edition of the *Evening Mercury* for Mitch. 'Our first duty is to respect the confidentiality of our clients. If Mirry Vesey's life was in danger, something really extreme like that, well, it's a different matter. But that wasn't the case. You were wrong, Mitch. I really can't see your line of reasoning.'

'No.' Mitch couldn't argue with her. She hadn't acted on a logical premise. She doubted she'd have acted at all if she hadn't seen the little teenage whore in Bootsie's council flat; Mirry had climbed out of a life like that. Surely you've got to have some respect for such a woman, give her a helping hand? She could see why Tommy and A.J. would never agree with her. She could even see herself that what she had done was wrong. The trouble was that nothing in life ever presented itself in the abstract. Faced with reality, Mitch did what her bones told her to. It was all very messy and unsatisfactory. She'd never make first base as an idealist. She sighed and then said: 'Dr Bateman has at last got back to me. She did have it out with Dr Rainbow, asked him what he was up to pinching something from a file, but she is not going to tell us what it's about. Patient confidentiality. It's hard to credit, isn't it? When we're spying on a whole bunch of them!'

'Is he trying to hide something or is he on to something?'

'I simply can't understand her reasons for not telling me what it's all about.'

'She doesn't want you to control the information. She intends to be in the driving seat, not have her hand forced if and when she's any decisions to make,' said A.J.

'I suppose you're right.' Mitch sighed again. 'God, something is really nagging at me, you know? But I feel so dreadful this morning... Psychiatrists take histories, don't they? Where you were born, brought up, what's the state of play with Mum and Dad. What if one of the members of his group said something that didn't gel with the history? Or he thought it didn't and wanted to check?'

'Why didn't he tell Dr Bateman?'

'Maybe he wanted to be sure of his ground first.'

'Do a bit of detecting on his own account? But it could have been his file he was pulling something out of, couldn't it?'

'Well, we'll never know, apparently, because the bitch won't tell us.'

A.J. put the *Evening Mercury* on Mitch's desk. 'There's more about the explosion at Lucy Lessor's funeral. There's a possibility it could have been caused by fireworks.'

'Fireworks?' Mitch's scalp contracted; the tingling iced her skull.

'They are working on the theory that someone put fireworks in the coffin. Even so, the explosions might have been contained except for some fault in the flues. There were fireworks at the murder scene, weren't there? As nut cases go this one's top of the mega-league. But how did he get the fireworks in the coffin?'

'I should think it more likely they were hidden in Lucy's corpse after the post-mortem. Far more people have access to a hospital mortuary.'

'It's as though he's pursuing her after death. It's really creepy.'

'I got on to Jean Black earlier. She's the woman I'm liaising with about this care in the community programme for Radio Brum. She told me that there had been some sort of rum goings-on at Jenny Bone's bungalow. She doesn't know what but the police are involved. She can't get hold of Jenny. Apparently she's staying with friends.'

'She was sitting in Lucy's chair. You know, at the group meetings. Is sitting in Lucy's chair. You told me.'

'Well, what does that add up to?' She was irritated. 'A row of beans.'

'I think the police believe both Lucy and Carole Carmichael were lured to their deaths,' said A.J. 'Surely that's got to mean the guy was known to both of them? Lucy, for instance, apparently had a dinner date and got her mother to babysit. She drove off in her own car but she never came back and they still haven't found the vehicle.'

'I saw the police appeal for the car on television. It's amazing it's not come to light. It's not at all easy to hide a car. Abandon it in a car-park or on the street and sooner or later someone notices it. And who would be foolish enough to stick such a piece of incriminating evidence in their own garage? There is something which links the two cases, though. The caduceus. God's messenger. Probably much more, but we only have a few of the details.'

'Surely the odds are, too, after this second attack . . . well, it has to be a member of the group, hasn't it?' A.J. said.

'I've thought of all that. I've even thought of how to solve it. Show the photos Tommy took of the members of the group to Sandra Wilkinson. She knows this Doc, doesn't she? If they are one and the same . . . but the social security lot have stashed Bootsie's little Pagan away and I've had no luck in tracking down Chrissie Hill and this Maltese guy Lino either. The house in Ada Road is shut up. They've done a bunk.' She shook her head and then said: 'Something else is nagging me, too. Really, we got this guy when we traced him to Ada Road, and if we have the police must, too.'

'You just think it's a question of getting Sandra Wilkinson or Chrissie for that matter saying which member of the group it is?'

'That's it. So what the hell is holding the police up? Why haven't they arrested the guy? God, if I didn't feel so awful . . . I've had it. I'm off. I've got a lunch date with Inspector Jack Briggs. It's a bit early but I need some fresh air. I don't know what it is. I seem to have snapped my elastic. There's no go in me today.'

'Business or pleasure?'

'What?'

'Your lunch date.'

'More in the line of business as usual.'

'Oh, right.'

'God. Would you look at my face?' Mitch had opened her compact and was staring aghast into the mirror. She snapped it shut and went to get her coat. 'I haven't got a headache. I don't want to throw up. I've got a nice lunch date to look forward to. Why do I feel like shit?'

'You're tired.'

'Of what?' And as Mitch clattered down the stairs in her peacock-hued shoes, she asked herself the question again. Occasionally she did suddenly fall into holes of gloom, hands clutching out for reasons but coming up with thin air. While the gloom lasted it was like being trapped in an oubliette. She expected to be carried out feet first. That is, if her bones were ever found.

Shutting the bureau door behind her, she was immediately buttered all over with warm sunlight. Though her coat was scarlet, she knew herself to be the only black thing in the golden day; the speck in the eye of light. In her experience there was nothing like brightness for crystallising the dark side of the soul. If you weren't careful you could reach the other side of black.

She plunged her hands in her pockets. Whistling to try and resurrect her spirits, she found herself wandering in the direction of the chapel which would be her home if she got planning permission to convert it from its current use. The gable end of the chapel, built by the congregation of the United Reform Church towards the end of the last century, butted on to the towpath. Kenny Colville, who had run his In Print business from here, had gone bust just as the recession ended and now the building mouldered behind blocked-up windows, a discarded relic of both God and the enterprise culture.

Even in full sunlight the chapel was charmless, home for all the fungi which grow in gloom and dankness.

Do I really think I can convert this dump into my home?

I hated going to that congregational chapel when I was a kid. Do I seriously plan to live in something similar? For a start, there's not a religious bone in my body. I have no talent for grace with a small g never mind a capital one.

Actually, from this angle the building looks more like an upturned boat than a chapel.

But it is really a chapel. And a complete dump.

You don't want to live here. Do you?

There were some questions it was better to leave unanswered. Let fate in the shape of the planning committee decide. She gloomily took herself off to the car-park, stuck her scarlet-coated body into the driving seat and drove her scarlet-coated car off to Chez O, there to be faced by the tiled picture of a cow with the biggest, softest, gentlest eyes Mitch had ever seen. How could you eat me, asked this cow which presided over what had once been a butcher's shop. Mitch had never yet managed to order a steak at the Chez O.

Jack Briggs wasn't there.

She took off her coat and sipped white wine at the bar.

My policeman's not going to come, she suddenly thought.

That's the kind of day it is.

If he does come he won't look the same. Not today. He'll have shrivelled to four foot nothing, his face will be like a half-chewed walnut and foot-long hair will sprout out of his ears.

She then wondered if her gloomy periods were getting worse as she got older and whether in the end she'd be one long whinge.

Even reflecting on this and knowing it wasn't true didn't cheer her.

'Ding dong bell . . .' mocked the mocking words in her head, 'Pussy's down the well . . .' And not the fine pussy it was, she mourned. It's getting thinner. I'm losing my lustrous pelt. 'Who pushed her in . . .'

'Hello there. Penny for them,' said Jack Briggs.

'Oh, hi.'

'Something the matter?'

She didn't answer that one. 'It's the most gorgeous day,' she said. She was studying him while trying not to appear to do so. First she felt relief that he wasn't four foot nothing and then she mourned that there was some grey in his hair. In her mind it was brown and stood up like the ruff of a displaying gorilla.

'Wonderful weather.' He was beaming all over, totally in tune with the beaming day. 'We found her car this morning. Lucy's Toyota. It was in the long-stay car-park at Birmingham Airport. Right under our noses all the time, so to speak. Want another of those before lunch?'

Mitch was about to shake her head and then changed her mind. Maybe the grape would work some miracle and she'd be a happy little sunbeam, too. 'That's great.'

'Well, to be honest, not as great as all that. The first law of evidence. It deteriorates. Fingerprints are ninety per cent water, you know. They tend to become useless to us after twenty-four hours and the car's been sitting there for well over a month. Anyway, it's with the forensic boys now. All we can do is wait. Not that we're doing nothing. Plenty of other lines of enquiry have opened up. But every good copper deserves a slap-up lunch now and then. Cheers.' He was looking at her more closely. 'There is something the matter.'

'What? Oh, no. Not really. Just a bit under the weather. Probably hatching a cold or something. Nothing serious, I promise you.'

'We'll get some food in you. Let's take our drinks to the table and order.'

He's so wonderfully tall and chunky. When you get over this fit of the blues you really are going to see him in a different light. A fucking good light. I promise you. She glanced down at his thighs. Hmm, she thought, not so gloomy as to be entirely blind to all the latent possibilities of well-packed muscle riding easily on nicely balanced bone.

She looked round the restaurant but saw nobody she knew. She recalled she'd last been here with Josh Hadley, the antique dealer who had once been her lover. He'd dumped her for a brainy blonde bimbo. There she was. Going on digging. Making the hole she was in deeper. 'I'll have something light. Fish, I think.'

'Chardonnay?'

'Fine.'

'Actually, I wanted to ask you about a dead man. A man who was apparently a fan of yours.'

Mitch stared at him.

'Have you ever heard of a Dr Edward Lucy?'

'It does ring a bell. A very distant bell. A court case. Maybe five or six years ago.'

'I'll have the blanquette of veal,' he told the waitress. 'And to start, Mitch?' When they had completed their order, he said: 'Actually it's twelve years ago.'

'I do wish time would stop flying,' said Mitch. 'It can get to be quite scary.'

'He was a pathologist at the Princess Eugenie Hospital in Gloucester. He must have been around thirty then, nice wife, baby. He killed a prostitute called Patsy Parker Snell.'

'It's coming back. It was plastered all over the tabloids at the time. Wasn't she a bishop's daughter? Something to do with black magic.'

'She called him Luxie. Short for Lucifer. But there was no real black magic element. It was straightforward S and M. He got done for manslaughter.'

'So it wasn't murder.'

'That was what the verdict was. Patsy had a house in the Cotswolds, rather remote. She spent most of her time in London but she organised weekend parties for like-minded boys who were willing to pay high prices to the girls. Edward Lucy became an occasional weekender less than a year after he married.'

'My God. I remember now. He was a firework nut. They found her chained up in the barn with all these burnt-out Roman candles ... There was some kind of mock catafalque, some oak coffer doing duty as an altar ... but I can't remember how she died.'

'Patsy Parker Snell had a massive stroke. She was just thirty-six at the time, and apparently in robust health. She didn't mess with drugs and was a very moderate drinker. Her turn-on was kinky sex. It was a test case. The prosecution alleged she'd been scared to death. Apparently it's easily provable in animals by research scientists, you can literally scare any creature to death, but it's never been proved in humans for obvious reasons. Fear releases a vast surge of adrenalin into the bloodstream to prepare us for flight or fight. Blood pressure rises dramatically and there is an increase in heart rate. This can result in either a stroke or a heart attack or uncontrolled fibrillation of the heart muscles. Stupid scientists have even managed to scare cockroaches to death. This woman had burn marks in the most ... well, I won't go into that. But anyway the upshot was the prosecution couldn't make murder stick. However, he was found guilty of the lesser charge of manslaughter. He got five years.'

'Game-playing that got totally out of control,' said Mitch. 'I do remember. Weren't the other guests having a high old time laughing, joking and drinking in the house while she was being tortured? What happened to Edward Lucy?'

'In 1987, having been moved from the open prison at Bredon Hill back to Gloucester for psychiatric evaluation, he petitioned for a judicial review and managed to get himself relocated to an open prison near Stafford. He then absconded even though it was likely he'd have been out within the next twelve months anyway.'

'Wife trouble?'

'She did remarry in 1989. But, actually, there is no record that he ever went near her. The theory is he hit some kind of psychological barrier when he was transferred back to the jail at Gloucester. He couldn't cope with prison any more.'

'He couldn't stand it? He had to get out?'

'He didn't need to top himself if he got back to an open prison. He could literally walk out. Apparently at that stage you were presenting a consumer television show. He was quite a fan of yours. Pin-ups of you all over his wall.'

'Considering he's dead, you're taking an awful lot of interest in him.'

'The police computer threw him up. We were looking for sex offenders with a kink for fireworks. We didn't immediately realise he'd died last year . . .' He paused and then went on: 'There was something else a very diligent sergeant, who read all the old press reports, came up with . . .'

'Well, go on, honeypot, go on . . .'

'Did you know we'd found a cuff link shaped like a caduceus at the Lucy Lessor murder scene?'

'Colin Parsons told me.'

'The emblem cropped up again when we were investigating Carole Carmichael's death. It was drawn on a pad next to the telephone. We'd questioned Carole during our enquiry into Lucy's death. Just before she went missing she rang the telephone number I'd given her. A detective constable took her call but she wouldn't talk to him. Only I would do. When I rang later I just got the answer phone. Our theory is that Carole drew the emblem on the pad – it was among other doodles – while she was waiting to get put through to the incident room. We think that maybe she'd realised where she'd seen the emblem before. If our theory is correct, she was going to point a finger at the killer.'

'But what's this got to do with this man you say is now dead? This Dr Lucy?'

'There was a colour piece in one of the Sundays just after the trial. It mentioned these cuff links of his shaped like the caduceus.'

'You are sure this fellow is dead?'

'There's a grave with his name on it.'

'But you maybe have one or two niggling doubts?'

'Why do you say that?'

'You wouldn't be telling me about him if you were absolutely sure,' said Mitch. 'My God. I don't believe it.' She was silent for a moment. 'Are you asking me if the bastard has been in touch in some way? With me? Jes-us-s-s.'

'Look –'

'If he's not dead what the hell is he doing turning up in Birmingham? That's what you're thinking. Why Birmingham? Isn't it? And then you thought of me. Perhaps he is still a fan of mine. Jesus Christ –'

'Look, Mitch, calm down, will you –'

'Calm down! Are you out of your mind?'

22

Sammy Pink saw that the group members had left the door open for him. He realised he wasn't an outsider any more. He was one of them. It made him feel very strange, as if he were on the point of melting.

He looked at the door again. Well, no need to go overboard. It was ajar. No more.

Am I one of them? he asked himself. Is that how I am now?

Sammy saw himself by a chunk of smouldering masonry, miraculously unscathed and knowing it, yet almost screeching in terror because he couldn't see Jenny. Then he spotted her, hatless, hair awry, hand touching her breast as if to discover if her heart had survived. The bitch, he knew it, was looking for Dr Rainbow. And then this Lazarus rose up from the dead, shaking off torn petals, scorched leaves, and wearing a pair of suede loafers, too. The cheek of it, nipping into Sammy's shoes, just as if he owned them, just as if they were his.

He sidled towards his seat, settled down with a sigh, then like any navigator, took his bearings. Something was unsettling them. Was this a result of some of them being patched up in some way, perhaps uncomfortable, even in pain? Ted Coveyduck's arm was in plaster and he wore a surgical collar, his head roosting like a bird on this improbable nest. Joan Ridley had two fingers taped up and was holding herself very stiffly. Edwina had a large crepe bandage about her calf. She'd brought a cushion to rest her leg on.

But no. He didn't think the group was uneasy because of the many injuries it had sustained.

He began to notice Cherry, the co-therapist. The girl no longer had the air of a child forced to attend church parade. She was staring at them all with a curiosity which verged on the indecent. Sammy, shocked, realised that the Thursday afternoon group had now achieved some celebrity status, at least within the Glick Hope Clinic.

And then he understood what the trouble was.

Dr Rainbow wasn't telling them their story. How could their session be declared open if the psychiatrist didn't give them a small snapshot of his family's life, Mrs Rainbow washing chair covers, a bird trapped in the Rainbow chimney? He wondered if this was a form of punishment. They had inveigled their leader into going to Lucy Lessor's funeral, hadn't they? He was furious with them because they'd got him blown up. But surely he only had to gaze about him to see they'd got their just deserts. Look at the yards of bandages, the weight of plaster-of-Paris. It was more like a war zone casualty station than a psychiatric clinic.

Or could it be that the blast had blown all Dr Rainbow's stories clean out of his head? Sammy had to admit he'd been feeling a bit peculiar on and off since it happened. It was as if pieces of his brain were still up in the air and those chunks which had come down didn't seem quite in the same place any more.

No, he's peeved with us, Sammy decided. Thoroughly browned off. Perhaps his bosses have carpeted him. After all, a lot of taxpayers' money is being spent on trying to turn us into proper people. Just what the hell is he doing, letting us all get ourselves blown up? It's not good enough. The man's a menace.

Sammy ventured another glance. The doctor outwardly seemed placid enough, relaxing in his chair, legs apart, cigarette dangling about in that nancy boy holder.

Still, he wasn't telling them their story. Was he?

That spoke louder than words.

That spoke volumes.

But volumes about what? The trouble was you could never really tell what went on in the head of a fellow like that. They weren't called trick cyclists for nothing.

One by one they turned to Joan Ridley. She broke their silences for them. She'd better start earning her keep otherwise the group's anxiety would not just send each of them right up the wall but rocket them into outer space. When she leaned forward they leaned forward as well, encouraging her.

'Of course,' she said, 'fillings are damn dangerous, too.'
They stared at her.
'I read about it in the paper,' she said. 'On average we all have five fillings. If all our remains are incinerated on the same day that releases twenty-five pounds of mercury into the air. Imagine that.'
They continued to stare.
'Mercury plays silly beggars with your central nervous system. I mean, "mad as a hatter" comes from hat-makers going crackers after they were exposed to mercury fumes. You know?'
'What has that to do with anything?' Ron Saffia's eyebrows were still hoisted, reminding Sammy of propped-up washing lines.
'Well, it does make you think, doesn't it? It's not only fireworks. Crematoriums are very dangerous places altogether. I think we can agree on that.'
'I never knew that about fillings in teeth. Perhaps the proper thing to do is to go to the dentist. I mean, when one is – if one knows . . . you know what I mean,' said Ted.
'It's all wrong. That's all I know,' said Joan. 'You can't go about making funerals unsafe, can you? Apart from anything else, where's the dignity? When that goes, what's left?'
'Actually, a neighbour of ours keeled over when he was planting phlox on Tuesday,' said Ted. His voice was thinner, as if he had to squeeze it up through the surgical collar. 'Dead as a door nail before he hit the ground. There's no way you'll get me to his funeral. I just couldn't face it.'
'They build in failure these days,' said Joan. 'That's the trouble. Nothing's built to last.'
'If someone fills a fucking crematorium chimney with fireworks and then ignites the gas what do you expect? It's a miracle we're here,' said Ron.
'I read that a furnace blew out at Burnt Green crematorium some years ago,' said Mirry. 'That was caused when they left a pacemaker in the remains. But apparently it was very small beer. Simply couldn't compare it with ours.'
'I wish you hadn't told me about fillings, Joan,' said Edwina. 'I've got a mouthful. I mean you don't want to be worrying about a thing like that on your death-bed. Do you?'
'It's all our own fault. We would go,' said Ted. 'I think you'll recall, I raised objections at the time. We aren't supposed to meet each other outside the clinic. Rules aren't made without good reason, you know.'
'No one expects to be cremated with the corpse when they go to a funeral, Ted,' said Mirry. 'Whoever heard of that?'

'Show a bit more respect,' Ron said. 'It's Lucy we're talking about and no one can say it was her fault.'

'I don't know why she ever became a member of the group,' said Joan. 'She'd already been an in-patient here, hadn't she? What did she want to join our group for in the first place? If you ask me too much is not enough for some people.'

'Christopher wasn't to know what was going to happen,' said Mirry. 'If he had I'm sure he wouldn't have let us get mixed up with her.'

'Lucy didn't kill herself any more than she stuffed fireworks up that chimney,' said Ron. 'They ought to hang him.'

'Got to catch him first, haven't they?' said Maurice. 'He's running rings round the coppers. That's the feeling I get.'

'There's always one firework which doesn't go off when it should. Have you noticed that?' asked Ted.

'A sleeper,' said Jenny.

'Actually, it was a shrieking eagles salvo jumbo Roman candle,' said Ted. 'It was the one Jeremy liked best at the Radio Brum bonfire.'

'As nut cases go this one takes the fucking biscuit,' said Ron. 'What's his game? But then you realise he's not in the same world as the rest of us and the game's up.'

'He wasn't mad when it came to getting in my house,' said Jenny. 'He just jemmied the lounge window. And then stuck it back up with chewing gum so I wouldn't notice. And I didn't.'

'Even if you don't think about what happened at the crematorium, you've got to be mad when you start sticking dead people under other people's duvets, haven't you?' said Mirry.

'I wonder what he did?' asked Ted.

'Lucy was strangled so I expect poor Carole was too,' said Ron Saffia.

'It's what might have happened to them first which makes me shiver,' said Mirry.

'The trouble is there's no money any more. They can't afford to keep them in. Only the other week they shut down Cold Ash,' said Joan. 'They're all out stabbing people in trains and taking an axe to their mummies and daddies.'

Suddenly they found themselves looking at each other, realising they wouldn't be here if any doctor had marked them present and correct. Then Sammy became the centre of attention. He understood from this that the others thought him the oddest of them all. The strange thing was that there was nothing hostile in the way they focused on him. It was more the protective eye of a mother looking out for her idiot child. 'But I'm not an idiot,' he wanted to tell them. He knew he wasn't but he said nothing for he really didn't know where to begin.

'Anyway, as it turns out only one person was badly hurt in the explosion,' said Ted. 'And it said in the *Birmingham Sentinel* that he came out of intensive care on Friday.'

'Who was that?' asked Cherry. Today she wore her burnished curls on top of her head like a rose-gold crown.

'I don't know what you'd call him. The baker chap . . .'

'He means the stoker guy,' said Ron.

'I sent him some roses,' said Mirry. 'Well, you've got to, haven't you?'

'That was very nice of you,' said Jenny.

'I didn't agree with those white roses on Lucy's coffin,' said Joan. 'They ought to have been lilies.'

'It's going to cost a million pounds for a replacement crematorium,' said Mirry. 'Did you read that? It makes you wonder where they get their figures from. And what of those poor folk who'll be forced to hold their funerals after their tea? Apparently it's the only way the other crematoriums will be able to cope with the work load now one is out of action. After tea! Well, I ask you. Funerals are something to get done with, aren't they? You don't want to be hanging about all day long.'

'However hard we try we don't seem to be able to get past poor Lucy, do we?' Ted asked. 'And now there's the black kid, too. It's growing all the time. I thought when we went to Lucy's funeral, that would be it. We could move on. Here we still are and now it's far worse. Christopher hasn't even told us our story yet.'

'That's absolutely true,' said Maurice and they all looked at the psychiatrist.

'It went completely out of my mind,' said Dr Rainbow. He was startled and Sammy could see that he now began to silently question himself about this.

'That's what blowing up does for you,' said Joan. 'Puts you all at sixes and sevens.'

'At the funeral you told me Duncan had collected his clothes,' said Jenny.

Joan's eyes grew and Sammy realised it was because a large tear was welling in each. 'It hurts,' she said.

'I know,' said Ron. 'It's a funny feeling. It's as though someone's stuck a suction pad on your stomach and is tugging your guts out.'

Joan wiped away the two tears with the back her hand. She'd painted the nails on her uninjured fingers a bluey shade of red.

They looked to Sammy like shell-shaped holes through which the blood in her veins had drained away. 'A friend of mine rang to tell him about the explosion. You know, that I'd been in it. So he rang me to ask how I was.'

'What did he say?' asked Dr Rainbow.

'He said Dodo and he were very concerned. But what concern is it of Dodo's?'

'The cruel bastard,' said Ron.

'You wouldn't take him back now, would you? Much better off without,' said Mirry.

'I'll tell you one thing,' said Joan. 'He's not having that Magimix and he can smarm up to me as much as he likes.'

'Would you have him back if he knocked on your door tomorrow?' asked Jenny.

'Of course I would.'

'Why?'

'He's mine.'

'That's how I felt about Irinia,' said Ron. 'I know no other human being is supposed to belong to you and of course they don't. But it feels like they do. Even now in the supermarket I find myself putting unsalted butter in the basket because she wouldn't have salted. I mean . . .' He stopped and then shrugged. 'But you get over it and that's even worse in a way. There you are believing this was the most meaningful thing in your life and then wham! you realise it didn't matter very much anyway. It seems to make everything else not matter very much, either. It's all insignificant.'

They were silent. Sammy could feel himself shrinking, becoming insignificant. But he was quite stoical about it. After all, he was used to it. The others, he could see, didn't like it at all. They weren't prepared to dismiss either themselves or their affairs as being of no account. Maurice was actually getting bigger, huffing, blowing out his cheeks. Sammy then realised there was something bigger about him altogether. He's getting fatter, he thought. But no, it wasn't that. It was as though someone had put a large chunk of coal under the flame of him and now he was dancing up. Sammy remembered Maurice telling the group that his nose poked into everything he saw and suddenly found this comforting. There are some people, Sammy Pink, who are a hell of a sight odder than you are.

'Actually, Sandra's being marvellous at the moment,' said Ted. 'The tops. Broken limbs are something she understands. She's broken one or two herself and knows how hellish it is. The pain . . . you know . . . it's all so real to her.' He was grinning.

'My God, you're really motoring now, aren't you?' Jenny asked him.

'Spades in?' asked Maurice.

'As it's my right arm that's broken she has to help me eat . . . and she dresses me . . . and, of course, undresses me . . . One thing leads to another, if you see what I mean.'

'All I can say is that anyone who has it away with a broken arm and his neck in a surgical collar deserves the DSO. And Bar.' Ron was breaking into a sweat at the thought. 'All that juddering around. Jes-u-sss. And it's hardly a *modus vivendi*, Ted. First she starts to fancy you again because the police came round. Now she fancies you because you're a bloody cripple. But from what you say when you're just boring old you, it's thumbs down.'

'It's a beginning, you've got to admit that. When she looks at me as if she fancies me . . . well, the ideas come flowing and you begin to perk up. When things have ground to a halt, you've got to start somewhere, haven't you?' He was looking fondly at his plastered arm. 'Came up beautifully on the X-ray. Fractured to hell. Anyway, it wasn't Sandra who turned me into a cripple,' said Ted. 'It was going to Lucy Lessor's funeral that did that.'

'Did you hear her father cry out?' asked Jenny. 'I'll never forget that.'

'Pain is totally pure,' said Maurice. He turned to Dr Rainbow. 'Wouldn't you say?'

'How do you mean?' Dr Rainbow asked.

'Nothing else impinges on it. Not when it's sharp.'

'A lot of things impinged when Irinia left me,' said Ron. 'Though most of all I wanted to crawl into a little hole and shrivel up.'

'Lucy said she cried so much she thought she'd turn into a prune. You know, all her juiciness would dry out. She'd shrivel up.'

'Actually, I was talking about proper pain,' said Maurice. 'Real pain. Flesh pain.'

'That's really terrible,' said Edwina. 'You don't want any of that.'

They fell silent again. Sammy was thinking of Lucy's funeral and suddenly he knew they all were, even Cherry Bye Byes who was of a different generation. But even so Sammy felt isolated from them for how could he tell them that the stars that sang in the sky when the chimney collapsed had shone in Lucy's hair when she'd thrown her glittering glass dick at the wall? 'We certainly can't ever see each other outside the group again,'

Sammy was surprised to hear himself saying. And then he knew what he had been struggling to come to terms with for the past two or three days. He was not going to go round spying on these ladies any more; somehow they'd got mixed up with his Aunt Ada. They were off limits. He stole a glance at his dark goddess. Well, you're not missing much, he tried to console himself. Need a microscope to find her knockers. Jenn-ee-ee. Her name flew off on an outing, stirring up his bones, giving his muscles a polish and then hopped back into his heart. There's plenty of other women you can look at, he thought, trying to cheer himself up. The world out there is full of knockers and bums and you can take your pick. There's that Mitchell bitch for a start, now she's got a pair of swingers. Over-ripe? Well, yes, but that, Sammy, is how you like your fruit, isn't it? Sweet, sweet, sweet, the sweetest of all, no more than a second away from going off.

'Do you suppose we're going to get blown up every time we meet outside the group?' Jenny was teasing him, laughing, and then they were all laughing, including Sammy. As his chest expanded it filled every crease in his shirt. He saw she was so full of merriment that even her feet were shaking. He was reminded of birds, of how when they sang their folded wings spread out a little and their tail feathers fanned out, too, vibrating with the sound of their music.

'I won't be coming next week,' Maurice said, straightening his tie. The sound of their laughter had died and they'd guiltily eyed each other. After all, they'd not long come back from a funeral, had they? And, anyway, they weren't here for the fun of it. Still, didn't an injury or two earn you a little respite?

Enmeshed in this, it took them a moment or two to take in what Maurice was telling them.

'We're going to Venice.'

'We're?' Ron queried.

'Brian. A friend from work.'

'Are you gay?' asked Ron.

'He's not a bit gay,' said Joan. 'You can see that.'

'Well, you're wrong there. I am a bit. But Brian isn't,' said Maurice.

'I don't believe it,' said Mirry.

'He should know, shouldn't he?' said Ron. 'He's not married, is he? He's never mentioned a girlfriend. Has he?'

'Nor has Sammy,' Maurice said.

'I'm not a bit like that. Honest,' said Sammy. 'I like a bit of . . .'

'The other,' said Maurice, looking at Dr Rainbow. Maybe,

Sammy thought, Maurice fancied the doctor? After all, he's always in consultation with him. He frowned. What Maurice had told the group made him feel a bit wriggly, uncomfortable. He looked at him again. You'd never think he had trouble with his nose, Sammy thought. You'd never think he was a proper pervert. Why, he's practically brimming over with something or other. He's big with it. Expectations? That Brian, thought Sammy, had better watch out. He'd better not turn his back on Maurice for one instant.

'I think you'll find going to Venice pretty painless,' said Ron. 'Quite romantic, I should think. Sitting in gondolas and all those statues of pretty boys. Maybe conventional, but romantic.'

'Makes a change from exploding crematoriums. That kind of thing. Wouldn't you say?' said Maurice.

Sammy, who had earlier seen how deeply Dr Rainbow had considered all those circumstances which had gone into his forgetting to tell them their story, had hardly listened to this exchange. He had been worrying about this lack of the psychiatrist's story. It just didn't seem right. If Dr Rainbow was going to become unreliable one of them would have to take it on. But if he was going to tell them a story he'd better watch out, hadn't he? If he weren't careful he'd land back in a police cell.

He found himself clearing his throat. He said: 'I used to live with my Aunt Ada but she had to go in a nursing home.' He paused. It was so easy to overlook something important. He was sweating. 'The estate agent came round yesterday because the house that we live in has to be sold to pay for her fees.' He looked round to make sure they were following him.

'But, Sammy, where are you going to live?'

'The trouble is I need such a lot. I not only need a roof over my head but some soil. I grow things, you see.'

'That's too bad.'

'What are you going to do?'

'I'll have to think of something.'

23

'Do you think the shit was winding me up?'

'No.'

'Then why would he tell me about this Dr Lucy? The man's dead all right. You can be sure I checked that out. It turns out he was born in Tewkesbury so I got on to the local rag. They carried all the stuff about the trial, of course, and then last year a bit about him being killed in a car crash in Greece. He's buried in some foreign graveyard. And Jack Briggs was practically asking me if I've heard from him because he used to be a fan of mine! Am I going crackers, Tommy? Or is he?'

'He could be thinking of something like copy-cat killing.'

'Thanks a bunch.' Mitch lifted the telephone and began walking up and down. 'What the hell are the police playing at? All this silence . . . this nothing is happening . . . is plain scary. Surely they have a good description of this Doc. What's happened to such quaint little things as identity parades?'

'You don't know? A.J. was told by Ian Pritchard that this chap always turned up at 18 Ada Road in motor-bike gear. You know, the helmet and leathers.'

'You're not telling me he performed with a helmet on!'

'A different kind of mask, actually. The sort they use in operating theatres.'

'You've got to be kidding.'

'And one of those hat and gown things. That was what he was togged up in under his motor-bike gear. I mean, it's the norm for that kind of thing, isn't it? I don't mean operating theatre clobber but dressing up. Dressing up is often part of the ritual.'

'I thought this man was into fireworks.' She paused. 'Fireworks are bad enough.'

'Maybe they're his laser beams. You know. No one is saying he's sane. Are they?'

'And this man's a fan of mine?'

'Mitch, the real Dr Lucy is dead. You said so yourself.'

'But a copy cat wouldn't be that if he didn't copy exactly. Would he?'

'He's not copying exactly, is he? There's all this add-on stuff. Motor-bike gear. Operating table stuff.'

'He was a practising doctor when Patsy Parker Snell died of fright. That was his work. Maybe the two have somehow fused together now for playpen games.'

'You are still talking as if this Lucy chap is still alive. Look, as there has been no arrest we must suppose that the police have eliminated the group members. They don't think it is one of them. We're back to Mr A.N. Other. Why don't you come and live with me for a bit until this blows over? I've got a spare bedroom.'

'No male shit's going to make me abandon my nest. I'm sorry, Tommy. Most of the time I'm quite all right. Quite rational. Sensible. You know? It's just now and then paranoia sweeps over me. I just wish they'd catch this bastard. Jesus Christ. He went to a brothel in this city. What better lead could they have? Think of their resources ... and still ... Sorry, sorry ... What I'm going to do, honeypot, is have a couple of large gins and fall into bed. I've always found gin to be a great steadier. I'm at the radio station all day tomorrow. You can catch me there if anything vital turns up.'

'Mitch –'

'I'm all right, honeypot. Honestly. Thank you for listening to all this raving paranoia. It was good to get it off my chest.'

But Mitch, when she put the phone down, found she'd not been able to club all the snakes of dread. One or two were lurking around there in the undergrowth.

Lucy, Lucy, Lucy, she was thinking. All the Lucys. Like a game of mirroring Frankenstein.

In the end she didn't have the gin. Dread had made her too queasy. But she did make herself go to bed and sleep came surprisingly easily.

She pitched into a sitting position. She was sheeted in sweat which was already cooling. The only sound she could hear was her heart; d-d-d-d-ddddd and then the strokes colliding together and falling, her vision swimming. She placed a hand down on each side of the duvet and took in long breaths of the cold air.

No, she decided, it hadn't been a dream. She was already half awake when Lucy Lessor had come to her, the scene far more vivid than when she'd seen it in reality. There were the baby blue painted bars, the pink chintz curtains, the curve of a hard, waxy buttock, blood pooling under the skin, marbling belly and thighs where they touched the grey thermoplastic tiles, legs splayed, feet pigeon-toed, arms out in front of her. Her hair was dreadfully alive, bouncing black curls yellow with sunlight, stirring in a sudden draught. She had thought Lucy was going to lift her head. She had thought Lucy was going to look up at her. When she did Mitch had known she'd be looking into her own eyes.

She forced herself to breathe very slowly, concentrating on each breath, perfecting it. Her skittering heart began to find its rhythm again. It was a slow process, almost like teaching a young child how to stay on a two-wheeler bike.

And now there it was, that securely steady beat which promised her she might still be alive in five minutes' time, and now she was aware of the cold. Her arms had grown so chilled in her short-sleeved nightshirt she was getting goose bumps. She propped another pillow behind her back, drew up her legs and the duvet and then plunged her arms under its warmth, wrapping them round her shin bones. She rocked herself a little.

It wasn't as though she hadn't seen grisly sights before. Why, alone amongst them, had Lucy come back to terrify her?

Her hair is like mine, thought Mitch.

He couldn't leave her alone even when he'd killed her.

A weird kink in his training as a pathologist? Needing to do something with dead people? Pull yourself together, Mitchell, she told herself. Dr Lucy is dead.

'Roman candles,' Digger had said. She could see him now with the card in his hand, holding it away from him: 'Enjoy,' and Jarvis Jackson dipping into the box.

You are building something out of nothing, she told herself. You weren't the only presenter to receive fireworks from a listener. If you're not careful you *will* scare yourself to death, you idiot.

But now she felt impelled to get up. She put on her new red Chinese dressing-gown with the embroidered back. She hadn't yet let herself know she'd bought it to entertain Jack Briggs in; she'd only told herself that her old dressing-gown was too scruffy for words. It had cost her a sinful price, well over a hundred pounds, so perhaps it was as well it was scarlet, though in the filtered neon-washed light of her bedroom it fell about her in folds of glistening purple. She put on the backless leather sandals she was using as slippers and padded over to the bay window.

She hesitated a moment, not wanting to pander to what she thought of as morbid fears. The curtains were made of unlined cotton, the material almost as limp as bandage. She twitched one back and peered down the street. What do I hope to see? This is ridiculous.

What she saw was the concrete street lamp on the other side of the road. Unlike the red light district, in this neighbourhood the old Victorian lamps had not been conserved. The paving slabs had vanished, too. The neon strip lit the tarmac on the pavement and the road and the back end of a Mazda that she knew belonged to a family further up the street. There were other cars parked against the kerbs but if she wanted to check them she'd have to get dressed and go out. She then noticed a black and white cat stalking along a front garden wall. It jumped off and leapt the five feet which separated the wall from the front door and began sniffing, not with the enthusiasm of a dog, but daintily.

It began to rain. Within a few seconds the cat had vanished under a bush.

As night scenes go, Mitch thought, this is about as peaceful as you're going to get. Shivering in the cold, she let the curtain go. She didn't bother to turn on the bedside lamp for the curtains were so thin and the street lighting so good, she could see her way round the furniture quite clearly. She went and put the kettle on.

She was not out of bed long. When I get up in the morning I'll read in the paper that they've got him, she thought. In the beginning, she remembered, Lucifer had been a she. Venus the wondrous light bearer, Venus in her mantle of star of the morning. Christianity had turned Venus into a he, into the prince of darkness. I wonder if any priest in that chapel I plan to make my home ever preached on the text? 'How art thou fallen from heaven, O Lucifer, son of the morning.' And now sleep was closing her eyelids and she snuggled into her limbs.

Of course, Venus was a good time girl, she thought, didn't she cuckold Vulcan and jump in the sack with Mars and any of the demi-gods who took her fancy? She was smiling a little when sleep took her. Those Romans!

If the morning star were around it would take more than the Mitchell and Orient Bureau, or any other detective agency, to find her, Mitch thought when her alarm clock woke her. All the buttery sunlight was gone and the day was chill and overcast.

She felt rather ashamed of succumbing to childish fears the night before. But at least me and Tommy seem to have made it up after that frightful Mirry Vesey row. He even offered to take me in. She knew their relationship would never be quite the same though; the honeymoon period was over.

Arriving at Radio Brum later that morning, Mitch spent the next two hours avoiding Freya Adcock. The station manager eventually caught up with her in the washroom. Standing side by side they put on new faces in the mirror which ran wall to wall over the row of wash basins. It seemed to Mitch that Freya was doing exactly what she was doing only two seconds later. When two pairs of lips were a satisfactory shade of scarlet, Mitch said: 'Have you had time to listen to my care in the community tape?'

'Excellent. No quibbles.'

Mitch found her just darkened eyebrows rising.

'Of course, it only deals with one aspect. There's more to care in the community than what is happening to our psychogeriatrics. But I listened to the tape again only an hour ago. You can't cut any of what you've got. What about making this the first in a mini-series?'

'I won't do that.'

'Why not?'

She would have liked to look Freya straight in the eye and let her have it but the fact was that the station manager was six inches taller and Mitch felt it was impossible to both look up at someone and look them straight in the eye.

'I don't want to.'

'Oh. Oh, OK.'

Mitch was reduced to incredulously watching the back of the station manager as she walked out of the washroom, the gilt chain of her little pink plastic handbag dangling from the rosebud pattern of her long-sleeved lawn blouse.

It just can't be that easy, she told herself as she snapped her handbag shut. She was still feeling a little dazed as she emerged into the corridor.

'What have you and Killer Driller been concocting in the ladies' room?' Digger Rooney was trundling along towards the studios, a tape box under his arm.

'Actually, she can be very reasonable really,' said Mitch.

'Contradiction in terms. Driller Killers aren't reasonable.' Digger waved the tape box in his podgy hand and chugged round the corner towards the studios. As Mitch walked back towards the production office Digger's phrase remained in her head. She reinvented it. As Edward Lucy is dead he can't be the killer. But he's not dead. Is he? She realised the thought had been in her head for days but that she had never wanted to examine it. 'He's a fan of yours,' Jack Briggs had said.

It's all right though, she had thought, he's dead.

She had wanted to believe that. She'd almost managed to make herself believe it.

But why had Jack Briggs mentioned it? Had this been one of his theories about the case and he'd mentioned it to warn her? Just in case?

He must have checked it out and all the evidence must appear to be watertight. Edward Lucy has to be dead and yet something is niggling him. Could it be that something is niggling Dr Rainbow too? As you've mentioned before, psychiatrists take histories of their patients. Say something said in his group does not tally with the history one of the members has given him? Why has Dr Bateman clammed up on it all?

The young pathologist who stood trial would look very different from the middle-aged man he'd be today if he's still alive. And if he is alive, who is in his grave?

Is the pathologist a member of Dr Rainbow's group?

I'm going to go with him being alive and being a group member. Right? Suddenly she was filled with energy. I'm going to go with he picked out Lucy not quite randomly but because her name was the same as his, right? He then picked on Carole because he thought she knew something, could point the finger at him. The caduceus, right? She'd suddenly remembered she'd seen something and rang the police. The group photograph? Something on that? But surely that picture was now in police hands. She picked up the phone and began by ringing A.J. 'Got a pencil? Find out if the woman in the bottom flat at the Great Wire Street house gave the photograph of the group to the police, will you? Secondly, find out which city hospital carried out the post-mortem on Lucy Lessor.' Those were only the first of her instructions.

In between editing tape she also set afoot her own investigations. By six in the evening, though she and A.J. had set a train of enquiries off, not much of the information she wanted was in. 'We've got to find a short cut,' she told A.J. 'This is taking too long. Pack it in for now but first thing in the morning I want you to look at every detail we have on both Dr Rainbow and the male members of the group. The answers have got to be in there somewhere. I'm going to be working late here. I want to clear the decks so I can concentrate on the case.' It was after nine that evening, just as she was about to leave the building, when her phone rang. Someone else was working late. 'It's only me. Put down some thoughts on paper for this mini-series. No big rush, kiddo. By tomorrow evening will do,' said Freya. 'While I'm on, where did you buy those peacock-coloured shoes of yours? They're really nice. You know?'

Mitch ground her teeth and put the phone down. She struggled into her coat as she made her way through the building to the back entrance. It was raining. She turned up her collar and made a dash for the car-park.

Why don't I tell Freya Adcock what to do with her job, she thought as she squirrelled down into the driving seat of her TVR. She turned on the ignition and headed for home. Thinking of her job set another train of thought off. She was trying to remember how the male members of the group made their living.

Suddenly she gave a whistle. He'd been in shirt-sleeves on the group photograph, too.

Could it be?

She was hearing A.J. telling her: 'He's been travelling on the Continent for five years with a friend of his called Eddie.'

She parked the car and sprinted to the flat. The bulb in the hall had gone but the wash of neon from the street lighting enabled her to find the door easily though she had some trouble in putting the key in the lock. 'Shit,' she said and eased down on to her knees so she could peer more closely.

Tommy saw pictures of them both on the mantelpiece, she was remembering.

She dropped her bags, slammed the door shut and felt about for the light switch. An arm went round her neck. 'Hello, Lucy,' he said. Her heels started out of her shoes. She twisted, her arms beginning to flail. Her mouth opened as terror grew.

The arm tightened against her windpipe. She choked on it.

'We are walking over to the armchair and you are going to sit down because if you don't I'm going to squeeze the life out of you.'

Her mouth was still open, now searching for air. Shoulders heaved, muscles squealed. Tears burned.

'Don't make me apply too much pressure, there's a good girl. I wouldn't want that. I'm a bit of a fan of yours.'

She was aware of something happening above her head, something snaking down over her face. Prickly, obscene. Pressure cut off the beginnings of her scream.

'What I am doing now is dropping a rope over your head. Don't move! Very shortly I'm going to remove my arm. If you try to scream again, if you try to fight, if you even move I'm going to pull the rope tighter. That will cut off the air supply. You do understand? I'm sure you do, a clever girl like you. We wouldn't want to strangle you, would we?'

She felt his arm slide away. She involuntarily fell forward. She gasped as the rope bit into her neck. 'I did warn you. It's a kind of slip knot, you see. I can apply as much pressure as I like when I like. Now I want you to sit down, hands on your lap, feet together. Hands on your lap! On your – there's a good girl.'

Mitch was trying to fight through the heaving, gasping squeal of her panic. If she could suddenly spring a hand. Get it between her neck and the rope.

'I'm transferring the rope to my left hand now. I'm pretty good with that too, almost ambidextrous. If I see any part of you move I will apply pressure. What I'm going to do is give you a little injection . . .'

Her squealing fingers clawed at the rope.

He tightened it.

Her body convulsed.

'I did that with my left hand,' he said as he eased it and she heard him even though she was gasping and panting, her tears mingling in the rivers of her sweat. 'There is nothing to worry about. It will just make you the tiniest bit sleepy. It will help you, I promise you. I prefer to give an injection with my right hand. You'll hardly feel a thing. We'll use the neck. Our sphere of influence, so to speak.'

Even as the rope was searing into her neck she felt the almost delicate prick of the needle. 'Still now, absolutely still. There. There now. Who's a good girlie? Just enough to thoroughly relax you but hopefully not send you to sleep. We wouldn't want that, would we?'

Mitch found her voice and then didn't recognise this croakiness as hers. 'What are you going to do?'

'When we're really completely relaxed I'm taking you for a ride. I'd love to examine those little titties while we wait but we've plenty of time. I wouldn't want to spoil the show. No point in going off half cocked.'

She was aware of a drowsiness beginning to overtake her. Her hands half rose, as if to bat it away, but the room was blurring.

Another picture formed. She saw the Amy Johnson ward nestling in the centre of rose gardens, but it wasn't winter now. It was high summer. All the roses were out. 'I wouldn't mind a stay in Amy Johnson myself,' she was saying again. Out loud? In the distance she was aware of her skin being pinched. Pricked? Another injection? 'Don't do that!'

'You're going to have a little trouble walking so we'll just set up the wheelchair. That's right. You have a little nap. Just leave this to me. I'm jolly good at this sort of thing. Used to wheeling people about.'

Her hand jerked in alarm and then sank to nestle at her side as her eyelids closed. Almost as if it were the same instant she became aware of wheels running over the pavement, of night air, a snatch in which she struggled to move but found she couldn't. I'm not in my flat any more? She was searching for limbs which weren't there. 'Let me tell you, Amy Johnson is the place to be.' Who had said that? Someone had said it. But he wasn't a porter.

The next thing she was aware of was part of a driving wheel and, though she knew she was in a car, this man in a motor-cycle helmet was looking down at her. He was withdrawing his leather-gloved hand from her face. 'Comfy? There's my girl. I'm really pleased with you. Taking that nasty medicine and not so much as a whimper. Won't be long now, Lucy . . .'

She tried to lift her head a fraction and found she couldn't. 'I've given you a muscle relaxant, my dear. Help with our operation, so to speak. Combined with a little tranquilliser. I knew you'd want to be *compos mentis*. Down but not out, eh? You wouldn't want to miss a thing, would you? A curious little girl like you. Don't get much practice these days so we're flying by the seat of our pants, so to speak. Gave that black bitch too much. There we are. We live and learn.'

She opened her mouth. No sound came out.

Though she was fading in and out of consciousness, when she came to her thought processes were far too clear.

Pathologists cut people up.

Lucy Lessor wasn't cut up.

After playing with fireworks, he strangled her.

But he wasn't copying exactly. Who had said that? Who had said: 'There's all this add-on stuff. Operating table stuff.'

She was aware of the sound of the engine and suddenly she was bathed in light. A cold distant voice a million miles from where she floated in these clouds told her: 'Mitchell, wake up. Mitchell, do you hear me?' She knew she had to make the cold surrounding that tiny voice bigger. But it wasn't getting bigger. It was shrinking to a pinprick. 'Help me!' she wanted to yell but she had no voice to yell with.

She knew she wasn't in the car any more because it wasn't warm and she was bumping along and there was a smell she recognised. It was damp and musty and somehow reminded her of home. She could hear wheels rattling somewhere out there, far, far away in the real world. She was being pushed briskly along because she had not got any limbs any more and this puzzled her. 'Mitchell!' she heard the voice shouting at her again. She knew what she must do. Make the cold around the tiny voice bigger.

You can wake yourself out of a dream. You know how to, the tiny voice said. You tell the dream it is a dream and that makes you wake up. But she could not seem to make the magic work. The dream was too big. It wouldn't release her.

If you don't wake up you're dead.

The parquet flooring in Amy Johnson House turned into a conveyor belt and was bearing her away. It was far too hot. The oven would explode and bring the chimney down.

In a blink she realised she was in her own home. She smelled the damp and dimly saw the wooden Victorian gothic arches which held up the roof. A wash of neon city night showed in the skylights Kenny Colville had cut out of the Welsh slates. It was taking a tremendous effort to push her head round; it was almost immovable. At first she had wondered if she were dreaming she was in the United Reform Chapel by the canal side but then she saw him. He'd left her in the well of the floor, on a lighter patch where one of Kenny's printing machines had once stood. He had taken off the motor-cycle helmet and was shaking out his hair. It was thick and swept to cover his forehead. When he shook it back his face wasn't young at all.

Hair out of his eyes, Maurice Pincing looked at her. 'Not quite the girl of one's dreams. But then nothing is quite what one imagines.'

He began to light candles placed along the side wall. The riding leathers were tight and he almost minced. The flames began to cast his shadow across the floorboards. As he moved up the row she noticed that between each wax candle an unlit Roman candle had been placed. He gave her a little wave as he jauntily strolled in front of her to the wall on the other side of the chapel, his shadow ahead of him, leaping up the wall to the ceiling. He started to light a second row of candles.

Mitch was in the middle of his flight path.

All the candles lit, he gave her a little bow.

She opened her mouth. A strange whirr of a sound came out.

He was now at the top of the chapel lighting storm lanterns on a plinth affair which was covered in white sheeting. On it were a number of objects. She could make out a washing up bowl and now the last lantern was lit she saw it was a cherry red colour and hanging neatly over its rim was a pair of rubber gloves, fingers pointing down. Next to it were covered steel trays and though Mitch couldn't see one she knew the trays to be laid with dreadful instruments. Next to them was a bundle of clothes; they were theatre green. In front of the plinth and placed so it formed a T shape was a long table which was also shrouded in white. At the bottom end, facing the well of the hall, were drum-style kitchen steps.

She opened her mouth wider. The whirring noise she made was louder.

'With you in just a tick,' he said.

Where have my limbs gone? Why can't I move?

She knew her body was still there, though, still about her; a solid, placid weightiness of being.

He was now lighting paraffin heaters, four of them, placed at each end of the long draped table.

A flight path, she thought drowsily, and now a plane on it, all fuelled and ready to go.

I won't be coming back.

That is why he's allowing me to see his face.

He wants the kick of letting me watch him getting into his theatre outfit.

He turned and came round the table towards her. He was holding a camera.

'One for the front of our case history, eh? I like to get in a shot before we begin. We'll do a little bit of photographic work in the middle. A snap or two at the end. Demonstration purposes. You know, teaching aid? Splendid. Splendid. Knew you'd agree.' He stopped just in front of her and stood examining her, very grave. The flash went off once, twice and then he put the camera on her knee. 'Hold that for me, will you? There's a good girl. Silly me. You can't hold anything, can you? Still. It seems nicely balanced. Must get in the old working gear.' He began unzipping the leather jacket. She could see the pin-stripes of his shirt, the whiteness of the detachable collar, the correctness of his tie. She opened her mouth again and the same strange inhuman noise came out. She blacked out.

'With us again, my dear. Good show. I see we've been perhaps a little too heavy-handed with the tranquilliser. While we wanted you to be *compos mentis,* so to speak, we didn't want you to be a nuisance. Mrs Lessor was an absolute pest. The trouble I had with that bitch. We certainly couldn't go through that again. We simply had to find a new *modus operandi*. Afraid I overdid it with the black tart. Talk about whoops! But this time we do seem to have got the muscle relaxant absolutely spot on. A little movement there, not entirely flaccid, not quite lost your voice. I must say it has worked out far better than I dared hope. Still, that's what trial runs are for. I'm really rather pleased with you. You're shaping up very well.'

She could now only see a patch of his hair. The effort of moving her head seemed absurd. She had plunged into peacefulness. The fact that he was going to kill her was of no importance.

'Better run over the routine with you. First of all we're going to get you out of all that nasty clobber. Then I'll get out of the rest of mine, put on the working clobber and we'll get down to it, shall we? We're going to pop you up on the examination couch. Give you a thorough going over. Absolutely nothing to worry about. No horrid instruments or anything like that.' He was holding his fingers in front of her so she could see them. 'Just these little pinkies. My feeling is we'll find nothing wrong, my dear. Jolly good biological material, I'd wager. Just these little pinkies and Mr Fee Fie Foe Thumb. I expect he'll want a good root round. Actually, I think you'll quite like him. Most ladies tend to. He'll make sure everything is in working order. I don't doubt it myself, dear. But best to be on the safe side. Wouldn't you say?'

She managed to look up at him. He was smiling. 'Of course, if it's not we might have to perform a little operation. Just minor surgery. Nothing too major, one hopes. Do you know, I don't think I've introduced myself. My name's Doc.' He leaned forward and gave her cheek a playful pinch. 'I hope you're going to do exactly what the doctor orders? Good girl! I know we're going to be really pleased with your progress. Just do as you're told and you'll be all right. A clever little thing like you is bound to pick up things quickly. We'll make a start, eh? Get you out of that coat. You'll have to bear with me, my dear. No nurse to help, I'm afraid, and I can be a bit of a clumsy beggar at this sort of thing.'

He laid a finger across her silent scream.

'What a fuss. You've got to be a brave girlie. Stiff upper lip and all that. When you've done really bad things, when you've been really naughty and got Mr Fee Fi Foe Thumb into the most terrible trouble you've got to take your punishment like a man, haven't you? But it'll be all right. You'll see, my dear. Nothing like a taste of pure pain to make one mend one's ways.'

He gave her cheek a pinch. 'This is case clickerty click. The body is that of a well-developed, well-nourished fifty-year-old Caucasian female with black hair and brown eyes. The body is sixty inches long and weighs a hundred pounds. Now let me see, how did she die? What has caused rigor mortis to be present in these delightful extremities? Are there any burn marks? Cuts? Bruises? Fractures? What will I put in my report? Not at all sure. And that is the truth. One does so like to keep one's options open. Extemporise. Good Lord. Silly me. Do you know, I forgot to lock the door? We don't want any interruptions, do we? Always best to go by the book. Doctor/patient confidentiality and all that.'

Mitch heard his footsteps on the oak plank floor receding from her and then stared at her flight path, at this small white-winged craft which would carry her out of this world into Never Never Land.

She tried to move; somehow, by some trick, she must magic herself out of this trap of flesh.

Suddenly, in the far distance, she heard disturbing sounds. Scuttling.

'I can't hold him for long! Run for it!'

She began to struggle in a quicksand of air.

'Run for it, you stupid bitch!'

Suddenly she saw a man in a green anorak with blue and yellow insets in the shoulders. Air bellowed under them. On wings he sailed towards her.

She made a gigantic effort. It was as if she was uprooting the tree of herself. She heaved her wood out of the ground. The wheels of the chair spun from under her. Her limbs smacked into the floor-boards.

24

She was wearing her pin-striped trousers, little black jacket with white silk shirt underneath and a red silk cravat woven high up round her neck. A felt fedora was perched on her curls and a trench coat swung from her shoulders. A.J. said: 'You're not supposed to be up.'

'Honeypot, if I stay in that flat any longer I'll scream and I'll scream until I'm sick. I don't want to be rude, but are we now branching out and running a flower shop on the side?' Two enormous bunches of flowers, one in an orange plastic bucket, the other in a cherry red washing up bowl, were lined up on the wall side of the reception desk.

'Actually, they're for you. One from Tommy and one from me. We were going to come and see you after work tonight. You look frightful.'

'Considering how I feel, I look fucking fantastic.'

'You'd better sit down.'

'I'm going up to my office. Bring the post. Oh. And I think the flowers are terrific. Really.'

Mitch had to hold on to the banister rail. Her knees were wobbling and a thin sheen of sweat was forming between her shoulder blades.

She began whistling and then she broke into song.

> 'There's no discouragement
> Shall make him once relent
> His first avowed intent
> To be a pilgrim.'

She sailed into her office, tugged open the sash window and pulled her Italian black leather chair towards it. She stuck her feet on the windowsill and listened to the rumble of traffic, sniffed the city smells. Better than wine, she told herself. Oh, oh. Is that a whiff of diesel? She shut her eyes while she recuperated. She should have stayed in bed.

'You'll get pneumonia.'

Mitch turned to see A.J. bringing in a tray with a mug of coffee on it and the morning's post. 'It smells so good.'

'The Nescafé?'

'Everything.'

'Was that a hymn I heard you singing as you went up the stairs?'

'Sure was.'

'I knew you still weren't at all well. You're as white as death.'

'My make-up really must be slipping. Anyway, there's nothing morbid about a jolly good hymn tune.'

'You've got it!' said A.J. 'The planning permission has come through.'

'Had a phone call from the architect this morning. The committee sat last night.'

'But . . . well . . . won't you . . . You're still going ahead?'

'Absolutely.'

'I don't think I could. Not after what's happened.'

'Most people's cupboards are bulging with rattling skeletons. Mine happens to contain a great big serpent which hisses and hisses. Don't get me wrong. Scares the socks off me. The strange thing is that as I was being trundled along in that wheelchair doped up to the eyeballs I knew I was going home. It seems there are some things you've got to live with.'

'All that pitch pine and damp, too.'

'You don't like it, do you?'

'It's hardly sunny.'

'Trust in my architect, trust in me. It's no good, A.J., I'm not a bungalow type. Even if I had the dosh, which I don't, I can't see myself in a cosy Elizabethan farmhouse, either, or a Georgian rectory. I'm the Bunyan type.' She began whistling and then broke into song again.

> '... his first avowed intent
> To be a pilgrim.'

'Come on-n-n,' said A.J.

'Well, maybe Bunyan wouldn't have recognised me. Say I fit into that category. More or less. Don't look at me like that. The United Reformed Church and I ... well, we'll deal comfortably together, you'll see. Suits the other side of my nature.'

'What other side?'

'The side which tells me to go easy on the gin and not jump into bed with twenty-five-year-old little squirts like that erstwhile assistant of mine Marco Rice.'

'Didn't stop you having it off with him.'

'No. But it tried to. See what I mean?'

'No,' said A.J. 'Actually, I see you living in a suite of rooms at Claridge's. If you really want to know.'

'I'm not saying a little bite of that cherry now and then wouldn't be absolutely terrific. But on a long-term basis? Wouldn't please my soul. Really. I can be very picky. I see you've opened the post. Still, I suppose it is well after eleven o'clock. Anything I should see?'

'Bills and no-nos like that.'

'Then you can just pass the coffee over. Where's Tommy?'

'He's gone to tie up a deal with a prospect in Wolverhampton. He hopes.'

'Not only is he talking to me again, he's offering to put me up and sending me flowers. Do you think it's possible he's forgiven me? Really, really, I mean? Two dozen red roses do not come cheap.'

'If you really want to know what I think, I think the honeymoon period is over.'

'That's exactly what I thought.' Mitch sighed. 'You know, I completely misjudged him. It wasn't just the colossal strop he got in. I kept seeing all this steeliness glinting beneath. Still, if you're born in the arse end of Hong Kong and land up where Tommy is you're no push-over, are you?' She paused and then said, 'Jack Briggs came over and made me breakfast this morning.'

'I'll bring my coffee up,' said A.J. and went to get it. When she came back she shut the window and settled herself in a chair opposite Mitch. 'So who is in their cells? Maurice Pincing or Edward Lucy? Don't tell me. Lucy.'

'They met when Maurice Pincing's family moved from Tewkesbury to Norfolk when Maurice was about sixteen. They became best friends when he was sent to the same school as Edward Lucy and though they eventually went to different universities they remained very close. Maurice Pincing was a homosexual, Edward Lucy says he wasn't. The two did drift apart for a while. Pincing went into insurance, Lucy eventually became a pathologist. He worked for a while in America but came back to marry an English girl he'd met. He'd always had peculiar sexual tastes and consorted with prostitutes both before and after his marriage. Funnily enough, it wasn't until late on in Lucy's prison sentence that the two got in touch again. Lucy's wife had by then made it clear she was going to divorce him and Lucy was looking for a place to go after he came out of prison. Pincing had always been in love with him, you see. By then Lucy was completely cracking up. He couldn't at all cope with prison life. Things weren't too rosy with Pincing at the time. In his own way, he'd got gate fever too. Couldn't stand his job. Both his parents had died, one very shortly after the other, and left him quite a lot of money. The pair of them decided not to wait any longer. Lucy managed to get himself transferred to an open prison and literally walked out. The pair of them first went to Brazil. While he was working in American hospitals, Lucy had been down there and liked it. They managed to get themselves into America for a while and then came back to Europe. Pincing died in a car crash in Greece around fifteen months ago. By that time Lucy was fed up with roaming. He decided to come back to England and start a new life. He just switched passports, medical cards, the lot. He said it was easy. He just identified the body as that of Edward Lucy and gave the Greek authorities all the documentation they wanted. He also, of course, took over Pincing's bank account and there was still enough in it to buy a house when he got back here.'

'So the photos that Tommy noticed on the mantelpiece must have been taken when the two of them were on their travels. And Tommy was right. One of them was a homosexual. But why on earth did he join the group?'

'He said that not long after he got back to England the old urges started again. He was afraid of doing something, afraid of landing in jail. Last time he hadn't been able to cope with the prison regime. But he went to see Dr Rainbow as Maurice Pincing. He had to pretend, for instance, that he was homosexual because that might at some time have been noted on Pincing's medical records. Psychiatrists take histories and Lucy did make one or two mistakes. He was actually born in Norfolk but as the real Pincing was born in Tewkesbury that's what he told Dr Rainbow. More than once in a group session he said he'd been born in Norfolk. There were one or two discrepancies like that.'

'That's why the doctor took some of the file? To check up on him?'

'He's a scrupulous man. He didn't want to rouse any suspicions until he'd thoroughly checked himself. Lucy as Pincing told Dr Rainbow he was unsure that he was gay. He was confused about his sexual orientation. The psychiatrist said he was confused, too. Pincing didn't seem to add up! When the group formed Pincing met Sammy Pink. He'd seen a piece about Sammy's exploits in the paper and suddenly saw he might get away with murder. Sammy had his own little harem. The women he peeked at. He tracked Sammy tracking them. These were to be Lucy's victims and Sammy was to get the blame. But he didn't want the finger pointed at Sammy too soon. Lucy wanted his fun first.'

'A diabolical game of Grandma's footsteps. Surely when they bang him up in Broadmoor they'll throw away the key.'

'As far as I'm aware Sutcliffe, the Yorkshire Ripper, is doing time in an ordinary nick.'

'Lucy's not over the edge but in outer space! That business at the crematorium? Maniacs make me shudder. Maniacs with imagination make me pass out.'

'Yes, well . . .' said Mitch.

'Oh, my God. Oh, I shouldn't have said that. Not after –'

'To be honest, what happened doesn't seem to mean much at the moment. I suppose I'm still in shock.' Mitch was considering. She might have been a clinician objectively examining her case. 'But I know, somehow, it's sort of imprinted itself into my flesh. That's why I decided to go ahead and buy the chapel. It doesn't matter where I take myself, it'll still be there. Some experiences are like that. They mark you for life. I don't quite know yet how this has marked me. I only know it has. What can I do about it? I've somehow got to live with it. That's all.'

'It can't be that easy.'

'When you're as old as I am you already have to live with quite a lot. Anyway, I'm determined. No nutter called Edward Lucy's going to ruin my life. Soon I'm going to be too busy to even think about it, aren't I? What with working here and at the radio station and stepping into the ring to fight brickies and carpenters and bawling out my architect, buttering up my bank manager ... For sure there's not going to be much time to mope, is there? Honeypot, how do I really know how I'm going to be? I'll have to wait and see ... Lord, that's Tommy coming over the bridge. He doesn't usually come the pub way.'

A.J. got up and looked out of the window.

'Do you think he has ever in his life worn an anorak?' asked Mitch. Shoulders back, charcoal Harris tweed overcoat busily flapping about him, Tommy Hung was crossing the Gas Street Basin. Behind him, beyond the moored canal barges, was Teddy's, the neo-Edwardian pub, its reflection wobbling like an unbalanced jelly in the water.

'Tommy? Not the type,' said A.J. 'When he carries an umbrella a funny old-fashioned word comes into my mind. Gamp.'

'For a Chinaman he certainly puts on a good show as an upperclass English gent,' said Mitch and then remembered the roses. 'One dozen red roses. OK. That's nice. Two dozen? I suppose really he is a gent. Some of the time.'

They heard the bureau door open and then Tommy coming up the stairs. 'I think we've got that Wolverhampton client,' said A.J.

'You can tell that just by his tread?'

'Sort of gets bouncy.'

'My dears ...' said Tommy as he came through the doors, his arms outstretched as if, like a conjuror, he'd just produced the pair of them. Mitch found beady eyes checking her over. 'One is reminded of Popeye.'

'Popeye?'

'What you need is a good dose of spinach. You shouldn't be out of bed but I knew nothing would keep you flat on your back for more than twenty-four hours. In fact, I've just booked lunch for the three of us at Teddy's.'

'You must be psychic,' said A.J.

'Absolutely not. I bumped into Jack Briggs. After going to Wolverhampton I popped over to see Sammy Pink. I thought one ought to thank the chap and it worried me a little. I didn't want you getting in touch with him, Mitch. Even though he saved your life we have to bear in mind he is a peeping Tom.'

'You were warning him off, I bet!' said A.J.

'Not at all. I truly admire the way he got stuck in. He knocked out two of Lucy's teeth. Did you know that? Turned out to be quite a little tiger. Of course, he'd be very fit. I'm told he's something of a jobbing gardener. It was a jolly good show and we had to show our appreciation. But, in all the circumstances, I felt it was better I did it.' He paused. 'I left Jack Briggs to warn him off. He was arriving as I was leaving.'

'Well, I'm truly grateful, Tommy. I had been wondering how I was going to approach that one. If only one's guardian angel would live up to expectations. Trust mine to be a pervert. When I was a child I had four of them, all strapping wonderful fellows with wings who kept me from the demons of the night. "Matthew, Mark, Luke and John, bless the bed that I lie on . . ." '

'One should never turn up one's nose at the chaps the gods send along. As snobbery goes, that's the very worst kind, my dear.'

'I'm honestly, truly, humbly grateful,' said Mitch.

'That's exactly what I told Sammy.'

'Though I still don't see why my guardian angel couldn't have been six feet six in his stockinged feet with long blond hair and a forty-four-inch chest. Though I'm honestly, truly, humb –'

'All right, all right,' said Tommy. 'And anyway Sammy Pink does have blond hair. Have you really looked at him?'

'I should think he's done enough looking for both of us. Well over the legal limit, I'd say.'

'Maybe this group therapy will help him,' said A.J.

'Perhaps I should be thanking my lucky stars it hasn't! If that little shit had become a reformed character he wouldn't have been out there trying to get an eyeful. He wouldn't have seen Lucy bundle me off and tracked us to the chapel.'

'One has to admit it's hard to see what, if anything, people get out of all this looking,' said Tommy.

'I suppose what really put the police completely off the scent was that their most likely candidate, this Edward Lucy, was dead. His first victim, Patsy Parker Snell, knew him as Doc, you know . . . and then the caduceus. Of course, after he'd killed Lucy he knew he'd lost one of his cuff links . . . and when the group picture – which the woman in the bottom flat had never thought to give the police – fell into their hands they were able to enlarge it sufficiently to make out the cuff links Maurice was wearing on that day.'

'That's why poor Carole was killed. He was after a piece of incriminating evidence,' said A.J. 'Carole must have noticed the cuff links as she was arranging the photo she was going to take. Maurice was afraid the police would blow the picture up, which, of course, they did.'

'I wondered if Carole told him I had the photograph. I wondered if that was why he came after me in the end. The police say not. Among all the awful photographs they found in his house were some old pin-ups of me. From the days when I used to work on television.'

'I wondered why a man like that became a porter,' said Tommy. 'I mean, he was used to professional status.'

'Access to drugs, I bet. It wouldn't take long for a man with a brain like his to worm his way through the defences of the hospital pharmacy.'

'There's instruments, too. And the thrill of working with dead bodies, even if he's only trundling the things along,' said Mitch.

'Well, I suggest you two put on your bonnets. No reason why we shouldn't take an early lunch. I would have made it dinner but Inspector Briggs told me he was taking you out tonight, Mitch. Are you sure that's wise?'

'Probably not. I've never dated a copper before. It could work out if I end up on top.'

'Literally or figuratively?'

Both Mitch and A.J. stared at Tommy. 'He's pulling our leg,' A.J. suggested.

'Maybe that American lady of his is a bad influence. I'm told these Yanks are pretty basic.'

Tommy was grinning.

'If he wasn't the wrong make I'd say that was a very Mona Lisa smile,' said Mitch, getting up. 'Shit. Legs still a bit wobbly.'

'You should cancel tonight.'

'If I have a little rest after lunch I'll be OK.' She tentatively perched her fedora on her curls. 'Oh, chums. It does make one go cold on and off. Every now and then my insides turn to jelly.'

'Why did he start killing again after such a long gap?' A.J. wondered.

'A year before the Patsy Parker Snell affair Lucy's mother died. This began after Maurice Pincing died,' said Mitch.

'People can get in a fearful rage when their nearest and dearest pop off,' said Tommy. 'What exercised me is how he got the fireworks in her coffin. He didn't. The post-mortem was carried out at the North-East Birmingham hospital –'

'Where he worked as a porter,' said A.J.

'He simply slipped into the mortuary one night after the autopsy had been performed and used some of his old skills as pathologist to insert a carefully constructed waterproof package of fireworks into Lucy's corpse.'

'I always thought it was going to be a member of the group,' said A.J. 'But it turned out to be the wrong member. My money was on Dr Rainbow.'

They had reached the bottom of the stairs. 'The flowers really are lovely,' said Mitch. 'Lord, there're lilies, too.' She stared at their greeny whiteness. 'Jack told me that the creep always wore the same suit at his trial. Day after day, this suit. It's the one he always wore when he went to the group meetings.'

'I noticed that. I'd no idea what it meant, of course,' said A.J. 'That funny old-fashioned suit. Somehow it makes you feel rather sorry for him.'

'Speak for yourself,' said Mitch.

'Careful!'

'Sorry. It's just . . . they look so lovely. Gorgeous. I wonder why flowers are sent to funerals. Is it because it's a celebration?'

'Put funerals out of your head,' said Tommy. 'Hang on to me.'